LEAGUE
OF
TRAITORS

Other books by Keith Hoar

<u>Zach Templeton Thriller Series</u>:

EDGE OF MADNESS

RAGE

DEADLY SECRETS

<u>NONFICTION:</u>

DECEIVED The Assault of Revisionist History

LEAGUE
of
Traitors

INSPIRED BY A TRUE STORY
A TALE OF ESPIONAGE & TREASON

Keith Hoar

First Edition

Zhetosoft Publications

Published by: Zhetosoft Publications

LEAGUE OF TRAITORS is a work of historical fiction based on a true story drawn from testimony given before the Privy Council of the Royal Commission on February 5, 1946, regarding the discovery of espionage and treason that occurred in Canada and the United States near the end of World War II.

Library of Congress Cataloging-in-Publication Data

Hoar, Keith.
LEAGUE OF TRAITORS/Keith Hoar.
Library of Congress Control Number: 2020924520

ISBN(13): 978-1-7362761-0-5 (paperback)
ISBN(13): 978-1-7362761-1-2 (eBook)

To Kathie,
The love of my life.

[AUTHOR'S NOTE]

This novel is set in various locales in Canada. Seemingly incorrect grammar contained within quotes may reflect broken English used by a foreign character. For example: "You read. Much important." would be typical speech for someone who has a poor command of the English language.

While *LEAGUE OF TRAITORS* is based on actual, historical events, many events, dates, names, characterizations, incidents, locations, and dialog have been added and/or changed for dramatic purposes. The fictionalization of events, locations, or names is not intended to reflect on the actual, historical characters, or events. This novel is simply intended to *entertain*. Any resemblance to persons living or dead is purely coincidental.

Deciphered messages and notes (pgs. 91, 102, 136, 140, 168, 216) that would have been written in Russian are shown in English for understandability. Examples of some of the originals are shown in Appendix I.

Thank you for reading *LEAGUE OF TRAITORS*. The author is very grateful for fans of his books, and would love to correspond with readers. Sample prologues and/or first chapters of current and upcoming books can be viewed on his author website at www.keithhoarbooks.wixsite.com.

You are encouraged to reach out to the author through his author email address at kahoarauthor@email.com.

Prologue

North River Road
Ottawa, Ontario, Canada

Run!

The voice of fear screamed in Yuri Antonovich Aleksandrov's mind. Raw, primal fear churned inside him. "Run! Run Now," blind fear shrieked in his mind.

"They're watching me. They are always watching," Yuri's mind protested, as he battled mightily against the urge to take flight and flee headlong into the darkness. *"Running would be foolish,"* he tried to convince himself because running would only attract attention and then he would be doomed for certain.

"I should have kept my mouth shut," he whispered. "Why did I let Pasha talk me into this?"

Paralyzed by indecision, he drew back into the shadows, leaning against the wall of an old, abandoned warehouse. For what seemed like an eternity, he stood frozen on North River Road just short of the bridge over the Rideau River. In the darkness, he tilted his head back toward the fog shrouded street. He held his breath, straining, listening for the slightest sound. Nothing. All was quiet.

Yuri squinted, trying to see through the heavy, mist-laden fog that obscured everything except one lone streetlamp, standing at the beginning of the bridge. A dim halo of light glowed around the streetlamp. Cautiously, he stepped out of the darkness and headed toward the dim light of the street-lamp. He pulled the collar of his heavy, wool overcoat up around his neck and rushed through the meager light streaming from the streetlamp. He stopped, leaning against the damp, concrete balustrade, waiting for his eyes to readjust to the darkness.

He took one step and froze. Scraping. He whirled around attempting to locate the source of the sound, but saw no one behind him. Scanning the foggy gloom in all directions, he tried to locate the source of the scraping sound, his heart pounding inside his chest, beating wildly against his rib cage. There it was again. Scraping. This time followed by a faint splashing sound. He listened. Again, he heard the scraping sound. The sound became louder as it grew closer. Glancing over the top of the bridge's concrete balustrade, he saw a dim light bobbing on the water below.

He breathed a sigh of relief, realizing the scraping sound had come from a fisherman rowing his boat along the edge of the river. Yuri tugged his overcoat tightly around him and turned to continue across the bridge.

Footsteps. He froze momentarily. Unable to suppress the rising fear any longer, he let go of his overcoat and bolted. Dragging his right hand along the concrete balustrade for balance and as a guide in the darkness, he raced full speed across the bridge.

A reckless, backward glance over his shoulder to see who was chasing him caused him to lose his balance. Slipping on the wet cobblestones, he fell face first onto the bridge's walkway. He grabbed for his hat as he slid up against the concrete balustrade, but he was a second too late. The hat flew between the columns and floated down to the river below.

Yuri leaped to his feet, expecting to be grabbed at any moment. Feeling disgusted and somewhat foolish, he discovered the bridge was completely empty except for himself. He straightened his overcoat, brushed himself off, and hurried across the bridge.

Stopping at the end of the bridge, he spotted the street sign for Fountain Place, a narrow street that ran along the edge of Besserer Park, his destination. As he approached the streetlamp, he heard a muffled pop and the tinkling of glass on the cobblestones. The streetlamp went dark. A hand grabbed his shoulder as something cold and hard was jammed forcefully against his neck.

"Yuri, why are you running?" a gruff voice asked.

Yuri gulped, instantly recognizing the familiar voice.

"Come on, Yuri," the man urged. "If you are running, you must have something to hide. I ask again. Why are you running?"

"I was frightened," Yuri stammered. "I thought someone wanted to rob me."

"Yuri, do not lie to me. It will go very badly for you."

"I… I…," Yuri stuttered.

The man spun Yuri around and backhanded him, sending him flying.

Yuri grunted as he hit the ground forcefully, the wet surface soaking his overcoat. He scrambled to his knees, his bleeding palms pressing against the rough cobblestones.

Another pair of hands jerked Yuri upright and turned him around to face the man that had struck him.

"My patience is wearing thin, Yuri," the man growled. "What have you seen and who were you going to meet?"

"I saw nothing," Yuri whimpered. "I was not going to meet anyone."

"Do not take me for a fool?" the man roared, backhanding Yuri even harder, sending him flying again.

Yuri sucked in his breath as he slammed onto the ground. Yuri moaned and struggled to his knees. Another muffled pop, followed a few seconds later by a large splash.

Chapter One

In a drab, nondescript building on the outskirts of Moscow, Viktor Sergeyevich Zakharov sat hunched over his assigned Fialka M-125 cipher machine. Working feverously, he glanced back and forth between the machine and the highly classified code book and the detailed operating instructions that had been provided to all students several days earlier.

Viktor arched his back and leaned his five foot nine inch frame back in his chair, trying to relieve his tired muscles. He ran his hand through his wispy-thin, ash-brown hair. His eyes, pale blue, the color of ice water, peered out from above prominent cheek bones. A straight, moderately protruding nose completed his face, the result of slavic features inherited from the Finno-Ugrian heritage of his father, Sergey Bogdanovich Zakharov. Fortunately, Viktor's face was more round and his nose less prominent than his father's due to the influence of his mother, Svetlana Leonidovna Zakharov.

Viktor snatched the operating instructions from the rickety old desk sitting beside the cipher machine, turned to the beginning of the coding section, and reread the instructions for a third time. Still hopelessly confused, he shook his head and wiped the sweat trickling down his forehead on his sleeve. Growing fear and much frustration hindered his ability to think clearly.

Viktor had to get his current task completed correctly and quickly. He could not allow himself to fail. In the Russian military, failure was simply not tolerated. At best, failure would result in exile to some wretched gulag in Siberia, or, at worst, a bullet in the back of the head and disposal in some horrid refuse pit. Viktor was well aware of the rumors that the latter option was, by far, the preferred penalty meted out by Major Dmitri Kostya Maksimov, Commandant of the intelligence training unit Viktor was currently assigned to.

Major Maksimov was a brutal despot, drunk with the power afforded to him by his rank. A pudgy man of average height, Maksimov had dark, close set eyes. Round, chubby cheeks only enhanced his nasty disposition, making him look as if he was perpetually squinting. He had risen to his current rank, not by performance or merit, but through his family's connections, being the nephew of a high-ranking party official.

Everyone feared Maksimov and did their best to avoid him. More than once, Viktor had witnessed another student being whipped severely for a simple mistake or infraction of the rules. To resist or fight back only angered Maksimov and made his attacks more vicious. Two students had died of injuries inflicted by Maksimov, inflamed because they had raised an arm to deflect the blows from his whip. Nothing ever happened to Maksimov. Quite the contrary, he would likely receive a medal because many of the officers above him were even more brutal than he was.

Viktor became increasingly nervous as the seconds ticked away. His current task was the final practice session before he would be required to take the final exam.

"You have five minutes, you ignorant simpletons," Major Maksimov screamed, slamming his whip down on an unoccupied desk.

Startled by Maksimov's sudden outburst, Viktor dropped the instruction book he had been holding. He scrambled to pick up the book and place it on the desk.

"What's the matter, Zakharov?" Maksimov yelled, stomping across the room toward Viktor's work area.

"The sudden noise startled me, Major Maksimov" Viktor answered. "I was concentrating on the instructions."

Maksimov raised the whip he always carried as if to strike Viktor, but instead smacked the desk beside Viktor. "Get busy and finish your task, you imbecile" Maksimov yelled. "You now have only four minutes."

"Yes sir," Viktor responded, turning back toward his assigned cipher machine.

Time had run out. He could no longer study the instruction book. Viktor would have to depend on what he had already learned. The Fialka M-125, setting on the desk in front of him, was the latest rotary type cipher machine. Similar to the German enigma machine, the M-125 used electromechanical cipher wheels to scramble letters as they were typed onto a keyboard. The device had ten rotors, each with thirty contacts along with mechanical pins to control how each rotor stepped through the coding sequences. Just one pin out of place and the message would not encode properly, a prospect Viktor did not want to think about.

Viktor blinked the sweat out of his eyes and finished the setup of the machine as he remembered it from his study of the instruction book. Viktor shoved the last pin into place and leaned back in his chair, exhausted from the mental strain.

"Time," Major Maksimov shouted ten seconds later, once again slamming his whip across a desk. One by one Major Maksimov went around the room inputting a test message into each cipher machine. He then took the resulting punched card and ran it through a decoding machine. Major Maksimov gave no indication whatsoever of whether any of the results were correct or not. When he had finished testing all fifteen machines, he walked to the front of the room and faced the terrified students.

"Four of you simpletons have failed," Maksimov announced, shaking his head. "When I call your name, come and stand here by the door. Senior Lieutenant Ivanov will escort you to my office where you will wait."

Viktor would feel concern for the four unfortunate souls that would soon feel Maksimov fury, but still, inside him a voice begged, "*Not me. Please not me.*"

One by one Maksimov called off the first three names, stopping as he was about to reveal the fourth and final name.

Maksimov stared directly at Viktor. Fear gripped Viktor's heart as Maksimov continued to stare at him. Time stood still. Viktor couldn't breathe. After what seemed like an eternity, Maksimov turned toward another student and announced the final name.

Viktor's breath escaped in a rush as he watched the fourth man, visibly shaking, get up from his seat and join the others. Senior Lieutenant Ivanov marched the four men out of the room. Viktor knew Maksimov hated him because he also came from a highly respected family and he was smarter than Maksimov.

For nearly a year, Viktor had silently endured Maksimov's insults and taunts. Growing up during the Stalin regime, Viktor had learned to keep his mouth shut, to trust no one, and to do exactly as he was told.

Viktor's high marks in the GRU's cipher school had prevented Maksimov from inflicting anything more than verbal insults, taunts, and extra work. Only one more hurdle remained, the final exam, and then he could escape this miserable place and, he hoped, never see Maksimov again.

After being dismissed for the day, Viktor stopped at the security station and waited as one guard physically searched him while another one went through his lunch pail. Students were not allowed to remove anything from the building, not even a scrap of paper. Any student needing after-hours study, would require Maksimov's approval and a security escort as long as they were in the building. Very few requests were made and even fewer were approved.

Viktor hurried out of the building, crossed Stromynka Street, and hurried the ten blocks to the Yaroslavsky Railway Terminal where he joined the long line of people waiting for the next train to arrive. Twenty minutes passed before the train, behind schedule by fifteen minutes, chugged into the terminal and screeched to a stop, hissing and billowing great clouds of steam.

Viktor shuffled along with the long line of people boarding the train. He presented his military pass and stepped up into the train, passing through three cars before he found an empty seat. He sat in the aisle seat in the next to last row and cradled his lunch pail in his lap. Deep in thought, he repeated in his mind the steps required to configure the cipher machine as the train lumbered along. Looking out the window occasionally, he watched for Kuskovsky Park, the landmark warning him that his stop, Veshnyaki Station, would be next.

When Viktor saw the cluster of trees in Kuskovsky Park, he stood up, made his way to the closest exit door, and held onto the overhead rail. In a hurry to get home, he stepped off the train and jostled his way through the crowded station. Viktor exited the train station, dashed across Kaznasky Prosek, and walked seven blocks down Kuzminskaya Street. At the end of the street, he turned left onto Topolyovaya Alleya. In the middle of the block, he pushed the door open to the tenement building in which he and his wife, Annusuka Goranovna Zakharov, and their one-year old son shared a tiny, three-room apartment. Hesitating at the stairway, he looked up at the worn stairs, wondering if he had the strength left to make it up the four flights to their dingy, cramped apartment.

Puffing from the exertion of climbing the stairs, he trudged down the hallway and opened the door to his and Anna's apartment. Too tired to go another step, he pushed the door shut, dropped his lunch pail on the floor, and collapsed into a ratty upholstered chair, a small wisp of dust curling up from the frayed fabric covering the arm. He drew in a breath through his nose, sampling the mouth-watering aroma wafting in from the tiny kitchen. He didn't need to ask what Anna, short for Annusuka, was preparing. It was definitely not shchi, cabbage soup, with boiled potatoes, their usual fare. It was something much better.

Viktor stared at Anna in the kitchen as she momentarily stopped what she was doing, brushing a wayward strand of hair back into place. She was not doing anything, except standing there leaning against the counter. It reminded him of the very first time he had seen her. He had been instantly smitten. Even from across the room, he saw something different in the beautiful young girl. At the time, she had just turned nineteen. It had taken Viktor nearly two years to win her heart. He smiled, remembering the first time he had touched her hand. Although five years had passed, in his mind, it seemed like yesterday. Anna wore her hair straight, refusing to curl her hair like a lot of Russian women did to attract men's attention. Her cheeks were faintly dotted with freckles, inherited from her mother who was born of parents from the Udmurt Republic.

"What?" Anna called out from the kitchen, noticing Viktor smiling from ear to ear.

"I was just thinking about the first time we met and I took your hand in mine." Viktor answered.

"That seems like so long ago," Anna sighed.

"Not to me. I remember it like yesterday. You were wearing that pale blue dress I love so much. I saw you across the room. You are the most beautiful woman I have ever seen. Annusuka Goranovna Zakharov do you know how much I love you?"

"Oh, Viktor," Anna stammered, blushing and turning red. She turned back toward the stove and busied herself with finishing their supper.

Anna did her best with the meager wage Viktor earned. If you were not one of the first dozen or so customers in line when the market opened, cabbage and potatoes was all that would be left. Once a week, Anna would leave their apartment long before sunrise, make the trek to the market, and stand in line for two hours. On one of those rare good days, she would be able to purchase a couple of beets, a small bunch of carrots, and maybe even some millet. On a *really* good day, if she was near the front of the line, she might score a chunk of meat. More gristle than meat actually, but meat nonetheless.

With a few precious vegetables in her knapsack, she would make the trek back to their apartment. That morning, smiling as she had begun the long walk back to the apartment, a chunk of meat lay safely stored in the knapsack.

On Viktor's next-to-last day in training, Anna had slipped quietly out of the apartment earlier than normal to be certain she snagged a spot near the front of the line, hoping to score a chunk of meat. It had been nearly a month since there had been any meat in the Zakharov's diet. Anna had been excited when she arrived at the market and found herself to be sixth in line. Her excitement had been short lived when she had arrived at the meat counter and found it to be completely empty. Unable to bear the crushing disappointment, Anna had begun to weep quietly.

"Psst, psst," she had heard coming from behind the empty meat case.

A man in a blood-stained apron had motioned her to the end of the meat case. "I am a friend of Katerina," the man had confided. "She told me you would be coming today and that it was a very special day."

"Yes. My husband has worked so hard and is finishing his training," she had answered. "I had so much wanted to fix his favorite meal tonight, but now I cannot because there is no meat."

All the other customers had noticed people turning away from the empty meat counter and had not even bothered to walk by. The man had bent over, retrieving something from underneath the display. After checking to be certain no one was watching, he had slipped Anna something wrapped in white butcher paper.

"Quick, add it to your items. No one must see," the man had warned. "I saved the best piece we had today."

"Oh, thank you, thank you," Anna had answered, on the verge of tears.

"Yes, yes, but you must hurry and continue your shopping. No one must know."

Anna had turned away quickly, heading for the far side of the market to gather the other items she needed.

By the time she returned to the apartment, Viktor would already be gone, having left for the train ride to the GRU intelligence training facility. Fortunately, Katerina Vasilyovna Kozlov, their neighbor from across the hall, would be there to watch little one-year-old Nikola. When Anna opened the door and entered the apartment, Katerina stood there smiling. Anna had dropped her knapsack on the floor and had rushed over and hugged Katerina, telling her how kind and generous she had been to speak to her friend the butcher.

Soon after a paltry lunch of crackers with a little dab of cheese and a cup of weak tea, Anna had read to Nikola from a book her mother had given her and then had put him down for a nap. She had then gathered the items purchased earlier and had begun preparing borscht, Viktor's favorite dinner.

Viktor lifted himself out of the ratty chair and followed the enticing aroma into the kitchen.

"Anna, you have done it again," Viktor said as he spun Anna around and hugged her so tightly she squealed.

"Viktor, stop," she protested, pushing him away. "Do you want the borsht to burn?"

"I do not care," Viktor said as he grabbed her again and kissed her. "I do not deserve such a fine wife and cook as you are."

"Viktor, it must not burn," she protested again. "These few vegetables cost an entire week's allowance and we have meat for the first time in a month. We must be careful. It will have to last us four days."

"Meat, really," Viktor exclaimed.

"Yes. Katerina spoke to the butcher and he hid a piece for us."

"That is great. Let me help you. I am starving."

While Anna dished up two bowls of borscht, Viktor opened the cabinet and pulled out a hunk of bread wrapped in a towel. He picked off and discarded several spots of mold and then tore off two fist-sized chunks and set them on the table beside the bowls.

"How was Nikola today?" Viktor asked as he pulled out his chair and sat down at their rickety dining table.

"Katerina said he was very good," Anna replied. "He didn't finish his lunch. After lunch, I put him down for a nap, but he only stayed down for a few minutes. He was cranky and underfoot all afternoon. You are lucky you have any borscht."

Anna smiled. Viktor had stopped listening, his attention fixed on the rich, red borscht sitting in front of him.

They ate in silence, savoring the rare treat. Viktor took the last morsel of his bread and swirled it around the bowl to soak up every last drop.

"Would you like more?" Anna asked.

Viktor's eyes darted back and forth from Anna to the pot of borscht sitting on the stove and back to Anna. "Oh, yes," he answered. "It is absolutely delicious, but only two spoonfuls. As you said, we must make it last."

Viktor hungrily slurped up the second helping of borscht, tipping up the bowl and licking the last drop off the rim.

"Viktor, you have the manners of a pig," Anna scolded.

"Sorry, but it is so good. I do not want to waste a single drop." Viktor said, smiling and licking his lips.

Viktor pushed his chair back, picked up his bowl, and bent over and kissed Anna on the neck. He added her bowl to his and set the two bowls in the sink. Returning to the tiny living room, he sank down into the ratty, old chair. Within five minutes, Viktor was snoring softly. Anna walked into the living room and stood watching Viktor for several minutes. He was a kind and thoughtful man and he deserved better than to be constantly screamed at by that swine, Maksimov.

She leaned over, brushed a strand of his ash-brown hair out of the way, and lightly kissed his forehead. "*Life had been so much better before Viktor was conscripted into the Red Army and we were sent to this miserable place*," Anna thought as she sat down on an old, scarred and worn rocking chair, the only other piece of furniture in their tiny living room. Rocking gently, she daydreamed about those better times.

Anna sat in the old rocker, rocking back and forth wondering what life would have been like if Viktor had been allowed to finish his education as an architect. She worried about what the future would hold for them. Undoubtedly, in his job as a cipher analyst, Viktor would have access to many secret messages. That fact, she realized, would make him both valuable *and* also dangerous to the Soviet government.

"*What does the future hold?*" she asked herself.

Anna awakened in the dark to find Viktor's side of the bed empty. She slipped out of bed as quietly as she could to avoid waking Nikola, eased through the bedroom door, and found Viktor hunched over the dining table.

"What are you doing Viktor?" she asked. "It is the middle of the night."

"I'm going over the process of setting up the cipher machine," he answered. "Today is the final examination. I hope drawing these diagrams will help me remember the many options. I will not have access to any instruction books. They have all been locked in a safe that is guarded twenty-four hours a day. Maksimov will assign me to a random machine and then I will have only one hour to determine the correct code plan, complete the settings, and then encode a test message.

"An hour seems like a long time," Anna mused.

"Not so," Viktor protested. "The code plans change constantly and the cipher machine is very complex. Yesterday, Maksimov told us he expects that at least half of us will fail."

"What would happen then?" Anna questioned.

"I have heard that those who fail end up being sent to a labor camp," Viktor asserted "*And* very few ever return."

"You had better get back to your study then," Anna advised. "I will make you some tea."

"Thank you," Viktor said as he returned to his drawing.

Two hours later Viktor tore the papers he had been drawing on into tiny little bits. He brushed the bits of paper off the table into his hand, dropped them into a bowl, and covered them with water. Once he had shaved and changed into his uniform, he would grind the contents of the bowl into mush. If he were to be caught with any drawings of the cipher machines or notes regarding the coding sequences, it would mean a firing squad.

Returning to the kitchen, clean shaven and dressed in his uniform, he dumped the old tea leaves from the tea Anna had brewed earlier together with the mass of soggy paper onto an old newspaper and rolled it up.

"Wish me luck," he said as he hugged Anna and gave her a kiss on the cheek.

"It is not luck you need, Viktor Sergeyevich Zakharov," Anna declared. "It is confidence and determination."

"As always, you are right, Anna, but wish me luck anyway."

"Ни пу́ха, ни пера́", Anna offered, the Russian equivalent of "break a leg", as Viktor turned and headed for the door.

Viktor smiled, as he grabbed the rolled-up newspaper to be dropped in the garbage bin behind the building and left the apartment.

One hour and ten minutes later Viktor stood facing a stern-faced Major Maksimov. Maksimov pointed to cipher machine number eight, handed Viktor a code designation, a message to be encoded, and told him he had exactly one hour to complete the coding process.

Viktor grabbed the materials from Maksimov's hand and rushed over to cipher machine number eight and began his assigned task. First he studied the code designation. Looking at the letters of the code string, he divided them into three letter sequences and then derived the proper code definition to use. Certain he had derived the correct definition, he began the tedious process of aligning the encoding rotors and placing the stepping control pins into their proper locations. With two rotors left to align, Viktor glanced at the large clock at the front of the room, alarmed to learn he had less than twelve minutes left. He should have at least fifteen minutes left, considering it should take no more than four minutes per rotor.

He did not want to take the time to recheck the alignment of the first eight rotors, but he dared not move ahead until he was certain. Once the ninth rotor was aligned it would not be possible to inspect those deeper within the machine. As quickly as he could, he rechecked the first eight rotors.

"Good grief," he exclaimed.

One of the stepping control pins on rotor number five had been incorrectly placed. After easing two fingers into the mechanism, he carefully wiggled the incorrectly positioned pin out between his fingers. As he began to withdraw his fingers, the pin began to slip out of his fingers. He froze.

If the pin fell down into the mechanism, all the rotors would have to be removed to be able to reach it. Removing and reinstalling all the rotors would take over twenty minutes and less than twelve minutes remained.

Ever so slowly he tried again to slide his fingers out of the mechanism. The pin caught against the edge of the rotor.

"No! No! Just another inch," Viktor begged as the pin slipped even further.

GRU Intelligence Directorate
Office of the Commandant
Moscow, Russia

Colonel Vasily Yevgenovich Sokolovsky, acting commandant of the GRU Intelligence Directorate, nodded off, his elbow slipping across the desk's surface, knocking a stack of folders off onto the floor. Blinking his eyes and yawning deeply, he laid the folder he had been reviewing down on the desk. He stood up, stretched, and poked his head through the doorway of his office.

"Evgeni, I need some tea," Colonel Sokolovsky called out. "Brew a fresh pot and bring it to my office right away,"

"Yes, Sir. Right away, Colonel," Senior Lieutenant Evgeni Pavelovich Ivanov, Colonel Sokolovsky's adjutant, answered.

Senior Lieutenant Ivanov groaned and pushed himself back from his desk and walked into the small kitchenette attached to Sokolovsky's office. "A senior lieutenant in the Army with twelve years service and all I do is answer phones and prepare tea for that ogre," Ivanov muttered, making certain he spoke softly enough that Sokolovsky could not hear.

Ivanov dumped two large spoonsful of tea leaves into a white china pot and then poured in boiling water. He let the tea leaves steep for two minutes. After straining the tea into a sterling silver serving pot, he placed it on a silver tray along with a bowl of sugar and a small pitcher of milk. Backing through the kitchenette's swinging door, he carried the tea service into Sokolovsky's office and set it on a small, round table just to the right of Sokolovsky's desk.

"Anything else, Colonel?" Ivanov queried.

"No, just some privacy," Sokolovsky answered with a dismissive wave of his hand.

"*Not even a thank you*," Ivanov complained to himself as he exited the office and pulled the door shut.

Colonel Sokolovsky, if standing straight with only his left foot on the floor and not his normal tilt to the right, stood five foot eleven inches tall. He had dark-colored eyes shaded by bushy, curved eyebrows. Several jagged scars marred the leathery skin of his face. The corners of his mouth turned down in his ever-present scowl. Everyone that knew him claimed his face would break if he ever smiled. However, no one ever said that to his face.

At the age of fourteen, Vasily Yevgenovich Sokolovsky entered an elite military-engineering school as a cadet private. Quickly becoming popular with his peers and his teachers, he proved himself to be highly intelligent and captured the attention of several high-ranking officials. After graduation and entry into the Red Army as a Junior Lieutenant, he demonstrated immense bravery in combat. Assuming command of his infantry battalion upon the death of the commanding officer, he literally shoved his men forward into battle, thereby, saving the entire unit and winning a decisive victory for which he was meritoriously advanced to the rank of Major. Continuing to demonstrate cunning and courage in battle, he was soon promoted to the rank of Colonel.

Months later, during a fierce battle against a superior force, a large caliber bullet shattered the lower bone in his right leg. Left for dead, he survived the night and was rescued by a medical evacuation unit. After months of recovery in a military hospital, his leg healed. However, the doctors had to remove a large number of bone fragments, leaving his right leg one-half inch shorter than the left. Upon his discharge from the hospital, Colonel Sokolovsky was informed he would not be allowed to return to an active infantry command. However, in honor of his gallantry, he was assigned to the Intelligence Directorate to oversee their training facilities. Discouraged and angry, and left with little choice, he accepted the position.

Sokolovsky opened the folder he had laid on the desk, revealing page one of a confidential report compiled by the *Narodnyy Komissariat Vnutrennikh Del,* The People's Commissariat for Internal Affairs, abbreviated NKVD. All functions of the Soviet Union's secret police had been absorbed by the NKVD in 1934, giving the NKVD an absolute monopoly over law enforcement activities. Therefore, the NKVD had jurisdiction over investigations into anyone's background; civilian, government, or military. Everyone outside the NKVD feared it because of its enormous, unchecked authority and power. Frequently abusing that power, the NKVD was responsible for the mass executions of untold numbers of Soviet citizens, often without trials or evidence. The dreaded Gulag system of forced labor camps and reeducation centers, the brainchild of the NKVD, effectively muzzled any and all dissent.

Absentmindedly, Sokolovsky stirred a spoonful of sugar and a dollop of milk into his tea as he flipped past page one. He flipped past the introductory pages he had already reviewed, stopping at the section describing the subject's early years.

The subject of the report had been born to peasant, potato farmers from Northern Russia. Both parents were of Finno-Ugrian descent. The young man had joined the Komsomol, formally known as the All-Union Leninist Young Communist League, at the age of sixteen. The Komsomol was the youth organization of the Communist Party. In addition to teaching the values of the Communist Party, it stressed moderation and discipline, and highly discouraged activities such as smoking and drinking. Those activities were considered "temptations of bourgeois life" and were to be avoided.

The Komsomol had had a huge impact on the subject. He excelled in the organization and quickly became a leader. Noticed by school officials, his enthusiasm and graduation at the top of his high school class earned his entrance into Moscow's highly-esteemed Architectural Institute.

As a student at the architectural institute, the subject had excelled in all his classes, becoming the institute's top student. With only one year remaining before graduation, this time noticed by a senior Politburo official, the subject was conscripted into the Soviet Red Army.

Despite the lack of a lower degree, the subject was assigned to a post-graduate program at Kuibishev Military Engineering Academy. Despite losing his place in the architecture institute, the subject distinguished himself, finishing in the top five of his class.

The rector of the architectural institute had noticed the subject's superior intellect and had advised the Politburo's Central Committee. Overriding the objection of the engineering academy's commandant, albeit a weak objection, the Politburo Committee chairman insisted the subject be accepted into the engineering academy. Because of the subject's initial lack of a lower degree and despite his top-five finish, upon graduation, he was assigned the lowest officer rank of junior lieutenant.

After five months of investigation by the NKVD, the subject was granted the proper clearances and was transferred to the Main Intelligence Division of the Red Army to begin his secret training as a cipher analyst.

Colonel Sokolovsky flipped back to the front of the folder and stared at the photograph of the subject. "Junior Lieutenant Viktor Sergeyevich Zakharov, you will do very nicely," Colonel Sokolovsky said as he closed the folder, rose from his desk, and left his office.

Chapter Two

Beads of sweat began to form on Viktor's forehead. He held his hand still, took a deep breath and held it, then very slowly slid his fingers out of the mechanism. He exhaled, relieved to see the pin still between his fingers. Repositioning the pin between his fingers, he took another deep breath and slowly slid his fingers back between rotors five and six. Careful to not bump the pin. he aligned it over the correct position. Once the pin was started in the hole, he used the tip of one finger to push the pin all the way.

He pulled his fingers out and glanced at the clock. Only five minutes remained. There would not be time to verify the stepping pin placement on the remaining three rotors. He aligned each of the last three rotors and inserted the stepping pins according to the diagram fixed in his mind. With time running out, he pushed the master locking lever that engaged the machine's gears, slid the cover closed, typed in the test message, and pulled the encryption lever.

He leaned back in his chair and gasped, glancing at the clock one last time. Fifteen seconds remained. Exhausted and shaking from the mental exertion, Viktor sat staring at the machine, waiting for the encrypted, punch card to drop into the output tray.

"Time," Major Maksimov shouted, slamming his leather whip on one of the desks.

"Okay, Zakharov, let's get your failure out of the way first," Maksimov sneered, pushing Viktor out of the way.

Maksimov retrieved the punch card from Viktor's cipher machine and walked to the front of the room. He pushed the card into the decryption machine, certain it would indicate Viktor had failed. Tapping his leather whip against his leg, he waited for the card to pass through the machine.

"What?" Maksimov bawled as he stared at a perfectly decrypted test message. "This can't be." He grabbed the card and ran it through the machine again, producing the same result. A third time he reran the card with the same result as the first two times, a perfectly decrypted message. Angrily, he pulled the master control card from his jacket pocket and ran it through the machine. He couldn't believe it. The machine was working correctly.

Watching the spectacle unfolding at the front of the room, Viktor could not suppress the smile growing on his face.

Maksimov glanced at Viktor and saw the grin on his face. "You have cheated," he shrieked, rushing toward Viktor. "I will have you shot for cheating." Upon reaching Viktor, Maksimov raised his leather whip, intending to whip a confession from him.

"Now, you will feel the sting of my whip you lying dog," Major Maksimov bellowed.

"Maksimov," Colonel Sokolovsky shouted from the front of the room. "What do you think you are doing?"

"I was about to teach Junior Lieutenant Zakharov a lesson for cheating," Maksimov responded.

"How could he have cheated?" Colonel Sokolovsky asked. "Did you not watch the students while they performed their final exam?"

"Yes, Colonel, I watched them. That is my duty," Maksimov replied, standing at attention.

"Well then, Major, if any of them cheated, which I doubt, it was your stupidity that allowed it," Colonel Sokolovsky barked. "Either Junior Lieutenant Zakharov here performed the test correctly or you are stupid. Well, which is it Major?"

"But, he….,"

"Shut up you stupid imbecile!" Colonel Sokolovsky roared. "I don't want to hear anymore of your pathetic rantings. Barely half of the students in your classes have passed their final exams. Your performance here has become unacceptable. You are hereby demoted to the rank of Captain. Get out of my sight before I demote you to junior lieutenant.

Maksimov started toward the door in the front of the room. Colonel Sokolovsky stopped him and held out his hand, waiting for Maksimov to hand over Viktor's final exam card. Maksimov relinquished the card. As Maksimov, rage boiling within him, reached the front of the room, Colonel Sokolovsky called out, "Oh, *Captain* Maksimov, I neglected to inform you of your new duty assignment. You have been relieved from your teaching position and are being sent to an infantry unit. Do not shoot yourself."

"Выродок," Maksimov snarled angrily under his breath, calling Viktor something akin to a despicable creature so vile and degenerate even its own mother would abandon it. He shot Viktor a menacing glare, turned, and left the room. "He will pay for this outrage," Maksimov growled as he stomped down the hallway.

"Junior Lieutenant Zakharov, follow me to my office," Colonel Sokolovsky ordered. "I have an important matter to discuss with you.

Colonel Sokolovsky pushed the door to his office open, waited for Viktor to enter, then pushed the door shut.

"Sit," he said as he walked around his desk and sat down. "Have some tea, Junior Lieutenant, in honor of completion of your cipher encryption training." Colonel Sokolovsky poured a cup of dark, red tea and pushed the steaming cup across the desk toward Viktor.

"Thank you, Colonel Sokolovsky," Viktor responded.

"I have read your file and I have been watching you," Colonel Sokolovsky announced, taking a sip of the dark, steaming tea. "I allowed that imbecile, Maksimov, to remain as commanding officer of the training unit as a test. I wanted to see if you could hold up under his insults and abusive behavior. You responded admirably. In spite of his constant attempts to provoke you, you passed every test perfectly. I have great need of someone like you."

"Thank you for noticing, Colonel."

"Next week I am being assigned to one of Russia's most important embassies where I will be responsible for security which includes encryption and decryption of all incoming and outgoing message traffic. I will need a top-notch cipher analyst. Therefore, I have directed General Petrovsky of the Military Council to have you assigned to the embassy as well."

"But I have just finished my training," Viktor asserted.

"Do not worry, Junior Lieutenant. I have confirmed the quality of your work here and you are more than qualified. Besides, it is not really a request."

"Yes, Sir," Viktor acknowledged, knowing that to argue would be considered disrespectful. "Where is it we will be assigned?"

"Ottawa, Canada, Lieutenant Zakharov," Colonel Sokolovsky replied, handing Viktor new rank symbols for his uniform. "At my request, you are being promoted to full lieutenant."

"When will I be assigned, Colonel?" Viktor asked.

"You will accompany me when I travel there next week. I will need you to start your duties immediately. The current cipher analyst has disappeared and is no longer there. A replacement is urgently needed."

"What about my wife and son?"

"They will be allowed to come later, once arrangements have been made and their security clearances are in order. Any other questions, Lieutenant?"

"No sir."

"You may take the rest of the day off. I have much to do to get ready. Please let yourself out, Lieutenant Zakharov."

Viktor rose from the chair and exited Colonel Sokolovsky's office. To say the just concluded meeting left Viktor stunned would be an enormous understatement. The sudden, and well deserved, demotion of Major Maksimov, the transfer to Canada, and then the unexpected promotion. His mind was spinning.

"Canada? Anyplace but Canada," he complained. "It is always cold and frozen in Canada."

As he rushed down the stairs two at a time, he wondered what Anna was going to say when he broke the news.

Zakharov Apartment
Topolyovaya Alleya
Moscow, Russia

Viktor leaned on the stair railing, breathing hard from the climb up the four flights of stairs. He started down the hallway but stopped, going over in his mind what he was going to say to Anna. She was not going to like being transferred so soon and a move would be especially difficult with a one-year old. On top of all that, the move would be all the way across the Atlantic Ocean to Canada and she would have to travel alone as he would be leaving next week.

"I'll wait until after supper," he muttered as he trudged down the hallway toward their apartment. Reaching the door to their apartment, he slid his key into the lock, twisted the key, and pushed the door open. He put on a smile, hoping his face would not show the anxiety that was churning inside him.

"Da, Da," little Nikola babbled when he saw Viktor enter the apartment. The toddler scrambled toward Viktor as fast as his wobbly, little legs could carry him. He stood holding his arms up, waiting to be picked up.

"How is my little Nicky," Viktor cooed as he reached down and scooped the little boy up in his arms.

"Viktor, what are you doing home?" Anna asked, stepping out of the kitchen into the living room. "It is not even lunch time yet."

"I passed my final exam, perfectly I might add," he answered, smiling from ear to ear. "Colonel Sokolovsky was pleased and told me to take the rest of the day off."

"Colonel Sokolovsky?" Anna remarked, a puzzled look on her face. "I thought Maksimov was in charge."

"Oh, Anna, you should have been there," Viktor chuckled. "Maksimov is no longer the commandant."

"What happened?"

"When the exam period ended, Maksimov ran to the cipher machine I had been assigned. He grabbed the punch card, returned to the front of the room and ran it through the master decryption machine. I know he was certain I had failed."

Nikola began to squirm in Viktor's arms. Viktor leaned over and put him on the floor, watching him head for the rag doll Anna had made shortly after he was born.

"It was hilarious, Anna," Viktor continued. "I wish you could have been there to see it. Maksimov became furious when the card decrypted correctly. He grabbed the card and fed it into the machine two more times. Each time it gave the same result. Then he fed the master control card into the machine. I suppose he thought the machine was defective. That decrypted correctly as well. He turned around and saw me smiling. I couldn't help it, Anna. It was so funny."

"But that swine Maksimov is so vicious. What did he do then," Anna asked, a look of concern on her face.

"He screamed that I had cheated and came charging toward me. He raised the leather whip he always carries and was going to strike me. That's when Colonel Sokolovsky walked into the room. Maksimov tried to convince him I cheated, but Sokolovsky said if anyone had cheated it was because he was stupid."

"What did Maksimov say?"

"Nothing. Colonel Sokolovsky cut him off. He demoted Maksimov and told him he is being sent to an infantry unit."

"Good," Anna spat. "I hope someone shoots that miserable pig."

"I can't say I disagree," Viktor added. "There is more. Colonel Sokolovsky asked me to his office and gave me tea in honor of my completing the cipher training."

"Really," Anna remarked. "You must feel very proud to be honored by such an important man."

"Yes, I must admit I do, but there is even more."

"More? How can there be?" Anna asked, a shocked look on her face.

"Anna, Colonel Sokolovsky promoted me to Lieutenant," Viktor beamed, holding out the new rank symbols but leaving out the news about the transfer to the embassy in Canada.

"Oh, Viktor, that is wonderful news," Anna gushed, grabbing Viktor and giving him a big hug.

"It is such a great day let's take Nikola and go have a picnic in the park," Viktor announced. "We can pick up a few items at the market. Today we will celebrate."

Three hours later Viktor and Anna returned to their tiny little apartment with a thoroughly exhausted, sleeping Nikola. While Anna put the little boy down for a nap, Viktor brewed a pot of tea with some special tea he had splurged on at the market. He poured tea into two cups, carried one of them into the living room, and handed it to Anna. As he straightened up, he cradled Anna's face in his hands and kissed her. He returned to the kitchen, grabbed his cup of tea, and rejoined Anna in the living room.

While drinking their tea, they discussed Maksimov's demotion, Viktor's successful completion of cipher training, and the promotion along with a much needed increase in pay. With the tea finished, Viktor picked up the cups, took them to the kitchen, and returned to the living room. He joined Anna in the ratty upholstered chair. It was a tight fit, but he didn't care. He intended to take full advantage of his rare day off. Soon they were both asleep, wrapped in each other's arms.

Viktor awoke with a jerk. He sat up and put his face in his hands. The dream that had awakened him had seemed so real it left him shaking. In the dream, he was standing on a raised wooden platform with a noose draped around his neck. Not far away, Maksimov, with a maniacal grin on his face, stood with his hand poised on the release lever that would send

Viktor plummeting to his death. *"Must have been the menacing glare Maksimov gave me,"* he thought as he rose from the chair and walked into the kitchen.

"Viktor, what is the matter?" Anna asked, following him into the kitchen.

"Just a dream," Viktor answered. "It is silly. I don't know why it startled me."

"What's really bothering you, Viktor?" Anna pressed. "Something else is troubling you. I saw it on your face the minute you walked in the door."

"But....,"

"Don't try to fool me, Viktor Sergeyevich Zakharov," Anna interrupted, staring directly at him. "You may be able to fool those oafs in the Army, but you can't fool me. Now, out with it. What have you not told me?"

Anna was partly able to read Viktor's frame of mind because she loved him so much and having learned over the years how to read even the subtle changes in his expression, and partly because he let his guard down when not in the presence of superior officers of the Red Army.

"I wanted to wait until evening to tell you," Viktor replied. "I did not want to spoil the great day we are having."

"Viktor, what is it?" Anna asked again, a look of worry clouding her face.

"I am being reassigned to an international posting," he announced, looking down at the floor.

"It can't be any worse than this miserable place. We will be together. Where are they sending you, I mean us?"

"To the Russian embassy in Ottawa, Canada."

"Canada?" Anna gulped. "Oh, Viktor, no. It's so far away and it's so cold there *and* all that snow."

"They tell me it is quite beautiful there in the summer," Viktor countered. "It gets quite warm there in the summer, even hot, I am told."

"But my parents, Viktor. They will not get to see little Nikola grow up," Anna protested, turning away. "Why does it have to be you?"

"I'm sorry," Viktor stammered, a pleading look on his face. "Colonel Sokolovsky said he has been watching me and I am the best cipher analyst available. He personally wants me to accompany him. There is nothing I can do. The Red Army says go; you *must* go."

Anna turned and looked at Viktor, her heart melting when she saw the disheartened look on his face.

"I'm sorry, Viktor," Anna said. "I don't mean to be difficult. I know there is nothing you can do. When must we leave?"

Viktor hesitated, not wanting to tell Anna that he would be leaving the following week, alone.

"Viktor, is there more?" Anna questioned.

"Sokolovsky wants me to travel with him next week," Viktor answered sheepishly.

"What?" Anna bawled. "You mean I will not be able to go with you?"

"No. No," Viktor blurted out. "You will be able to go to Canada, but it will be later. There is much paperwork required for civilians. Sokolovsky, himself, said you would be able to come once all the clearances are in order. Maybe three or four weeks. Perhaps, a little longer."

"But what will I do with this?" Anna questioned, waving her hand toward their few meager possessions.

"Give it away or just leave it," Viktor answered. "You will only be allowed to travel with three suitcases. Two for you and one for Nikola. Sokolovsky said we will be assigned a small apartment in the consulate housing complex. He promised he would do his best to get us what we need."

"I wish you had never been forced into the Army," Anna complained. "This is just awful. I don't know if I want to go. Maybe I will go home and live with my parents."

"Anna, do not say such a thing," Viktor choked. "What would I do without you?"

Anna turned away and rushed into the kitchen. Leaning against the counter, she began to cry. The news of the reassignment had produced exactly the reaction Viktor had feared.

He laid his hand on Anna's shoulder and gently turned her around.

"Anna, please don't be upset," Viktor pleaded. "It won't be forever."

"I'm sorry, Viktor," Anna sniffled. "I know there is nothing you can do. You must obey. But, Canada?"

"Yes, I know, but someone told me food is plentiful in Canada. They say you can buy meat everyday in the market."

"Every day?" Anna responded, a look of surprise on her face.

"Besides, it cannot be as bad as this place," Viktor added, glancing around the small, dingy apartment.

"I hope you are right. I…" Anna started to answer, interrupted by Nikola's wail coming from the bedroom.

Viktor watched Anna disappear into the bedroom, trying to imagine what life would *really* be like in Canada.

What had been a truly good day for the Zakharov family, had ended on a sad note. "*Would Canada really be better than this place?*" Viktor wondered, glancing at the ratty, worn furniture and peeling paint.

"I certainly hope so," he muttered as he headed for the bedroom to help with Nikola.

Chapter Three

Baltiysky Railway Station
Moscow, Russia

Still dark, Viktor looked up at the impressive Baltiysky Railway Station as he stood across the street waiting for traffic to clear. Hopefully, he would be early and Colonel Sokolovsky would not already be there waiting. Colonel Sokolovsky, an impatient and quick-tempered individual, was known to scream at anyone inconsiderate enough to cause him to have to wait, especially someone of junior rank.

Viktor stepped into the street, his attention distracted. Startled by a loud horn blared to his right, he lurched backward out of the street, barely avoiding a speeding truck as it roared by. The truck's front tire dropped into a large pothole as it swerved to avoid running Viktor over.

"Just great," Viktor complained, looking down as muddy water from the pothole soaked the legs of his trousers. "Just absolutely great!"

His mind had been replaying the heart-wrenching scene when he had said goodbye to his beautiful wife, Anna.

Two hours earlier, Viktor had attempted to slide out of bed without disturbing Anna. His lone bag, packed and ready, sat waiting beside the door. He had given himself extra time to sit and have a cup of tea and half a biscuit, knowing the trip to the seaport would be long and tiring. Having very little money, he would need to save it for when he arrived in Canada. Unless Colonel Sokolovsky felt generous, he would have nothing to eat until they boarded the steamship bound for Canada at Königsberg. Colonel Sokolovsky had informed Viktor the steamship would provide one meal a day.

Deep in thought, Viktor jumped, startled when Anna walked up behind him and laid her hand on his shoulder.

"Viktor, were you not going to say goodbye?" she asked.

"You were sleeping so soundly I did not want to wake you."

"But, Viktor, I may not see you for weeks. Maybe even months."

"I'm sorry," Viktor said. "Sit. Join me while I finish my tea and biscuit."

"How long will it take you to reach Canada?" she asked, watching Viktor shove the last chunk of biscuit into his mouth.

"I am told it will take nearly a full day to reach the seaport. Then four or five days by steamship to reach the coast of Canada. Then another day or so by train to reach the city of Ottawa. All that adds up to at least a week," he groaned. Tipping up his cup, he drank the last swallow of his tea, sat the cup on the table, and dug in his pocket for his pocket watch. He flipped it open and sighed deeply.

"It is time," he said as he pushed his chair back and stood up. "I must leave."

"Oh, Viktor," Anna wailed as she jumped up and hugged him tightly. "I am frightened for you. The things I hear that are happening in Prussia are dreadful."

"Colonel Sokolovsky says the war is over," Viktor explained. "What is happening there is because of a lack of control of the Red Army. He says the seaport is tightly controlled and we will be safe. We will be escorted from the train station to the seaport by a heavily armed squad of soldiers."

"I will miss you," Anna sniffed, trying hard to control the tears threatening to flow.

"I will miss you too," Viktor responded. "I will post a letter as soon as we reach Canada. I'm sorry, but I really must go if I wish to beat Colonel Sokolovsky to the station."

Viktor hugged Anna tightly for a long time. He released his grip, whispered something in her ear, and headed for the door. She smiled and watched Viktor exit the apartment without looking back.

"*I must be more careful,*" Viktor told himself, doing his best to brush off his trousers. He looked both ways down Suschevsky Street. Seeing a break in traffic, he raced across the street and stopped in front of the large building housing the Baltiysky Railway Station. Opened in September of 1901, the station sat at the edge of Rizhskaya Square, at the crossing of 1st Meshchanskaya Street and Suschevsky Street. Baltiysky Station, Moscow's least busy station, was also Moscow's only connection eastward to the then Prussian city of Königsberg, eleven hundred kilometers to the east. Less than two years in the future, as would be decreed by the Allied Control Council, Prussia would be declared officially dissolved and Königsberg would then be renamed to Kaliningrad.

Viktor selected the far door to his left and entered the station. Locating his train number on the large board displaying arriving and departing trains, he proceeded to the track number indicated. He handed the ticket Colonel Sokolovsky had provided him to the ticket agent.

"Papers please," the ticket agent ordered.

Viktor withdrew his travel and identity papers from the inside pocket of his uniform jacket and handed them to the ticket agent. The heavily armed guard standing next to the ticket agent slid his hand down and rested his index finger on the trigger guard of his PPS-43, Pistolet-Pulemjot Sudaeva submachine gun, suspiciously watching every move Viktor made.

The ticket agent shifted his eyes back and forth between the papers and Viktor's face several times.

"Destination?" the ticket agent asked."

"Königsberg," Viktor answered, knowing it wise to give no more information than required. The ticket agent shot Viktor a questioning stare. "And then on to Canada by steamship."

"By who's authority?" the ticket agent demanded.

"I am accompanying Colonel Vasily Yevgenovich Sokolovsky to the Russian Embassy in Ottawa, Canada. I am early and Colonel Sokolovsky has not yet arrived."

The ticket agent stared at Viktor for some time, uncertain if he should allow Viktor to pass. "Stand over there," he said, pointing to the spot beside the guard.

The guard took a step sideways to make room for Viktor. As ordered, Viktor dragged his heavy bag out of the way and stood beside the guard. For fifteen minutes, Viktor stood waiting, occasionally shifting his weight from one foot to the other. A piercing whistle announced the arrival of the train bound for Königsberg. The huge, black locomotive lumbered into the station and screeched to a stop, billowing huge clouds of steam. The conductors opened the doors and positioned step stools on the platform as scores of passengers disembarked.

Viktor pulled out his pocket watch and looked at the time, becoming worried that if Colonel Sokolovsky did not arrive soon, they would miss the train. Three more minutes passed.

Aroused by a flurry of activity coming from the station's concourse, the ticket agent watched as an elite Imperial Russian Guard unit marched to the front of the line. The guard standing beside Viktor immediately came to attention.

"I am in a hurry," Colonel Sokolovsky barked at the ticket agent, handing him his travel papers. "I must not miss that train."

Colonel Sokolovsky stood there glaring impatiently at the ticket agent. After a few seconds, he bent over and reading from the nameplate pinned to the ticket agent's uniform said, "Agent Vorodin, are you having trouble reading the papers. I assure you everything is in order. Do you wish to make me late for my train? Would you like to find yourself reassigned to Novosibirsk. It is quite cold there *and* very inhospitable."

"No, sir, Colonel Sokolovsky," Agent Vorodin squeaked. "I do not wish that. Here are your papers. You may board your train, Colonel."

"Wise choice," Colonel Sokolovsky smirked as he grabbed the papers, turned, and headed for the train. "Lieutenant Zakharov, follow me. Hurry. The train is already boarding."

Viktor snatched the handle of his bag and hurried after Colonel Sokolovsky. Together they handed their tickets to the conductor waiting by the first car behind the locomotive. The conductor first looked at Colonel Sokolovsky's class of travel.

"Sir, you may board and take any open unit in the first four cars," he said as he punched the Colonel's first-class ticket. "Lieutenant, your ticket is third-class so you must board one of the last four cars."

"Lieutenant, meet me on the platform at the front of the train when we reach Königsberg," Colonel Sokolovsky said as he climbed up the steps and into the first car.

"Yes, sir," Viktor answered, grabbing his bag and racing toward the end of the train. "Wait. Wait," he shouted, seeing the conductor bend over and pick up the step stool.

"Hurry," the conductor shouted.

Viktor leapt onto the first step and threw his bag up into the car. The conductor followed Viktor up onto the first step and waved his arm. The huge locomotive spun its enormous wheels several revolutions and then began to chug out of the station, belching clouds of thick black smoke from its boiler.

Lugging his heavy bag, Viktor passed through the first three cars before finding a spot in the last car where both seats were unoccupied. He propped the bag in the seat by the window and plopped down in the aisle seat, glad to be off his feet. He would leave the bag in the seat unless someone demanded the window seat.

Viktor glanced out the car's northeast-facing window and saw that the sun had just begun to rise above the horizon. The sparse streetlights quickly faded to none as the train passed through the outlying areas of Moscow and into the countryside. The conductor walked through the car announcing the estimated time of arrival at their first stop, Smolensk, three hundred sixty-nine kilometers distant, as being six hours and forty-five minutes away.

"*Seven long hours*," Viktor moaned internally, knowing that would only be one-third of the way to their destination. The seat was hard, angled oddly, and very uncomfortable. He shift-

ed his weight, found a mildly uncomfortable position, and settled against his bag, hoping he would be comfortable enough
he could sleep. If not, it was going to be a very long, very miserable trip. Lulled by the swaying motion of the car and the
rhythmic clackety-clack of the wheels passing over the joints in
the rails, Viktor soon drifted off to sleep.

Viktor slept almost five hours leaning against his bag.
Awakened by a sudden jolt as the train passed over an old siding switch, he straightened up and winced in pain. Sleeping in
the odd position had given him such a stiff neck he could not
turn his head sideways. He lifted himself out of the seat and
stood in the aisle. With his hands on seats on both sides of the
aisle, he stretched one way and then the other, trying to work
the knots out of his back and neck muscles.

Returning to his seat, he pulled out his pocket watch and
checked the time. In a little over an hour, the train would make
its first stop in Smolensk. He would get off and stretch his legs
and, hopefully, at least be able to get a drink of water at the
station.

Just as the conductor had announced, six hours and forty-
seven minutes after the train departed Moscow, it pulled into
the Smolensk station and stopped. The conductor announced
the train would be at the station for only fifteen minutes while
it took on water and coal.

Viktor stepped off the train and made a beeline for the
station facilities. At the end of the station's platform, Viktor
spotted a large water bucket and dipper. He waited his turn
and then drank two dippers full of water. Wiping his mouth on
his sleeve, he started back toward the end of the train.

"Lieutenant, have you any money?" Colonel Sokolovsky
asked, standing not far away.

Viktor turned and answered, "Very little, Colonel. Only
enough for when I arrive in Canada."

"Would you like a sandwich?"

"Yes, but I will have to save my money."

"I am feeling generous," Colonel Sokolovsky said. "Here, buy yourself something in the station's market," he said, dropping a few coins into Viktor's hand.

"Thank you, Colonel," Viktor beamed. "You are most generous."

"Yes, but do not grow to expect it," Colonel Sokolovsky asserted as he turned away and climbed back up into the car.

Viktor hurried back into the station's small market, selected a pre-made sandwich, and paid for it with coins the colonel had given him. He rushed back out onto the platform, climbed onto the train, and took his seat. Hungrily devouring the sandwich, Viktor gazed out the window as the train chugged out of the station, resuming its journey toward Königsberg.

Viktor lurched forward, about to take another bite from his sandwich. He turned to see what had banged into him.

"I am most sorry, sir" a tall, rail-thin man in a Red Army uniform apologized. "The train is swaying so badly I lost my balance. I have checked all the third-class cars and that seat beside you is the only one that is not occupied. If you would be so kind as to move your bag. Otherwise, I will have to stand."

Viktor looked up at the man who had to be at least six foot four inches tall, but could not weigh over eighty kilos. The man's skin was pasty white and his face was drawn and hollow with sunken eyes rimmed with dark circles, a sure sign the man was malnourished.

"I did not expect anyone would board the train at Smolensk," Victor responded. "If you give me a hand, we can shove it up in the overhead rack."

Together, the two men grabbed the bag and hoisted it up into the overhead rack.

"I am Junior Lieutenant Borislav Gordanovitch Ismaylov," the man said, holding his hand out toward Viktor. "I am being sent to the embassy in Ottawa, Canada. I am told they are increasing security."

"Nice to meet you," Viktor replied, shaking the man's hand firmly. "I am Lieutenant Victor Sergeyevich Zakharov. I am being sent to the embassy as well."

Viktor stepped out of the way, allowing Junior Lieutenant Ismaylov to take the window seat. As the man sat down and leaned against the wall of the car, Viktor noticed him glancing at the remainder of his sandwich.

"Would you like a portion of my sandwich?" Viktor asked.

"I apologize," Ismaylov answered. "I didn't mean to stare. I have not eaten since yesterday."

"Someone provided this for me. It is only right if I also share with you," Viktor asserted as he tore of a piece of the sandwich and handed it to Ismaylov.

"You are most kind, Lieutenant Zakharov. I am deeply grateful."

"You are quite welcome and please call me Viktor. If we are going to work together at the embassy, we should become friends."

"I agree. You may call me Borislav, or Boris for short."

Boris turned toward the window, stuffed the portion of sandwich Viktor had given him into his mouth, and took an enormous bite. The two men sat in silence as they finished their sandwiches.

Port of Pillau
Königsberg, Prussia

Fourteen hours later, the train slowed as it entered the outskirts of Königsberg, founded in 1255 by the Teutonic Knights during the Northern Crusades. Situated on the southeastern corner of the Baltic Sea, the city had developed into an important seaport for the entire Baltic region.

Boris poked Viktor in the arm, interrupting Viktor's efforts to write legibly on the note paper he intended to post to Anna as soon as they reached the seaport at Königsberg.

"Viktor, Viktor, look," Boris exclaimed excitedly. "The destruction here is beyond words. I had heard the battle for Königsberg was quite brutal, but this... This is unbelievable!"

Viktor turned and looked out the window and audibly gasped. He also had heard the same reports as Boris, but nothing could have prepared either man for the devastation their eyes beheld. Viktor shook his head, his mind trying to comprehend the enormity of the wreckage and the horrible despair on the faces of the poor souls milling about looking for anything they could salvage.

Viktor rose out of his seat and kneeled alongside Boris to get a better look at the heartrending scene. Viktor and Boris gazed in unbelief as the train passed through the city. The train tracks had been cleared and repaired, but on either side of the track the devastation spread out for as far as the eye could see. Most of the city had been reduced to rubble, first by RAF bombing and then by the relentless pounding of Soviet artillery. Thousands of civilians had died, but in many respects that was just the beginning of the horrors that would be visited upon the surviving German population.

The commander of *Fortress Königsberg*, left with little choice as supplies of ammunition ran out and Soviet forces overwhelmed their positions, decided all was lost and surrendered the remnants of his forces to the Russian Army. German soldiers not loaded into cattle cars bound for concentration camps were simply shot were they stood.

The train passed into a residential neighborhood, the houses burning and smoking. Any houses that remained standing had been ransacked. Household furnishings, musical instruments, cooking utensils, children's toys, and clothes had been thrown out into the streets. Nearly everything had been reduced to rubble. Those buildings left standing were mere shells, burning and smoking, missing one or more walls.

Most unsettling of all, were the faces of the few German civilians that had not yet been rounded up to be exiled to Siberia or some miserable labor camp. Their once happy faces were empty, hollow, soulless, as they poked among the ruins. Carcasses of dead horses littered the streets, stripped of all edible flesh by the starving inhabitants of the once thriving city. Clouds of foul-smelling, black smoke hung over the city like a dark burial shroud.

Victor and Boris both flinched when they heard gunfire ring out. They stared open-mouthed as the train passed into another scene far more horrifying than anything they had seen.

Amongst the inconceivable carnage, Russians soldiers, drunk from alcohol looted from liquor stores, danced wildly in the streets, shooting into the air. Many, too drunk to stand, staggered and fell into the carnage. Those still able to stand brutalized and murdered the wandering civilians, ripping anything of value from their dead bodies. Weeping girls and women were dragged into houses despite their pleas for mercy. Children screamed for their parents. Victor and Boris stared transfixed, sickened by the brutality, but unable to look away.

Two drunk Russian soldiers viciously clubbed an elderly German nun with their rifles. Laughing like hyenas, they picked up her unconscious body and flung it into the street. Further down the street, two women and three small children ran screaming out of a house with their hands raised beseechingly. Three Russian soldiers ran out after them and shot them in the back. One of the soldiers rolled the bodies over, ripping off clothing as they searched for anything of value.

"This is unspeakable," Viktor groaned.

"Yes, Viktor, this is horrible," Boris agreed

"How can soldiers do such things, Boris? This is unbearable. I can watch no more of this."

Not waiting for an answer, Viktor turned away from the horror taking place outside the window and returned to his seat, revolted by what he had just witnessed. Swallowing hard, he fought desperately to hold back the burning vomit rising in his throat as he tried to strip from his mind the images of children being shot and stripped naked.

"*What if it had been little Nikola?*" he asked himself.

He bent over and covered his face, pressing his hands hard against his temples as if he could squeeze the sickening images from his mind. Through tightly closed eyes, tears seeped out onto the palms of his hands. "*Children. How could they shoot defenseless children?*" his mind screamed.

Neither man spoke nor looked at each other for the remaining twenty-five minutes. The train screeched and hissed to a stop as it reached the end of the track. Viktor and Boris grabbed their belongings without speaking and exited the train onto the platform. Colonel Sokolovsky quickly gathered Viktor, Boris, and two other men in uniform and hustled them over to a heavily guarded troop transport and ordered them up into the back of the truck.

The driver slammed and hooked the endgate, hurried to the cab, started the engine, and drove away from the station. Two armored vehicles, armed with .50 caliber machine guns, one in front and one behind, escorted the troop transport as it headed toward the seaport spread out along the banks of the Pregolya River.

The troop transport rumbled along through the rough streets occasionally bouncing over a piece of debris. Twice they stopped at military checkpoints to have travel documents verified. Finally, the troop transport arrived at the seaport and the four men were ordered out of the truck and lined up to receive further instructions. Colonel Sokolovsky informed the men of their assigned berthing areas and that the steamship would sail in just over two hours. He gave the men permission to browse the few shops that still remained open along the seaport and purchase anything they could find as long as they were on board the ship prior to sailing. He warned them explicitly that to miss the sailing would mean court-martial and a likely death sentence.

Viktor agreed to meet Boris somewhere along the line of shops and then hurried off to find the place he had been told he could post his letter to Anna. One-half hour later, Viktor came running back along Ulitsa Portovaya, the street running between the train tracks and the seaport docks, panting and out of breath. Hurrying toward the end of the line of shops, he saw Boris waving frantically at him.

"Viktor, you must be quiet and hear this," Boris spoke softly as soon as Viktor reached him.

Boris grabbed Viktor's arm and pulled him along. Together, the two men strolled to the end of the last shop in the line, pretending to look at something in the window. Viktor turned his head and listened to a group of infantry soldiers talking and laughing. Viktor quickly turned away and ran toward the steamship with Boris running after him.

"Did you hear what they said?" Boris questioned.

"Yes, I heard," Viktor snapped. "I had to run away. I did not want the soldiers to see the disgust on my face."

"I too felt anger and disgust," Boris asserted.

Viktor had seen first-hand the atrocities being committed by the Red Army, but to learn that as a reward, the commanding general had given official permission for two days of rape and looting stunned Viktor.

"This is not the way soldiers are to act," Viktor growled.

'Yes, I agree," Boris added. "But, what are we to do?"

"We will keep our mouths shut and say nothing," Viktor barked. "Or, we will end up like the Germans."

The two men abandoned their browsing and rushed back to the ship, displayed their travel papers and tickets, boarded the ship, and located their assigned berthing area. For an hour, Viktor laid silently in his bunk, trying desperately to push what he had seen and heard from his mind, but the revolting images refused to go away. They danced and swirled in his mind. The laughing soldiers taunted him. He couldn't take it anymore. Pushing himself up, he sat on the edge of the bunk with his face in his hands.

Part of him wanted to scream and cry out against the sadistic brutality he had witnessed, but Viktor knew even the slightest aspersion directed against the Soviet Army would bring swift punishment. He would bury what he had seen and never speak of it.

Viktor was the first to feel the subtle vibration in his feet as the steamship's two large screws began to churn the water, creating a muddy plume in the river.

"Boris, we are moving. Can you feel it?"

Boris placed his palm on the steel deck and cocked his head. "Yes, I can feel the vibration. I will be glad to be far away from this terrible place."

"I, too, will be glad, but how will we ever forget what we saw? The horrible stench. As long as I live, I will never be able to forget such atrocities."

Boris just shrugged his shoulders, laid back in his small bunk, and closed his eyes.

Slowly, the large steamship slid backward into the river's main channel. The steamship pivoted in the water and steamed down the river. Twenty minutes later, the steamship entered the deepwater Vistula Lagoon, headed for the wide channel at Baltiysk and the entrance to the Baltic Sea and eventually the open waters of the Atlantic Ocean.

The days at sea were long, monotonous, and boring. During the day, Viktor spent most of his time sitting on the deck or standing at the ship's railing staring off into the distance. At night, the images from Königsberg that were seared into his memory haunted his sleep. Every night the same vivid dream would awaken him: his precious, little Nikola shot in the back and then trampled by drunken soldiers. Drenched in sweat and unable to sleep, he would climb out of the cramped bunk and make his way topside. He would stand at the bow railing staring down at the dark water. Tired of standing in one spot, he would walk back to the stern of the ship and then back to the bow. Many nights he would make a half-dozen trips back and forth. Finally, in desperation, he would sit on the deck and hug his knees, begging the visions to stop.

On the sixth day, Boris could not help but notice the dark circles under Viktor's eyes and the hollow, empty expression that clouded his face. He had started to mention the horrors in Königsberg. Viktor shot him an angry glance, shook his head, and turned away. From that day onward, the distressing subject was never mentioned again between them.

Chapter Four

Early on the morning of the eleventh day after leaving Königsberg, the passenger steamer S.S. Tadoussac, owned by Canada Steamship Lines Limited, on a heading of due north, sailed just east of the rocky coast of New Brunswick. Viktor and Boris, leaning against the port railing, watched as the steamship entered the Honguedo Strait, passing between the eastern tip of Quebec's Gaspé Peninsula and Anticosti Island. The steamship made a slow gradual turn toward the southwest and headed down the Saint Lawrence Seaway.

The two men watched for an hour as the seaway narrowed and then headed below deck for their one meal of the day. It would take another full day before the steamship docked at Trois-Rivières, Quebec, the end of their travel by ship. From there Viktor and Boris had been told they would complete the final leg of their journey to Ottawa by train.

Up early the following day and anxious to get off the steamship, Viktor and Boris stood at the forward railing and watched as the ship captain skillfully eased the large steamship up to the dock. The deck hands threw the large hawsers to waiting workers on the dock who looped the hawsers over large cleats on the edge of the dock. Soon, the steamship was secured fore and aft and the gangway was lowered.

Viktor and Boris, hoisting their bags up on their shoulders, joined the line waiting to disembark the ship. Both men were quite relieved as they stepped back onto solid ground and away from the constant swaying of the ship.

Trois-Rivières, Quebec, derived its name from the French, meaning 'three rivers', because of the fact the Saint-

Maurice River had three mouths where it met the Saint Lawrence River. The city, lying on the north shore of the river and located at the confluence of the Saint-Maurice and Saint Lawrence rivers, prospered greatly as a major shipping center because of its location. Viktor and Boris were immediately struck by the heaps of fruits and vegetables displayed in front of the shops that lined the waterfront.

"Viktor, come quick," Boris called out. "You must see this. Can you tell me what these are?"

Viktor trotted up to the shop where Boris had gone to browse. Boris pointed to a large stack of crates sitting in front of the shop, waiting for Viktor to answer his question.

"да иди ты!" Viktor exclaimed as he ran over and stood gawking at the stack of crates. The closest translation of Viktor's exclamation into English would be like saying "Are you kidding me?"

"What is it, Viktor?" Boris asked.

"Only once in my entire life when I was a young boy did I see one of these," Viktor answered. It is called an orange. Because of its color, I think."

Viktor picked up one of the oranges, held it beneath his nose, inhaled deeply, and said, "Wonderful. I remember the look on Papa's face when he handed me and my sister each an orange just like this one. Those two oranges cost him a day's wages each. It was the only time I ever saw one. All these years later, I can still remember the taste. Katerina and I licked our fingers till every last drop of the delicious juice was gone."

"Let's buy some," Boris insisted.

"Buy Some? Are we allowed?" Viktor questioned. "Surely we cannot. It is such an extravagance."

"Look, here is a… a…," Boris said pointing at a piece of paper sticking up from the end of the crate.

"It is called a label," Viktor explained. "It is to tell you how much something costs."

"What does it say, Viktor?"

Viktor bent over and pushed the tag backward so he could read the numbers. "It says forty-eight something. I do not know what that symbol after the numbers is."

Viktor noticed someone standing in the doorway of the shop and asked, "Sir, I ask you. What mean symbol here?"

"It means 'cents'," the man answered. "The oranges are forty-eight cents."

"Forty-eight cents each?"

"No. They are forty-eight cents for a dozen. A whole sack for forty-eight cents."

"Surely this cannot be," Boris exclaimed, crowding closer to Viktor. "A whole sack for such price? In Russia you not buy fruits like these for any price."

"Yes, sir, that is the correct price," the man confirmed. "Would you like to buy some?"

"Yes, yes, very much. I like to buy," Boris replied. "I wish buy two sacks. Do I have right money?" Boris reached in his pocket and held out a handful of coins.

"Yes, you have enough money," the man answered, picking through the pile and taking a dollar's worth of coins. He dropped the coins into the pocket of his apron, retrieved four pennies, and dropped them into Boris's hand.

"Money left?" Boris said, an incredulous look on his face. "I not believe such bounty and for such small price."

Viktor watched as the man placed a dozen oranges into each of two paper sacks and handed one to Boris and one to him. They thanked the man and started back toward the dock where the steamship was tied up. Viktor stopped beside a stack of discarded, wooden pallets and sat down.

"I cannot go one more step. I must eat one of these oranges right now."

Boris watched as Viktor set the sack between him feet, pulled out an orange, and dug his fingernails into the orange skin, squinting as the oils from the peel squirted him in the face. Boris sat down beside Viktor and repeated what he had seen Viktor do.

Viktor quickly ripped off the peel, dropping the pieces into the sack at his feet. The segments went into his mouth whole. Happy memories of that day many years ago played in his mind as he savored the sweet juice and flesh of the orange. Unable to resist, he reached into the bag and devoured a second orange.

Just like he had done in his Papa's house, Viktor licked his fingers until not even a hint of juice remained. He turned toward Boris, "Thank you for your generous purchase. I will save the rest of the oranges for the journey to Ottawa."

"Umm…," Boris mumbled as he stuffed two segments from his third orange into his mouth, juice running down his chin and dribbling onto his shirt. He finished chewing and added, "I have never seen such wonderful things in my entire life and I have never tasted anything so delicious. Perhaps, I am going to like Canada?" He smiled and stuffed more segments into his mouth.

"We should be on our way," Viktor said, slapping Boris on the back. "Come on my friend, or we will miss the train."

Colonel Sokolovsky and the other two men had already departed, having been picked up by private vehicle at the dock. Viktor and Boris lugged their bags the twelve blocks to Rue Saint Philippe Street where they expected to find the train terminal. Unable to locate a train terminal, Viktor walked several blocks in each direction while Boris watched their bags. Still unable to locate the train terminal, Viktor asked a man seated on a bench where he might find the train station. The man suggested he ask at the bus terminal two blocks further down the street. Inside the bus terminal, Viktor learned the first hour and one-half hour portion of their journey would be by bus to the city of Drummondville. There they would have to wait for an hour then board a train for the final four hour portion of their journey to Ottawa.

Victor hurried back to where Boris waited, hollering as he approached, "Come quick. We must board a bus here. The bus will take us to where we will board a train. Hurry. The bus will start boarding in five minutes."

They snatched their belongings from the sidewalk and raced off toward the bus terminal. Inside the building, they purchased tickets and flew out the door toward the waiting bus. The bus driver motioned frantically at them to hurry and climb aboard, already two minutes past the scheduled departure time. The driver punched their tickets and they located a pair of empty seats near the back of the bus.

Viktor dove into the seat by the window. Boris fell in a heap in the aisle as the driver gunned the engine. The old Greyhound bus roared out of the parking lot onto the street, belching thick black smoke. As Boris fell, his arm banged into the seat back causing him to lose his grasp on his bag of oranges. The three remaining oranges bounced out of the bag and began rolling toward the front of the bus.

"Stop them," he shouted, attempting to grab the escaping oranges.

A man seated five rows closer to the front of the bus stuck his foot out and stopped two of the oranges, but the third one rolled all the way to the front of the bus and bounced down the stairs, coming to rest against the door.

"I am thanking you," Boris bleated, scrambling after the wayward fruit. He snatched the two oranges from the floor and stumbled his way toward the front of the bus.

"Sir, you must sit down," the bus driver warned.

"I am begging pardon, kind person," Boris babbled. "I must get wonderful fruit."

"Be quick and then get back to your seat," the driver barked.

Boris got down on one knee, retrieved the orange, and headed back toward his seat. "Is wonderful, sweet fruit. I must not lose," he explained as he swayed down the aisle. Hugging the three oranges against his chest, he slumped down in the seat next to Viktor.

"Hold please," he said, handing the three oranges to Viktor. He reached down, retrieved the bag, and held it out while Viktor dropped the oranges into it. He took the bag from Viktor and held it to his chest.

"Is that all you have left?" Viktor asked.

"Yes. I know you think me a pig, but they are so delicious. I ate six while you hunt for train station."

Viktor patted his bag of oranges and leaned back in his seat.

Ottawa Train Station
200 Tremblay Road
Ottawa, Ontario, Canada

Six and one-half hours after leaving Trois-Rivières, Quebec, "Royal Hudson", Locomotive Number 2822, built in 1937 by the Montreal Locomotive Works, thundered into the train station at Ottawa and squealed to a stop, hissing and spewing great clouds of steam.

Viktor and Boris gathered up their belongings and stepped down off the train. Pushing their way through the crowd, they walked along the platform, searching for an information window where they could inquire about a taxi.

"Down there." Boris announced, pointing toward the eastern end of the platform.

"I see it," Victor announced as he turned, walked to the end of the platform, and joined the line waiting at the window. He waited for the two people in front of him then stepped up to the window.

"Is there taxi to Russian embassy?" Viktor asked.

"Yes. There is a taxi stand around on the other side of the building," a man seated on the other side of the window answered.

"What is cost?"

"Between three and four dollars Canadian," the man answered. "Half that much again if your friend over there goes with you. It's a little over four kilometers if you decide to walk."

"Thank you kind sir," Viktor said, tipping his hat.

"What did man say?" Boris asked when Viktor rejoined him.

"He said there is a taxi to the embassy, but it would cost us over five Canadian dollars," Viktor answered, digging in his pocket for what money he had left. "How much money do you have left?"

Boris dug in his pocket and held out the few bills and coins he had left. Viktor added up the total amount of money they had between them. "Boris, it would take almost all the money we have," Viktor moaned.

"**ВОПИЮЩИЙ!**" Boris exclaimed. "We shall walk," he added, remembering they were to speak English whenever they were outside the embassy.

"But, Boris, the man said it was a little over four kilometers."

"Then, we must get started," Boris advised as he picked up his bag and started toward the street.

Viktor stuffed the paper bag with his remaining oranges into his large bag, hoisted it up onto his shoulder, and hurried after his new friend.

Russian Embassy
285 Charlotte Street
Ottawa, Ontario, Canada

One hour and twenty-eight minutes after beginning their trek from the Ottawa train station, sweat running down their faces, Viktor and Boris rounded the corner from Laurier Avenue East onto Charlotte Street.

"Look. Down there. I can see the embassy at the end of the next block," Viktor announced excitedly.

"I am glad," Boris declared. "My feet hurt and I am soaked to the skin."

The large, ornate manor, formerly belonging to a wealthy lumber tycoon, that housed the Russian embassy, had been given to the Soviet Union in 1942. Even though the building and grounds were located in Canada, the embassy stood on official Russian soil. Located along the western bank of the

Rideau River, it sat directly across the street from Strathcona Park.

The two men walked up to the security entrance, pushed the call button, and waited for a security guard to unlock the gate and let them in. Junior Sergeant Alexander Nikolaevich Yakolev, barely twenty-three years old, exited the embassy building, walked up to the gate, and saluted the two officers standing on the other side of the fence. He looked through the vertical bars of the iron gate at the two men and asked, "What business do you have here?"

"Junior Lieutenant Borislav Gordanovitch Ismaylov and Lieutenant Victor Sergeyevich Zakharov reporting for embassy duty per order of Colonel Vasily Sokolovsky," Viktor responded, handing his and Boris's travel orders through the bars of the gate.

"I will need your identity papers as well," Junior Sergeant Yakolev ordered.

Viktor held out his hand and waited for Boris to retrieve his papers from the inside pocket of his uniform jacket. He added Boris's papers to his and handed them through the bars.

"One moment, sirs, while I verify your papers," Junior Sergeant Yakolev advised, turning his attention to the clipboard in his hand. The young security guard spent several minutes scrutinizing the papers and comparing them to entries on the clipboard.

"Sorry, but very strict security has recently been imposed," Junior Sergeant Yakolev apologized as he repeated the verification process a second time. Satisfied the two men were expected and they were who they said they were, he unlocked the gate and held it open. "Your papers are in order. Welcome to the embassy, sirs. Please present your orders to the duty officer at the end on the center hallway."

"Thank you, Junior Sergeant," Viktor said as he grabbed his and Boris's paperwork. They marched up the steps, entered the embassy, and headed toward the large desk positioned at the end of the center hallway.

Viktor and Boris came to attention in front of the desk. Viktor held out their orders toward Captain First Rank Grigorii Michailovitch Bagoran, the embassy duty officer.

A squinty-eyed man with deep creases across his forehead and an angry-red scar that began high on his left cheekbone and ended at the corner of his mouth looked up from the desk.

"Orders, please," Captain First Rank Bagoran said indifferently, raising his hand without lifting his elbow from the desk.

Viktor placed their orders in Captain First Rank Bagoran's outstretched hand and waited.

"Which one is Zakharov?" Captain First Rank Bagoran asked as he laid the sets of orders side by side on his desk.

"I am Lieutenant Zakharov," Viktor replied.

Captain First Rank Bagoran rearranged the orders to match the order Viktor and Boris stood before the desk. After several minutes of flipping through the orders, he looked up at Viktor.

"You wish to ask me something, Lieutenant Zakharov?"

"I'm sorry, Captain, sir. I did not mean to stare."

"Everybody does. The wound on my face is not yet fully healed and is quite conspicuous A nasty and unwelcome gift from a German soldier, who is now very dead," Captain First Rank Bagoran sneered.

"I am sorry, sir. This war has made many people suffer."

"You are quite correct, Lieutenant," Captain First Rank Bagoran acknowledged as he pushed his chair back from the desk, stood up, and hobbled over beside the desk. "My leg is now stiff. I was sent here to the embassy because I am no longer fit to command an infantry unit."

"I…."

"Never mind, Lieutenant. What is done is done," Captain First Rank Bagoran declared as he sat back down in his chair and scooted up to the desk. "Junior Lieutenant Ismaylov, you are to report to the security unit. Go up one flight of stairs and turn to your left and go down the hallway. It is the last door on the right."

Captain First Rank Bagoran handed Boris his orders and waited. Boris shook hands with Viktor, said goodbye, and headed for the stairs. Captain First Rank Bagoran handed Viktor his orders and instructed him to sit in one of the chairs and wait. He picked up the phone, rang the operator, and waited to be connected to Colonel Sokolovsky. After a short conversation, he replaced the phone and waved Viktor back up to the desk.

"Colonel Sokolovsky was about to leave for the day, but he wants to see you immediately in his office. His office is on the top floor at the east end of the building. Be quick. He is waiting."

"Thank you, Captain First Rank Bagoran," Viktor said, drawing to attention and giving the man a crisp salute. "May your wounds heal quickly." Viktor turned and hurried off toward the stairs.

After rushing up the stairs two at a time, Viktor stopped in front of the door to Colonel Sokolovsky's office, drew in two deep breaths, and knocked loudly on the door jam.

"Enter."

Viktor strode into the office, came to attention, and said, "Lieutenant Victor Sergeyevich Zakharov reporting for duty, sir."

"You are soaked," Colonel Sokolovsky observed, returning Viktor's salute. "Have you been running?"

"I and another officer, Junior Lieutenant Ismaylov, walked all the way from the train station. The taxi would have cost us too much. I am afraid we splurged and bought two bags of oranges. Only once before as a child had I ever tasted one."

"Yes, I also saw those. A great extravagance in Russia, but here they are cheap. I ordered some to be sent to my residence. Sit Lieutenant Zakharov," Colonel Sokolovsky said, pointing toward a chair sitting in front of his desk.

Viktor dropped his bag on the floor as he sat in the chair. He leaned forward and handed his orders to Colonel Sokolovsky. The colonel took the orders, signed them in two

places, and placed them in a shallow, wooden tray to be filed
later. He looked up at Viktor and said, "You must listen carefully. What I am about to tell you is very important. Security
regulations have been greatly increased and must be followed
precisely. Failure to follow the new rules will result in swift
punishment. What I tell you will not leave this room. Do you
understand Lieutenant?"

"Yes, sir, I understand."

"Some time ago Sergeant Yuri Antonovich Aleksandrov,
one of the embassy's two cipher clerks, disappeared. Ultimately, he was found floating in the Rideau River. He had been
shot in the back of the head. As you would expect, Ambassador Volkov is very concerned. An audit of the last two months
of the embassy's message traffic was performed immediately.
The audit did not reveal anything was missing. However, the
remaining cipher clerk, Corporal Gennadi Turov, has poor
cipher skills and we cannot be certain his audit was accurate.
He is really nothing more than an errand boy. That is why you
are here, Lieutenant Zakharov. I personally requested you as
soon as I was informed I was to be sent here to Ottawa to improve security."

"I understand Colonel Sokolovsky," Viktor acknowledged. "I will do whatever I can to assist you."

"It is late and I have a dinner engagement so I will only
give you brief instructions for now," Colonel Sokolovsky continued. "Every inbound communication will be personally verified by you. Once complete, all originals, copies, notes, or
work papers will be immediately placed in the safe. All encoding or decoding of messages will be completed in a locked
room guarded by someone from the security unit. Only the
person decoding or encoding will be allowed in the room. Violation of any security protocols will mean prison. Instantly.
There will be no trial. Is that clear?"

"Yes, sir, Colonel."

"Corporal Turov will be assigned to assist you, but only
for non-message duties. Until another cipher analyst arrives
from Moscow, you will be responsible for *all* message traffic.

You will likely work very long hours, Lieutenant, so I suggest you get some rest. I have directed Captain First Rank Bagoran to assign you a bunk and storage locker in the officer's berthing quarters until your wife and child arrive. He will be waiting for you at the main desk. Now, I must go or I will be late."

"Yes, sir. Thank you, sir," Viktor answered as he stood up, grabbed his bag, and exited the office.

"I will work all day and all night with such strict requirements," Viktor moaned as he started down the stairs.

Viktor trudged down the three flights of stairs and waited for Captain First Rank Bagoran to finish with the man already standing at the desk. When the man walked away, the captain motioned Viktor over to the desk.

"What can I do for you, Lieutenant?"

"Colonel Sokolovsky said you would assign me a temporary bunk in officer's berthing."

"Yes, it is already done. Follow me."

Viktor followed the captain to the lower level. Along the way, the captain grabbed a set of sheets and a musty, wool blanket from a linen closet. At the end of the narrow hallway, he pushed the door to the berthing room open and walked to the far side of the room.

"Here," Captain First Rank Bagoran said, tossing the sheets and blanket on a bunk in the corner. He noticed the disgusted look on Viktor's face. "It is the last bunk available," he explained. "It looks bad, but it is much better than what the enlisted men have. At least in this room there is a fan to move the air around."

"Thank you, Captain. It will do."

"You may use the locker beside the bed for your belongings. Breakfast, such as it is, will be at zero-six hundred. If you are not one of the first to arrive, there may not be anything left. If you need anything, someone will be at the main desk."

With that, Captain First Rank Bagoran turned and left the bunk room. Viktor stood staring at the thin mattress and musty old blanket. He picked up the blanket and held it to his nose.

"Phew, this is horrible," he growled. "I will not be able to sleep under this stinking rag." In disgust, he threw the smelly blanket in the corner, deciding he would speak to Colonel Sokolovsky in the morning. He unpacked his bag and changed into dry clothes, draping the wet clothes over the bed rail. The evening meal had already passed and he did not wish to go into town in the dark. Poking around in the locker, he grabbed two of the oranges he had saved. Sitting on the edge of the bed, he peeled the oranges and savored the sweet juice and flesh. He was still hungry, but the rest of the oranges he would save for another day. After gathering up the peels, he exited the bunk room and found a trash can at the opposite end of the building. He did not want anyone else to know he had oranges or they would be stolen for certain.

Stopping in the lower level's only bathroom, he washed his face and hands and returned to the bunk room. Sitting on the bed with a note pad in his lap, he started a letter to his beautiful Anna. First, he told her about the train ride and meeting Boris, telling her he felt certain Boris and he would become good friends. He scribbled two more lines, beginning to describe the horrible things he had seen in Königsberg. Shaking his head, he tore off the page, crumpled it in his hand, and began the letter again. The things in Königsberg were just too horrible. Mere words on paper could not begin to describe it. Maybe he would tell Anna when she arrived.

Thirty minutes passed while he completed the letter. With nothing else to do, he decided to go to bed early. He returned the note pad to his locker, spread the sheets on the bed, climbed out of his clothes, and slid under the top sheet. He wanted to be certain he arrived early for breakfast, not wanting to go another day with only oranges to eat. Soon he was asleep, snoring softly.

Viktor had been asleep less than an hour when two drunken officers burst into the room. Despite his efforts to filter out the racket with his pillow, sleep was impossible. An hour later, the raucous laughing and joking died out only to be replaced by loud snoring. For another hour, Viktor tossed and turned, trying to ignore the snoring. Finally, exhausted from the day's travel and the long walk from the train station, Viktor fell into a nightmare plagued sleep.

As usual, Viktor's was awakened by the same horrible nightmare. He swung his feet out from under the sheet and sat on the edge of the bed in the dark, rubbing his tired, gritty eyes. The berthing room was overly warm and the air was filled with the stench of the drunken officers' breath. Knowing any further sleep would be impossible, he snatched his clothes from the bed rail, quietly slipped out of the room, and headed for the bathroom. At least he would be able to take a shower before the hot water ran out.

Somewhat refreshed by a hot shower, he shaved, dressed in his uniform, and headed to the dining hall to wait for breakfast. As he passed the main desk, the duty sergeant called out, "Lieutenant, the dining hall will not be open for another forty minutes. There is a small sitting area behind the building where officers sometimes wait."

"Thank you, Sergeant," Viktor acknowledged, turning on his heels and heading the opposite direction toward the rear entrance. He pushed the rear entrance door open and stepped out into the pre-dawn twilight.

"Viktor," a voice called out from the semi-darkness.

"Who is it?" Viktor asked.

"It is me Boris. Come sit while we wait for breakfast."

"You could not sleep either," Viktor remarked as he sat down beside Boris.

"I had nothing to do, so I climbed into bed as soon as I was assigned a bunk," Boris replied. "What about you?"

"I was assigned a bunk in the basement," Viktor complained. "It was hot and stuffy and then two drunken officers came in. The noise was horrible and the air was filled with their drunken breath. I'm telling you, Boris, the stench was worse than the wrong end of a mule."

"I am sorry, Viktor. I heard from someone in the security unit that the officers here have been given much discretion and they believe they can act however they wish. I also heard that

Colonel Sokolovsky intends to change that. How long before your wife and child arrive?"

"Colonel Sokolovsky says it will be four or five weeks. I am told married officer's quarters are a bit better. At least there is more privacy."

"There is something else I must tell you, but you must swear to tell no one else."

"Will you get in trouble for telling me?"

"If someone were to find out, perhaps. But you are my friend and you must know this."

Boris stood up and scanned the entire property behind the embassy. Seeing no one, he sat back down and leaned close to Viktor.

"Something serious has happened. I do not know what because everyone seems afraid to talk about it. The former head of the security unit did not come in one day. He just disappeared. Nobody knows why, or at least they will not say. A friend I knew from back in Moscow is also here. He told me if I see anything, I must keep silent. He said even the senior officers seem tense. Now, everyone is watched constantly."

"Is that all he said?" Viktor questioned.

"Yes, that is all he would share," Boris answered. "My friend said even the slightest disobedience results in brutal punishment. Viktor, you must be very careful. Keep your eyes only on your own work. Someone is always watching."

"Thank you for the warning, Boris," Viktor said. "Let's go get something to eat."

Viktor felt uneasy as they entered the embassy and walked toward the dining hall. His new friend seemed quite nervous and concerned over the information he had shared. Viktor had also sensed something the previous evening. Colonel Sokolovsky had changed. There was something different about the colonel's eyes. Viktor had noticed it immediately.

"*I agree with Boris. I must be very careful,*" he thought as he pushed the door to the dining hall open.

Chapter Five

Russian Embassy
285 Charlotte Street
Ottawa, Ontario, Canada

On the first day Viktor reported to duty in the cipher unit, the huge volume of message traffic waiting to be deciphered shocked him. Colonel Sokolovsky had informed him the disappearance of the previous cipher clerk had created a large backlog, but what Viktor found more resembled a mountain.

Even worse than the mountain of work facing Viktor, was the nearly constant line of officials screaming for their messages to be deciphered. A few officials, refusing to accept any explanation for the delays, threatened Viktor with being sent back to Russia and then a gulag somewhere in Siberia.

The massive amount of new security restrictions further added to Viktor's workload and growing frustration. The day Colonel Sokolovsky had arrived he had issued an order that all documents arriving at or leaving the embassy were to be classified, with no exceptions.

Entered through double steel doors, the cipher room occupied one of eight rooms on the second floor in the east wing of the building. Guarded constantly, the cipher room's windows were covered by iron bars and steel shutters which were closed whenever message traffic was present due to Colonel Sokolovsky's demand for complete secrecy. In a separate room, a large steel safe housed all cables, telegrams, and messages not in the cipher room along with Military Intelligence Directorate documents.

Each day it would take Viktor several hours just to catalog the inbound traffic and assign each scrap of paper a classified tracking number and then enter the information into the cipher books.

Before he could start deciphering the backlog of messages, Colonel Sokolovsky had instructed him to conduct a complete audit of the last two months of embassy message traffic. Not one scrap of paper could be removed from the safe until Viktor completed the audit. With an armed guard stationed in front of the door, Viktor opened the door and entered the secure file room and stopped halfway into the room. He stared at the monstrous safe standing in the center of the room.

"How did they get that huge thing in here?" he questioned out loud.

"You should have seen it," the guard answered, having overheard Viktor's question. "They had a huge crane beside the building. A large hole was cut in the outside wall and in the doorway. If you look carefully, you can see where they patched the wall."

Viktor rubbed his hand across the wall and felt the ridge two feet from the door jamb where the wall had been patched. Viktor used the note pad in his hand to shield the dial on the safe as he entered the combination. He twisted the release lever, swung the heavy door open, and groaned. There had to be at least two hundred cables, telegrams, and various memorandums piled haphazardly on the middle two shelves waiting to be catalogued and deciphered. Viktor's quick count of the stacks of waiting messages revealed there were two-hundred twenty-seven items waiting.

For six long hours, Viktor stood in front of the safe. First he went through all the previously deciphered items, comparing them to the master routing list. The count of deciphered messages did not match the number of items on the master list. Viktor repeated the comparison two additional times. Each time, the comparisons were off by the same number, indicating three messages were missing. The scrawled entries on the master list for the missing items were so illegible, it would be impossible to know the subject or the intended recipient. Viktor did not relish the thought of telling Colonel Sokolovsky, knowing he would be furious.

Viktor pushed the safe door closed, spun the dial several times, and exited the secure file room.

"Sergeant, Stay here. I'm going to Colonel Sokolovsky's office and will be right back.

Twenty minutes later Viktor returned to the secure file room after having listened to Colonel Sokolovsky yell for most of that time. In no uncertain terms, the colonel had made it clear to Viktor that he was to do his best to find those missing messages. Viktor had no idea how he was going to do that. He had already scoured the safe three times. Complicating the matter, he had not been at the embassy when they went missing. Rather than inform the colonel of that fact, he stood silently and took the tongue-lashing rather than the sting of Colonel Sokolovsky's whip.

"I heard the yelling clear down here," Sergeant Mikhail Olegovitch Barkov remarked. "What are you going to do?"

"I will keep searching. I will find nothing and then I will get yelled at again," Viktor conceded, pointing at the door.

Sergeant Barkov unlocked the door, waited for Viktor to enter, and took his place in front of the door.

Viktor unlocked the safe and pulled the heavy door open. With the audit completed and delivered, he drew a line across the page below the entries he had audited, added the new items to the master list, and sorted the random piles into groups based on assigned priorities. He signed out the first ten items, locked the safe, and tapped Sergeant Barkov on the shoulder.

"Let's go," Viktor ordered.

Sergeant Barkov locked the secure file room door and followed Viktor to the communications center. Viktor entered the coding room and pulled the door shut. Sergeant Barkov once again assumed his position in front of the door. Following the strict new security protocol, only one cipher analyst at a time was allowed to sign out items and no more than ten at a time. In addition, only one cipher analyst or clerk at a time was allowed in the coding room which was to be guarded whenever classified communications were present which now meant everything.

Viktor spent the rest of his day, except for a short twenty minute break for the evening meal, ferrying batches of ten message items to be decoded back and forth from the safe to the coding room and then back to the safe. By the time he made it back to his bunk, he was bleary-eyed and far too tired to write anything to Anna. He climbed out of his clothes, slipped under the sheet, and was asleep in less than five minutes. For the first time since passing through Königsberg, Viktor slept through the night without being awakened by his usual recurring nightmare.

For the next five weeks, the days blended together into one big blur. Seven days a week Viktor would be one of the first ten in line for breakfast. After finishing breakfast, he worked furiously, without a break, until the evening meal. Taking no more than twenty to twenty-five minutes to wolf down the meager, evening rations provided, he would hurry back to the cipher unit for two more hours of work.

Some days he made progress, decoding more old messages than new messages that arrived during the day, but on the other days the backlog of messages increased. No matter how diligently he worked, he could not eliminate the backlog, but he had reduced it.

At the end of the sixth week, he had reduced the number of items in the message backlog to sixty-one. Colonel Sokolovsky still grumbled because of the backlog, but he did admit that Viktor had made progress. Because of his hard work, the colonel granted Viktor a half day off the following week to meet his wife, Anna. Anna's and Nikola's clearances and travel papers had finally been approved and they were scheduled to arrive the following Tuesday, just past mid-day. Excitement had been building in Viktor's heart ever since he had been informed. He would be so happy to hold Anna in his arms and to finally move out of the overcrowded and stuffy officers' berthing.

Ottawa Train Station
200 Tremblay Road
Ottawa, Ontario, Canada

Viktor sat down on a wooden bench on the train station platform and fanned himself with a train schedule he had grabbed
from a display near the station's information window. Rather
than spend the cost of a taxi, he had walked the four plus kilometers from the Russian Embassy.

Growing impatient, he stood up and walked to the edge
of the platform. Rising up on his tiptoes, he peered down the
railroad track. Nothing. No headlamp. No sound of a locomotive approaching. He returned to the bench and sat down. Another twenty minutes passed and still no train.

Viktor slipped his hand in his right trouser pocket and
pulled out a silver pocket watch. He thought of his papa as his
fingers gently caressed the well-worn pocket watch. The vision
of his papa, a tall man with light brown hair streaked with gray,
was as clear as if he were standing right in front of him. Fair
skinned with a prominent nose and light blue eyes the color of
ice, all traits inherited from his Finnish parents. While Viktor's
papa had been considered a peasant, he was a fiercely proud
man who believed in hard work and honesty.

The pocket watch had been his papa's most prized possession. Viktor's mother had placed it in Viktor's hand after his
papa's death. "Your papa made me promise you were to have
this if something happened to him," she had told him on the
day they buried Sergey Bogdanovich Zakharov.

Viktor held the pocket watch up to his ear and listened to
the rhythmic ticking. He remembered sneaking into his par-
ent's bedroom as a small child to hold the watch and listen to
its ticking. One time in particular he remembered lifting the
watch from its place in the top dresser drawer, marveling at its
beauty, the back engraved with fine crosshatching and the
front adorned with a beautiful double-headed eagle. He had
flipped the front open and rubbed his finger across the en-

graved inscription, "**Не забудьт**". Engrossed in admiring the watch, he had nearly fainted when his papa had laid his hand on his shoulder.

"It is quite beautiful, but you must be careful," his papa had warned him. "It is very old and the case is solid silver. It belonged to my papa."

"I am sorry, Papa," Viktor had squeaked. "It is hard to resist. I wanted to read the inscription. It feels so good laying in my hand."

"Yes, I understand, Viktor," his papa had acknowledged. "It is what ties us to our past. You must always remember your past. Now, put it back, carefully."

Viktor's mind returned to the present. Glancing at the time, he wondered why the train was already over twenty minutes late. He snapped the lid closed, kissed the back, and returned the pocket watch to his pocket. Rising from the bench, he walked over to the information window and inquired as to when the train would arrive.

"Excuse sir. Train from Trois-Rivières late. When you expect it arrive?" Viktor asked.

"The truck delivering coal to the station in Trois-Rivières broke down," the man answered. "I am told the train is running an hour behind schedule." The man inside the window turned and looked at the clock on the wall and said, "If there were no other delays, the train should arrive in another twenty-eight minutes."

"Thank you," Viktor said as he turned and headed back toward the bench. He sat down on the bench, leaned back against the building, crossed his ankles, and watched a switch engine moving cars on the opposite side of the rail yard.

Viktor sat bolt upright, startled by the sound of a train whistle, having drifted off to sleep. He leapt off the bench and hurried to the edge of the platform and looked down the track. In the distance, he could see the headlamp of the approaching train. He ran to the eastern edge of the platform, anxiously awaiting the train's arrival. Knowing she would be in one of the third-class cars, he watched as the train rumbled by and screeched to a stop.

His heart leapt within his chest when he saw little Nikola's face pressed against one of the windows. Waving frantically, he managed to get Anna's attention. She smiled and waved back. Viktor pointed, crowded his way to the car's doorway, and waited as other passengers exited the train, greeting waiting family and friends.

Anna stepped off the train and rushed to where Viktor stood waiting. Holding Nikola with one arm, she hugged Viktor with the other and kissed him.

"This nice man offered to carry my bags," Anna said.

"Thank you sir," Viktor beamed. "You most kind to help wife with heavy bags."

The man smiled and tipped the bill of his hat. He turned and rushed off toward the station.

"It has been so long," Anna exclaimed as she hugged Viktor again.

"Yes, it has been much too long," Viktor agreed. "The nights have been long and empty without you. Come, there is something I must show you."

Viktor picked up the two bags and headed for the far end of the station with Anna and Nikola trailing behind.

"Viktor, slow down. Where are we going?" Anna asked.

"There is a vegetable market along the street beside the station," Viktor called out. "Such things they have. You must see it to believe it."

"Viktor, never have I lived where you could obtain such things so easily," Anna exclaimed as she looked up and down the row of vegetables and fruits displayed in front of the market. "And there is such great quantity." Anna stopped, bent over, and picked up a bunch of bananas. She held the bananas to her nose and sniffed. "Incredible. Viktor, I have only heard about these… These… How you call them?"

"They are called bananas," Viktor answered, smiling. "You will not believe the taste. Here, put them in this bag. We will buy them."

"Viktor, no," Anna exclaimed. "They must be very expensive. Surely you must have to show ration card and we cannot afford such extravagance."

"No. No ration cards or coupons. I have been saving and they cost much less than you might think."

Anna and Viktor continued to walk along admiring the fruits and vegetables. Several that Anna asked about Viktor had never seen and he had no idea what they were called. Viktor hurried ahead of Anna, beckoning for her to follow.

"Anna, look at these," Viktor said, pointing at a crate of large, round, orange fruits.

"Oranges. I cannot believe it," Anna blurted out. "Twice as a little girl I saw what were called oranges in the market back in Moscow, but they were much smaller and shriveled and priced way beyond papa's meager income. I remember dreaming about how they must taste."

Viktor smiled, already knowing what they cost, and said, "Well then, you shall have some. In fact, we shall buy an entire sack full."

"And the bananas?" Anna stammered, a shocked look on her face. "Viktor, surely we cannot afford them both."

"I am sorry, Anna," Viktor apologized. "I already know what these fruits cost. I wanted to see if your reaction was the same as mine. You should have seen the look on your face."

"You are awful," Anna scolded, punching Viktor in the shoulder.

"Come. Watch me as I pay. You will see."

Viktor and Anna, with Nikola propped on her hip, walked into the market. Anna watched as Viktor set the fruit on the counter and waited for the clerk to total up his purchases. A fresh-faced boy of no more than sixteen looked up at Viktor. Underneath a mop of the curliest red hair Viktor had ever seen, a broad smile spread across the boy's face, covered with hundreds of freckles.

"Good afternoon, sir," the boy greeted. "Is that all for you today?"

"Da… I mean yes," Viktor answered.

"Okay. One dozen oranges, fifty three cents and two point six pounds of bananas, thirty-two cents," the boy announced, placing the fruit into a large paper bag. "Your total is eighty-five cents, sir."

Viktor pulled a small wad of bills from his pocket, peeled off a one-dollar bill, and handed it to the clerk. The boy placed the bill into the tray of a large, brass cash register and dug out two coins.

"Fifteen cents is your change.," the boy said as he dropped the coins into Viktor's hand. "Is it okay if your little boy has a piece of candy?"

"No thank you. Wife and son just arrived. We must be careful with money."

"Oh, I'm sorry. I meant for free."

"You would just give to Nikola?"

"Sure, my treat as a welcome to Ottawa."

The young boy pulled a penny from his pocket, dropped it into the cash drawer, and selected a stick of red and white striped candy from a glass jar behind the counter.

"Here, Nikola. It is called peppermint," the boy said.

"Thank you. Is very kind of you."

"You're welcome. Have a nice day, folks. I hope you enjoy our city." The boy waved and stepped sideways to wait on the next customer.

"Come, let us go," Viktor said, guiding Anna past the waiting customers and toward the door.

Once outside, Viktor directed Anna and Nikola to the same stack of discarded, wooden pallets where he and Boris had feasted on their oranges seven weeks earlier. He set the suitcases on the ground and took the paper sack from Anna. Reaching inside the bag, he broke off one of the bananas.

"You must taste this first," he said as he stripped the bright yellow peel off the banana. He broke off half and handed it to Anna. She sniffed the chunk of banana and then took a bite, a look of utter delight lighting up her face.

"This is amazing," she mumbled as she took another bite, still chewing the first. "I have never tasted anything so delicious in my entire life." She broke off a small piece and handed it to Nikola. Immediately, it went into his mouth. Both his hands flew out, begging for more of the delicious fruit.

"May we have another?" Anna begged.

Viktor reached into the bag for another banana. He peeled it and handed the whole banana to Anna. With great joy, he watched as they devoured the delicious fruit.

"Now you must taste one of these," he said pulling out a bright, shiny orange. Digging his fingernails into the peel, he squinted as juice squirted up into his eye. After rubbing his face on his sleeve, he finished peeling the orange, separated it in half, and handed half to Anna. She watched as Viktor pulled of a segment and stuffed it into his mouth. She repeated Viktor's action and immediately a smile, broader than before, spread across her face.

"I cannot believe it," she gushed. "It is far better than I had dreamed. Just to taste these marvelous fruits alone has made the long trip worthwhile."

"What about me?" Viktor questioned, a sad look on his face.

'Oh, Viktor. You know what I mean."

"Yes, I know. That is the exact same reaction Boris and I had. I met Boris on the train to Königsberg. He is posted here at the embassy also. You will like him. We sat in this very spot and ate oranges the day we arrived."

Licking her fingers, Anna asked, "How much money was that bill you handed the young man in the market?"

"It was one dollar Canadian money."

"How much is that in Russia?"

"I believe the exchange rate is between twenty-five and twenty-eight rubles per Canadian dollar."

"That is all," Anna remarked. "In Moscow such things would cost ten times that much, if you could get them at all. Viktor, never have I seen such abundance. How can that be with the war and rationing?"

"It is a mystery to me as well," Viktor replied, shrugging his shoulders. "And the people I have met have been so friendly. You would never guess there has been a war."

"Yes, I know. People on train were so friendly. A man got up and gave me his seat. Because I had Nikola people let me through first. It was nice to not have to push and shove."

"We should catch a taxi and get to our apartment and get settled," Viktor announced as he grabbed the bags and pointed Anna toward the station.

"Apartment?" Anna questioned. "I thought all embassy people must stay at the embassy."

"Not here," Viktor answered. "There is a high-ranking party official that hates children. He refuses to listen to crying. So, we have been assigned to civilian housing."

As Viktor was about to hail a taxi, Anna asked, "Can we afford to do this?"

"Yes. I have saved money. It is too far to walk. It is over four kilometers. When Boris and I arrived, we walked to the embassy because we did not have enough money. It was awful."

Viktor waved at the next taxi in line. The driver pulled up to the taxi stop, jumped out, and opened the trunk. Viktor handed him the bags, told him the address, and opened the door. "Yes, *how nice it was to not have to push and shove*," Viktor thought as he climbed into the back seat. The driver jumped behind the wheel and sped off toward the address.

Zakharov Apartment
Somerset Street
Ottawa, Ontario, Canada

After being dropped at the curb in front of the apartment building on Somerset Street, Viktor had lugged the bags up to the second floor. He set the bags beside the door and dug in his pocket for the key Captain First Rank Bagoran, the embassy duty officer, had given him the previous day. Viktor shoved the key into the lock and twisted, but it would not turn. Shaking the key sideways, he tried again. Still the key would not turn. He pulled the key out and repeated the process two more times. Each time the key refused to turn.

"Anna, the key will not turn. The door will not open," Viktor complained.

"Try jiggling it," Anna suggested.

"I have already tried that," Viktor snapped, getting frustrated. "I'm sorry. I do not want to have to walk all the way to the embassy and back."

Viktor turned around when he heard the door behind him open. A short, squat man entered the hallway and walked toward Viktor.

"I heard the ruckus and thought I'd see if I could help. My name is Martin Clavet," the man announced, offering his hand to Viktor.

"Hello. My name Viktor Zakharov," Viktor responded, taking the man's hand and shaking it vigorously. "This is wife Anna and son Nikola. We moving in."

"If you'll let me, I can show you how to get that lock to work. The previous tenant had the same problem."

"Thank you, Mister Clavet," Viktor said as he pulled the key out of the lock and handed it to the man.

"Call me Martin. Now watch. Push the key all the way in then pull it back just a little. Pull the door knob toward you to take the pressure off the lock then twist. See. Easy as pie."

"What mean, 'easy as pie'?" Viktor asked, a puzzled look on his face.

"It means 'very easy' or 'nothing to it'," Mr. Clavet answered.

"Okay, I understand." Viktor pulled the door shut and repeated Mr. Clavet's instructions and the door opened the first time. "Thank you. Easy as pie," Viktor declared with a big grin on his face.

"Glad I could help," Mr. Clavet said. "My wife, Sylvie, and I helped the previous tenant move out. The furniture in the apartment is a bit worn, but the place is clean. If you're not too tired, once you get settled, knock on our door. We'd be glad to have you join us for some cake and coffee."

"Is kind offer. We like very much."

"Great. We'll expect you then. Come over whenever you are settled. Welcome to the building."

Mr. Clavet turned, walked back into his apartment, and pulled the door closed. Viktor pushed the door to their apartment open and stood aside waiting for Anna to enter.

Anna walked into the apartment and exclaimed, "Viktor, is this what people in Canada call worn?" She walked over to a couch sitting against the wall, set Nikola on the couch, and sat down beside him. Against the other wall sat two upholstered chairs with a table and lamp sitting between them. The smile on her face widened as she looked around the apartment, noticing a kitchen, large enough to hold a small dining table.

Three doors opening off the living room piqued her interest. She rose from the couch and poked her head into the door closest to the kitchen.

"Viktor, come look," she exclaimed. "This is the biggest bathroom I have ever seen. It is so clean. It looks new."

"Very nice," Viktor agreed, looking over her shoulder.

"What is this door," she asked as she poked her head into one of the remaining doors. "It is a bedroom. Oh, Viktor, I love the colors. They are so inviting." She hurried to the last door, poked her head in, and cried out, "I cannot believe it. There are two bedrooms!"

"Two bedrooms!" Viktor remarked. "It cannot be."

"Well, come look for yourself."

Victor quickly poked his head into the first room and then walked up beside Anna. "We can have our own bedroom and Nikola can have one as well," he beamed. "Never have we had so many rooms. I was so worried when I was first told I was being sent to Canada. It seems I was worried for nothing."

"I too was worried," Anna added. "I know the winter will be cold, but this wonderful apartment will make up for it. Here in Canada we will be a happy family."

"Yes, you are most correct. It is wonderful to be together again." Viktor kissed Anna and hugged her tightly.

"Viktor, where is Nikola?" Anna asked, noticing the little boy was no longer sitting on the couch.

"There he is by the door," Viktor laughed. "He is trying to get the peel off a banana."

Laughing quietly, they both stood watching as the little boy grunted and pulled at the banana. Unable to get the peel off, he came running toward them holding the banana out.

"Should he have another one?" Anna asked as she bent down and picked him up.

"Why not. It is a special day. We should enjoy it."

Anna set Nikola at the dining table, peeled the banana, and handed him half. With Nikola busy, Anna and Viktor dragged Anna's suitcase into their bedroom and put her meager assortment of clothes into a five-drawer dresser sitting against the wall opposite the bed. When they were done, three drawers still remained empty.

"Doesn't look like much," Anna observed.

"I must agree," Viktor acknowledged. "The strict travel limit said only one bag per person. Tomorrow I will bring my things from the embassy officers' berthing. When I have some time off we will go to what the local people call department store and buy some new things."

"That will be much fun. I have not had any new clothes for five years."

Viktor returned to the kitchen and entertained Nikola while Anna carried Nikola's suitcase into the second bedroom and put his things away. Finished with the clothes, she pulled the curtain back and glanced out the window. She raced into the kitchen. "Viktor, you will not believe it," she blurted out. "There is a park just across the street."

"That will be nice for you and Nikola," Viktor said. "Now, let's go meet our neighbors."

Two hours later, Anna, Viktor, and an exhausted Nikola returned from the Clavet apartment. Martin and Sylvie loved children, but had been unable to have any of their own. They had spent much of the two hours bouncing Nikola on their knees, playing peek-a-boo, or some other child's game. Viktor had learned by experience that Sylvie was a fabulous cook, partaking of two large pieces of the luscious banana cake she had baked that afternoon. The coffee Martin had served had been dark and bold, the best Viktor had ever tasted. In Russia, to stretch their meager budget, Anna often reused coffee grounds a second time adding just a dab of fresh grounds.

"Did you see in the Clavet's refrigerator?" Anna asked.

"Anna, you should not snoop," Viktor admonished. "The Clavets were very kind to invite us."

"I didn't look on purpose," Anna answered in defense. "Sylvie opened it right in front of me. There was hardly anything inside. It was the same in their cabinets. When she opened one to get sugar for your coffee, it was almost bare. I believe the sugar she put out was the last they had. I think they may be more poor than we are."

"And I ate like a pig," Viktor choked. "I will have to apologize."

"You'll do no such thing," Anna barked. "They freely offered. Didn't you see the pleasure it brought them. We must not embarrass them."

"Yes, you are right," Viktor agreed. "Even though they have very little they are happy *and* they share what they have."

"I am puzzled, Viktor. In spite of the war and many shortages, the people here in Canada seem so happy and friendly. Back home, in Russia, people are distrustful and hateful. I wonder what makes the difference?"

Viktor shrugged and shifted a sleeping Nikola from one shoulder to the other.

"After I put Nikola to bed, we will have a light supper and then we will sleep in our own bed in our own bedroom. We are most fortunate."

Russian Embassy
285 Charlotte Street
Ottawa, Ontario, Canada

Viktor walked through the embassy's security gate twenty minutes early and entered the main building. Still puffing from the forty-five minute walk from his apartment, Viktor signed the entry log and started toward the stairway. Halfway down the hallway he heard someone whispering his name.

"Viktor, over here. Do not acknowledge me or look at me."

Viktor stopped, leaned against the wall, and mopped his face with a handkerchief, turning his ear toward the sound.

"It is me, Boris. I have learned some disturbing news. Meet me outside in five minutes. Usual place."

Viktor nodded his head slightly and continued on down the hallway. He walked into the first floor bathroom, stopped in front of one of the sinks, and splashed some cold water on his face. After drying his face with a paper towel, he exited the bathroom, walked to the rear door, and exited the building. He walked over to a wooden bench and sat down.

Two minutes later, Boris came around the other side of the building and sat down beside Viktor.

"I'm sorry, but I had to be certain to not be suspicious," Boris said. "I exited the other side of the building and waited to be certain no one was watching."

"Boris, you know someone is always watching," Viktor pointed out. "You are in security. Surely, you must know that."

"You are correct," Boris answered. "But between watch changes, I am the only security guard on duty."

"Well, then. Make it quick before the general staff officers arrive and someone notices us."

"I got this information from Junior Sergeant Alexander Nikolaevich Yakolev. He is a junior security guard here. He has been here almost a year. I also learned he is my cousin. Otherwise, he would never have confided in me."

"I'm listening. Hurry up. We don't have much time."

"The previous cipher clerk, a man named Aleksandrov, discovered something and was silenced."

"What do you mean silenced?"

"Come now, Viktor. You know. He was murdered. Yakolev thinks he knows who did it, but he will not tell me."

"People get silenced all the time back in Russia," Viktor said, hiding his shock and surprise. "What does that have to do with me?"

"Yakolev said the order to silence Aleksandrov came from someone in Moscow. Someone who was on his way here. Only three people have arrived here at the embassy in the last three months. You, me, and Colonel Sokolovsky."

"Colonel Sokolovsky mentioned this man, Aleksandrov, but he said he disappeared. He made no mention that he was murdered. How did Yakolev know he was murdered?"

"Yakolev was there when they fished him out of the river. He had a large hole in the back of his head."

"Did Yakolev say anything else?"

"Yes. He said all security staff was instructed to be vigilant and report the slightest breach of the security protocols. He said they were warned any individual, no matter his rank, would be sent back to Russia to face a firing squad."

"Colonel Sokolovsky has said none of this to me."

"Everyone in the security unit is frightened. Something unusual is happening. Yakolev told me unauthorized packages are being sneaked in and out of the embassy. He thinks Aleksandrov may have discovered this. The next day he was murdered."

"Mention this to no one, Boris," Viktor warned. "Keep your eyes open, but be very careful. If you see or hear something unusual, rub your right eye when we are at breakfast. We will pick a time and place so you can tell me what you have learned."

"Agreed," Boris said. "You be careful as well, my friend. I will leave first. Wait two minutes and then report to your work space."

Viktor watched as Boris stood up and disappeared around the corner of the building. Glancing at his watch occasionally, Viktor waited two full minutes, got up from the bench, and hurried back into the building. Taking the steps two at a time, he rushed up the stairs and into the cipher room with three minutes to spare.

Zakharov Apartment
Somerset Street
Ottawa, Ontario, Canada

After a long, tiring day, Viktor trudged home in the fading twilight. After climbing the stairs to their second-floor apartment, he pushed the door open, dropped his bag beside the door, and collapsed onto the couch. He crossed his feet, leaned his head back against the wall, and closed his eyes.

"Viktor, you are home late," Anna observed, coming out of the kitchen. "Will you always be this late?"

"Yes, probably for some time," Viktor yawned. "It is because of the backlog of message traffic waiting to be deciphered. I'm starving, but I'm so tired I don't know if I have the strength to pick up a fork."

"Come, you must eat," Anna urged. "Your supper has already been waiting over an hour. If it sits any longer, it will not be fit to eat."

"Yes, Anna, I am coming," Viktor answered, rising from the couch. Viktor stretched, plodded to the dining table, and sat down heavily. "It smells delicious."

Anna lifted a glass pie plate from the oven and set it on the table.

"We are having desert first?" Viktor joked. "Is this what they do in Canada?"

"Is called Lord Woolton Pie," Anna chided as she dished out a portion onto Viktor's plate. "Sylvie from across the hall gave me recipe. We walked together to the market today. She said she often made this when rationing and shortages made many things hard to find. She still makes it because her husband loves it, so I thought I would make for you."

"Well, it certainly smells good," Viktor remarked, holding the plate up to his nose, breathing in the enticing aroma. He broke off a portion, loaded it onto his fork, blew on it, and then stuffed it into his mouth. "Hot. Hot," Viktor bawled, shoving the hot food back and forth in his mouth to keep from burning his tongue. He finally managed to chew the bite and swallow it. "Water, please," he begged.

Anna grabbed a glass from the cupboard, filled it with water, and handed it to Viktor. "You must be careful. Food is hot when it comes out of the oven."

"Ha, ha, very funny," Viktor responded, setting the nearly empty glass on the table. With his fork, he broke the pie into pieces, watching the steam curling up as he blew on the entire mass. After testing the temperature with his finger, he again loaded his fork and shoved it into his mouth.

"This is delicious," he mumbled, quickly shoving another forkful into this mouth. "If we eat like this, I will like Canada very much." Viktor devoured the slice of Lord Woolton Pie and held his plate out for another.

Anna scooped another piece onto his plate along with a piece of bread and said," You must also taste this brown bread. Sylvie showed me how to make it. I cannot believe the wonderful smell."

Viktor smeared a dab of butter on the bread and took a bite. "Incredible. What is that taste?"

"It is something called molasses. Sylvie said it is made from beets. I have never seen such things as they have here."

"Never in my life have I had such a wonderful meal," Viktor gushed. He pushed the chair back, stood up, walked to the other side of the table, and kissed Anna. "You will make me as fat as old General Zabotin was when he dropped over dead from a heart attack."

Unable to resist, Viktor returned to his chair and gobbled down two more portions of Lord Woolton Pie and three slices of brown bread. Both stuffed to the gills, Viktor and Anna left the dishes sitting on the table and moved over to the couch.

"How was your day?" Anna questioned.

"Nonstop work, as it is most days," Viktor replied. "I only took two short five minute breaks and still I cannot get caught up. If I don't catch up the backlog soon, Colonel Sokolovsky will send us back to Russia."

"Viktor, say this is not true," Anna protested. "We have only just arrived."

"I'm sorry, but it is true. Boris warned me. He said….,"

Anna stared at Viktor, waiting for him to finish his sentence. After a long delay, she said, "You said Boris warned you. Warned you about what? Finish what you were saying."

"I must not. It is better that you do not know."

"No, Viktor. We are happy here. You must tell me what has you worried."

"I cannot," Viktor answered as he stood up and started toward the kitchen.

Anna followed him, grabbed his hand, and pulled him back to the couch. She said, "Sit. Tell me what is going on. I know you work with classified things, but we must not have secrets between us. Do you believe you can trust me?"

"Yes, I trust you, but this is…," Viktor stopped talking again, afraid to continue.

"I do not believe you trust me," Anna snapped. "Otherwise, you would tell me."

Viktor saw the pained expression on Anna's face and relented. "Okay, but you *must* promise you will not speak a word of this to anyone and I mean *anyone*."

Anna took both Viktor's hands in hers and gave him her full attention. Viktor told her about the strange packages Boris had told him were being sneaked in and out of the embassy. Not leaving out a single detail, he told her about Sokolovsky's warning to the security staff and that the former cipher clerk had been murdered.

"Viktor, that is frightening. What are you going to do?"

"It gets worse, Anna. Today, I saw one of those packages in the security safe. Nobody else was in the room and the package was not sealed, so I looked in. It was a document that should not be there. An hour later the package was gone. The room is guarded and there is an entry log that must be signed. Nobody had been in the room but me and Colonel Sokolovsky."

"Sokolovsky is a despicable pig," Anna sneered. "I do not like him."

"Anna, you must *never* say that outside these walls," Viktor commanded, tightening his grip on Anna's hands.

"I know. I hear many women talking back in Moscow in that horrible place they called housing. They say Sokolovsky is a ruthless tyrant, but only to those who are weaker or less important than he is."

"This is likely true, but, other than the Russian Ambassador, he is the highest ranking official here."

"What do we do, Viktor?"

"We will be careful and we will keep our mouths shut. Boris is a lieutenant in the security unit. He has promised to keep me informed of any changes or new dangers."

"Promise me you will be careful. Sokolovsky is very dangerous."

"I promise. Now, come, it is time for bed. Morning will come soon."

Chapter Six

"Stupid machine," Viktor muttered, bent over the newly in-stalled Fialka M-125 cipher machine. "Why won't this thing work?" The machine was brand new and just like the machine he had trained on at the GRU Cipher Training Unit, but no matter what Viktor tried, he could not get the machine to deci-pher a test message correctly.

When the backlog of message traffic encoded using the old type machines had been deciphered, the old cipher machine had been disassembled and moved to the lower level. Viktor had been tinkering with the new machine for over two hours. Message traffic had increased over the past few weeks and the backlog was growing. If he did not get the cipher machine working soon, Colonel Sokolovsky would be furious.

"I just don't understand," Viktor whined. "Everything is aligned correctly. Why won't it work?"

Viktor turned back to the desk, flipped back to the begin-ning of the instruction manual section on initial setup and re-read the instructions for a third time. Completely out of ideas, he slammed the manual closed out of frustration. He had fol-lowed the manual's instructions precisely. There was nothing left to try.

"I have to be missing something, but what?" he fumed.

He grabbed a lamp from the table sitting beside the ma-chine, removed the shade, and held it over the machine. All the gear sprockets were engaged. The cipher wheels and rotors were all aligned properly. He wiped the beads of sweat running down his forehead on his sleeve. As he turned his head back toward the machine, he saw something shiny flash in the bottom of the machine.

"What is that?" he exclaimed as he slipped his hand between the rotors and the machine's outer case. "Why didn't I see that before?" He wiggled his hand to get it deeper into the machine, but the object remained just out of reach. "Almost," he sputtered. "Just a little more and…"

"Zakharov," Colonel Sokolovsky yelled, barging into the room. "I have officials in my office complaining they are not getting their messages. What are you doing?"

"Yeow!" Viktor cried as he yanked his hand out of the machine, a large red scrape on the back of his hand oozing blood. He grabbed an old rag from the table and wrapped it around his hand. "The new cipher machine will not decode correctly," Viktor answered.

"Why isn't that machine working?" Colonel Sokolovsky demanded. "The machine was installed yesterday. What is taking so long?"

"It looks like one of the shipping pins fell out and lodged in the bottom of the machine. It must be binding on one of the rotors."

"Show me," Colonel Sokolovsky said as he walked over to the machine and peered inside. "You are mistaken. I don't see anything."

Viktor repositioned the lamp over the machine "Tilt your head and look here," he said, pointing at the back of the machine.

"Yes, I see it. How long will it take to get the pin out and the machine working?"

"If I have to remove any of the rotors to be able to reach it, it could take an hour or longer."

"Too long. You have thirty minutes to have the next batch of messages deciphered and on my desk. Do you understand?"

"Yes sir," Viktor replied.

Colonel Sokolovsky turned and stomped out of the room. Not only did Viktor not have an hour to remove the pin and finish the setup, he had only thirty minutes to do that *and* decipher and deliver the next batch of messages. Viktor shook his head and went back to work getting the pin out of the machine.

Thirty-five minutes later, soaked in sweat and puffing from running up the stairs, Viktor stood in front of Colonel Sokolovsky's office door. He slapped the wall three times and waited.

"Enter."

Viktor rushed into the office, stood at attention in front of the colonel's desk, handed him the sealed cipher bag, and said, "The next batch of messages deciphered and verified, sir."

"You are fortunate, Lieutenant Zakharov," Colonel Sokolovsky taunted. 'I was just about to come looking for you."

Colonel Sokolovsky unsealed the bag, pulled the stack of papers out, quickly flipping through the pile. He pulled out two telegrams, put them in the middle drawer of his desk, and locked it.

"I will deliver these messages personally. Get back to work. Now that the new cipher machine is working, I expect more progress toward eliminating the backlog."

"Yes, sir," Viktor acknowledged. Viktor turned on his heel, exited the office, hurried back down the stairs, and signed into the cipher room.

"Ты шутишь, что ли," Viktor gasped (roughly translated - *Are you joking?*) when he saw the original messages still lying on the table beside the cipher machine. He ran over to the table, jammed the stack of papers into a backup cipher bag, and rushed out the door, headed for the secure file room.

After signing the entry log, the guard stepped aside and allowed Viktor to enter the secure file room. Viktor entered the combination and pulled the heavy safe door open. Peeking around the side of the safe, he made certain no one else was in the room. One by one he located the message reference numbers in the master routing list and entered the time returned as two minutes before he had run out of the cipher room, headed for Colonel Sokolovsky's office.

He piled the original encrypted messages on the lower shelf with the others that had been deciphered earlier. Grabbing the next group of ten messages, he stuffed them into the cipher bag, sealed the bag, closed and locked the safe, then headed back to the cipher room.

Back in the cipher room, the process of deciphering the next group of messages went quickly now that the Fialka M-125 cipher machine was setup and working properly. He placed the original messages in the cipher bag along with the deciphered messages. On his way to deliver the latest batch of deciphered messages to the indicated recipients, he passed his friend, Boris, in the hallway. Boris deliberately bumped into him while rubbing his right eye.

"You were supposed to….,"

"Bathroom, ten minutes," Boris interrupted.

Before Viktor could say anything, Boris hurried down the hallway and turned the corner. Viktor glanced at his watch and continued his task of delivering the deciphered messages. Hurrying as fast as he could without drawing attention, he delivered all the messages. After he delivered the last message, he looked at his watch. Eleven minutes had passed. He wondered if Boris would still be waiting. Taking the steps two at a time, he reached the ground floor, ran down the hallway. and rushed into the bathroom.

Boris was not in the bathroom. About to leave, Viktor saw Boris peek over the wall of the last stall. Boris pushed the stall door open and walked toward Viktor with his finger pressed to his lips. "*Read later,*" he mouthed without making a sound. He placed a small, folded piece of paper in Viktor's hand and exited the bathroom.

Hearing another stall door opening, Viktor quickly slipped the folded paper in his pocket, tucked the cipher bag under his arm, and washed his hands. Nodding at the officer walking up to the sink next to him, Viktor dried his hands, tossed the used paper towel into the trash can, and left the bathroom. He climbed the stairs and headed back to the secure file room to mark the original encrypted messages as complete and collect another group of ten.

As he signed the entry log, he noticed that Colonel Sokolovsky had entered the file room while he was delivering deciphered messages. Glancing up at the wall clock, he scribbled his entry time on the appropriate line and walked into the secure file room. He entered the combination and pulled the heavy door open.

Surprised, he noticed an odd envelope lying on the second shelf from the bottom that had not been there before. According to the log book, no one else had been in the room, so the envelope had to have been placed there by Colonel Sokolovsky.

The colonel had signed out of the file room only seven minutes earlier. Assuming the colonel would not return anytime soon, Viktor decided to read the note Boris had placed in his hand. He pulled the note out of his pocket, unfolded it, and began reading.

> *I see suspicious activity. An intelligence officer not report for duty. S and G getting messages A knows nothing about. Officer see something he not supposed to, sent back to Russia and was shot. Everyone warned that is what happens to people who not follow rules. B*

Viktor refolded the note and slipped it down into his sock as far as it would go. As he straightened up his gaze fell on the odd envelope. He lifted the envelope off the shelf and examined both sides. Nothing on either side indicated what it contained or where or who it was from. Sliding his finger under the flap, he discovered the envelope was not sealed. He poked his head around the side of the safe and saw no one in the room and there was no one signing in. Giving in to his curiosity, he decided to have a quick peek in the envelope. He opened the envelope and slid out one single sheet of paper.

Chapter Seven

Russian Embassy
Senior Military Attaché Office
Ottawa, Ontario, Canada

Colonel Sokolovsky unlocked the middle drawer of his desk, lifted out one of the messages Viktor had delivered earlier, and laid it face down on his desk. He got up from his desk, closed and locked his office door, and returned to his desk. Turning the message face up, he began reading.

> *On previously communicated data with respect to Frank, it is known to us he received instructions from his director to get in touch with your corporation.*
>
> *At present Commander needs to know more details about candidates proposed by Frank and therefore it is desired that you should in written form enlighten us with possibilities.*
>
> *Contact the Neighbor with regard to any previous suggestions by Frank. Take no action until permission by Commander.*

Colonel Sokolovsky returned the message to the middle drawer and locked it. Pushing back from his desk, he stood up, walked over to the window, and pushed the curtain aside. Deep in thought over the content of the message, he stared out at Strathcona Park, directly across the street from the embassy.

Donated by Lord Strathcona in 1909, the park had originally been a swampy and unusable floodplain located along the Rideau River. Unfit for building, the site first had become home to a rifle range, where soldiers had trained before departing for the Second Boer War. That history was preserved in the name Range Road, which formed the western border of the park. In the distance, Colonel Sokolovsky could see a group of young boys playing on the ball diamond near the southern end of the park. Closer, along the riverbank, he watched a group of shirtless boys screaming and jumping into the shallow water.

"*Undisciplined. Boys that age should be in training program. I'm surprised Canada didn't lose the war,*" Colonel Sokolovsky thought as he turned away from the window and returned to his desk.

He stood in front of his desk for several minutes deciding how he should respond to the message he had just read. After reaching for a small notepad, he bent over, scribbled a few words on the top sheet, and stuffed the sheet of paper in an envelope. He unlocked the door, opened it, and poked his head through the doorway.

"Captain Moroshkin, come into my office," Colonel Sokolovsky ordered as he backed away from the door and waited. As soon as the captain entered, he said, "Captain Moroshkin, close the door and stand in front of it.

Yegor Feodorovich Moroshkin, Colonel Sokolovsky's Adjutant , did as instructed, waiting for further orders.

"Take this note and deliver it to Frank. No one is to know of this and no one is to see you deliver note. Same location as before. Indicate in the embassy log you are going to pharmacy to get medicine for me. At the *Dubok* change out of your uniform. Wait for Frank to reply then return to *Dubok* and change back into your uniform. Go to pharmacy and see Albert. He will give you package. Return as soon as you can."

"Yes, sir, Colonel Sokolovsky," Captain Moroshkin replied. "I will return quickly." Pivoting on his right heel, Captain Moroshkin yanked the door open, and rushed out of the office, headed for the stairway. At the bottom of the stairs, he turned left and hurried to the front desk. He signed out of the embassy as instructed, exited the front gate, and hurried off in the direction of his first stop.

Colonel Sokolovsky had returned to his desk and had begun writing out the required information requested in the message. He wrote furiously for several minutes. Suddenly he lifted the pencil from the paper and stopped writing. Staring blankly at the paper, unable to remember the list that had been provided, he would need the original communication. He unlocked the middle drawer and rifled through its contents. The message was not there. A quick search among the papers on his desk turned up nothing. "Where could it be?" he grumbled out loud. After searching every surface in his office, he remembered having been in the secure file room.

"It has to be in the safe," he complained as he exited his office and headed for the file room.

Russian Embassy
Secure File Room
Ottawa, Ontario, Canada

Viktor stared at the sheet of paper in his hand, confused by what he saw. "This cannot be," he whispered.

"Where is Zakharov? I did not see him in the cipher room as I passed by," Colonel Sokolovsky's irritated voice echoed from the outer room.

"He is in file room collecting more messages, sir," the duty security guard answered, snapping to attention. The guard stepped sideways in front of the colonel and said, "You must sign the entry log before entering sir."

Colonel Sokolovsky stopped and glared at the security guard. "But, sir. It is your orders," the guard offered in defense. "You said absolutely no one, not even you may enter without signing."

"You are correct, Junior Sergeant," Colonel Sokolovsky said as he bent over the table and scrawled his name on the entry log. "Enter the current time next to my name."

During the brief exchange between the colonel and the guard, Viktor tried desperately to slip the sheet of paper back into the envelop. His hands were shaking so badly he could not get the paper in. The sound of footsteps entering the room made his hands shake even worse.

"Zakharov, what are you doing?" Colonel Sokolovsky demanded, stepping around the open door of the safe. "What is that in your hand?"

"It is the master routing list, Colonel Sokolovsky," Viktor answered, quickly sliding his right hand into his trouser pocket and holding out the master routing list with his left hand. "I'm verifying the master routing list. The message count was off. One of the messages in the last batch must have had an incorrect control number."

"And who assigns the control numbers?"

"I do, sir. First thing in the morning, all newly arrived messages are assigned a control number. I was in a hurry to get started. I have finally been able to reduce the backlog of message waiting to be deciphered."

"Is this problem corrected?"

"Yes, sir. I have corrected the control number and now the counts are in agreement."

"I will overlook your error this time, but you must be more careful in the future. I do not have time to instruct you in the necessity of accurate counts. As soon as Captain Moroshkin returns from the pharmacy with some medicine, I will be leaving. Any new messages addressed to me will be kept in the safe until I return tomorrow. Is that understood?"

"Yes, sir."

Colonel Sokolovsky turned, started toward the door, and stopped. He walked back to the safe. "Hand me that envelope. The yellow one on the second shelf."

Inside, Viktor cringed. If the colonel found out there was a message missing from the envelope, he would be sent back to Moscow. Visions of a firing squad swirled in Viktor's mind. Viktor lifted the envelope off the shelf and handed it to Colonel Sokolovsky. Colonel Sokolovsky folded back the flap, pulled the entire stack of messages partially out of the envelope, and began flipping through them. Stopping on the fourth message, he pulled a single sheet out and shoved the rest back into the envelope.

"This one is all I need," he said as he folded the sheet into fourths and shoved it into his pocket. "These are highly classified. I will drop them in the incinerator on my way back to my office. Now, get back to work, Lieutenant Zakharov. I expect to see much progress when I return tomorrow."

"Yes, Colonel Sokolovsky. I will stay late if I must to assure there is progress on reducing the backlog."

Without another word the colonel turned and left the file room. Viktor breathed a sigh of relief. With the threat of discovery gone, his hands shook worse than before. He took two deep breaths then pulled the sheet of crumpled paper from his right trouser pocket. He had been careful to keep his right side turned away from the colonel so he would not see the bulge in his pocket.

Viktor laid the crumpled paper on one the shelves, smoothed it out, and folded it into fourths. He unbuttoned one of the buttons on his shirt, slid the message under his shirt, and redid the button. After signing out the next group of ten messages and stuffing them into the cipher bag, he closed and locked the safe. He exited the file room and stopped to enter his exit time in the entry log.

"The colonel is very difficult man," the security guard observed.

"That is understatement," Viktor agreed as he wrote down the time and rushed off toward the cipher room.

Zakharov Apartment
Somerset Street
Ottawa, Ontario, Canada

Six hours later, Viktor walked into his and Anna's apartment completely exhausted. Shuffling over to the old, gray overstuffed chair, he collapsed into it and leaned his head back. His mind raced with the thought of how close he had come to being caught with Colonel Sokolovsky's secret message in his hands. He squeezed his eyes closed tightly as if that would chase away the terrifying memory.

"Viktor, you are much later than usual," Anna observed, stepping out of the kitchen. "You look exhausted. Did you have a bad day?"

"I stayed later because Colonel Sokolovsky is not happy with the progress on reducing the backlog of messages."

"Sokolovsky is a pig," Anna hissed. "Did he yell at you again?"

"Of course he yelled. That is all he ever does. But that's not…." Viktor started to say something about the message under his shirt, but thought it best not to tell Anna about it.

"Yes, Viktor, go on. You were going to say something else."

"It is best if you do not know."

"Viktor, you should tell me. I do not know how to help if you do not."

"I'm sorry. I cannot."

"We agreed there would be no secrets. You will feel better if you tell me."

"I cannot," Viktor said again, shrugging his shoulders.

A wounded look clouded Anna's face. She turned away and started toward the kitchen. Viktor rose from the old chair and hurried after her. He grabbed her arm, turned her around, and hugged her. "I'm sorry. You do not understand. It's…."

Still hurt, Anna pushed away from Viktor. Her arm pressed against his stomach as she pushed away, rustling the paper hidden under Viktor's shirt.

"What do you have under your shirt?" she asked, reaching for a button on Viktor's shirt.

"No, you must not," Viktor protested, backing away from Anna's outstretched hand.

"Victor Sergeyevich Zakharov, you must tell me. Are you stealing documents from the embassy?" Anna demanded with her hands on her hips.

Viktor had seen the look on Anna's face before. That look and the use of his full name meant she would not relent until he explained.

"I want to tell you, but I fear for your safety," Viktor countered, hoping to end the conversation. "It will put you in great danger."

"I do not care," Anna argued. "We will not move from this spot until you tell me what has you so upset."

Viktor knew he had no choice *and* Anna was right. He would feel better if he could share his concern with her. He bent over, slipped his fingers into his sock, and retrieved the message Boris had passed to him in the bathroom.

"Boris whispered at me in hallway. He said to meet him in bathroom in ten minutes. He passed me this note."

After Anna finished reading the note, Viktor explained, "In note, 'S' means Colonel Sokolovsky, 'A' means the Soviet Ambassador, Leonid Grigoryovich Volkov, and 'G' means Ilya Karpovovich Liminov, Second Secretary of embassy. Volkov is mere figurehead. Man named Liminov is real head of power. Liminov runs a secret political system and answers directly to the Central Committee of the Communist Party in Moscow. I have learned he is head of N.K.V.D. in Canada"

"What is N.K.V.D. you mention?"

"It stands for Narodnyy Komissariat Vnutrennikh Del. In English it means The People's Commissariat for Internal Affairs. They are the secret police. They also run the labor camps back in Russia and they are responsible for the execution of thousands of Russians, all without trials."

"They operate here in Canada?" Anna asked.

"Yes, they are everywhere and they watch everybody. Liminov uses code name 'Gisel' in all messages. I discovered that after deciphering many messages. Sokolovsky and Liminov get many messages that are not catalogued and no one else knows about them."

"But you know these things, Viktor," Anna added with a worried look on her face. "Does that not make you a threat?"

"I believe Colonel Sokolovsky trusts me. He knows my background in the Komsomol and the Leninist Young Communist League. I am certain he believes I am faithful communist."

"And you are not?" Anna questioned.

"I was until I came here," Viktor answered. "Since arriving, I am no longer certain. I am amazed by complete freedom individuals have here. It is amazing the things on sale in the market. Remember the unbelievable variety of fruit at the market. People here are allowed to buy whatever they want. And the elections here have more than one name you can vote for. Back in Russia, this is not how they describe life is in democratic countries."

"Yes, I too have seen these things," Anna agreed. "Why were we not told these things?"

"Anna, the hardliners have lied to us. They have other motive."

Viktor unbuttoned one button on his shirt and pulled out the folded sheet of paper.

"After Boris handed me note, I went to secure file room to get more messages. When I opened safe in secure file room, I see odd envelope lying on one of the shelves. I slipped this paper out and had it in my hand when Colonel Sokolovsky came into room."

"Viktor, did you get caught?" Anna asked, a look of horror on her face.

"No. I did not get caught. Security guard challenged him and made him write name in entry log. That gave me time to slip paper in pocket."

"But Viktor, you *must* not do this! Sokolovsky will find out paper is missing."

"He will not know. As he was leaving file room, he said he was going to put envelope in incinerator on his way back to office. Without envelope, I had no place to put paper, so I had to hide it under shirt. What is on paper proves what I have said. You will not believe what else I have to say, but you must read this first."

Viktor unfolded the paper and handed it to Anna. She reached out, took the paper, and began reading.

"What is Comintern?" she asked, looking up at Viktor.

"Comintern is short for Communist International," Viktor answered. "Is like headquarters that directs activities of Communist Parties across whole world. I have been told there is a file at Comintern office in Moscow; for every communist in whole world."

Anna nodded her head in acknowledgment and continued reading.

To: Comintern - *After reading, burn.*
~~Benson~~ *has agreed to my original requests and has pro-*
vided the material for the attached report. He offers to fill
in any missing details re: military movements. ~~Benson~~
and ~~Gray~~ *feel the need for maintaining a very high de-*
gree of security and taking increased precautions at their
normal meetings is necessary. Since they are currently not
labeled with any political affiliations, they are concerned re:
introduction of new members to the group, and feel it might
compromise their own secrecy. Please check ~~Walter~~,
~~Leader~~ ~~Foster~~ *and* ~~Benson~~ *through the Comintern and reply.*

"Why are names crossed out?"

"I met Boris as I walked home. I show him paper. He said handwritten names are cover names. Real names are crossed out, but as you see, whoever did this was in a hurry or was very careless. It is not difficult to read original names."

"Do you know any of those names?"

"No, but Boris was shocked when he see name under 'Leader'. Name scratched out is 'Gardner'. Boris say this has to be man by name of James Gardner. Boris overhear two men in security unit talking. One say he see this man meeting with

Colonel Sokolovsky at night outside of embassy. Man hand colonel piece of paper and then disappear quickly."

"Who is he? Did Boris know?"

"Boris say he see man's picture in local newspaper. He is squadron leader in Royal Canadian Air Force."

"Why would such a man meet with Sokolovsky?"

"I do not know, but I do know they should never meet secretly. Over two years ago, Central Committee in Moscow said Comintern was being disbanded. It appears only name was disbanded. This paper proves Comintern still exists and is involved in espionage work. Canada is said to be ally not enemy. Something is very wrong."

"What do you think all this means?" Anna asked as she walked into the living room and sat down on the couch.

Following her into the living room, Viktor answered, "I think someone is passing classified information to Sokolovsky and maybe others. Then it is sent to Central Committee in Moscow. I only see this one paper. I do not know what was on report it mentions, only that it had to do with military movements. Last part of the message talks about adding new members. That must mean someone is recruiting locals to work as spies for the Soviets."

"But, Viktor," Anna countered. "Even during a time of war, the Canadian people have such freedoms, they can buy whatever they want. They are happy people. Why would they spy on their own country?"

"I am as puzzled as you," Viktor exclaimed, shaking his head. "I have no answer. I do not understand how people can betray their own country."

"What are you going to do with paper?"

"I will hide paper until I can discover what all this means and who other names are."

"Viktor, you must not," Anna protested. "If you get caught with Embassy papers, they will send you back to Russia and you will be executed."

"Here, cut open seam," Viktor said, grabbing Nikola's favorite stuffed toy. "We will hide paper inside stuffed bear. No one would think to look there."

Anna grabbed a pair of scissors from her sewing basket and snipped open a three inch portion of the side seam. Viktor refolded the paper and stuffed it inside the bear. Anna threaded a needle, repaired the seam, and fluffed the fur. Viktor grabbed the stuffed bear and examined it. Satisfied no one would notice the repaired seam, he tossed the bear into the overstuffed chair.

"Let's have supper now, if it is not ruined. Tomorrow I will look for more suspicious things as I decipher messages."

"Viktor, you must be extremely careful. Sokolovsky is a sadistic monster. If he catches you, he will have you executed."

"I will be careful, my beautiful wife. I am not stupid."

"Let us hope so for both our sakes," Anna added, turning toward the stove to dish out their supper.

Chapter Eight

Russian Embassy
Dining Hall
Ottawa, Ontario, Canada

Early, before most embassy staff had arrived, Viktor had signed into the embassy. One of the first five to line up at the dining hall door, he met Boris and sat down for a quick breakfast. After shoving the last spoonful of oatmeal into his mouth, Viktor pretended to scratch at his right ear. As he moved his hand away, he tugged at his ear lobe. He looked at Boris to see if he had noticed. Boris nodded slightly and went back to finishing his breakfast.

"It will be a long day," Viktor announced. "I have many messages to decipher."

"Will you get a break?" Boris asked, shoveling a forkful of what appeared to be scrambled eggs into his mouth.

"If I get one at all, it would likely be two in the afternoon."

Viktor looked around the dining hall to see if anyone might be watching. Only fifteen other embassy staff members had arrived early and were seated around tables on the opposite side of the room. Reaching down into his sock, he retrieved a small, folded piece of paper. With the note concealed in his hand, he leaned on the table and pushed the note under the edge of Boris's plate.

Viktor rose from his chair and walked over and stood on the other side of Boris to shield him from view of the others in the room.

"May I take your dirty dishes?" Viktor asked.

"Please, take them away. I am finished," Boris replied as he laid his left hand on top of the note. While Viktor stacked the dishes together, Boris pretended to knock a fork off onto the floor. As he reached down to retrieve the fork, he slid the note into the top of his sock. He picked up the fork and dropped it onto the stack of dishes.

"Perhaps I will see you on your break," Boris said as he pushed his chair back and stood up.

"If I can afford the time, I will meet you in usual place," Viktor responded.

Viktor headed for the front of the dining hall to deposit the dirty dishes. When he turned around, Boris had already left, stopping in the lower level bathroom. In the relative privacy of the far stall, he slipped out the note, read it, memorized the five names written there, tore it into tiny pieces, and flushed it.

"*What have I gotten myself into,*" he asked himself as he left the bathroom and headed for the security office.

Russian Embassy
Cipher Room
Ottawa, Ontario, Canada

Two hours after leaving the dining hall, Viktor, for the second time, finished resetting the Fialka cipher machine to use a new master cipher code. Several days earlier, Colonel Sokolovsky had informed him that the Central Committee in Moscow had ordered the master cipher code should be changed every day instead of weekly. The elaborate new security protocol required an additional code book to determine the master cipher code for each day. All new messages received from Moscow included a new keyword on each message to indicate the day on which it had been encoded.

Adding to Viktor's workload was the fact that messages did not always get transmitted to the embassy on the day they were encoded. The first group of messages Viktor retrieved from the safe, had messages using two different keywords. Fortunately, he had noticed the different codes before resetting the cipher machine. After splitting the messages into two groups, he deciphered the first group, reset the machine, and then deciphered the second group.

He slid the originals and deciphered messages into the cipher bag. After delivering the messages, he headed for the secure file room to store the originals and pick up another group of ten messages. As he bent over to sign the entry log, he noticed that Colonel Sokolovsky had been in the file room. "*That's odd,*" he thought. Colonel Sokolovsky was supposed to be out of town, but he had signed into the secure file room eighteen minutes earlier. Viktor signed in, unlocked the safe, and marked the originals as complete in the control log. He stacked them on top of the other deciphered messages and grabbed the next five messages waiting to be deciphered.

"What?" he exclaimed, noticing the first message was not the next one listed on the master routing list. He lifted the top ten messages off the stack and compared all ten messages to the master routing list. They were all in order, exactly as he had left them, but two messages were missing. He entered the time for the ten messages and slid them into the cipher bag.

Squatting down, he checked the lower shelves to see if the missing messages might have been placed on the wrong shelf. He saw another yellow envelope just like the one he had seen the previous day. Sitting on top of the envelope was Colonel Sokolovsky's secret diary. Giving in to curiosity, he picked up the diary, flipped it open to the first page, and began to read.

"Zakharov, are you in here?" Colonel Sokolovsky hollered as he walked around the open safe door.

Viktor dropped the diary back on the envelope and started flipping through a stack of messages on the bottom shelf.

"What are you doing?" Colonel Sokolovsky demanded.

"I'm looking for two missing messages," Viktor lied. "They were here yesterday. I am certain of it."

"Lock the safe and follow me."

"Yes, sir, Colonel," Viktor responded, thinking Sokolovsky must have seen the diary in his hand. Viktor straightened up, retrieved the cipher bag from the top shelf, pushed the heavy door closed, and spun the combination dial.

"Sign us both out," Colonel Sokolovsky ordered, standing in the doorway waiting.

Viktor looked up at the clock, wrote down the time beside both names in the entry log, and hurried after Colonel Sokolovsky as he stomped down the hallway, the heels of his highly-polished boots echoing loudly. Expecting to follow the colonel to his third floor office, Viktor was surprised when Colonel Sokolovsky turned, walked down the second floor hallway, and entered the cipher room.

"Close the door and lock it."

Viktor did as ordered. Quaking inside, Viktor fully expected to be the recipient of Colonel Sokolovsky's rage.

"Do not look so frightened, Zakharov," Colonel Sokolovsky chided as he pulled two sheets of paper out from under his uniform jacket. "You are not in trouble. I have the two missing messages here. Moscow informed me these messages are very highly classified and no one but me is to see them. Reset the cipher machine to the proper cipher code and I will run the messages through myself."

With shaking hands, Viktor took the first message, read the keyword, and determined the appropriate master cipher code to use. Sokolovsky watched while Viktor reset the cipher machine and deciphered a test message to verify the setup.

"The machine is set to the correct code and verified, Colonel."

"Very well. Step to the other side of the room and face the wall."

Colonel Sokolovsky waited until Viktor had done as told. He ran the first message through the cipher machine and read the deciphered message then repeated the process for the second message. He folded the messages in half and slid them underneath his jacket.

"Zakharov, I am finished. You may now resume your normal duties. The next time you are in the cipher room mark the two messages as complete. I will burn the original messages myself."

"Yes, sir," Viktor answered to Sokolovsky's back.

Viktor watched as Colonel Sokolovsky unlocked the door and left the room. He slumped down into a chair, pulled a handkerchief from his pocket, and wiped the perspiration from his face. Anna's warning echoed in his mind, "*Viktor, you must not do this.*" Her warning had nearly come true. He had come within two seconds of getting caught with Sokolovsky's diary in his hand. He vowed from that point on to exercise more caution.

Perhaps Boris would be able to provide some information about the five names he had passed to him in the note. The identity of those individuals, might explain the reason behind the strange envelopes and the sudden increase in security. If he was going to be able to take a break, he would need to get back to work and make up the time lost while Sokolovsky deciphered the two classified messages. He pushed himself up from the chair, grabbed the cipher bag, and went to work deciphering the messages.

Over the next five hours, Viktor averaged just under two hours to decipher and deliver a batch of ten messages. Finished deciphering the third batch of messages, he glanced up at the clock. He had slightly less than twenty minutes to deliver the messages and get to the seating area behind the embassy by two o'clock. He jammed the messages into the cipher bag, headed for the door, and hurried down the hallway.

Viktor pushed the embassy's rear door open at three minute past two. Looking to his left, he saw that the seating area was empty. Boris was not there. Shaking his head, Viktor walked over to the bench and sat down, winded from his rush down the stairs and out the rear door.

"Sorry, I'm late," a voice called out.

Viktor looked up to see Boris heading his way. Boris sat down on the bench beside him. He took several deep breaths and said, "I was busy and didn't realize what time it was."

"I just got here myself. I know it's been a short time, but were you able to learn anything?"

"Yes, but I could only learn the identity of two of the five names on the paper," Boris whispered. "I will need more time to see if I can learn who the other three are. You will not believe what I have learned."

"Who are they?"

"Not here. Is too dangerous. Take off hat and scratch your head."

Viktor did not know what Boris intended, but he did as instructed. Viktor reached up with his left hand, pulled off his hat, and scratched the top of his head with his other hand. Boris stretched, deliberately knocking the hat out of Viktor's hand.

"Sorry, I am clumsy oaf," Boris exclaimed. "Let me get it." Boris bent over and as he picked up Viktor's hat, he slipped a small, folded piece of paper under the inside band. "Here, it is not dirty." As he leaned toward Viktor, he whispered, "Under band inside hat."

"I must go," Boris announced. "I am busy and have many things to do."

"Me too," Viktor added. "I will see you at breakfast tomorrow."

Both men got up from the bench and left the seating area in different directions. Viktor hurried back to the secure file room to collect another batch of messages. He signed the entry log, entered the file room, and unlocked the safe for the fourth time that day. As he pulled the heavy door open, his eyes settled on Sokolovsky's diary

He lifted his hat off his head and felt around inside the band for the paper Boris had placed there. His finger touched the paper, but he decided it was much too risky to read the note in the file room. He laid the hat on top of the safe and picked up the diary. "*No, this is too risky,*" his mind cried as he started to open the diary. He put the diary back on the envelope and stared at it. Battling with inner turmoil and the desire to find out who was collaborating with Russian agents, he picked up the diary again.

"*No. No. Do not do this.*" His mind balked, knowing he would be executed if he got caught. He laid the diary back on the envelope and signed out another batch of messages. He picked up his hat, closed and locked the safe, and headed back to the cipher room, deciding he would read Boris's note first and see if anything on the note would let him know if the risk of getting caught was warranted.

Chapter Nine

Marion Dewar Plaza
Ottawa, Ontario, Canada

Viktor trudged across the Rideau River Bridge on Laurier Avenue, exhausted from another long day of deciphering telegrams, memorandums, and various other communications received from Moscow. The delay caused by Colonel Sokolovsky's demand to decipher two messages himself had put Viktor behind schedule. In order to decipher more messages than were received, he had had to work late, again.

Even though he was eager to get home, his desire to read the note Boris had passed him overrode the hunger gnawing at his stomach. Desperate to reduce the backlog, he had not taken the time for even a short break. Despite the success of reducing the backlog by nearly a third, the suspicious activity he had stumbled across nagged at him. Deciding to take the time to read the note before returning to the apartment, he looked for a place away from prying eyes.

Just past the end of the bridge, he stopped at the intersection with Queen Elizabeth Drive. Seventy-five meters ahead he saw the edge of Marion Dewar Plaza, a public space featuring a well-maintained landscape, wide, sweeping paths, and a shallow fountain. Turning left, he walked down Queen Elizabeth Drive then turned right at the second entrance into the plaza. He walked past Lisgar Field and took a seat on a concrete bench next to the fountain.

Normally the plaza would be teeming with people, but late in the day with all the businesses closed, the plaza was nearly deserted. Viktor waited while a young couple, walking arm in arm, passed by and left the plaza. A quick survey of the plaza satisfied Viktor that no one was watching. He slipped the note out of his pocket, unfolded it, and began reading. The sun had begun to set, making the note difficult to read. Turning sideways he angled the note upward to catch the last fading rays of the sun.

> *Friend, Kony, miss work today. Word is he was beaten*
> *by S. No more details.*
>
> *Only able learn about 2 names.*
>
> *Gray (Holland) - Dept. of Munitions, Mgr.*
> *Leader (Gardner) - Sqd. Ldr., R.C.A.F.*
>
> *Is much danger. 2 security off. sent back to*
> *Russia. Be much careful. Trust no one. B*

Viktor shook his head. The nickname 'Kony' that Boris used was short for Konstantin Ilyonovich Bogdanovitch, a junior sergeant in the communications division. Viktor had talked with Konstantin many times as he picked up incoming messages. During those conversations, Viktor had learned they had similar backgrounds. Konstantin came from the same region as Viktor and he had a wife, Ludmila, a year younger than Anna. He also had a young son, but Viktor could not remember his name.

Viktor refolded the note, slipped it in his pocket, and pushed himself up from the bench. He walked west through the plaza and turned left on Laurier Avenue, an idea forming in his mind. Knowing a twenty minute walk remained, he quickened his pace, trotting for three or four blocks, then he would walk for a block and begin trotting again.

Zakharov Apartment
Somerset Street
Ottawa, Ontario, Canada

Arriving twelve minutes after leaving the plaza, Viktor hurried up the stairs and burst into the apartment.

"Anna, where are you?" he called out, slamming the door behind him.

"I'm in Nikola's room," she answered back.

"Grab Nikola's bag," Viktor panted as he stuck his head into Nikola's room. "We need to go visit someone."

"Who?"

"Boris's friend Konstantin Bogdanovitch. He did not come to work today. Boris said he was beaten."

"But, Viktor, it is late."

"I know, but it is important. I know him. They have a young son also. We must see if we can do anything for them. They live only a few blocks from here. Come, let's go."

"Okay. You get Nikola's bottle from the refrigerator and I'll grab a toy."

Viktor dashed into the kitchen, got Nikola's bottle, and ran to the door. He was standing at the door waiting impatiently when Anna came out of the bedroom. Pushing Anna out the door, Viktor pulled the door shut and the three of them hurried down the stairs. They exited the apartment building and turned east on Somerset Street. At the end of the block they turned south onto Lyon Street North.

"Here, let me take Nikola," Viktor insisted.

"Viktor, slow down. I cannot walk as fast as you do," Anna protested.

With difficulty, Viktor slowed his pace. Three blocks to the south they turned east onto James Street. In the middle of the block they stopped in front of a red brick apartment building. Viktor scanned the list of tenants, seeing Konstantin and Ludmila Bogdanovitch listed as apartment three-zero-eight. They entered the foyer and climbed the stairs to the third floor. At the end of the hallway to the left, they stopped in front of apartment three-zero-eight. Viktor rapped on the door and waited. No answer. Viktor rapped on the door again.

"Who is it?" a female voice asked through the closed door.

"It is Viktor and Anna Zakharov," Viktor shouted. "I know Konstantin from the embassy. His friend, Boris, said he did not come to work today. Anna and I came to see if he is okay and to ask if there is anything we can do for you."

The door opened a small crack and a round face peered at them. "It is rather late," the woman inside said.

"I am sorry, but I felt it was important to let Konstantin know we are concerned for him. We will not stay long."

"Well, okay," the woman shrugged as she pulled the door open and stepped back. "I am Ludmila Bogdanovitch."

"Yes, I know. Konstantin has told me about you. He is very much in love with you."

Ludmila blushed a deep red as she pushed the apartment door closed and directed Viktor and Anna to a couch in the living room. Awakened by the noise, Konstantin slipped off the bed and walked into the living room.

"Viktor, I am surprised to see you," Konstantin mumbled through swollen lips as he took a seat on a chair across from Viktor and Anna.

Viktor immediately noticed the bruises and swelling that made Konstantin's normally thin face round and puffy. Hints of purple and red were beginning to show around his swollen eyes. Ludmila walked over and stood beside Konstantin and laid her hand on his shoulder.

"Boris told me you did not come to work today. Anna and I came to see if there is anything we can do for you."

"That is very kind of you," Konstantin answered, dabbing the cut at the corner of his mouth with a handkerchief. When he pulled the handkerchief away, it was stained with blood.

"Boris told me what happened. Your face looks very painful."

"Yes. I make stupid mistake. I should not have left telegram lying out. I know better."

"That is all that you did to receive such a beating?" Viktor exclaimed.

Uncertain if he should answer Viktor's question, Konstantin shrugged his shoulders and dabbed at the cut again. Ludmila squeezed Konstantin's shoulder and looked at him with great sadness in her eyes.

Viktor looked at Anna then at Ludmila and said, "Konstantin and I must talk in private."

"Please come," Ludmila said. "Your little boy can play with our son, Oleg. He is playing in the bedroom."

Viktor waited for Ludmila, Anna, and Nikola to disappear into the bedroom and for Ludmila to pull the bedroom door shut.

"Konstantin, is leaving one telegram lying out all that caused this beating? Surely there must be something else."

"Yes, just the telegram. Nothing else. Otherwise, I perform job duties well."

"Boris also told me it was Colonel Sokolovsky that beat you. Is that true?"

"Yes, it was him. I…." Konstantin stopped, afraid to say anything more.

"You may speak freely, my friend," Viktor coaxed. "I think Sokolovsky is a despicable pig. I have learned things recently that make me think something improper is going on."

"Viktor, I hate Sokolovsky and the monsters above him. I am afraid. Sokolovsky threatens to send me back to Moscow. I am not to leave apartment until he comes for me. You know what will happen to me if I am sent back. I am good Russian. I do not deserve this. Ludmila is also very frightened. I do not know what to do."

"You must be careful where you say these things. Sokolovsky has many ears."

"Yes, I know, but I am so angry it is hard to be silent."

"Why is one telegram so important?

"The telegram was not coded. That is why Sokolovsky was so furious."

"I see," Viktor said, leaning forward. "Can you describe the telegram?"

"It was sent by Sokolovsky addressed to 'The Director'. I do not know who that is.

"I do," Viktor asserted. "It is the Director of Military Intelligence in Moscow. I have seen that title many times. Continue. What else do you remember?"

"I only got a quick glance at it. What I can remember is that it said something about a parallel system of agents. I believe it also mentioned something about United States."

"Anything else?"

"I remember one line. It said, '*Imperative Leader approved and connecting with Gisel*'."

"I know the name, 'Leader'. It is a cover name for someone in Canada. Someone very important."

"Who is it?" Konstantin asked.

"It is better if you do not know. Continue describing telegram."

"The last I can remember is the last line. It said, '*I think it is better to get rid of him, or to give him to the Neighbor*.' Who is Neighbor?"

"I have also seen name 'Neighbor', but I do not know who it refers to."

"That is all I can remember," Konstantin said. "Do you know what any of it means?"

"Not yet, but I intend to find out," Viktor answered. "What was the date of the telegram?"

"It was sent the day before yesterday. Sokolovsky grabbed the telegram from the counter and stomped out."

"When do you think Sokolovsky would send you back to Moscow?" Viktor asked.

"He say no more than one week," Konstantin answered, grimacing as he pressed the handkerchief against the corner of his mouth.

"I am sorry you were treated so badly."

"Viktor, he was like a madman," Konstantin whimpered. "He beat me with his walking stick and he kicked me. I really thought he was going to kill me."

Viktor opened his mouth to speak but stopped, afraid to put to words the thought that entered his mind. He repeated the words in his mind. Could he really say that? Should he? Two diametrically opposed loyalties, safety of his friend rather than obedience to his country, battled for control of his mind. He sat there staring blankly at Konstantin as the battle raged.

"Viktor, what are you thinking?" Receiving no answer, he waved at Viktor and asked again. "Viktor, what are you thinking?"

"What would happen to Ludmila and Oleg if you are sent back?"

"Sokolovsky said they would have to go back as well. Ludmila has no other family. Her father was killed in the war and her mother died a few months later from lung disease. My precious Ludmila and little Oleg would end up destitute."

Viktor could endure a lot, but that was too much. The simple mistake of leaving one telegram lying out should not carry such a high price. He could not believe he was going to say what was in his mind, but the decision was made.

"Konstantin, you must promise to tell no one what I am about to say. Do you agree?"

Konstantin thought for a few moments and then answered, "I swear I will not speak one word to anyone."

"Good. Now, listen very carefully to what I am going to say. Would you consider not returning to Russia?"

"What are you saying? How could I do such a thing?"

"I believe I know someone who could help you stay in Canada permanently, but it means you could *never* go back to Russia?"

"Ludmila and Oleg also?"

"Yes, of course."

"I do not know what to think. I do not want to die, but to never be able to return home. That is unthinkable."

"If you get sent back, you will be executed. Then what will happen to your wife and child?"

"But to never see Russia again."

"You will be dead and your family will starve. Is that what you want?"

"No, is not what I want."

"I need your answer, now. I will not talk to person I know unless you commit to stay in Canada."

"May I talk to Ludmila and see what she say?"

"Can you trust her to not say anything?"

"Yes, I am certain. She hates Sokolovsky more than me."

"Okay, you may talk to Ludmila, but you must do so quickly. Anna and I will watch Oleg while you talk. We are leaving in ten minutes."

Viktor walked to the bedroom door, tapped lightly, and opened the door. Stepping into the bedroom, he told Ludmila that Konstantin needed to talk to her privately. Viktor waited for her to exit the room and then pushed the door shut. Putting his finger to his lips, he said, "They must talk privately. I will explain later."

Viktor went over to where Nikola and Oleg were playing, sat down on the floor, and helped Oleg stack wooden blocks. When a stack reached five or six blocks high, Oleg would push the stack over and giggle wildly. About to build a stack for the twentieth time, Viktor looked up when the bedroom door swung open.

"We are agreed. Our answer is yes," Konstantin announced as Ludmila nodded her head vigorously in agreement.

"I am glad. Stay inside and go nowhere," Viktor instructed. "I will contact you later. Come Anna. It is late and we must return home."

Anna picked up Nikola, said goodbye to Ludmila, and followed Viktor out of the apartment. Starting down the stairs, she asked, "What was that all about?"

"Not here," Viktor said. "Wait until we are back in our apartment."

The three of them hurried home in the darkness. Viktor scanned every shadow to see if anyone was watching. He felt great relief when they reached the relative safety of their apartment. Viktor brewed a pot of tea while Anna put Nikola to bed. Needing something strong and satisfying, he dumped an extra scoop of tea leaves into the pot and poured boiling water over them. He waited two minutes for the tea to steep, positioned a strainer over a cup, and poured the dark red tea into the cup. Holding the cup up to his lips, he blew across the steaming liquid, and carefully took a sip. As he sipped the hot tea, he began to finalize the plan to help his friend.

Anna slipped up behind him and gently touched his arm. He poured her a cup of tea and pointed her toward the couch in the living room. After several sips of tea and a deep breath, Viktor began his explanation. As Viktor's plan unfolded, Anna's expression grew more and more stunned. He did not hold anything back: Boris's note, the beating, the telegram, his suspicions, absolutely everything.

As Viktor finished his explanation, he took a sip of tea, leaned back, and said, "That is all I know for now."

"For now?" Anna questioned. "What does that mean? Viktor you must stop. You will receive the same beating as Konstantin, or worse if you get caught."

"I have more access than Konstantin did. I will be able to learn what all this means. I will be very careful to not get caught."

"I do not like it. It is too dangerous."

"But we must help Konstantin and Ludmila," Viktor insisted. "Do you not agree?"

Anna had developed an instant bond with Ludmila and little Oleg was a joy to be around. "Viktor, you are awful. You know I must say yes."

"That is why I love you, my sweet wife. Come. Let's go to bed. Morning will come soon."

Viktor picked up the tea cups, rinsed them, and set them in the sink. He checked the apartment door to be certain it was locked, peeked into Nikola's room to be certain he was asleep, and then walked into their bedroom. Dropping his clothes beside the bed, he slipped under the covers. Anna rolled over against him and draped her arm across his chest. Soon, they were both sound asleep.

Russian Embassy
Cipher Room
Ottawa, Ontario, Canada

Viktor finished his fourth batch of messages and stuffed the originals and deciphered copies into the cipher bag, arranging the messages so that the last one to be delivered would be on the first floor of the embassy. He pulled the cipher room door shut and headed to the third floor and the first message's intended recipient. After delivering the last message on the first floor, he walked by the entry guard's desk and deliberately knocked something off the desk. As the guard bent over to retrieve the item, Viktor leaned over the desk and quickly scanned the entry log.

Just as he had hoped. Earlier, while delivering messages on the third floor, he had noticed Colonel Sokolovsky's office was dark. Colonel Sokolovsky's name was on the next to last line of the entry log. He had signed out seventeen minutes earlier. Viktor looked up at the clock. The clock said eleven forty-six. Viktor assumed the colonel had left the embassy for a lunch engagement.

"Sorry," Viktor called out to the guard. "I'm in a hurry. Not even time for lunch."

Viktor rushed down the hallway and ran up the steps. Stopping at the entrance to the secure file room, he signed the entry log and entered the file room. As quickly as he could, he entered the combination and pulled the heavy safe door open. Before marking the messages in the cipher bag as complete, he searched through the stack of deciphered messages from two days earlier, looking for anything that might match the telegram Konstantin had described.

Viktor flipped through the stack twice and found nothing that matched the telegram Konstantin had described. Colonel Sokolovsky's private diary was still lying on the large yellow envelope. Knowing he could not afford to spend any more time looking for the telegram, he decided to have a quick peek at the diary. He raised up on his tiptoes to see if anyone was about to enter the file room. Satisfied he was alone, he lifted the diary off the envelope and started flipping through the pages. Stopping at the last page that contained writing, he read the first few lines. Nothing interesting. The six previous pages contained notes about various meetings, reminders to requisition needed supplies, a note to buy something for his wife's birthday, but nothing of real interest. He stopped on the eighth page and read the note about two-thirds of the way down the page. Sokolovsky's handwriting was so sloppy, Viktor had to read the note three times.

> *Possible second security breach discovered. Efforts must not be discovered. Request instructions from Director. Should K I B be given to Neighbor or returned.*

Viktor repeated the note several times in his mind. Holding his finger in the page, he closed the diary and repeated the note again. Satisfied he had the words firmly in his mind, he replaced the diary exactly as he had found it. He logged the batch of messages in the cipher bag as complete, added them to the stack of deciphered messages, signed out another batch, and stuffed the new messages into the cipher bag. He pushed the safe door closed, spun the combination dial, signed out of the file room, and hurried back to the cipher room.

Viktor opened a desk drawer and pulled out a blank sheet of paper. After looking over his shoulder to be certain he was alone, he wrote down the note he had memorized from Colonel Sokolovsky's diary. He folded the note and slipped it under his shirt.

Working as quickly as he could and still accurately deciphering the messages, he completed the batch of messages and shoved them into the cipher bag. Hopefully, he would be able to catch Boris after he delivered the deciphered messages.

Viktor delivered the last message and exited the back door of the embassy. He turned left and headed toward the small bench at the north end of the building where he and Boris often met. Boris was walking away, about to turn the corner and go behind the building. Boris glanced to his left and saw Viktor waving at him. Pivoting and walking back to the bench, he bent over and pretended to retrieve something he had dropped. He turned and said, "Viktor, I did not expect to see you."

"I just completed my fifth batch of messages," Viktor answered. "My eyes are tired and my back hurts. I needed a break."

"Sit. I will join you for a few minutes."

For several minutes, Viktor and Boris chitchatted about the weather, family life, long hours, and various other mundane topics. Finally, Boris said, "I must go. I cannot be gone too long."

Viktor looked at the Boris and tugged at his earlobe.

"Yes?" Boris inquired.

"Do you know who Neighbor is?" Viktor whispered.

"Where you hear this name?" Boris shot back.

"I saw it in Sokolovsky's private diary."

"Viktor, have you lost your mind? If Sokolovsky were to find out, you would be shot immediately."

"It's important. Do you know this name?"

"Yes, but I am not supposed to. I hear rumors. Some say that it is a code word for the N.K.V.D. The secret police."

"The secret police? Here in Canada?" Viktor asked with a look of shock on his face. "But they should not be here. Why would the embassy need secret police?"

"I cannot answer that. Many things have changed here since Sokolovsky arrived."

"In the diary I see note that said something about turning someone over to Neighbor. I believe it is someone I know. What would happen to them?"

"You know the answer to that. Just what you would expect. They will never be seen again. Is that all? I must go."

"Yes, that is all. Thank you, Boris."

"You should know, two more security officers are being sent back to Russia. Everyone is frightened. Be very careful. Mention that name to no one."

Viktor watched Boris get up from the bench and disappear around the corner of the building. Viktor rose from the bench, walked to the south end of the building, and entered the embassy. About to start up the stairway, he heard Colonel Sokolovsky's voice.

"Zakharov, Where have you been?"

"I have already deciphered five batches of messages today. My eyes were tired and my back hurt. I needed a breath of fresh air."

"There is no time to waste," Colonel Sokolovsky snarled, his fingers tightening around the walking stick in his right hand. "Get back to work."

Before Colonel Sokolovsky could even think of striking out with his walking stick, Viktor turned and ran up the stairs two at a time.

Viktor's first stop was the secure file room to check in the batch of messages he had just deciphered and collect another batch.

Back in the cipher room, Viktor dropped the cipher bag on the desk and sat down in the chair, still shaking inside from his encounter with Colonel Sokolovsky. He bent over the desk and leaned on his elbows, trying to make sense of what he had discovered. Strange envelopes, clandestine meetings, nonsensical security protocols, the N.K.V.D., secret messages, embassy staff being sent back to Russia, his friend severely beaten over a simple telegram. He was certain his friend, Konstantin, was a good son of Mother Russia. *"Why would Sokolovsky want to have him murdered?"* he asked himself. Viktor's fear of Sokolovsky began to be replaced by anger. None of what he had learned made any sense. Unless....

A sudden insight flashed in Viktor's mind. There could only be one possible explanation. In that brief instant, Viktor's frame of mind changed. He vowed he was going to uncover the reason behind the strange events, but first he had to find a way to make his friend, Konstantin, and his family disappear before Sokolovsky or the N.K.V.D. did.

Chapter Ten

Zakharov Apartment
Somerset Street
Ottawa, Ontario, Canada

"Viktor, you are home early," Anna called out from the kitchen when she heard the apartment door open and close. She placed the dish she had been washing in the rack, dried her hands, tossed the dish towel over the dishes, and walked into the living room. "What is wrong?" she asked, seeing the look of concern that clouded Viktor's face.

"Oh, Anna, it is much worse than I thought," Viktor answered as he grabbed Anna and hugged her tightly. He released his grip and stepped back. "Konstantin and his family are in much trouble. We must help them."

"Is Sokolovsky sending them back to Russia sooner?"

"Worse than that," Viktor exclaimed, pulling the folded sheet of paper out from under his shirt. "Here, read this."

Anna read the short note quickly and looked up at Viktor. "What does K I B mean?"

"I believe those letters stand for Konstantin Ilyonovich Bogdanovitch. Those are his initials."

"Okay. Who then is Neighbor?"

"I talked to Boris at the bench behind the embassy. He said many rumors say it is a code word for the N.K.V.D."

"You mean the secret police you told me about" Anna asked, a puzzled look on her face. "Why are they here in Canada?"

"I do not know. Boris did not know either, but he said to be very careful. A number of the security officers are being sent back to Moscow, presumably to be shot. I suspect the security officers will be replaced by secret police."

"When will Sokolovsky do this terrible thing?"

"I have no way of knowing, but it could happen as soon as tomorrow. Anna, we must do something to hide Konstantin and his family."

"Hide them? How would we do that?"

"I have an idea. I think Martin Clavet, you know the man across the hall, would agree to help."

"You can't be serious," Anna exclaimed. "What makes you think he would agree to do that?"

"When we were in their apartment and you were talking to his wife, Sylvie, He told me on several occasions he has seen senior officers from the embassy in town. He said they were very rude to the store clerks and mean to the junior officers that were with them."

"Yes, so."

"Mister Clavet seemed quite angry. I found out that he speaks passable Russian, but I won't repeat what he said. I will just say that he has a great dislike for the senior officers. He believes Canada should throw the Russians out completely."

"Do you think it is safe to ask Mister Clavet to help?" Anna questioned. "What if he were to tell the authorities?"

"The Clavets have been so kind to us and have helped us in the past. I think it is a risk we have to take," Viktor answered. "If we do nothing, they will be sent back to Moscow. Konstantin will be shot and Ludmila and Oleg will starve. Anna, he is a friend. We cannot let that happen."

Anna nodded her head and said, "If Sokolovsky finds out, it is you that will be sent back to Russia. I know you are right, but I am frightened for little Nikola."

"As am I. I must do this quickly. Is Nikola sleeping?"

"Yes. I gave him his supper and put him to bed just before you came in. I will check on him." Anna walked over to Nikola's bedroom door, eased the door open a tiny crack, and peeked in. She turned around and whispered, "He's sound asleep."

"You stay here with Nikola and I will go talk with Mister Clavet."

"Viktor, be very careful."

"As always, my sweet wife," Viktor answered, touching two fingers to his lips.

Viktor opened the apartment door quietly and slipped out into the hallway. Across the hallway, he could see light under the Clavet's apartment door. He stepped in front of their door, drew in a deep breath, and rapped his knuckles on the door. Footsteps. The door opened.

"Mister Zakharov, what a pleasant surprise," Sylvie Clavet greeted. "Please come in." Sylvie Clavet stepped back allowing Viktor to enter the apartment. She pushed the door shut and directed Viktor to a dark tan sofa in the living room.

"Anna is not with you. Is she okay?"

"Yes, she is fine. She had just put Nikola to bed and did not want to wake him. I came to talk to Martin if that is okay."

"Certainly. Martin is in the back bedroom. I'll go get him."

Viktor stood up and offered his hand as Martin entered the room. Martin took Viktor's offered hand and shook it vigorously.

"Sylvie said you wanted to talk to me," Martin said, pointing at the couch. "Sit down and tell me what you need."

Viktor sat and put his hands between his knees. He stared at the floor. In his mind it had been easy, but now the words would not come. He did not know how to start the difficult conversation.

Martin looked at Viktor struggling to start the conversation. He looked up at Sylvie and jerked his head toward the bedroom. Sylvie turned and left the living room. "Viktor, it is obvious you are troubled. When you have something difficult to say, it is best to just say it. Tell me what is troubling you."

"I have need of your help, but am afraid to ask."

"Sylvie and I loved meeting you and Anna and that precious little Nikola. I believe we have already become friends. Why would you be afraid to ask me for help?"

"It might be dangerous. It would entail a great risk. I would not ask, but Anna and I do not know anyone else here."

"Dangerous, huh," Martin smirked. "Does it have something to do with those despicable senior officers at the embassy? I have seen how they treat the people beneath them. Viktor have they threatened you?"

"No, not me. It is for a friend. The Military Attaché at the embassy is threatening to turn my friend over to the Soviet secret police or send him back to Russia. Either way he will never be seen again."

"I have heard people talking about this *'disappearing'*," Martin sneered. "Is that what happens in Russia to someone officials do not like? They suddenly *disappear.*"

"Yes, too often that is what happens. I do not want this to happen to my friend. He has a beautiful wife, Ludmila, and a little boy, Oleg, about the same age as my Nikola. They would all be sent back to Russia. My friend, Konstantin would *disappear* and then Ludmila and Oleg would starve."

"Well now, we can't let that happen," Martin announced. "How can I help?"

"Konstantin was beaten for simply leaving a single telegram lying out. He was then told to not leave his apartment until someone came for him. I told him I would find a way to hide them. He talked to Ludmila. They both agree. They do not want to return to Russia, ever."

"How soon does this need to happen?"

"They could come for them at any time, so it would be best if it happened tonight," Viktor said, waiting for Martin to throw him out of the apartment at any time.

"You took quite a risk telling me all this. What makes you think I won't turn you over to the embassy police?"

"I heard what you said about the senior Russian officers when Anna and I were here before. I had to take a chance. I do not know any other way to help my friend. And I know you speak some Russian. My friend and his family do not speak any English."

"I hope this man knows how good a friend you are, Viktor," Martin confided. "How far do they live from here?"

"Only four blocks. The apartment building on James Street."

"Okay, Viktor, I will help your friend. Here is what has to happen. I have a small cabin in the woods about ten kilometers from here. I can hide them there for a short time and then I can make other more permanent arrangements. Tell them to leave their apartment tonight at ten minutes before ten o'clock so that they arrive at the swings in the park just off Maclaren Street at *exactly* ten o'clock. Is that understood?"

"Yes, I will tell them. Is there anything else?"

"Tell them they must take absolutely nothing except the clothes they are wearing. Sylvie and I will get them whatever they might need later. Viktor, listen to me. I will be driving my black Buick. Make sure they know they *must* be there at exactly ten o'clock. When I drive by, if they are not there, I will keep driving. Make certain they know that."

"I will make certain they understand," Viktor said as he rose from the couch "Mister Clavet, I cannot begin to tell you how grateful I am for your help."

Martin followed Viktor to the door and said, "Do not mention this again. I will let you know when they are safe."

Viktor grasped Martin's hand and pumped it frantically and thanked him again.

Martin opened the door and let Viktor out. He closed the door and hurried toward the bedroom to inform Sylvie of the little adventure that awaited them. "*Is Sylvie ever going to be surprised,*" he thought as he pushed the bedroom door open.

Viktor hurried down the stairs and exited the apartment building. Staying in the shadows and avoiding streetlights, he made his way to the Bogdanovitch apartment. As quickly as he could, he gave Konstantin Mr. Clavet's instructions, stressing the need to follow those instructions exactly. He wished Konstantin good fortune and said he hoped he might see them sometime in the future.

Twenty-five minutes after leaving the Clavet apartment, Viktor returned to his and Anna's apartment. Anna had been pacing back and forth, waiting for him to return. She let out a huge sigh of relief when she saw the door knob turn and Viktor walk through the door.

"Viktor, what took you so long?" she asked. "I was worried Mister Clavet had turned you over to the police."

"No, nothing like that. Mister Clavet agreed to help right away. He is going to hide them tonight. I went to Konstantin's apartment to tell him where they should meet Mister Clavet."

"That is good news. How is he going to hide them?"

"He is going to take them to a cabin he owns. It is far from here in the woods. He will pick them up in less than an hour. Mister Clavet said we should never talk about this again."

"I understand," Anna acknowledged. "Now come to bed. You must get up early for work."

"I could not possibly sleep until I know they are safe. If I turn the lights out, I can see most of the park across the street. That is where they are to meet Mr. Clavet."

"Wake me and tell me what happens," Anna said as she kissed Viktor on the forehead. "You are a good man, Viktor Sergeyevich Zakharov."

Viktor smiled and watched Anna disappear into the bedroom. "*What would I do without such a wonderful wife?*" he asked himself as he walked over to the door and punched the light switch. In the darkness, with his hands in front of him, he felt his way over to the window in the south wall of the apartment. He sat on the floor, raised the shade two inches, and stared at the park across the street.

Viktor's stare became more focused as the minutes ticked off. Time dragged. Minutes seemed like hours, but he dare not look away for fear he would miss something. After what seemed like hours, the clock in the living room chimed ten o'clock, but there had been no activity in the park. He feared they might have been caught. Viktor laid his chin on the window sill and squinted. He saw car headlights coming down Maclaren Street. The headlights stopped for no more than three seconds and then sped off. It had to be Mr. Clavet. Viktor continued watching for five more minutes. No more headlights meant they were not being followed. He breathed a sigh of relief, knowing they were safe.

He pulled the shade down and felt his way around the furniture. Easing the bedroom door open, he slipped inside and pushed the door partway closed, leaving it open a crack so he would be able to hear Nikola if he were to wake up during the night.

Viktor slid under the covers and nudged Anna "I saw a vehicle stop for a few seconds and then continue down the street. No one followed them. I believe Konstantin, Ludmila, and little Oleg are safe now."

"I am glad," Anna mumbled. "They are nice people. They deserve to be happy and live in freedom."

"Yes, I agree," Viktor answered as he rolled over and laid his head on the pillow.

Russian Embassy
Cipher Room
Ottawa, Ontario, Canada

Viktor glanced up at the clock on the wall. It was just past noon as he finished deciphering the fifth batch of routine cables and telegrams. As he had done many times before, he shoved the originals and deciphered copies into the cipher bag. He exited the cipher room to deliver the deciphered copies and then return the originals to the secure file room. One thing was different this time however. Viktor had a smile on his face. Only two more batches of messages and he would be caught up. The backlog would finally be eliminated.

With the last deciphered copy delivered, Viktor climbed back up the stairs to the second floor, headed for the secure file room. As he had done so many times before, he signed the entry log, entered the file room, spun in the combination, and pulled the heavy door open. Standing behind the safe door, he entered the times in the master control log and piled the original messages on the stack with the other deciphered originals.

Sokolovsky's private diary was still lying on the second shelf from the bottom. Curious as to what else might be in the diary, he lifted the diary off the shelf and began to browse through the pages.

Viktor's heart skipped a beat when he heard Sokolovsky bellow, "Zakharov, are you in there?"

He dropped the diary back on the shelf and answered, "Yes, Colonel Sokolovsky. I am signing in the batch of messages I just finished deciphering."

"Close and lock the safe and get our here, now."

Viktor complied without delay. Sokolovsky's voice had a different, more menacing tone than usual. He sounded agitated and very angry. Viktor stepped through the door, entered the time on the entry log, and stood at attention in front of Colonel Sokolovsky.

"Zakharov, you will accompany me to my office immediately," Colonel Sokolovsky demanded. "There are serious questions you must answer. Follow me."

Viktor fell in behind Colonel Sokolovsky and followed him to his third-floor office. The colonel entered first and waited for Viktor to enter. As soon as Viktor passed through the doorway, Colonel Sokolovsky slammed the door and pushed Viktor down in the chair sitting in front of his desk. Sokolovsky walked around the desk, stood behind it, and slammed his cane on the desk's surface. Viktor flinched, startled by the sudden violent action.

"I see you are frightened," Colonel Sokolovsky taunted. "You would do well to be very frightened, Lieutenant Zakharov."

Viktor sat silently, knowing better than to challenge Sokolovsky, especially when he was in fit of a rage.

"Nothing to say, Zakharov?"

"I do not know what this is about, sir."

"Do you know a Junior Sergeant Konstantin Bogdanovitch?"

"Yes, I have met him," Viktor replied. "I have spoken with him several times while picking up messages at the communications center."

"Those are the only times, Lieutenant Zakharov?" Colonel Sokolovsky questioned. "No other times? You have not talked with him outside the embassy?"

"No, sir, Colonel Sokolovsky," Viktor lied.

"Well, Junior Sergeant Bogdanovitch is missing. He was ordered to stay at his apartment, but he is not there. We cannot find him or his family."

"He is missing?" Viktor exclaimed, pretending to be as shocked as the colonel.

"Be very careful what you say next, Zakharov," Colonel Sokolovsky warned as he grabbed his cane, walked around the desk, and stood directly in front of Viktor. "I think you are lying. Save yourself from a beating and tell me the truth."

"I only know him from the embassy," Viktor repeated.

Colonel Sokolovsky grabbed Viktor by the shirt and yanked him upright, tipping over the chair. What about your friend Junior Lieutenant Borislav Ismayilov? I have reports of you two talking behind the embassy. What does he know?"

"I do not know if he knows Junior Sergeant Bogdanovitch," Viktor lied again.

"What do you and Ismayilov have to talk about?" Colonel Sokolovsky snarled, drawing Viktor closer until he could smell the stench of Sokolovsky's foul breath.

"Borislav and I are friends. We met on the train to Königsberg," Viktor offered in defense. "We talk about many things: food you can buy here in the markets, family, life back in Russia, but never about Bogdanovitch."

"You will talk, now!" Colonel Sokolovsky bellowed, releasing his grip on Viktor's shirt. Colonel Sokolovsky raised his cane in the air. Viktor stumbled backward and raised his arm to deflect the blow. Stepping backward, Viktor winced from the pain as the cane struck his arm. He stumbled over the chair and fell against the wall. Struggling to his feet, Viktor rubbed his arm, trying to relieve the pain.

"Pick up the chair you clumsy oaf," Colonel Sokolovsky yelled. "Bogdanovitch must be found. You are going to tell me where he is."

"I only talked with him here inside the embassy. I do not know where he is."

"You are lying!" Colonel Sokolovsky screamed, grabbing a leather riding crop lying on top of a file cabinet sitting in the corner. "I will beat the truth out of you if I have to. Your friend Ismayilov would not talk either. He is now on his way back to Moscow. He would not talk and will now pay the price for his lies, but you are going to tell me where Bogdanovitch is."

Colonel Sokolovsky walked to the door, and said, "Captain Moroshkin, I need privacy. Leave the office and go to the dining hall until I send for you. Lock the door on your way out."

Captain Moroshkin scrambled out of his chair, knowing exactly what was about to take place. He rushed to the door, twisted the lock, and pulled the door shut. Colonel Sokolovsky pulled the inner office door closed and locked it. He turned and looked at Viktor with fury in his eyes.

Viktor cringed and summoned all the courage he could muster. He, too, knew exactly what was about to happen.

Chapter Eleven

Viktor hobbled down Laurier Avenue West, stopping often to rub his injured arm or roll his shoulders to relieve the pain. He crossed the bridge over the Rideau River and sat on one of the benches in Marion Dewar Plaza. Tiring quickly, he could only walk a few blocks before he had to stop and rest. Even breathing was difficult. Anything other than half-breaths inflicted great pain because of the welts on his back, concealed beneath his clothing.

Sokolovsky had alternated between his cane and the riding crop as he attempted to beat a confession out of him regarding Borislav Bogdanovitch's disappearance. Sokolovsky had been well schooled by the GRU in interrogation techniques that would leave no visible marks. The only visible evidence of the beating Viktor had endured was the contorted expression of pain that distorted his face.

Finally, after nearly an hour of yelling and striking Viktor repeatedly with his cane or the riding crop, Sokolovsky had relented. Had it not been for Viktor's superior skills as a cipher analyst and the lack of anyone to replace him, he would likely already be on his way back to Moscow like Borislav. During the tortuous hour, Viktor had relied on the training he had received as a youngster when he was in the Komsomol, the All-Union Leninist Young Communist League. That training had instilled in him a deep sense of moderation, discipline, and focus. Committed to the safety of Konstantin and his family, Viktor had focused his mind on the safety of his own family, allowing him to be able to endure the pain.

Viktor struggled to push himself up from the hard bench. On wobbly legs, he took a few tentative steps. Cradling his injured arm, he shuffled down the street, carrying guilt and distress for his friend, Borislav. Had his friendship with Borislav cost the man his life? If he had not pushed him for information, would Borislav be on his way back to Moscow? "*No!*" he told himself. "*Sokolovsky is to blame. He accuses everyone of being a spy.*"

When Viktor began his journey to Canada, he had been proud to be Russian. With each step he took, the turmoil churning in Viktor's mind increased as he mulled over the events since he had boarded the train in Moscow: the horrors he had witnessed in Königsberg, strange messages and meetings, comrades beaten for no reason, his friend Konstantin forced into hiding, his friend Borislav sent back to Moscow to be executed, and, now, himself beaten.

With twelve blocks still to go as Viktor limped down the street, the turmoil he battled changed to anger. That anger grew more intense with each painful step he took. Not just for the pain he had endured but for his friend, Borislav. If Borislav was lucky, when he arrived in Moscow he would be shot. If not, he would spend the rest of his life in some wretched gulag.

At the end of the block, Viktor grimaced and turned left onto Elgin Street. Five grueling blocks later, nearing exhaustion, he stopped at the intersection with Somerset Street and leaned against a building to rest. A heavy overcast had turned dusk into darkness much earlier than usual. A light rain started to fall as Viktor pushed off from the building and continued his trek home.

"Only seven more blocks," Viktor wheezed as he pulled his collar up tight and started down Somerset Street. Summoning the last scrap of strength he had left, he focused on putting one foot in front of the other. The light rain turned to a steady, pounding downpour. Counting each step as a small victory and that much closer to Anna's loving arms, he slogged on, the cold rain penetrating his uniform jacket and soaking him to the skin. Viktor stopped twice to rest as he plodded the remaining seven blocks. Shivering against the cold, soaking rain, he winced because of the increased pain shooting through his bruised flesh.

He picked up his pace as he crossed the intersection with Lyon Street, seeing his destination only one-half block ahead. His face distorted by pain, he pushed the door to their apartment building open and limped toward the stairway. Stopping at the foot of the stairway, his rain-saturated clothing dripped a puddle on the floor. He looked up the long stairway, wondering if he had enough strength left to climb to the top. Cold, exhausted, and shaking, his wet hand slipped off the railing and he crumpled onto the stairs, too weak to even call out for help.

"Viktor, are you okay?" Martin Clavet called out, dropping the bag of trash he had been carrying. He kicked the bag of trash out of the way, rushed over beside Viktor, and laid his hand on Viktor's shoulder. Viktor flinched and pulled away. "What have they done to you?" Mr. Clavet questioned.

"At embassy.... Discovered my friend missing," Viktor panted. "Sokolovsky.... Interrogation...."

"Don't talk now," Mr. Clavet commanded. "Let's get you upstairs and into some dry clothes."

Viktor groaned as he tried to stand up. Mr. Clavet slipped his arm under Viktor's uninjured arm and helped him to stand upright. Viktor looked up the stairway and shook his head. "I can't do it," he whimpered.

"Come on," Mr. Clavet insisted. "I'll help you. Just concentrate on one step at a time."

Leaning heavily on Mr. Clavet, Viktor eased one foot up onto the next step then dragged the other foot up. One slow step after another Viktor struggled to the top of the stairs. Mr. Clavet leaned Viktor against the wall.

"Wait here. I'm going to go get Sylvie," Mr. Clavet instructed. He rushed down the hall and threw the door to his apartment and hollered, "Sylvie, grab the first aid kit and get out here."

Leaving the apartment door standing wide open, he hurried back to where Viktor leaned against the wall and helped him limp over to his and Anna's apartment door. Sylvie Clavet came running out of their apartment carrying a first aid kit in her hands.

"What happened?" she exclaimed when she saw the contorted look on Viktor's face.

"One of those animals at the embassy beat him," Mr. Clavet answered. "It has to have something to do with his friend from last night. Let's get him into their apartment and out of these wet clothes."

Sylvie Clavet pounded on the door to Viktor's and Anna's apartment while Martin supported Viktor. They heard the sound of the deadbolt being unlocked and the door swung open.

"Viktor you are really late. Did you forget your...." Anna stopped momentarily, frozen by the sight of her injured husband. "Viktor? What is this? What happened?"

"Not now," Martin barked. "We must get him inside so he can sit down. Grab a chair from the kitchen."

Anna turned and ran into the kitchen, grabbed a straight-back chair from the dinette set, and set it in the middle of the living room. Martin guided Viktor into the apartment and over to the chair. Viktor yelped as Martin eased him down onto the chair.

"I'm sorry, but this may hurt," Martin said. "We must get those wet clothes off of you."

Martin slid Viktor's uninjured arm out of his uniform jacket, pulled the jacket around behind him, and eased the jacket off his injured arm. He tossed the jacket on the floor.

"Anna, unbutton Viktor's shirt so we can get it off and see what injuries need to be tended to."

Anna kneeled down in front of Viktor, tears welling up in her eyes. Quickly she unbuttoned all the buttons and looked up at Viktor. 'Is it okay to remove your shirt in front of strangers?" she asked, knowing Viktor to be a very private man.

In great pain and well beyond any concern for modesty, he nodded his head. As carefully as they could, Martin and

Anna removed Viktor's shirt. Anna shrieked in horror when she saw the angry welts on Viktor's arms, shoulders, and back, already turning a deep, purplish red.

"My poor Viktor," Anna blubbered. "What have they done to you?"

"Sokolovsky. Interrogation," Viktor stammered through clenched teeth.

"But why?" Afraid to touch her beloved husband and cause him any more pain, she brushed away a strand of hair and kissed his forehead. "Mister Clavet, what can we do?" she asked, a pleading look on her face.

"Get me warm water and a cloth," he answered. "That may soothe the pain some."

Anna got up and rushed into the kitchen. She ran some warm water into an enamel pan and grabbed a clean washcloth from a shelf under the sink. Back in the living room, she handed the pan to Martin. Martin dipped the washcloth into the water, wrung it out, and gently placed it on one of the welts. Viktor gritted his teeth, refusing to cry out. Twenty minutes later, Martin had applied the warm cloth to all of the welts and dabbed on some salve from the first aid kit. He sent Anna back to the kitchen for a glass of water. When she returned, he shook out two aspirins and told Viktor to take them.

"At least there is no broken skin anywhere," Martin told Anna. "The bruises are going to be ugly and painful, but I don't believe there is any serious damage."

"Thank you, Mister Clavet," Anna blurted out as she reached out and hugged Mr. Clavet.

"We are glad to help, but you must call me, Martin."

"Okay, Martin," Anna answered. "I don't know what we would have done without you. Not just tonight but also last night for Konstantin and his family."

Martin blushed and said, "You're welcome." He turned and looked at Viktor and asked, "Viktor, you should not go to work tomorrow?"

"But I must," Viktor countered. "Sokolovsky allows no time off. Not for any excuse."

"What time do you leave for work?" Martin asked? "I will drive you. You can't walk all that way in your condition."

"It is too early. I cannot ask you to do this."

"Don't argue. What time do you leave?"

Viktor smiled weakly and said, "Five-thirty."

"I'll knock on the door. Be ready."

"I will be ready. Anna, get me some dry pants," Viktor said. "I will change after Martin and Sylvie leave.

"Come on, Sylvie, let's give them some privacy. See you in the morning," Martin said as he and Sylvie left the apartment and pulled the door closed.

Unable to lie in bed, Viktor had spent most of the night on the couch dozing fitfully. Anna did not sleep much either. Refusing to leave Viktor's side, she spent the night lying on the floor beside the couch. Every time Viktor changed position or moaned, she would awaken then watch and listen until Viktor settled down.

Once during the night, she awakened to find Viktor sitting up, unable to sleep. She went into the kitchen, filled the enamel pan with warm water, and applied a warm rag to his welts. Along with her empathy for Viktor, a deep, burning anger began to intensify within her. "*Viktor is a good Russian. Why would Sokolovsky do this*?" she asked herself.

An hour before Mr. Clavet was due to arrive, Viktor could no longer stand to be on the couch. He rose from the couch, limped into the kitchen, and sat at the dining table. Anna followed Viktor into the kitchen and put a pot of water on the stove to brew some tea. While the water heated, Anna dumped two aspirins out of the bottle Mr. Clavet had left. She filled a glass with water and handed it and the aspirins to Viktor.

"Here, take these," she said. "They will help with the pain. Was this because of Konstantin and his family?"

"Yes. Sokolovsky found out Konstantin was missing. He had their apartment searched. Somehow Sokolovsky knew we were friends. He wanted me to tell him where they were. I told him I did not know, but he did not believe me. So, he tried to beat it out of me."

"And you did not tell him even after the beating?" Anna asked as she turned and walked into the kitchen. She poured two cups of tea and carried them to the table.

"No, Anna, I dared not tell him," Viktor answered, blowing across the top of the steaming tea. "I knew what would happen to Konstantin and his family if they were caught. They would all be sent back to Moscow. Konstantin would be shot and then Ludmila and little Oleg would starve."

"Just because Konstantin left one telegram out?"

"Yes. Sokolovsky has become harsh and unforgiving about the new security protocols. Sokolovsky had Boris sent back to Moscow. He even laughed when he told me."

"Oh, Viktor, no!" Anna cried. "What about you? Will Sokolovsky also send us back to Moscow?"

"I do not think so," Viktor answered. "It is possible Sokolovsky believes I know nothing about Konstantin and he cannot do without me. I am the only cipher analyst here at the embassy. There would be no one to decipher the embassy's messages."

"Can't they send another cipher analyst from Moscow?"

"Perhaps, but it would take a long time."

Viktor's and Anna's conversation was interrupted by a knock at the door. Viktor pushed his chair back, stood up, and limped over to the door.

"Good morning, my friend," Viktor said as he pulled the door open. "Come in and sit."

"How are you feeling today, Viktor?" Martin Clavet asked.

"Better than last night. It only hurts when I move or breathe," Viktor joked, a strained smile on his face.

"Martin, we are so thankful for your help." Anna added, having joined them at the door. "Please thank Sylvie also."

"We are glad we could help," Mr. Clavet answered. "Sylvie told me to tell you to come over this morning for tea and cake."

"Martin, we must go," Viktor interrupted. "I have much work to do today and I will be slower because of the pain."

"Okay, let's go then," Mr. Clavet replied, backing out through the doorway and waiting for Viktor to follow.

Viktor kissed Anna, stepped through the doorway, and followed Mr. Clavet down the hallway to the top of the stairway. Viktor looked down the long stairway and sighed, knowing each step would be painful. He put his hand on the railing, took a deep breath, and started to step down.

"Here, let me help you," Mr. Clavet offered, grabbing Viktor's uninjured arm.

"No, you must not help," Viktor protested. "At the embassy there will be no one to help me. I must be able to do this by myself."

Mr. Clavet released Viktor's arm and started down the stairs in front of Viktor, staying two steps in front of Viktor as he hobbled slowly down the stairs. At the bottom of the stairs, Viktor stopped and rested, perspiration beading up on his forehead. Viktor drew in a deep breath, pointed toward the apartment building's back door, then followed Mr. Clavet out to the parking area.

Mr. Clavet walked up to his black, 1942 McLaughin Buick sedan and opened the passenger door for Viktor. Viktor eased his left leg in, slid into the seat, pulled his other leg in, then leaned gently back against the seat. The grimace on Viktor's face revealed the pain the exertion of climbing down the stairs and climbing into the car had produced. Mr. Clavet hurried around the car and slipped into the driver's seat. He started the engine, backed away from the building, and drove out of the parking lot.

Martin Clavet's *blackout* Buick left a thin cloud of blue-grey smoke as it rumbled down Lyon Street. Martin Clavet's old Buick was called a *blackout* version because the normally shiny brightwork, grill, door and trunk handles, headlight rims, and window trim, were painted a dull grey. Copper and nickel, two of the ingredients used to make chromium alloy, were in short supply, being diverted to the war effort.

Mr. Clavet turned left at the first intersection and headed east on Somerset Street. Five blocks later, he turned left again onto Elgin Street. Five more blocks and he turned right onto Laurier Avenue West and crossed the Rideau River, retracing Viktor's route home from the previous night. Slightly over a kilometer later he turned left onto Charlotte Street.

Seeing MacDonald Gardens Park in the distance, Viktor looked over at Mr. Clavet and said, "When you cross Rideau Street, stop quickly and let me out. I can't be seen getting out of your car near the embassy. If they see you, you will be next."

"But you will still have a long way to go," Mr. Clavet protested.

"Does not matter," Viktor asserted. "I will take shortcut through the park. You must not be seen."

As instructed, Martin Clavet slowed the car as he approached Rideau Street. A few feet past the intersection, Mr. Clavet stopped and Viktor struggled himself out of the car. Before shutting the door, Viktor leaned in and said, "Martin, you very good friend. Thank you."

Viktor pushed the door shut and the *blackout* Buick sped off into the early morning darkness, having stopped for no more than ten seconds. Viktor stood up as straight as he could and started toward the park. At the intersection with Tormey Street, he veered right, entered the park, and took the center walking path which exited the park directly across from the embassy.

Viktor crossed Heney Street, showed his papers to the gate guard, and entered the embassy through the main entrance. He limped down the hallway, signed the entry log, and headed for the dining hall. After loading a tray with his usual bowl of oatmeal and glass of milk, he headed for the seating area. As usual, he selected a table away from everyone else and sat down. He scooted the chair up and leaned back gingerly. As it was most days, the sugar bowl had been empty. With nothing else to enhance the oatmeal, he poured a third of the glass of milk into the bowl and stirred it into the thick, sticky oatmeal.

Glancing at the empty chair sitting beside him, reminded him of the breakfast meetings with his friend, Boris. Profound sadness filled Viktor's heart as he considered Boris's fate. Not just sadness plagued him as he stared at the empty chair. Guilt ripped at his heart. If he had not talked with Boris, maybe he would not have been sent back to Moscow.

Knowing he had much to do, he quickly finished the bowl of oatmeal and drained the glass of milk. After dumping his tray at the scullery, he exited the dining hall. To be certain he saw all message traffic to the embassy, he stopped at the communications center and collected all the previous night's messages. Before leaving, he asked the on-duty communications technician how often messages arrived. He advised the technician he would be back periodically to pick up all the incoming messages.

As best as he could, he stood up straight and headed for the cipher room, determined to stay out of Colonel Sokolovsky sight if at all possible.

Chapter Twelve

Viktor straightened up and stretched carefully to relieve his sore muscles. He rolled his shoulders, desperately wanting to remove the heavy uniform jacket. The jacket pressed painfully upon the angry welts, making work on the cipher machine very uncomfortable. Despite his desire, he dared not remove the uniform jacket. If Colonel Sokolovsky caught him without the jacket on, he would receive another beating. That unpleasant thought made Viktor shudder involuntarily.

Finishing his second batch of ten messages, he glanced up at the clock, shock registering on his face. It was nearly ten o'clock. The first two batches of the day had taken over an hour and three-quarters each. Colonel Sokolovsky would be furious if he found out. Some of the slowness was due to Viktor's injuries, causing part of the increased time required to decipher messages, but the other part was due to the fact that Viktor now read every message in its entirety.

Sorting the messages by floor, he made certain he would make only one trip down the stairs and then back up. Viktor jammed the originals and the deciphered copies into the cipher bag and hurried out the door as fast as his sore muscles would allow. After delivering the last message, he entered the communication center to pick up any new messages that might have arrived.

"Junior Sergeant Yakolev," Viktor exclaimed. "Sergeant Pasha Voronin works the communications desk during early mornings. What are you doing in communications? You are normally assigned to the front gate."

Junior Sergeant Yakolev handed Viktor the latest messages and pushed a clipboard across the counter for Viktor to sign. Yakolev let his right eyelid close very slowly as a warning signal. After Viktor signed for receipt of the messages, Yakolev bent over, pretending to verify Viktor's signature and whispered, "Pasha Voronin and Anatoly Gribkov have been sent back to Moscow. We do not know why. Be very careful." Junior Sergeant Yakolev straightened up and said, "Thank you Lieutenant Zakharov. All is in order."

Viktor nodded, picked up the new messages, and headed for the secure file room to log in the new messages and pick up another batch of messages waiting to be deciphered. With the next batch of messages sealed in the cipher bag, he signed out of the file room and trudged back to the cipher room.

Approaching eleven o'clock, Viktor was already exhausted, partly from the pain as he tore down and reset the cipher machine for each message and partly from the anxiety caused by reading every message. If he were to get caught, he would immediately be sent back to Moscow. Then he would be shot and dumped somewhere to never be found.

The first five messages of the current batch were routine and of no special interest. However, the sixth message stirred Viktor's interest. Glancing behind him to be certain he was alone, he read the message a second time.

He shook his head in disbelief as he reread the message.

"FRANK" identified as person willing to supply secret information. Has a belief in, or a sympathy for, Communist ideology. Recruited because he is a national organizer for the "Labour-Progressive" Communist Party of Canada. Has shown great ingenuity in getting prospective agents into the "NET".

Has established relationships with individuals who can be used as contacts that have inherent weaknesses which can be exploited. The methods of approach will vary with the person and with the position they occupy.

Has demonstrated uncanny success in recruiting highly educated individuals willing to betray their country and supply top secret information to which they have access in the course of their work to Soviet agents, despite their oaths of allegiance and of secrecy which they have taken.

"*Why would people betray their own country?*" Viktor asked himself as he laid the original message face down on the desk. He jerked and nearly slipped off his chair when he saw the marking on the lower left corner of the original indicating the message was a private message for Colonel Sokolovsky's eyes only. If he was caught with that message he would be a dead man for certain.

He folded the deciphered copy into fourths and stuffed it under his shirt. After cramming all the messages and deciphered copies into the cipher bag, he flew out of the cipher room, nearly falling as he rushed down the stairs. He raced down the hallway to the communications center.

"Junior Sergeant Yakolev, over here, please," Viktor called out after verifying the communications center was empty except for the duty clerk and himself.

"Yes, Lieutenant Zakharov, how can I help you?"

Viktor unsealed the cipher bag, slipped Colonel Sokolovsky's private message out of the bag, and slid it across the counter face down. Pointing at the mark on the bottom of the paper, Viktor asked, "What do you suppose that mark means?"

"Oh my," Junior Sergeant Yakolev exclaimed. "How did I miss that?"

"If I were to turn you in, you would also be sent back to Moscow. Do you realize that?"

"Yes, I understand. Colonel Sokolovsky would not tolerate such a mistake like this. Please do not turn me in. I swear it will not happened again."

"Do not worry, Junior Sergeant Yakolev, I did not decipher it," Viktor lied. "No harm has been done. Put the message away and pretend this did not happen."

"Yes, sir, Lieutenant Zakharov," Junior Sergeant Yakolev sputtered. "I am in your debt, sir. Anything you need, just ask me."

"Do not be frightened. Believe me, I dislike Sokolovsky more than you do."

Junior Sergeant Yakolev's shoulders sagged, knowing he had just escaped a severe beating and, perhaps, death. "Sir, I know you always arrive early. I have seen you arrive and go to the dining hall. I will meet you tomorrow and we will talk about home."

"That would be agreeable, Junior Sergeant Yakolev, I will see you tomorrow at six o'clock."

Viktor turned, exited the communication center, and hurried back to the cipher room to decipher the four remaining messages in the cipher bag.

Already past sunset, Viktor hobbled down the stairs, on his way to deliver the last batch of deciphered messages for the day. Viktor reached the bottom of the stairway to the first floor and heard someone calling his name.

"Lieutenant Zakharov, stop I wish to speak with you," a deep voice called out.

Viktor stopped, turned toward the voice, and waited for the man hurrying down toward him. The man was quite tall. Viktor guessed six foot three inches at least. He had a long, narrow face with pinched features and jet black hair that drooped over his forehead. The man's eyes were his most foreboding feature. Dark and penetrating, his eyes gave the man a sinister appearance. As the man approached, Viktor saw the Major's insignia on his uniform jacket. Viktor came to attention as the man stopped in front of him.

"I am Major Alexei Volodyavich Karpanov," the man announced. "I have just arrived from Moscow. I am to be Colonel Sokolovsky's new adjutant. Captain Moroshkin is on his way back to Moscow."

"I am Viktor Sergeyevich Zakharov," Viktor replied, hiding his surprise. "I am the cipher analyst for the embassy."

"Yes, I know who you are, Lieutenant Zakharov. Colonel Sokolovsky has told me about you."

Viktor did not answer, wondering just how much Colonel Sokolovsky had told Major Karpanov.

Realizing Viktor was not going to say anything, Major Karpanov continued, "I will be assuming control of all embassy message traffic, both inbound and outbound. If you have any issues or need anything, you are to report directly to me and to no one else. Is that understood?"

"Yes, sir, Major Karpanov," Viktor acknowledged. "If that is all, I am just finishing up the last batch of messages so I can leave for the day."

"That is all," Major Karpanov declared. "Go finish your task. We will talk again tomorrow."

Viktor turned and limped down the hallway before Major Karpanov could change his mind. The last message delivered, Viktor trudged back up the stairs to the second floor secure file room to sign in the original messages. He signed the entry log, entered the file room, unlocked the safe, and pulled the door open.

After entering the time returned for each of the original messages and placing them on the completed messages stack, he was about to push the safe door closed when he saw a five by seven card lying on a stack of old messages that had not been there earlier in the afternoon. He peeked around the edge of the safe door to make certain he was alone. Satisfied, he picked up the card and turned it over. Quickly scanning the card, he noticed a name he had seen just a few minutes earlier on Sokolovsky's private message that had mistakenly been included with normal inbound message traffic.

Viktor slipped the deciphered copy of Sokolovsky's message out from behind his shirt and unfolded it. After smoothing the creases out, he turned the blank side up, lifted a pen out of his pocket, and copied the information down exactly as it appeared on the card. He compared his copy to the original card.

REGISTRATION CARD
No. __27__

1. **SURNAME & NAME:** ___"Edward Manning"_____
2. **PSEUDONYM:** ___FRANK_____
3. **SINCE WHEN IN THE NET:**_____Feb. 9, 1945_____
4. **ADDRESS:**
   (a) **OFFICE:**_____
   (b) **HOME:** 870 Rue du Vigneau, Ottawa. Tel. Ll-7847_____

_____
5. **PLACE OF WORK AND POSITION:** LABOUR PROG. PARTY
   _____political worker_____
6. **FINANCIAL CONDITIONS:** Financially secure, but takes money.
It is necessary occasionally to help.

BIOGRAPHICAL DATA:
Detailed biography is available in the CENTRE in the COMINTERN.
Has an excellent knowledge of the Russian language.
Graduated from the LENIN school in Moscow.

Satisfied he had copied the information exactly, he refolded the sheet of paper, slipped it behind his shirt, then laid the card back on the stack of messages, positioning it exactly as he had found it.

Viktor put his hand on the safe door about to pull it closed. He jumped when he heard Major Karpanov bellow from the outer room, "Zakharov, what are you doing? Do not move."

The security guard started to step in front of Major Karpanov to challenge his entry, but stepped back when he saw the threatening glare from Karpanov's dark eyes. Major Karpanov rushed into the room and pushed Viktor out of the way.

"What are you doing? I thought you were leaving."

"I was just about to do that, Major Karpanov. I had to return and sign in the original messages. I was about to close the safe."

"Is that all you were doing?" Major Karpanov challenged.

"Yes, sir," Viktor answered. "I never touch anything but the new messages and the master control log."

"You had better not be lying," Major Karpanov threatened as he bent over and looked carefully at the five by seven card. He snatched the card off the pile of old messages and stuffed it behind his uniform jacket. Turning around, he fixed a menacing glare on Viktor. Both men stood still, staring at each other. Sweat began to trickle down Viktor's back. Major Karpanov was the first to break the stare.

"I will warn you only once, Lieutenant Zakharov. I am here to see that the new security protocols are followed to the letter. Even the slightest violation will result in the most severe punishment. Do you understand me?"

"Yes, Major Karpanov. I have been told about the new security protocols. I follow them exactly."

"See that you continue." Major Karpanov pivoted abruptly on his left foot and left the file room, his highly-polished boots echoing loudly as he stomped down the hallway.

Viktor breathed a sigh of relief. If Karpanov had arrived in the file room just a few seconds earlier, Viktor would have been caught red-handed with the card in his hands.

"*I must be more careful,*" Viktor scolded himself as he pushed the safe's heavy door closed. He signed out of the file room, trudged down the stairs, signed out in the building entry log, and left the building. Viktor groaned, not looking forward to the long, arduous walk home. He crossed Heney Street and took the shortcut through the center of MacDonald Gardens Park.

Exiting the south side of the park, Viktor limped down Charlotte Street. After only two blocks, he stopped and rubbed his sore leg. As he straightened up and started across the intersection with Besserer street, he saw Martin Clavet's *blackout* Buick slowly approaching the intersection from the East. The *blackout* Buick stopped only long enough for Viktor to jump in and slam the door.

"I thought you might appreciate a ride," Mr. Clavet said as he shoved in the clutch and shifted the car into second gear.

"You are quite correct, Martin," Viktor remarked, very happy to not have to walk the three kilometers home. "I was dreading the long walk, but how did you know when to be here?"

"I asked Anna. She told me when you normally leave the embassy. I've been waiting down the street. I saw you exiting the park"

Viktor hauled his bruised, aching body out of Martin Clavet's car and entered the back door of the apartment building. At the top of the stairs, he leaned against the railing, breathing heavily, not from the exertion but from the pain that flared up due to the long climb up the stairs. He walked over to the apartment door, unlocked it, and pushed the door open.

Anna, sitting in a chair waiting for Viktor to arrive, jumped up the moment she heard the door opening and met him at the door. Taking his uninjured arm, she led him to the couch and helped him ease down onto it.

"Mister Clavet stopped by earlier and asked when you usually left the embassy," Anna said. "Did he find you and give you a ride home?"

"Yes, he did," Viktor answered. "I am glad. I only had to walk a few blocks. I doubt I would have made it if I had to walk all the way."

"I am glad as well. Now, stay put. I will bring you a bowl of soup."

Anna rushed into the kitchen and returned carrying a bowl of steaming, vegetable soup and a crusty slice of bread. While Viktor started on his soup, Anna made another trip to the kitchen for a bowl of soup for herself. Seated beside Viktor, they ate in silence. Frequently, Anna would glance at Viktor to make certain he was okay.

"More?" she queried as Viktor set the empty bowl on the arm of the couch.

"No. I have had enough," he answered.

Viktor watched Anna gather the bowls and take them to the kitchen. She poured two cups of tea and carried them into the living room on a small tray. Viktor stirred a half spoonful of sugar into his cup of tea and gently eased back against the couch. Deep in thought, he sat staring into space as he blew across the hot, steaming liquid.

Anna recognized the look on her husband's face and knew something was troubling him. Rather than wait for Viktor to open up, she asked, "Did something happen at the embassy today? I can see that something is troubling you."

"Another person I know has been sent back to Moscow," he answered. "A man named Pasha Voronin. I knew him, but not well. He worked in the communication center. Alexander Yakolev, who is usually assigned as a guard on the front gate, was working the communications center desk. He told me Voronin had been sent back to Moscow. He also told me Captain Moroshkin, Colonel Sokolovsky's adjutant, had been sent back to Russia also. Yakolev winked at me very slowly so no one else would notice. As he bent over and pretended to verify my signature, he told me to be very careful."

"Viktor, what does all this mean?" Anna asked, a look of deep concern clouding her face.

"The man that replaced Captain Moroshkin, Major Alexei Karpanov, stopped me in the hallway. He informed me he is taking over control of all embassy message traffic. Anna, a major does not serve as an adjutant. Something very strange is going on."

What is this man, Karpanov, like?" Anna questioned.

"I only just met him, so, all I can do is describe his physical appearance," Viktor answered. "He is very tall and muscular with cold, dark eyes and a narrow, pinched face. The closest likeness that comes to my mind is *animal like*. I was startled when he glared at me. I felt as if he were going to snarl and then leap upon me like a wild animal."

"I am frightened," Anna quavered. "I am afraid they will send you back as well. Viktor, I do not want to go back to Russia, ever!"

"But, Anna, Russia is our home. Surely you do not mean that."

"Yes, Viktor, I do mean it," Anna countered. "The officers are cruel, sadistic, bullies. All of them! They trust no one. Everyone is watched constantly. Here, the people have freedom. They are friendly and kind. There is plenty of food for everyone. No one watches their every move."

Stunned, Viktor did not know how to respond. Even after the beating, he had never considered not going back to Russia when his duty at the embassy was completed. Still, he could not deny what Anna said because everything she had said was absolutely true. The officers were cruel, sadistic bullies and back in Russia everyone was watched. People would suddenly disappear never to be seen again, victims of the ruthless N.K.V.D.

As Viktor shifted his weight to relieve the pain in his back, he heard the folded sheet of paper crinkle under his shirt. If he showed Anna what he had discovered, it would only strengthen her desire to not return to Russia, but it did not matter. Anna read him like an open book. He would never be able to conceal the truth from her.

"Anna, there is more," he confessed. He unbuttoned his shirt, slipped the folded sheet of paper out, unfolded it, and handed it to Anna. He watched Anna's eyes flash back and forth as she read the message. When she stopped and looked up, Viktor said, "There's more. Turn the paper over."

Sweetland Avenue
Ottawa, Ontario, Canada

In the basement of an ordinary building at the intersection of Sweetland Avenue and Osgoode Street, a small group of mostly university students listened in rapt attention to the evening's speaker. Professor James Flemmings, a short, skinny, man with a thin, hawkish nose, curly, black hair, and close-set eyes, stood behind a flimsy wooden lectern skillfully extolling the virtues of communism.

Those attendees who had planned to arrive by car had been instructed to park on different streets at least six blocks from the meeting place to avoid announcing the existence of the meeting.

Professor Flemmings, dressed in a double-breasted, brown suit, expertly commanded the group's attention. Most of the attendees, dressed in the sloppy attire of college students, paid close attention to the information being presented. The Professor, a gifted speaker, captivated his audience with his extensive knowledge of capitalism and its alleged weaknesses. Building to the conclusion of his presentation, he stepped from behind the small platform and stood directly in front of the group. Carefully watching the faces of the two individuals that had been invited specifically because of their access to valuable information, he assessed their reaction.

Wrapping up his conclusion, he bowed slightly as applause began to fill the room, attendees rose to their feet, expressing their concurrence with his ideology.

"Please, no applause," the Professor admonished, holding his hands up. "We must not raise undue attention."

Outside the basement room, a rotund, balding man with a blotchy complexion had stood in front of the closed door to prevent entrance by anyone except the individuals that had been invited. Inside, a tall man dressed in civilian clothes, with his chair pushed up against the door, closely watched the attendees as they gathered around the professor to offer their praises and shake his hand.

The tall man stood and moved his chair aside. Moving over to the crowd around the Professor, the tall man tapped a young woman on the shoulder and told her it was time to leave. Two minutes later, he informed a young man it was time for him to leave. Repeating the process in two-minute intervals, the tall man gradually had instructed all but the last two attendees to leave.

The tall man interrupted the conversation between the last two attendees and the Professor. "Professor, I am known as Commander," the tall man said, offering his hand to the Professor. "Sorry to interrupt, but we must conclude the meeting soon."

"Yes, Commander," the professor acknowledged. "I saw you come in as we started. I was told you would be attending our meeting tonight."

"Who are your two special guests?" the Commander asked, despite already being fully aware of their identities.

"This is Frank," the Professor advised, pointing to a stocky man of medium height standing to his right. "He joined our group several months ago and has attended regularly." The commander reached out and shook Frank's hand. "The gentleman on my left is, Benson," the Professor said, pointing toward a short, skinny man standing on his left. "Benson, is attending for the first time tonight."

"I am glad to meet you, Benson," the Commander said, offering the man his hand. "I hope you will continue to attend our gatherings. Now, I am sorry, but I must ask that you leave separately. I have private things I must discuss with the Professor."

The Commander watched as Benson was the first to leave and then two minutes later Frank left. The commander pointed at one of the empty chairs and said, "Sit. Let us talk."

The Professor sat, crossed his legs, and asked, "What is it you would like to know?"

"Grant wishes to know how many in tonight's meeting would be useful to us?"

"None, except for Frank and the new man, Benson? The rest are young students from the university and are nothing but whiny, spoiled brats. They gather together and complain about whatever perceived injustice is popular at the moment, but they understand nothing. They are ideological idiots."

"Sadly, you are correct," the Commander agreed. "But we need them. If anyone discovers these meetings, they will appear to be nothing more than the usual complaining of rich university students."

"Yes, but it is difficult to put up with their smug, know-it-all arrogance."

"I know it is infuriating, but, as I said, it is necessary. Let me ask how Frank is doing in recruiting new members?"

"He says he has several important individuals that are in agreement with us, but he has been unable to get them to attend, except for Benson, who was here tonight."

"What do you know of this Benson?"

"I know who he is, but I pretended not to when Frank introduced him before the meeting. I did not wish to frighten him any further. As you probably noticed, he seemed quite nervous. I did notice him nodding his head in agreement several times during my presentation. If he agrees to help us, I am certain he can be quite useful."

"Please explain," the Commander insisted.

"His real name is Christopher Edmonds. He is a professor at the university and a former major in the Directorate of Artillery. Frank says he still has contacts in the directorate and might be able to influence others to join us."

"What of the man named Foster. I was told he would also be here tonight?"

"Frank said he decided at the last minute to not come. He is concerned these meetings are too public. He fears being caught. He will only agree to a private meeting."

"Is the information he can provide worth setting up such a meeting?"

"Yes, very much so. He was hired by Allied War Supplies Corporation and soon promoted to administrator at the Department of Munitions and Supply. His department regulates the production of armaments and also regulates scarce supplies that are essential to war production, such as gasoline and rubber for tires."

"Is there anything else?"

"He was hired at the insistence of his brother-in-law, K. S. Holland, code name Gray. Not only is Gray egotistical, he is stupid. He is having an affair with his boss's wife. We told him we would expose him. Now, he, *and* his greedy, bother-in-law will do whatever we tell them to do."

"Very well. Set up a meeting at Dubok Three for tomorrow. Tell Edmonds I will tolerate no excuses. If he is not there, I will turn them both over to the Neighbor. Understood?"

"Yes, sir," the Professor answered, nodding his head in agreement.

The two men shook hands. The Commander left the meeting room followed two minutes later by the Professor.

Russian Embassy
Ottawa, Ontario, Canada

Unable to dissuade Mr. Clavet, Viktor had relented, allowing Martin to drive him to within three blocks of the embassy. Viktor had jumped out of Martin's *blackout* Buick and had limped the last three blocks to the embassy. He greeted the security guard, displayed his identity papers, and waited for the guard to open the gate.

Inside the embassy, he limped down the center hallway, stopped at the main desk, and signed the building entry log. After hobbling down the stairway to the lower level, he made his way to the dining hall. His tray loaded with the usual bowl of oatmeal and glass of milk, he selected a table at the east side of the seating area.

About to shove a fourth spoonful of oatmeal into his mouth, he looked up when the chair beside him screeched as it was pulled away from the table.

"Good morning, Viktor," Alexander Yakolev greeted as he sat down. "I did not see you here for breakfast yesterday."

"It took me longer to walk than I thought. I was late getting to the embassy," Viktor answered. "I finished my oatmeal quickly and then went straight to the cipher room and started my work."

"Viktor, you need not lie to me."

"I'm not lying," Viktor protested.

"I also take the shortcut through the park. I saw you get out of a black car. Who was that, Viktor?"

"It was my neighbor. He has been so kind. Please, Alexander, you must tell no one."

"I promise I will tell no one. I saw you limping very badly. Sokolovsky beat you didn't he."

Viktor shook his head and stuffed a spoonful of oatmeal into his mouth, avoiding looking directly at his friend.

"Viktor, you need not lie. I also received a beating before you arrived here in Ottawa. The monster Sokolovsky replaced was even more sadistic and cruel. I still bear the marks on my back. I hear Sokolovsky is much more skilled in giving beatings that do not show."

"I am sorry, Alexander. No one should have to endure such things and for no reason."

"I made a simple mistake. What was the reason for your beating?"

"Did you know Konstantin Bogdanovitch?"

"No, I do not know him, but I have heard that he and his family are missing."

"Colonel Sokolovsky believed I knew where they were. He tried to beat the information out of me. He was like a wild animal. I believe, if there were another cipher analyst here to decipher the embassy's messages he would have beat me to death."

"I am sorry for you, Viktor. The senior officers are despicable savages. If I had a gun, I would shoot them all."

"Alexander, do not say such a thing. Not even in jest," Viktor admonished. "If someone should hear you, you will immediately be sent back to Moscow and a beating would be the least you would receive."

"I know," Alexander growled, biting off a chunk of dry toast. "I hate them, Viktor. I hate them all. I am never going back to Russia. I know I should not say such things," he added before Viktor could respond.

Viktor and Alexander spent the rest of their breakfast talking about life back in Russia before the war. Viktor learned that Alexander had grown up in a little village not far from Moscow.

Viktor also learned that Alexander's hatred of senior officers was driven by an incident that occurred while he was serving in an infantry unit. A group of drunken officers were pillaging from families in the countryside. Alexander's father had refused to give up what little they had. In a rage, they murdered both his father and his mother and set the small cottage on fire. When Alexander arrived home weeks later, there was nothing left but ashes and a few scorched timbers. Alexander's heartrending tale of misery rekindled the hideous images Viktor had witnessed as the train passed through Königsberg.

Viktor had grown concerned for Alexander as he told the horrible story. He laid his hand on Alexander's arm and said, "I'm so sorry, but you must let this thing go. The anger I see in your eyes will drive you to do something you will regret."

Alexander reached up and brushed a tear off his cheek. "It was over two years ago, but it feels as if it were yesterday," he stammered.

"We must go," Viktor urged. "If we do not, we will be late."

Alexander stood up and pushed a spoon off his tray. As he bent over to pick it up, he whispered, "Another friend, Leonid Zubkov, has disappeared. I hear from others that Karpanov is a brutal N.K.V.D. assassin. Everybody in the embassy has stopped talking. Great fear is evident in everyone's eyes. You must be very careful, my friend."

Viktor nodded his head in agreement and followed Alexander to the scullery to drop off their breakfast trays. Viktor had also noticed a change in people's eyes. Something had changed. The atmosphere was very different, and charged with fear.

Deep concern clouded Viktor's thoughts as he pushed the dining hall door open and headed for the cipher room. Troubling questions swirled in his mind. *"Why were so many embassy staff members suddenly disappearing or being returned to Russia?" "What was Karpanov's real purpose at the embassy?" "What do the suspicious messages mean?" "Is Russia spying on its allies?"* But most concerning of all, *"Who was to be feared most?"*

Heeding Alexander's warning, Viktor vowed to be more careful, but he grew even more determined to discover what was going on and who was behind it.

Chapter Thirteen

Zakharov Apartment
Somerset Street
Ottawa, Ontario, Canada

"Viktor, you are again troubled," Anna observed as she set a pot of potato soup on the small dining table. "I can see the worry on your face. I noticed as soon as you entered the apartment. Has Sokolovsky threatened you again?"

"No, I was busy the whole day and I did not see Colonel Sokolovsky even once," Viktor answered, looking down and focusing on the bowl of soup Anna had dished out and set before him.

Anna waited. When Viktor did not respond, she pulled the bowl of soup away and said, "Well, something is bothering you. You must tell me."

"It gets worse every day, Anna," Viktor groaned as he laid his spoon on the table and dabbed at the corners of his mouth with a napkin. Remember I told you Major Karpanov stopped me in the hallway and informed me he would be assuming control of all embassy message traffic."

"Yes, I remember and I asked what kind of man Karpanov was."

"He is not what he says he is," Viktor snapped. "He is a liar. Majors do *not* serve as adjutants. I learned from Alexander Yakolev that Karpanov is an N.K.V.D. assassin. Alexander told me everyone has stopped talking and they are very frightened. He warned me to be very careful."

"Viktor, you must stop looking at those messages," Anna begged. "If Karpanov finds out, you will be shot."

"But, Anna, I must," Viktor countered. "Konstantin and his family are in hiding and my friend, Boris, has been sent back to Moscow. Pasha Voronin is also on his way back. Alexander told me Karpanov had Captain Moroshkin sent back to Moscow. I only had a few conversations with Moroshkin, but he seemed like a decent fellow. Sokolovsky and Karpanov are hiding something. I cannot....."

Viktor stopped mid-sentence, pushed his chair back, and got up from the table. Pacing back and forth in front of the living room window, he reached up and grabbed the curtain, about to pull it closed. Hesitating for a few seconds, he stepped away from the window.

"Anna, turn off the light," he called out.

Anna rose from the table, rushed to the far side of the room and punched the light switch. Crossing the living room in the dark, she stumbled and fell against the couch.

"Are you okay?" Viktor asked from the other side of the living room.

"Yes, I am fine. What is the matter? Why did you ask me to turn off the light?"

"Someone is watching us," Viktor answered as he pulled the curtain shut. "Just now, I saw the same car that followed me as I left the embassy. When I exited the park and started down Charlotte Street, I saw a man get up off a bench and talk to someone in a car parked along the street. When I looked back, the man pointed in my direction. At the next intersection, I saw Mister Clavet waiting. I shook my head and mouthed the word 'no' and just kept walking."

"How do you know the car followed you?" Anna queried.

"When I turned onto Laurier Avenue, I saw the same dark gray car reflected in a store window. I stopped several times to rest. Each time as I got up to continue, I saw the same car sitting a block behind me. Now, the same dark gray car is sitting on the street just below our window."

"Viktor, are you certain?" Anna exclaimed.

Viktor held out his hand in the darkness. "Here, take my hand and sit beside me."

Anna felt her way in the darkness over to where Viktor was seated on the floor. She grasped his hand, eased down onto the floor, and leaned against him, looking over his shoulder. Viktor eased the curtain away from the window just enough to be able to see the street below.

"Yes, that is the same car," Viktor declared. "See, there near the end of the block."

"I see it," Anna said. "But who is it?"

"I do not know. I cannot see the man's face. It is too dark."

Viktor and Anna sat in the dark, staring out the window. For fifteen minutes nothing changed. Stiff from sitting, Viktor was about to release the curtain and get up. The gleam of headlights flashed as a car turned the corner and pulled up behind the car Viktor and Anna had been watching. The man in the second car turned off his car's headlights, stepped out of the car, and walked up beside the other car.

Viktor shrank back and released the curtain when the new man looked up at the apartment building and pointed at their window. Viktor carefully eased the curtain back again and saw that the new man was now talking with the man inside the car.

"Do you know the man that just drove up?"

"No, I do not know him, but his face seems familiar. I must have seen him somewhere, but I cannot remember where."

"I must get up and take care of Nikola," Anna said, hearing the little boy crying out from his bedroom.

"Turn on the small light in the bathroom only," Viktor advised as he helped Anna to her feet. He turned back toward the window and continued to watch. The two men continued talking for several minutes. The last man to arrive returned to his car and climbed in. The headlights on both cars came on and they drove off.

"*What reason would they have to follow me?*" Viktor asked himself as he let the curtain drop and leaned back against the wall. Deep in thought, Viktor did not stir until Anna returned from caring for Nikola.

"Viktor, may I turn the light on?" she asked.

"Yes, you may turn the light on. Both cars drove away."

"Were they from the embassy?"

"I must assume they were. Perhaps Sokolovsky still suspects I know where Konstantin and his family are."

"If they are following you outside the embassy, they must be watching you inside as well," Anna fretted. "It is not safe for you to copy Sokolovsky's messages. You must stop"

"I am very careful," Viktor argued. "I only do that when I am in the secure file room and am certain I am alone."

"Why do you continue to do this?" Anna probed. "There is nothing to be gained. Sokolovsky has eyes and ears everywhere. He will catch you. What happens to little Nikola and to me if you get caught? Have you thought about that?"

"Of course I have thought about the risk to you and Nikola. That is…."

"No Viktor," Anna interrupted, anger tingeing her words. "You must not continue to do this."

"Anna, please," Viktor pleaded. "You must not be angry. I do this for us."

"For us?" Anna cried, tears welling up in her eyes. "How can this be for us? You know what happens to those who are caught spying."

"But Anna…."

"No, Viktor. This must stop now." Anna turned and ran into the bedroom.

Viktor stood in the living room, unhappy and confused. Unhappy that he had caused his beautiful Anna such anguish and confused that he could not explain why this task was so important to him. Sokolovsky and the men like him were depraved and cruel. "*Why can't I explain it?*" he asked himself. Determined to make Anna understand, he headed for the bedroom.

Sitting on the edge of the bed, Anna turned toward Viktor when she heard him walk into the room. "I'm sorry," she sniffled, dabbing at her eyes. "I am very frightened for you and for little Nikola. I know what men like Sokolovsky do. I have heard the stories."

"I also have heard the stories," Viktor added as he sat on the bed and took Anna's hand in his. "Anna, I have seen brutal, hideous things firsthand."

"Viktor, when? What did you see?"

Viktor looked down at the floor, battling internally over how much he could or should tell Anna about the things he had witnessed. Even after months, just the thought of those horrific scenes sickened him. How could he tell Anna about such upsetting things. Viktor sat frozen with indecision.

"Viktor, is this what has been troubling you?" Anna insisted. "You must tell me what you saw."

Viktor looked up at Anna, the pain of those memories contorting his face. "No, it is too horrible." Viktor's shoulders sagged, his head dropped, and his stare returned to the floor.

Anna put her hand under Viktor's chin and lifted his head up. Staring directly into his eyes, she said, "Viktor, we have been through much together. When you were posted to Canada, we promised each other there would be no secrets. You must tell me what causes you such torment."

Viktor began his tale at the point he boarded the train bound for Königsberg. He described the long hours with nothing to do and then the meeting between himself and Borislav. All seemed routine until Viktor began to describe the grisly spectacle that confronted him as the train entered the outskirts of Königsberg. The bloated bodies of men and horses strewn everywhere. Block after block, smoking ruins stretched as far as he could see.

Viktor put his hands to his face and squeezed his eyes shut as tightly as he could, unable to continue, tortured by the images yet to come. "I cannot go on. It is too horrible," Viktor gasped.

"We must share this together," Anna choked, shaken by the things Viktor had described.

"No, it is too dreadful."

"You must, Viktor. I must know what haunts you."

Viktor dropped his hands to his lap, drew in a deep breath, and continued his tale. Not leaving out a single detail,

he described watching in shock as two drunken Russian soldiers chased a woman and a child not much older than their
Nikola out of a partially collapsed house and shot them in the
back. Shooting wildly into the air, the two soldiers ran up to
the lifeless bodies and searched their clothing for anything of
value. Angry that they found nothing of value, they kicked the
bodies into the street.

"When I got off the train, I heard a group of officers
laughing. I heard one of them say that as a reward for defeating
the Germans, the commanding general had given his official
permission for two days of raping and looting."

Viktor shook his head as tears streamed down his face.
"Oh, Anna. That is not the way soldiers are to behave," he
wailed. "Since that time, I am ashamed to call myself a soldier.
How can men do such things?" Viktor reached out and hugged
Anna, burying his face against her neck.

Shaken by the tale of depravity Viktor had shared, Anna
also wept. Together, they sat weeping silently. For a long time
they sat on the bed holding each other tightly, without saying a
word because there were simply no words that could explain
away the horror of such unspeakable wickedness.

Anna was the first to stir. She released her embrace and
said, "It is late. Perhaps a cup of tea would help us sleep."

"I hope so," Viktor replied, rising from the bed. "I am
sorry you had to hear about such horrible things."

"I do not understand how men could do such things, but
now I know what troubles you. Is Sokolovsky involved in such
things?"

"I do not know for certain, but I would not be surprised."
Viktor answered, stopping at the doorway. "Now, that the war
is over, you would think Russia's leaders would be concerned
with rebuilding our country and caring for the Russian people.
It is hard to believe but some officers in the embassy freely talk
about the fact that the Soviet Union is secretly preparing for a
third world war. They believe a general upheaval throughout
the world would allow them to establish Communism everywhere."

"Viktor, tell me this is not true," Anna exclaimed.

"I believe it is true," Viktor asserted. "I think what I have discovered shows that Sokolovsky and others are spying on Canada and also on the United States. They want to learn their secrets so they can defeat them in another war."

"What are you going to do?"

"I do not know," Viktor answered, as he turned and walked out of the bedroom. He walked into the bathroom and splashed cold water on his face while Anna went into the kitchen to brew some tea.

Russian Embassy
Cipher Room
Ottawa, Ontario, Canada

The next day, as he did every day, Viktor had arrived at the embassy early, wolfed down his usual bowl of oatmeal, then stopped by the communications center to pick the early morning message traffic. Smiling, he had headed for the cipher room with only a slight limp, carrying a smaller stack of new messages than usual.

After entering the early morning messages into the control log, he had stuffed the first group of ten messages into the cipher bag and hurried to the cipher room to begin his day.

Hearing footsteps, Viktor looked up from the cipher machine and watched as Major Karpanov sauntered into the room, followed by someone he did not know.

"Lieutenant Zakharov, stop what you are doing and come over here."

Viktor stopped, laid a code wheel on the table, wiped his oily hands on an old rag, and said, "Yes, Major Karpanov, what can I do for you?"

"This is Senior Sergeant Zinovy Fyodorovich Naumenko," Major Karpanov announced. "He is a newly trained cipher clerk. He has just arrived from Moscow. He will help you keep up with the increase in message traffic that we expect to start soon."

"It is my pleasure to meet you Senior Sergeant Naumenko," Viktor greeted, holding out his hand.

Being junior in rank, Senior Sergeant Naumenko came to attention, saluted, then took Viktor's hand and shook it. "Good day, Lieutenant Zakharov."

"You can exchange pleasantries later," Major Karpanov broke in. "I am busy so please listen carefully. I do not have time to say this twice. Security is being increased again. The increase in message traffic will be quite sensitive and we must be certain there are no possible leaks. A new cipher machine arrived with Senior Sergeant Naumenko and is being uncrated. As soon as it is installed, Lieutenant Zakharov you will assist in seeing that it is setup, tested, and functioning properly."

Major Karpanov held out his hand and waited for Senior Sergeant Naumenko to hand him the diplomatic pouch tucked under his arm. He ripped the security seal off the pouch and dumped two code books onto the table. Handing a book to each man, he continued, "These are new code books. They will be used for all new messages that arrive starting tomorrow. Zakharov, you be responsible for all messages already cataloged and those that arrive today. Once those have been deciphered, you will immediately destroy the existing code book. Is that understood?"

"Yes, Major Karpanov," Viktor responded. "It will be done."

"Once the new cipher machine is installed, a partition will be built between the two machines. You will not view each other's work and you will not discuss any details about your work. If you do, your punishment will be severe. Understood?"

After both men acknowledged understanding of his threat, Major Karpanov pointed at the books lying on the table and continued, "Those code books are extremely sensitive. Anytime you are not using them, they will remain secured in the safe in the secure file room. Only one of you at a time may enter the secure file room. I have instructed the security guards of the new rules. They will be monitoring your compliance. If you violate either of these last two security regulations, you will be shot. I have an important meeting outside the embassy and must go. I expect much progress when I return."

Major Karpanov turned on his heel and rushed out of the cipher room.

Dubok Three
Sandy Hill Road
Hawkesbury, Ontario, Canada

Major Karpanov's car pulled up and parked next to a weathered and dilapidated cabin at the end of a long tree-shrouded lane. Two other cars were parked out of sight of the lane behind the cabin. Located deep in the woods six and one-half kilometers southwest of Hawkesbury, the cabin was far away from prying eyes. In all conversations or communications, the Russians referred to any hiding place, or safe house, as a dubok. To assure secrecy, individual duboks were distinguished by simply adding a number.

After leaving his meeting at the embassy and taking time to change into civilian clothes, Major Karpanov had completed the one hundred eleven kilometer drive to Hawkesbury in just over one hour. Karpanov grabbed an umbrella and climbed out of his car. A light rain had begun to fall as Karpanov turned off Highway Thirty-four onto Sandy Hill Road. The gentle rain filled the air with the aromatic scent of pine trees. He stepped up onto the rickety porch, careful to avoid the broken floorboards. Tapping once then three times on the weather-beaten door, he waited.

The cabin's wooden door screeched on rusty hinges as it was pulled open. The Professor waited for Karpanov to enter then quickly pushed the door closed. Across the single room, two men were seated at a small round table next to the kitchen area. Karpanov recognized the man identified as Benson, but the other man he did not recognize. Karpanov strode across the room, stood next to the table, and waited for the Professor to join them.

"Professor?" Karpanov urged, waiting for the man to introduce the two men seated at the table.

"Benson you already know," the Professor announced. "The other gentleman is the man we shall call Foster."

"What of Gray?" Karpanov asked. "Why is he not here?"

"He said he was scheduled for a meeting and claimed he could not get out of it," the Professor answered.

"A likely story," Karpanov grumbled as he pulled out a chair and sat down. "Let us begin."

Karpanov glared at the man the Professor called Foster. Like his brother-in-law, the man was very large and very fat with a round, pulpy face. His mostly bald head sprouted a few clumps of scraggly brown hair. A brown and green striped tie, stained from sloppy eating habits, hung askew from the man's unbuttoned collar. Despite the coolness of the day, the man mopped sweat from his face with a handkerchief. Disgusted by the man's unkempt appearance, Karpanov could not imagine such a slovenly pig could offer anything of value.

The Professor, noticing the disgusted look on Karpanov's face, elaborated on what Foster could offer. "Foster here, is in charge of the distribution of war production at the Ministry of Munitions and Supplies. He directs the shipping of war supplies: guns, ammunitions, and other essential supplies."

"Do you know items, locations, and quantities for upcoming shipments?" Karpanov asked.

"That is highly classified information. I can't reveal that," Foster protested.

"Need I remind you of your brother-in-law's affair with his boss's wife?" Karpanov yelled. "If the company is made aware of his shameless behavior, he will be fired. We will also make certain they are aware of the items you are selling on the black market."

"What?" Foster sputtered. "You cannot know about that."

"You stupid fool," Karpanov roared. "You are not as smart or as careful as you think you are. We know everything. I advise you to choose your words very carefully, Mister *Foster*. I ask you again. Can you provide the information I desire?"

"I…. I…. No, I cannot. It is classified," Foster sputtered, sweating even more profusely.

Karpanov leaped from his chair and grabbed Foster by his tie and hauled him up out of his chair. "Agree to provide the information, or, perhaps, I will shoot you right now," Karpanov bellowed as he pulled out a Tokarev TT-33 pistol from under his coat with his free hand and jammed it against Foster's forehead. "This will make a big hole in your head and it will make a horrible mess on the floor. Well, what is your answer, Mister *Foster*?"

"Okay, okay," Foster cried. "I will give you whatever you want. Do not shoot me!"

"A wise decision, my fat friend," Karpanov declared. "I was about to lose my patience."

Karpanov slipped the Tokarev back into his shoulder holster and shoved Foster backward into the chair, causing the chair and Foster to fall over backwards.

"Benson," Karpanov barked, "You brought this buffoon to us. Get him up and get him out of here."

Karpanov watched as Benson scrambled out of his chair and helped the fat man up onto his feet. Foster straightened his jacket, dusted himself off, and headed for the door. As the door opened and the two men were about to leave, Karpanov added, "A word of advice to both of you. Do *not* change your mind. We have many friends in Ottawa and also in Montreal. You will be watched constantly. If you do not provide the information within two days or if you try to run, you will die a very painful death."

An ashen, trembling Foster turned and nearly stumbled as he rushed out the door. A few seconds later the two men still inside the cabin heard rocks and mud pelting the side of the cabin as Benson slammed his car into gear and roared between the trees.

"Will he follow through?" Karpanov asked.

"Yes, I think he will," the Professor answered. "Foster is stupid and greedy, but Benson is not. He will see to it that Foster provides the information as he said he would."

"Very well," Karpanov conceded. "Change of subject. I wish to know how you are progressing with your *special* students? Are there any new corporants being added?" Karpanov's use of the cover-name 'corporants' referring to any member of the Communist Party outside of Russia.

"The inevitable result of a deliberate emphasis on a conspiratorial atmosphere and behavior in our class political discussions and meetings, which are perfectly legal, is the gradual disintegration of normal moral principles such as honesty, integrity, and, especially, a respect for the sanctity of oaths," the Professor explained. "This technique has played a significant part in bringing in persons such as Miss Haven, Jensen, and Kimball. They have been indoctrinated to a state of mind where they will disregard the moral obligations they have undertaken in connection with their public duties."

Karpanov nodded his head and the Professor continued, "Most of these... Let's call them *agents* began their Communist associations through a burning desire to reform and improve Canadian society which they foolishly believe is failing them. Prolonged exposure to the conspiratorial methods and conditions of secrecy of the student groups these people join effectively isolates them from the Canadian people. Because of what they learn in these study-groups, some adherents, begin to feel that Canadian society is not equalitarian enough for their taste. Then, they gradually shift most, if not all, of their loyalties to another country. This shift happens even when the other country is actually far less equalitarian than Canada. As these idiots graduate and move into society and government, we will own them."

"That all sounds good in theory," Karpanov observed. "But does it work in practice?"

"Yes, absolutely. It works," the professor countered. "It worked perfectly with Professor Collins. He bragged that he gave top secret information to Frank despite the oath of secrecy which he had taken. He actually believes the information he provided the Corporation would further international scientific collaboration. His approach to the supposed goal of increasing international scientific cooperation was totally uninformed and unscientific. His motive was simply driven by his ill-formed ideology."

"Well then, Professor, I would ask that you keep up the good work," Karpanov said. "Now, I must get back to the embassy."

The professor and Karpanov shook hands. Karpanov left first, followed by the Professor five minutes later.

Chapter Fourteen

Dutton and Parker Dentistry
Third Avenue
Ottawa, Ontario, Canada

The fragrance of Eugenol, also called "Clove Oil", hung heavy in the air. Doctor James P. Dutton, dressed in a white smock that buttoned up the left side, had just dabbed a generous glob of the sweet-smelling paste on the upper gum of his patient. Dr. Dutton reached out his right hand and lifted a hypodermic syringe filled with Novocain from the tray beside him. Eyeing the needle, the patient cringed and squeezed the arms of the chair, his knuckles turning white.

"This won't hurt," Dr. Dutton advised as he grabbed the man's upper lip and tugged it up out of the way, about to insert the needle.

The man closed his eyes and mumbled something unintelligible. The needle just touched the man's gum when there was a knock at the patient room door.

Dr. Dutton stopped, pulled the needle away, turned toward the door, and asked, "I'm about to start a procedure. What is it?"

Lydia Hess, Dr. Dutton's receptionist, replied from the other side of the door, "There's a man named Lamont on the phone asking for you."

"Tell him I'm with a patient," Dr. Dutton hollered.

With his left hand, Dr. Dutton tugged at the patient's lip again and pushed the needle into the man's upper gum just behind his left maxillary second premolar. The patient whimpered, rising off the chair slightly. As Dr. Dutton withdrew the needle, a small amount of Novocain squirted out and dribbled down the patient's chin.

"Here, rinse and spit," Dr. Dutton instructed, handing the patient a small, paper cup filled with water.

Dr. Dutton laid the hypodermic syringe back on the tray. As he picked up a curved, right-angle scraper, another knock at the door again interrupted his treatment of the patient.

"Yes, what is it?" he barked, becoming annoyed at the continuing interruption.

"I'm sorry, Doctor Dutton, but the man named Lamont is insistent. He says it is urgent."

"Very well," Dr. Dutton responded, pushing his three-wheeled stool back from the patient. He stood up, looked at the patient and said, "Sorry for the interruption. It will take a few minutes for the Novocain to completely numb your mouth. I'll be right back."

Dr. Dutton dropped the curved scraper on the tray and left the room. At the end of a long hallway, he entered his private office and pushed the door closed. He picked up the phone receiver from the desk and put it to his ear.

"I told you to never call me in the middle of the day. I'm busy with patients," Dr. Dutton complained.

"It is most important," the man named Lamont replied.

"It always is. Hurry up and tell me what is so important. I have a patient waiting."

"Grant has requested that I obtain shoes for two people. They cannot be purchased locally. Therefore, we have need of your friend the shoemaker."

"I will need names and details."

"The details will be provided in one hour in the usual manner."

"How soon are these shoes needed?"

"They must be ready in two days."

"That is a very short time. The cost will be higher to rush their completion."

"Yes, we expected as much. An amount double the normal payment will be provided as before."

"Is there anything else?" Dr. Dutton asked.

Dr. Dutton waited for a response, but all he heard was the sound of the receiver being dropped back onto the phone followed by silence. He replaced the receiver, exited his office and returned to his patient.

"Let's see if you are ready," Dr. Dutton said as he walked back into the patient room. Selecting a mouth mirror and the curved scraper from the instrument tray, he rolled his stool close to the patient and placed the mouth mirror in the patient's mouth and poked at one his teeth with the scraper.

"Can you feel that?" he asked.

The patient mumbled something that Dr. Dutton assumed meant no. Replacing the curved scraper with a flat-edged calculus remover, he pushed the patient's gum upward to fully expose the cavity he intended to fill.

He lifted the dental drill off its storage hook and inserted a coarse, round burr. Bending over the patient, he stepped on the speed pedal then inserted the drill head into the patient's mouth and began grinding out the cavity. Realizing there would be no pain, the patient relaxed and released the arms of the chair.

Dr. Dutton had one more patient after his current patient. After that, he would change clothes and attend to Mr. Lamont's request.

Russian Embassy
Colonel Sokolovsky's Office
Ottawa, Ontario, Canada

Interrupted by a knock on his door, Colonel Sokolovsky looked up from the papers lying in front of him.

"Enter," he called out.

"You requested my presence, Colonel," Major Karpanov said, stopping in front of Colonel Sokolovsky's desk.

"Shut the door and lock it," Colonel Sokolovsky instructed as he closed the folder he had been working on and dropped it in a drawer of his desk. "I have a sensitive message you must read."

Major Karpanov turned around, pushed the door closed, and locked it. He returned to the desk and took the piece of paper Sokolovsky held out. Colonel Sokolovsky watched Karpanov's eyes as they darted back and forth across the paper as he read the message.

> *To Grant:*
>
> *Meet Alek tomorrow on street corner or in automobile in front of Montreal Museum of Fine Arts on Sherbrooke Street. Use extreme secrecy. Use only cover names. The time: 11 o'clock in the evening. Identification sign: A newspaper under the left arm. Password: Best regards from Mikel.*
>
> *Buy from Alek information from visit to secret Uranium Plant in Petawawa district. Information will be hidden in bottle of whiskey. Alek must not remain in Canada. Earliest, after completion of meeting, he is to fly to London where he will be contacted by Albert. Hand over to him 200 dollars for whisky and 500 dollars for travel expense.*
> *Director*

"You wish me to accompany you?"

"Yes. I wish to leave immediately," Colonel Sokolovsky replied. "We have other business there as well. I will need someone to convince the parties involved that we mean business. Grab enough personal items for three days. Meet me back here in one hour. On your way, inform Lieutenant Zakharov that he will be responsible for outbound messages as well as inbound."

"Yes, sir. I will see to it immediately.

Karpanov unlocked the office door and exited the office to gather his personal items and to inform Lieutenant Zakharov of the changes.

Russian Embassy
Cipher Room
Ottawa, Ontario, Canada

Hearing loud footsteps, Viktor looked up from the cipher machine as he tore off the deciphered copy of the last message from the current batch he had been working on. He stood, watching as Major Karpanov rushed into the room. "*What kind of tongue-lashing am I about to receive this time*," Viktor wondered.

Major Karpanov stuck his head through the doorway in the partition and barked. "Naumenko, get in here." He waited for Senior Sergeant Naumenko to enter the room then continued, "Colonel Sokolovsky and I have to travel out of town for some critical business. Lieutenant Zakharov, while we are away, you will be in charge of routing for all inbound and outbound messages. I expect there to be no problems, but should any arise, you are to contact Lieutenant Colonel Meliknikov, the Chief Assistant Military Attaché. Is that understood?"

"Yes, Major Karpanov," Viktor replied.

Major Karpanov turned abruptly and rushed out of the room.

"I wonder what that is all about?" Senior Sergeant Naumenko exclaimed.

"Better to not ask questions," Viktor advised.

Senior Sergeant Naumenko, shrugged his shoulders, turned, and disappeared through the doorway in the partition. Viktor stuffed the last deciphered message into the cipher bag, sealed it, and took off to distribute the messages.

About to start down the stairs, Viktor tuned when he heard someone shout his name.

"Lieutenant Zakharov, stop," a loud, gruff voice bellowed.

Viktor stopped and waited for the man rushing down the hallway. On the man's uniform jacket, Viktor recognized the insignia of a lieutenant colonel. The left side of the man's jacket was covered by many rows of ribbons. "*This must be Lieuten-*

ant Colonel Meliknikov," Viktor thought. "May I be of assistance, Sir?" Viktor asked, standing at attention as the man stopped in front of him.

"Yes, you may, Lieutenant Zakharov," the man answered. "I am Lieutenant Colonel Meliknikov. Major Karpanov should have informed you that I am to oversee operations while he and Colonel Sokolovsky are away."

"Yes, Sir, he did. Just a few minutes ago."

"Normally, these outbound messages would be included in the diplomatic pouch, but they are quite sensitive and must be encrypted," Meliknikov said, handing Viktor a sealed folder. "There are two messages in that folder. They must go out immediately. I will be in my office. Inform me when you have completed the task."

"Yes, Lieutenant Colonel Meliknikov," Viktor replied, standing at attention. "I will see to them immediately."

Rather than continue with the delivery of the deciphered messages, Viktor turned and headed back to the cipher room. After entering the cipher room, he poked his head through the doorway in the partition. "Senior Sergeant Naumenko, stop what you are doing and come out here."

Senior Sergeant Naumenko laid the message he had been deciphering on the table, covered it with a cloth, and stepped through the partition. "Yes, Lieutenant Zakharov, what is it?"

"Lieutenant Colonel Meliknikov handed me some very sensitive messages that must be encrypted and sent out immediately," Viktor advised. "I must be certain I have absolute privacy. You are to go to the dining hall and take a break. I will come get you when the messages have been submitted to the communications department."

"Very well," Senior Sergeant Naumenko answered, turning toward the door.

"Lock the door on your way out," Viktor added as Naumenko grabbed the doorknob. Viktor waited until he heard the door close and the locking bolt slide into place.

Sitting at the table, he broke the seal on the folder and flipped it open. He lifted out the first message and closed the folder. Positioning himself in front of the Fialka M125's thirty-character keyboard, he slid the three-position MODE lever to the CODING position. He opened the card reader on the left side of the machine and inserted a numbered punch-card for the current day of the month. The card reader then acted as an extra code wheel, consisting of a 30 x 30 contact matrix, which allowed permutations to the coding process based on the day of the month key.

Viktor consulted the outbound messages section of the daily key book, keyed in the proper day key and sequence number, then lined out the sequence number to prevent it from being used again. He positioned the message beside him and began punching in the message. Once the entire message had been entered, he advanced the paper and tore off the encrypted message. The message contained multiple lines of characters in groups of varying lengths. Without the Fialka cipher machine, the correct day key, and the proper sequence number the message was meaningless gibberish.

Viktor looked at the original message and shook his head, unable to see any need for encryption. The message described normal embassy activities and included a request for Moscow to transfer funds to purchase local food items for the dining hall. Hardly the top-secret information he had expected, considering Meliknikov's request for strict privacy.

After adding the encrypted message to the cipher bag, he flipped open the folder. He laid the first message aside and picked up the second message, quickly reading the handwritten memorandum.

> *To the Director, Reference No. 12293*
>
> *Lamont has been in contact with Oscar. Lamont expressed our urgent need for two pairs of shoes. Will transmit sizes and other detail to Oscar by routine drop. Requested the shoemaker deliver in two days. Oscar requires double payment in cash for rush. Product to arrive at Eaton's Store.*

> *Lamont advises that the money be sent in small sums in the usual manner.*
>
> *As is known to you, in the last two months we had to make heavy expenditures and therefore there will be nothing left in the private cash box. For shoes it is necessary to pay $2,400.00. I therefore beg you to send urgently needed operational sum of money.*
>
> > *Grant*

Viktor furrowed his brow and read the message a second time. "What would make two pairs of shoes cost $2,400.00?" he asked himself. The answer to that question was obvious. The message was *not* really talking about shoes, but Viktor did not know what it might refer to. 'Grant' was a name he had seen before, but who was 'Lamont' and who was 'Oscar'? Rifling through the messy pile of papers strewn across the table, he located a blank sheet of paper and scribbled down the important parts of the message. After tearing off the bottom half of the sheet of paper, he folded it and slid it under his shirt.

Switching to the chair in front of the Fialka M-125, he selected another sequence number from the daily key book and punched in the message. He tore off the second encrypted message and added it to the cipher bag. With Sokolovsky and Karpanov away for an unknown number of days he was determined to learn as much as he could. Carrying the cipher bag under his arm, he unlocked the cipher room door and headed for the dining hall.

"Senior Sergeant Naumenko," Viktor said as he tapped the man on the shoulder. "I have finished with the messages. You may now return to the cipher room and continue your work."

"Yes, Lieutenant Zakharov," Senior Sergeant Naumenko acknowledged.

"Senior Sergeant, after I submit the messages at the communications center, I have to deliver the last batch of deciphered messages and then I will return to the secure file room to double check and verify the master control log. I may be some time."

"Yes, sir," Senior Sergeant Naumenko answered.

Viktor followed Naumenko out of the dining hall and down the hallway. Naumenko turned and headed up the stairway while Viktor continued down the hallway to the communication center.

"Junior Sergeant Yakolev," Viktor greeted as he walked up to the communications center counter.

"Lieutenant Zakharov, what can I do for you?"

"I have two private messages that must be transmitted immediately."

Junior Sergeant Yakolev took the messages Viktor held out, assigned routing numbers to them, and entered them in the control log. "Wait while I give them to the telegraph operator," Yakolev said. He disappeared for a few seconds then returned. "Is there anything else, Lieutenant Zakharov?"

"Yes there is," Viktor answered. "Sokolovsky and Karpanov are away from the embassy for a few days. I have been put in charge of all inbound *and* outbound messages." Viktor heavily emphasized the word 'and'.

A slight smile crept onto Yakolev's face, quickly disappearing. "I understand," Yakolev replied, winking slightly.

"I will return later to collect any new messages," Viktor advised as he turned and left the communications center.

Back in the secure file room, standing in front of the open safe, Viktor was surprised to see Sokolovsky's private diary lying on the second shelf from the bottom. He walked over to the doorway. "Sergeant, I am cataloging highly classified documents," Viktor lied. "I must not be disturbed for any reason."

"I will see that no one enters, Lieutenant," the security guard responded.

Viktor returned to the open safe and lifted Sokolovsky's diary off the shelf, making note of exactly how the diary had been positioned. As he began to browse thru the pages, two folded sheets of paper slipped out from in front of the back cover and fell onto the floor. He bent over, picked up the papers, unfolded them, and began to read.

Unable to believe his eyes, he gasped and shook his head. "This is not to be believed," he exclaimed. Right before his eyes was proof that Colonel Sokolovsky was involved in a massive conspiracy against the Canadian government. Viktor started counting the names listed. He shook his head again. Fifty-six entries in all. The two-page list included cover names, actual names, workplaces, and titles. Viktor scanned the pages again, looking at the various places of work.

"Surely, this cannot be true," he whispered, bewildered by the high-level positions listed on the papers: a nuclear physicist, a newspaper editor, a major in the Canadian Army, someone from the Directorate of Artillery, several American scientists, a Soviet Military Attaché, a vice-president from the Bank of Canada, a Manager of the Department of Munitions, a squadron leader in the Royal Canadian Air Force, an agent in American Naval Intelligence, a university explosives expert, an assistant to the Canadian High Commissioner, at least fifteen high-ranking Russian embassy officers, and many others.

"*This list must be preserved,*" he told himself. "*But how?*"

An idea formed in his mind as he refolded the papers and shoved them into the cipher bag. He pushed the heavy safe door closed, spun the combination dial, hurried to the table in the entry room.

"I forgot something important," Viktor lied again as he signed the entry log. "No one is to enter the file room until I return and I mean no one. Is that understood Sergeant?"

"Yes, sir, Lieutenant Zakharov," the security guard responded. The security guard picked up his weapon, walked around the table, took a position in front of the door, and said, "I assure you, *no one* will enter that room."

"Very well, Sergeant. I will be back soon."

Viktor turned and headed for the cipher room as fast as he dared, not wanting to create any unnecessary suspicion. He walked straight to the cluttered table and sat down. Digging through the mound of books and papers, he pulled out two blank sheets of paper. Pushing some of the clutter out of the way, he made a clear spot where he could write. He unsealed the cipher bag, and slipped the folded papers out. After a quick glance around the room to be certain he was alone, he unfolded the papers, laid them on the table, and covered them with some other papers from the pile of clutter.

Flipping the cover papers up, he read an entry and then copied the information onto the blank sheet. Then he repeated the process, sweat trickling down his back as he scribbled furiously. After completing all entries on the first sheet, he slipped it into the cipher bag and started on the second sheet. About to lift the cover papers to read the third entry on the second page, he jerked when he heard Naumenko walk through the doorway in the partition.

"The paperwork never ends does it," Senior Sergeant Naumenko remarked, stopping beside the table.

"You are quite correct," Viktor answered as he slid a maintenance brochure over the sheet he was writing on.

"Are there any new messages waiting to be deciphered?"

"No. I have a discrepancy in the message count I am trying to resolve. I have not been able to stop by the communications center."

"I have completed all the messages that were assigned to me. If I have your permission, I would like to leave for the day. It would be nice for once to arrive at the dining hall before there is nothing left but burned soup."

"I have nothing else for you to do. You may leave, Senior Sergeant Naumenko."

Senior Sergeant Naumenko handed Viktor his code book, turned, and left the cipher room, leaving Viktor alone to finish copying the list of espionage collaborators. Viktor laid the papers he had used to cover the original list aside and quickly finished the task of copying the information. After folding the second sheet, he slipped it into the cipher bag with the first sheet. The duplicate sheets were folded into fourths and stuffed under his shirt.

Intending to leave the embassy as soon as he returned the collaborator list to Sokolovsky's diary, he would have to secure the cipher machines. He positioned the protective covers on each machine, locking them in place. A quick sweep around the room revealed no classified materials lying out. He grabbed his and Naumenko's code books from the table, stepped through the doorway, pulled the door shut, and locked it.

Viktor hurried back into the secure file room and said, "I am back Sergeant. I have corrected the earlier problem. As soon as I lock the code books and these messages in the safe, I will be leaving for the day."

Viktor signed the entry log and entered the secure file room. Quickly unlocking the safe, he retrieved the list from the cipher bag, made certain the sheets were in the proper order, placed them back into Sokolovsky's diary, and positioned the diary on the shelf exactly as he had found it. He pushed the safe door closed, spun the combination dial, and exited the room.

"Sergeant, after I leave, you may close and lock the outer door. If you have not other duties, you may go off duty."

Viktor turned and left the file room. After a quick dash to the first floor, he exited the embassy and started his long trek home.

Chapter Fifteen

Russian Embassy
Communications Center
Ottawa, Ontario, Canada

Having finished delivering his fourth batch of messages for the day, Lieutenant Viktor Zakharov pushed to door to the communication center open and walked up to the counter.

"Good afternoon, Lieutenant Zakharov," Junior Sergeant Alexander Yakolev greeted. "How are you this morning?"

"I am fine Junior Sergeant Yakolev," Viktor responded. "I am here to pick up the morning message traffic."

"Just one moment, Lieutenant. I will gather what we have so far."

Viktor waited while Junior Sergeant Yakolev disappeared through a door with запрещенный stenciled on it in large block letters. Two minutes later, Junior Sergeant Yakolev returned with a sheaf of papers in his hand.

"There are only five messages so far today," Junior Sergeant Yakolev commented, pushing a green, cloth-covered book across the counter. "This is a new custody log book required by Major Karpanov's orders. Please fill in the information on the first bank line and sign."

Viktor filled in the date, time, and number of messages. He signed his name and pushed the book back across the counter. Junior Sergeant Yakolev verified and initialed Viktor's entry, put the book under the counter, and laid the messages face down in front of Viktor, pushing the top five messages askew. Viktor looked up at Yakolev with concern after noticing Colonel Sokolovsky's private message indicator on the corner of the bottom message.

Before Viktor could protest, Junior Sergeant Yakolev bent over the counter, straightened the pile of messages, and whispered, "This message just arrived. More people have disappeared. Sokolovsky and Karpanov are not here. Go quickly. If you bring it back with the next batch of messages, no one will notice." He straightened up and said, "Good day, Lieutenant Zakharov. I hope your day goes well."

"Thank you, Junior Sergeant Yakolev," Viktor answered as he stuffed the messages in the cipher bag, turned, and hurried out of the communications center. He rushed down the hallway, up the stairs, and into the secure file room. After pulling the five new messages out of the cipher bag, being careful to leave Sokolovsky's private message inside, he added the new messages to the control log and placed them on the top shelf in the safe. He signed out a batch of ten old messages, slid them into the cipher bag, and headed back to the cipher room.

Viktor walked through the door to the cipher room, laid the cipher bag on the table, then poked his head through the doorway in the new partition that had been added, and called out, "Sergeant Naumenko do you need any assistance with the cipher machine?"

"No, I do not need any assistance, Lieutenant Zakharov," Sergeant Naumenko replied. "The new machine is working perfectly."

"I should inform you I just picked up all new messages. I added them to the master control log and placed them on the top shelf of the safe. I am just starting on the next to last batch of old messages. I do not wish to be interrupted."

"Very well," Sergeant Naumenko acknowledged, turning back toward his cipher machine.

"Very well what?" Viktor barked, pretending to behave like a typical Russian Army officer.

"Very well, *Sir*," Sergeant Naumenko shot back, coming to attention and offering a crisp salute.

Viktor sneered, pulled his head back through the doorway, walked over to the table, and sat down. After unsealing the cipher bag, he slid Colonel Sokolovsky's private message out just far enough to read the master control code, pushed the message back in, and resealed the bag. Running his finger down the list of control codes in the new code book Sergeant Naumenko had brought from Moscow, he located the matching sequence of numbers. "Surely I cannot be that fortunate," he muttered. A recheck of the master control code on Sokolovsky's private message verified the code was, in fact, correct. Smiling broadly, he was unable to believe his good fortune. The message's master code was exactly the same as the last message he had deciphered, meaning he would not have to tear down and reset the cipher machine.

After a cautious glance through the partition doorway to verify Naumenko was busy, Viktor unsealed the cipher bag, and pulled out Sokolovsky's private message. He sat in front of the Fialka M-125 and began to punch in the lines of character groups. After punching in the last character, Viktor grabbed the edge of the deciphered message protruding from the bottom feed slot of the machine, tore it off, and began reading.

"да не может быть!" Viktor shrieked, a Russian exclamation roughly equivalent to "That's impossible! That cannot be!"; a look of raw terror spreading across his face.

"Yes, what is it, Lieutenant Zakharov?" Sergeant Naumenko hollered.

"It is nothing," Viktor hollered back. "I pinched my finger in the machine."

With trembling hands, Viktor snatched the original message from the table and folded it and the deciphered message haphazardly into fourths. Nearly ripping the buttons off his shirt, he unbuttoned the two just above his belt, and jammed the folded papers under his shirt. He fumbled with the buttons, his hands shaking so badly he could not get them buttoned. Drawing in a deep breath, he leaned his arms against the table. Bracing from the table steadied his hand enough he managed to push the buttons through the buttonholes.

Dizzy from the flood of adrenaline circulating through his bloodstream, he sat down on the chair. After several deep breaths, he knew he had to get out of the room and get some air. Stopping beside the doorway in the partition, he blurted out, "Sergeant Naumenko, I feel sick. I'm heading to the bathroom." Before Sergeant Naumenko could answer, Viktor was out the door and running down the hallway.

"Sorry, sick," Viktor twice offered as an excuse as he raced down the two flights of stairs, smashing into a junior officer as he started down the first flight of stairs and then nearly knocking a secretary off her feet as he turned the corner on the lower floor. After a mad dash down the hallway, he shoved the bathroom door open and flew into the last stall against the far wall.

Panting and shaking from the dash down the stairs and the overload of adrenaline, he sat in the stall trying to regain control of his emotions. Gradually the adrenaline burned off and his breathing returned to near normal. "*You must not panic!*" his mind screamed at him. "*If you do, they will know.*" Never more in his life than at that moment he needed to rely on his training received in the Komsomol. From deep within his inner being, he summoned the strict discipline he had once learned. Pulling in as large a breath as he could, he held it for a full ten seconds then let it out very slowly through his nose. Twice more he repeated the calming breath exercise.

With a clenched jaw, he pulled the stall door open, walked over to the closest sink, and splashed cold water on his face twice. Water dripping from his face, he looked up into the mirror. "*What am I going to do?*" he asked himself. "*First, I must tell Alexander about the message,*" he answered himself.

He ripped two paper towels from the dispenser, dried his face, and headed for the communications center.

"Lieutenant Zakharov, I didn't expect…." Junior Sergeant Yakolev stopped mid-sentence and motioned Viktor over to the counter. "You do not look well, my friend. Is there anything I can do?"

Viktor scanned the communications center. Finding it empty except for Yakolev, he leaned toward his friend and whispered, "I cannot return the message."

"But you must," Yakolev protested. "When Sokolovsky returns he will find out. Then he will kill you *and* me."

"It does not matter. I'm sorry, but I must keep it."

"Why? You are risking your life and mine."

"You must cover for me for at least a day or two," Viktor begged. "It should be at least a week before the sender will question why there has been no response. I cannot explain further now. I will explain tomorrow at breakfast after I have had time to calm down and decide what I am going to do. Please Alexander, you must help me."

"Okay, Viktor, but only for a day or two."

Viktor turned and left the communications center before Yakolev could change his mind. As Viktor's back disappeared through the doorway, Alexander Yakolev wondered if he had just committed suicide.

Zakharov Apartment
Somerset Street
Ottawa, Ontario, Canada

Viktor stopped at the bottom of the stairway, rubbing his sore leg, having hurried home as quickly as his still-healing leg would allow. Not stopping once to rest, he had walked and limped the slightly over three kilometer distance from the embassy in just over an hour. He grabbed the railing for support and hobbled to the top of the stairs. After unlocking the door, he pushed the door open and entered the apartment.

Mopping his face with his handkerchief, Viktor collapsed onto the couch, breathing heavily and rubbing his leg again.

"Viktor, you are home late again," Anna called out from the kitchen. "I thought you told me you were getting caught up on the backlog of messages."

"The old messages are not the problem," Viktor answered. "It is much worse than that."

"What do you mea….," Anna's voice trailed off as she walked out of the kitchen and into the living room. She stopped in front of Viktor and exclaimed, "Viktor, you are soaked and you look deathly pale. Are you sick?"

"No. I wish it were only that I was sick."

"Is it Karpanov" Has he threatened you again?"

"No, it is not Karpanov."

"Well then, is it Sokolovsky?"

"No. It is much worse than that," Viktor groaned, putting his face in his hands.

"Viktor, you are scaring me," Anna cried. "You must tell me what has you so upset."

"Alexander Yakolev added a private message addressed to Colonel Sokolovsky to the today's inbound messages when I picked them up from the communication center."

"Viktor, we have talked about this," Anna sighed. "You must stop reading Sokolovsky's messages. If you continue, you will get caught. Then what will happen?"

"I know, but this time is different," Viktor protested. "If I had not read this message we would soon be on our way back to Moscow."

"On our way back to Moscow? What do you mean?" Anna sputtered.

"Here, read this," Viktor responded, unbuttoning his shirt and pulling out the folded pieces of paper.

Viktor unfolded the papers and handed Anna the deciphered copy of Sokolovsky's message. Anna grabbed the paper, her eyes darting back and forth as she read the words. She looked up, her face contorted with panic as she completed reading the message.

"Viktor, you are being recalled to answer charges of treason," she cried, her voice quaking with fear. "When will this happen?"

"I do not know," Viktor responded, holding up the original message. "I have the original encrypted message also. Karpanov and Sokolovsky are out of town. It will be some time before the sender of the message finds out the message did not arrive."

"But Viktor, what the message says is not true. You have not done these things You can fight this."

"Look at the initials at the bottom of the message."

Anna glanced down at the paper in her hands, then asked, "Who is DM?"

"I believe it is Dmitri Maksimov."

"The commandant at the cipher school you attended in Moscow?"

"Yes. It has to be him. He was furious when Colonel Sokolovsky embarrassed him during my final examination. He became even more enraged when Sokolovsky asked for me personally to accompany him to the embassy here. Maksimov blames me for his demotion."

"But the things in the message are not true," Anna protested.

"It makes no difference," Viktor declared. "Maksimov is from an important and highly respected family and he has friends on the Central Committee. I am afraid the truth is of little value when political ambitions are involved."

"What are we going to go?" Anna fretted.

Viktor did not answer, afraid to tell Anna the thoughts that had swirled around in his mind during the long walk home. First, he would show her the other message and the list he had copied.

"There is more," Viktor said, pulling the other sheets of paper out from under his shirt. He handed her the message about the shoes. "Here, look at this message."

"This does not make any sense," Anna blurted out after reading the message. "Two pairs of shoes cannot cost twenty-four hundred Canadian dollars."

"That is exactly what I said."

"Who are these people?"

"The name 'Grant' at the bottom is a code name for Colonel Sokolovsky."

"A code name? Why would Colonel Sokolovsky need a code name?"

"The same reason why two pairs of shoes costs twenty-four hundred dollars," Viktor answered. "It is obvious the message is not really about shoes. It refers to something illegal. Something Sokolovsky does not wish to mention openly. There is a very large conspiracy and I have proof Sokolovsky and Karpanov are involved."

"Viktor, how do you know this?" Anna asked, a skeptical look on her face.

"After I found out Karpanov and Sokolovsky were going out of town, I was in the secure file room and I saw Sokolovsky's private diary lying on one of the shelves. I picked it…."

"Viktor, you didn't," Anna interrupted. "Not his private diary."

"He is out of town and will never know," Viktor countered. "When I started to browse the pages, this fell out." Viktor held out the two sheets of paper he had copied.

"What is this?" Anna asked as she glanced at the two sheets of paper.

"It is a list of secret cover names for Russian officers and for Canadians who are spying on their government. Look near the top of the second page for the name 'Grant'."

Viktor watched as Anna flipped to the second page and ran her finger down the list, stopping one-third of the way down the page. Sliding her finger to the right, she came to Colonel Sokolovsky's name.

Seeing the recognition displayed on Anna's face, Viktor said, "See, the sender of the message about the shoes was Colonel Sokolovsky. Let me have the massage."

Anna held out the copy of the message. Viktor took it and read the first line of the message. "Look through the list of names and tell me what Lamont's real name is."

Anna flipped back to the first page and scanned through the names. Locating the name Viktor asked about, she answered, "It says here that name is Lieutenant Colonel Meliknikov."

"He is the Chief Assistant Military Attaché," Viktor exclaimed. "He answers directly to the ambassador. There is another name in the message. Who is Oscar?"

Anna looked several entries further down in the list and with a puzzled look on her face said, "That name is a Doctor James P. Dutton, Junior. It says here he is a dentist. Why would the military attaché use a code name for a dentist and why would he ask him for shoes?"

"Remember, I said the message is *not* about shoes. The word shoes is obviously a code for something else. Something important and very expensive."

"Viktor, I cannot believe the names on this list are spying on their own government," Anna commented. "These are very important people."

"That was my reaction as well," Viktor agreed. "Remember Boris told me about suspicious activities and I have seen other messages about individuals passing information to Russian agents. Remember the message we hid? Get Nikola's stuffed bear, quickly."

Anna tiptoed into Nikola's room, retrieved the stuffed bear from the toy box, and returned to the living room. She handed the ragged, stuffed bear to Viktor.

"Get me the scissors from your sewing basket," Viktor ordered, holding out his hand.

Anna rushed over to her sewing basket sitting beside a large, overstuffed chair and grabbed her scissors. Placing the scissors into Viktor's hand, she watched as he split the seam open and withdrew a folded piece of paper.

"I remember there were names that had been scratched out and other names written in," Viktor said as he unfolded the paper. "Let's see if we can find them on the list."

Viktor read off the handwritten names while Anna located them on the list. All five names were on the list. Anna became more and more bewildered as she located each name Viktor read from the message.

"Two of those names are directors of military weapons agencies," Anna stammered. "One is a squadron leader in the

Royal Canadian Air Force. How can this be? Surely people in such important positions would not betray their own country."

"The evidence you are holding is clear," Viktor insisted. "And I have seen more messages that are even more troubling. I believe this is more than simple spying."

"Oh, Viktor, what have you gotten yourself into," Anna moaned, letting the papers drop to the floor. "What are you going to do?"

Viktor did not answer. He could not. He rose from the chair he had been sitting on and paced back and forth in front of the window. Back and forth he paced, trying to put words to the thoughts flashing through his mind. He could not bring himself to speak the words. Not even to himself. He stopped pacing and carefully pulled back the edge of the curtain. The same car as before pulled up, stopped at the end of the block, and shut off its headlights. Viktor let the curtain fall back into place.

"The same car as before is parked at the end of the block," he informed Anna. "Come look so you will be able to recognize it." He pulled the curtain back just enough for her to be able to see out the window. Anna bent down slightly and peered through the window.

"I cannot be certain, but I think the man driving is the new cipher clerk, Zinovy Naumenko," Viktor said. "I do not trust him. He is just under six foot tall with curly brown hair. When you go out for anything, do not be obvious, but watch for him or the car."

"If we are being watched, do they already know you are sneaking messages out of the embassy?"

"I do not believe so. If they did, they would already have arrested me. But, it does appear they are suspicious, but they are suspicious of everybody. We may have a few days, but not more than a week before someone discovers the missing message that says I am to be sent back to Moscow."

"Then we must do something quickly. Viktor, what are we going to do?"

Viktor had been wrestling with that question ever since he had discovered the list of collaborators. He knew there was only one answer, but he could not bring himself to say it; not even to himself. It was unthinkable. Viktor walked over to the couch and sat down. Anna followed and sat beside him.

She laid her hand on his arm and asked, "Viktor, we do not have much time. What are we going to do?"

He agreed with Anna. There was very little time. "*We must do something, but what*," he asked himself.

He opened his mouth, but before he could speak, Anna blurted out, "Viktor, we must defect. Take some of the documents and go to the authorities. They will protect us."

"Anna, no!," Viktor objected. "We cannot."

"We have no choice," Anna responded.

"But, Anna, Russia is our home. I have no one but a few distant aunts, uncles, and cousins. But what about your parents? You will never be able to see them again."

"We else can we do?" Anna questioned. "What other choice is there?"

"I do not know," Viktor choked. "I love my country. I have served Russia well. They have instructed us that to defect is the action of a coward. Do you know what they do to those who attempt to defect when they are caught?"

"Yes, I have heard the stories."

"They are not just stories, Anna. Defectors are brutally tortured until they reveal who helped them. Their deaths are gruesome and extremely painful."

"If you get sent back to Moscow under a charge of treason, you will stand before a firing squad. Viktor, you have no choice."

Viktor rose from the couch and began pacing again. Anna remained seated, watching her husband in turmoil. Back and forth he paced. After several minutes, he stopped pacing and returned to the couch.

"Are you certain you wish to never return to Russia?"

"Yes, absolutely," Anna answered immediately. "The people here are happy and friendly. They have great freedom.

They do not have to always be looking over their shoulder. They do not have cars sitting outside their windows watching their every move. Canada's military officers do not condone raping and looting. They do not send people to a gulag for simply disagreeing with them. I am certain. I never want to go back to Russia, ever."

"After the sickening atrocities I witnessed in Königsberg and the spying I have discovered here, part of me also never wants to go back to Russia." He sat down beside Anna with tears in his eyes and said, "If I were to defect I would feel as if I would be abandoning my country. It is who I am. Russia is our home. Anna, how could I do that?"

Anna reached out and pulled Viktor to her and held him tightly. They sat in silence for a long time.

"I understand," Anna comforted. "You are a good man and a good son to Russia. Maybe if you defect and expose the evil men like Sokolovsky that are destroying Russia, you can do more good. Otherwise, you will be sent back to Moscow and you will die for nothing. This evil must be stopped."

"Perhaps you are correct," Viktor conceded. "There is also something I believe is far worse, but I must be certain before I tell you."

"You must do it quickly, before Karpanov or Sokolovsky return and discover what you are doing."

"I agree," Viktor answered. "Tomorrow I will begin to identify the most incriminating documents. If I have enough, I will decide whether I can go to the authorities."

Viktor rose from the couch and stretched, feeling some of the weight of indecision being lifted. However, that relief was replaced with a new fear. The fear of being caught before he could alert the authorities, knowing Anna and Nikola would also pay the price for his decision.

"Come, let's go to bed. I have much to do tomorrow."

Viktor reached out and took Anna's hand and helped her up from the couch. They walked arm in arm into the bedroom, each wondering secretly what the future held.

Chapter Sixteen

Russian Embassy
Dining Hall
Ottawa, Ontario, Canada

Viktor walked into the dining hall and looked around, trying to locate Junior Sergeant Alexander Yakolev. He saw Yakolev sitting by himself in their usual spot on the left side of the dining hall. He walked over and tapped him on the shoulder.

"Good morning, Alexander," Viktor greeted. "I'll go grab something and be right back."

Yakolev held up his hand, waved at Viktor, and mumbled something, his mouth full of scrambled eggs. Viktor walked over to the beginning of the serving line and grabbed a tray. Starting down the line, "*Something different today*," he observed, seeing an unusually large variety of breakfast items. The large variety of tasty looking items piqued the hunger growling in his stomach. As he pushed the tray along, he added a scoop of scrambled eggs, fried potatoes, and a piece of toast to his plate. He filled a glass with milk and stopped.

"Is that really bacon?" he remarked.

Hurrying down the line, Viktor stopped in front of a large metal pan containing dark brown strips that looked like bacon. With a set of tongs, he selected a piece and laid it on his plate. He picked up the piece of bacon, sniffed it, stuck it is his mouth, and bit off half. It was bacon. He jammed the remaining half in his mouth, grabbed the tongs again, glanced up and down the line, then added four more pieces to his plate. In large letters, the sign above the pan said, "Two pieces per person." Not wanting to get caught with the extra bacon, he pushed the toast over the bacon, turned, and headed back to the table where Yakolev was seated.

"Alexander, did you see the bacon?" Viktor asked as he pulled a chair and sat down.

"Yes. How many pieces did *you* take," Yakolev asked with a smile on his face.

"Four. No, five," Viktor answered, remembering the piece he had eaten at the serving line. "It has been so long since I have had bacon, I hardly remembered what it tasted like."

"I had five pieces as well. It is the first time they have served bacon since the day I arrived here six months ago."

Viktor sprinkled generous amounts of salt and pepper on his scrambled eggs then shoved a huge forkful in his mouth, a look of surprise spreading across his face. "I thought the eggs would be powdered as usual, but these are real," he remarked, shoving another large forkful into his mouth. Viktor did not hear much of what Yakolev said as he concentrated on devouring the food on his plate.

"That was really good," Viktor said, wiping a few morsels of eggs from the corners of his mouth. "I wonder why we are treated with such good food today?"

"I asked one of the cook's helpers, but he did not know," Yakolev answered. "I suspect tomorrow it will back to the same old slop."

"You are probably right," Viktor laughed as he picked up his glass and drained the last few swallows of milk.

"You seem different today," Yakolev observed. "Has something changed?"

"Yes it has," Viktor answered, lowering his voice. Viktor glanced around the dining hall to be certain no one was close enough to overhear what he was about to say. "I know you have noticed the difference since Major Karpanov arrived because you informed me that he is an N.K.V.D. assassin. I have discovered a large conspiracy."

"Who is involved?" Yakolev whispered.

"You would not believe how many. I cannot say more here. It is not safe. You once told me you were never going back to Russia. Did you truly mean that?"

"Yes, I did," Yakolev confirmed. "Never."

"How do you plan to do that?"

"As you said, it is not safe to talk here."

"You are correct," Viktor agreed, nodding his head. "But, I wish to know. We will talk later. Now, I must get to work as I have much to do. If there are any new messages from overnight, I will pick them up on my way to the cipher room."

"I have not been to the communications center yet. If you follow me, I will check with the night duty operator."

Viktor and Alexander pushed themselves away from the table and carried their trays to the scullery. The two men exited the dining hall and walked down the hallway. Viktor followed Yakolev through the door to the communication center and waited at the counter while Yakolev disappeared into the restricted area. A minute later Yakolev returned with a large stack of papers in his hand and laid them on the counter.

"It looks like you will be very busy," Yakolev announced as he began to count the messages. "There are seventeen messages here."

Viktor added the message count to the new log book beside the date and time he had already written in. He signed the entry and pushed the log book across the counter toward Yakolev. Yakolev verified the entry and handed the stack of messages to Viktor.

"Have a pleasant day , Lieutenant Zakharov," Yakolev offered as Viktor turned and left the communications center.

"*What will I find as I look through the old messages*," Viktor asked himself as he hurried down the hallway.

Montreal Museum of Fine Arts
Rue Sherbrooke East
Montreal, Quebec, Canada

A lone black car drove northeast along deserted Rue Sherbrooke East, slowing as it approached the intersection of Avenue Calixa-Lavalée. The car turned left and entered Parc

Lafontaine. The driver located a parking area just inside the park, pulled in, and quickly turned off the headlights. A brief orange glow illuminated Major Alexei Karpanov's face as he lit the cigarette stuck between his lips.

"We are early, Alexei," Colonel Vasily Sokolovsky, sitting in the passenger seat, observed. "How long must we wait for Alek to arrive?"

Major Karpanov held up his arm and drew in on his cigarette. The faint red glow provided enough light for him to be able to read the watch at his wrist.

"We have not quite twenty minutes before he is supposed to arrive."

"Then let us discuss what information we expect him to provide," Colonel Sokolovsky suggested. "I do not trust him. I understand he has become very difficult to work with."

"Yes, you are correct. He has become quite difficult to work with," Major Karpanov agreed. "especially after my request for a sample of Uranium 235."

"Why is that?"

"He claims it is nearly impossible to get the material in a sufficient quantity to be usable. When I pressed him, he tried to explain to me the theory of nuclear energy. He uses scientific terms which mean nothing to me."

"Did you ask him to write these things on paper so we can provide them to our scientists?"

"Yes, but he refuses to put anything down in writing and he also would not agree to take photographs or sneak out any information from the uranium plant."

"If he is so afraid to put anything in writing or take photographs, why has he agreed to help us?" Colonel Sokolovsky asked.

"He is an imbecile," Major Karpanov sneered. "He is like so many of the pathetic, naive students he teaches at the university. They are arrogant and blinded by their misguided passions. He told me the entire matter is extremely painful to him and he is not doing it for gain. He actually believes he is making a contribution to the safety of mankind. What a buffoon. I could hardly keep from laughing in his face."

"Why have we agreed to meet with him?" Colonel Sokolovsky asked.

"Because he is a high ranking member of the Canadian Association of Scientific Workers," Major Karpanov explained. "We will use his misguided intentions to identify and recruit like-minded scientists among the group. In spite of their years of education and many degrees, they are more easily manipulated then the naïve students they teach. Once the Party has gained enough adherents from among the scientists, the Communist Party will gain control. That will give the Party many espionage agents in key positions in Canada's national life."

"Yes, I see," Colonel Sokolovsky admitted. "As always, your logic is flawless."

Major Karpanov drew another lung full of smoke from his cigarette and glanced at his watch, nearly burning his fingers. He rolled the window down halfway and flicked the cigarette out.

"Stay here," Major Karpanov ordered. "I will go see if our friend has arrived."

The black car's door opened, Major Karpanov slipped out onto the dark street, and gently pushed the door shut. He walked down the street and turned left onto Rue Sherbrooke East. A figure hurried toward him from the far end of the block. Karpanov slipped his hand under his jacket and waited, his hand gripping a Tokarev TT-33 pistol. A middle-aged man with his collar drawn up tight moved to the edge of the sidewalk, rushed past him, and continued down the street. As the sound of the man's footsteps faded out, another figure stepped out of the shadows along the side of the museum, turned, and headed toward Karpanov.

Karpanov eased the Tokarev TT-33 part way out of its holster and waited. He relaxed somewhat when he saw the folded newspaper tucked under the man's arm, but he maintained his grip on the pistol.

"Greetings, Commander. Best regards from Mikel," the man said as he stopped in front of Karpanov.

"Alek, it is you," Karpanov acknowledged. "Come. Let us go to my car where we can talk freely."

The two men walked to the corner and turned right onto Avenue Calixa-Lavalée. When they reached the car, Karpanov opened the rear driver-side door and gestured for the man to climb into the car. The man poked his head into the car and hesitated when he saw someone sitting in the front seat.

"Do not be afraid," Karpanov said. "That is Mister Grant. He also wants to hear what you have to share with us."

Karpanov put his hand on the man's back, encouraging him to climb in. The man slid over to the center of the seat and waited for Karpanov to climb into the car as well.

"Well, Alek, do you have something for us?" Karpanov asked, looking directly at the man.

Again, the man hesitated, his eyes flicking back and forth between Karpanov and Sokolovsky.

"We do not have all night," Karpanov demanded. "The longer we sit here the more likely it is we will attract attention."

The man looked at Karpanov and began, "At the uranium plant, I have learned that the Canadians and the Americans have spent a great deal of money on atomic research. Specifically, the research is on the engineering and chemistry of producing nuclear material for bombs. At present, the work is on the nuclear bombardment of radioactive substances to produce enormous amounts of energy. This research is far more hush-hush than the work being conducted on new radar systems. Some of the work is being conducted right here at the University of Montreal"

"I have told you before what we wish for you to provide is the documentary materials for these atomic bombs. We desire the technical process, drawings, and calculations."

"I cannot," the man stammered. "Those materials are highly guarded. It would be impossible."

"If you cannot provide what we want, you will be no further use to us. If that is the case, we will alert the authorities and tell them you came to us, trying to sell us military secrets."

"You must not do that," the man cried. "I have helped you and have provided everything you asked for until now, but this, I cannot do. It is not possible."

"Well then, you will spend a very long time in prison or perhaps you will face a firing squad for being a traitor."

"No. No. Please don't!" the man wailed. "Wait. I forgot. I do have something to give you."

The man pulled a small gray, metal tube from his pocket and handed it to Karpanov and said, "That tube is lead. It contains a small amount of Uranium 235. I am told it is the same fissionable material the Americans used in the atomic bomb dropped on Hiroshima The material is very dangerous. You must not open it. It must be handled only by skilled scientists."

"This will be sent to our scientists in Moscow," Karpanov said as he reached out and took the small tube. "This will keep us from alerting the authorities for now, but we must have the drawings and calculations. Without them this material does not have much value. You will have three days to obtain the materials we ask for. Do you understand?"

"Yes, Commander, I understand. I will do my best to obtain them."

"Our meeting is over. Disappear quickly and do not be seen."

The man, Dr. Bradford Devin, a British nuclear physicist on temporary assignment at the University of Montreal, scrambled out of the car and disappeared into the darkness of the park.

"Do you think he can be trusted to keep his mouth shut?" Colonel Sokolovsky asked.

"I certainly hope so," Major Karpanov answered. "But I am taking no chances. I have two agents assigned to watch him twenty-four hours a day. If it looks like he is going to the authorities, they have orders to silence him, permanently."

"You are wise to do so. While we are here, what do you think of Zakharov, the cipher analyst?"

"I do not know much, except for what I read in his personnel file. I only met him once when I informed him we were to be out of town. Why do you ask."

"He was friends with Junior Sergeant Bogdanovitch, the one from the communications department that disappeared. I questioned Zakharov thoroughly. He left with many bruises, none of which were visible. He maintained that he knew nothing of the disappearance, but I am not certain he is telling the truth."

"Do you want me to interrogate him?"

"No. I do not believe he would survive another beating like that. He has a wife and young child. I believe we can put pressure on him through them."

"Do you want me to detain them?"

"I believe that is necessary, but first we have at least one day's business with Benson and Foster. The Director says we must gain more information on Canada's military capabilities and where and how they move munitions and artillery. If we have time we should also meet with Leader. He says he can provide information about their aircraft capabilities."

"Colonel, I hear Lieutenant Colonel Meliknikov may have found another source that may be leaking information from the communications department."

"Who might that be?" Colonel Sokolovsky asked.

"A Junior Sergeant Alexander Yakolev," Major Karpanov answered.

"What is being done with him?"

"I have not heard. I learned this just before we left the embassy."

"It is quite interesting that Yakolev and Zakharov are also friends," Colonel Sokolovsky observed. "Zakharov may be involved in more than just Bogdanovitch's disappearance. Before we leave in the morning, I will call Meliknikov and instruct him to hold Yakolev until we return. You can interrogate him then."

"I assure you I will make him talk," Major Karpanov asserted. "We are checked in at a small, *discrete* hotel on the edge of town. We will rest there for the night and leave to meet Benson and Foster in the morning. Once we arrive back in Ottawa, I will take Zakharov's family into custody. Then we shall find out what Zakharov knows."

Karpanov backed out of the parking area, drove down Avenue Calixa-Lavalée, and turned right onto Rue Sherbrooke East, headed southwest. Sokolovsky leaned his head back against the seat and crossed his legs while Karpanov drove toward their hotel.

Russian Embassy
Cipher Room
Ottawa, Ontario, Canada

Before going to the secure file room, Viktor had gone up to the third floor and had walked by Colonel Sokolovsky's office. Finding it still dark and the door locked, Viktor had felt assured Karpanov and Sokolovsky were still out of town. Then he had hurried down to the secure file room and had quickly logged the new messages into the master control log and added them to the stack of new messages in the safe. While collecting a batch of ten messages waiting to be deciphered, he had added ten old messages to the cipher bag as well.

When Viktor returned to the cipher room, he could not believe his good fortune. A handwritten note lying on the cipher machine informed him that Senior Sergeant Naumenko had tripped on the stairway and had landed very badly at the bottom of the stairs. The infirmary reported he had a severely broken arm and would require bed rest for at least two days.

No longer worried about interruptions or prying eyes, Viktor quickly worked through the batch of new messages. Finding two messages of interest, he made an extra copy of each one and hid the extra copies under a large pile of papers on the table. After stuffing the ten new messages and their deciphered copies into the cipher bag, he pulled out the old, al-ready-deciphered messages and sorted them into groups by sequence number and date, resulting in three separate groups of messages.

With the entire stack of day-of-the-month punch cards sitting beside the cipher machine, he inserted the appropriate day-of-the-month punch card and punched in each message from the first group. He repeated the process, resetting the cipher machine for each of the remaining two groups. Moving to the table, he put the original messages back into the cipher bag and scanned the deciphered copies. Unable to believe his eyes, he found a message revealing the spying was also occur-ring in America. He hid the third deciphered copy with the other two. The remaining nine messages that were of no inter-est would be dropped in the incinerator on his way to the se-cure file room.

The second and third groups of already-deciphered mes-sages yielded nothing of interest. The messages were typical requests, reports, and memorandums related to normal embas-sy operations. Viktor became worried, knowing the three mes-sages would not be enough evidence to convince the authori-ties. He needed more to corroborate his theory of a conspiracy. Adding to his concern was the fact that there were only two more batches of new messages left in the safe. If he did not find the evidence he needed in the next two batches, he would have no excuse to return to the secure file room. In a few days, the sender of the telegram requesting Viktor's return to Mos-cow would realize it had not arrived and would contact the embassy. Then, he would be on his way back to Moscow to stand before a firing squad.

It was late and Viktor was exhausted from the mental strain of fearing someone would catch him viewing Sokolovsky's private messages. Already an hour past his nor-mal quitting time, staying any later would likely raise someone's suspicion. He decided he would go home and return early in the morning. Senior Sergeant Naumenko would still be on bed rest, giving him the privacy he needed. He would decipher as many old messages as he could while finishing the last two batches of new messages. "*What if I find nothing of interest tomorrow?*" he asked himself. Not even wanting to think about that possibility, he sealed the cipher bag and hurried out of the cipher room to deliver the deciphered messages.

Rather than take the time to drop the deciphered copies of the old messages into the incinerator, he left them in the cipher bag, returned to the cipher room, and locked the cipher bag in the storage unit. He tore off a small scrap of paper and folded it into a small square. Wedging the small square of paper between the door and the jam, he pulled the door shut and locked it. The scrap of paper would let him know if anyone else had been in the cipher room.

Viktor hurried down the stairway and stopped at the main desk to sign out of the embassy.

The security officer looked up at Viktor and said, "Lieutenant Zakharov, you are late leaving the embassy today."

"Yes, I had trouble with the cipher machine," Viktor lied. "I had important messages that had to be finished."

"Very well," the security officer responded. "Sign out and be on your way."

Viktor signed the entry log and exited the embassy, eager to get home.

Chapter Seventeen

Zakharov Apartment
Somerset Street
Ottawa, Ontario, Canada

Viktor had been unusually quiet and uncommunicative after arriving home from the embassy. Anna thought it would be best to wait and let Viktor open up when he was ready, knowing he was under tremendous strain because of things going on at the embassy and learning that she never wanted to return to Russia. She put their dinner on the table, dished up two bowls of vegetable soup, and was about to begin when Nikola cried out from his bedroom.

"I'll be right back," Anna said as she pushed back from the dining table and headed for Nikola's bedroom.

Viktor dipped his spoon into soup and raised it to his mouth. Nervous and unable to eat, he dropped the spoon back in the bowl and stared at the wall. As Anna returned to the dining table, she noticed that Viktor sat motionless, his attention fixed somewhere far away.

"Viktor, I'm sorry, but I must know what you are worried about. You have hardly said five words since you walked in the door."

"I was able to work in privacy because Senior Sergeant Naumenko broke his leg. That allowed me to be alone in the cipher room all day. I repeated the deciphering process on many of the old messages, but I was only able to find three that provide evidence of the conspiracy. One of the messages indicates the conspiracy is even larger than I first thought."

Viktor unbuttoned his shirt and withdrew the three messages. He unfolded them and handed Anna the message he had just referred to.

"That message proves the conspiracy extends even into the United States," Viktor remarked.

Anna took the piece of paper and quickly read the message.

> *To Grant:*
> *Frank is to tie up with Berger and depending on the circumstances is to make a proposal about working for us or for the corporation. Make contact in Washington with Frank's person to work out arrangements for a meeting. Send coded telegraph with arrangements. Provide 600 dollars for necessary travel. If Frank should be unable to go to U.S.A. contact Bagley for transfer of research details.*
> *Director*

"Who, again, is the corporation?" Anna asked, looking up from the paper.

"According to the list we looked at earlier, that code name refers to the Communist party here in Canada," Viktor answered.

"I remember the names Frank and Director, but who are Berger and Bagley?"

"I do not know those names. I have not seen them in any other messages. Perhaps, they will be on the list. I will grab the stuffed bear from Nikola's toy box. You get the scissors."

Viktor tip-toed into Nikola's bedroom and lifted the stuffed bear from the overflowing toy box and returned to the dining table. Anna was already seated with scissors in hand. She handed the scissors to Viktor as he sat down and laid the bear on the table. After a few quick snips, Viktor spread the seam open and pulled out a wad of folded papers. He separated out the two page list of cover names.

"What is the first name in the message?" he asked.

"The first name is Berger," Anna answered.

Viktor ran his finger down the list, stopped at the line that contained that name, and read out loud the information, "That code name is for William Kincaid. It says he is an American scientist. That's all. There is nothing else for that name. What is the second name?"

"The second name is Bagley."

Viktor moved his finger up two entries and said, "That code name is for Thomas Cain. It says here that he is an electrical engineer and that he is on the National Research Council here in Ottawa."

"Viktor, these are important people. Why would they be talking to people from the Communist Party and why would they want a meeting with scientists?" Anna questioned.

"I suspect they are attempting to gain detailed information about the atomic bomb the Americans have invented."

"This should not be!" Anna barked. "How can free and intelligent people do such things? Do these fools not know the ultimate aim of the Communists is world-wide revolution."

"The Communist Party uses very subtle methods to convince people to join them," Viktor explained. "Once these people have provided classified information to their agents, they are blackmailed and threatened if they even think about leaving the Party. There are stories about some being found murdered."

"What are you going to do?" Anna fretted.

"Karpanov and Sokolovsky are still away from the embassy. I will continue to look at as many messages as I can. Hopefully, I will find more that provide evidence of the conspiracy because I cannot go to the authorities with only three messages. They would never believe me."

Viktor looked at Anna, frustrated and sad that he could not offer her more hope. He reached out and took her hand in his and said, "We must be very careful. I have not looked out the window today, but I suspect they are still watching us."

"What will you do if you do find the messages you are looking for?"

Without giving much thought to the consequences of the thoughts swirling in his mind, Viktor answered, "I am not certain. It will depend on what I find, but we must be ready to leave at a moment's notice. When I come home tomorrow, I will talk to our friend Martin Clavet. I think he would be willing to help us."

"Is it safe to leave the apartment? I need to go to the market tomorrow. We have very little food."

"As long as you are careful. Remember, Sokolovsky's men are watching us. Make certain to look for the car or the man who has been watching us. When I come home from work, we will make a final decision about what we will do next."

Russian Embassy
Cipher Room
Ottawa, Ontario, Canada

Viktor had gone to bed battling terrifying images of standing in front of a firing squad. As the rifles were readied, his precious little Nikola was dragged out and strapped to a pole beside him. He begged the images to stop, but they only became more vivid. Finally, after lying awake for hours, his body gave into exhaustion and he had fallen into a fitful asleep. As a result, he had overslept and had arrived at the embassy an hour later than usual.

Viktor signed into the building, hurried to the dining hall, and poked his head through the door. As expected, his friend, Alexander, was not sitting at their usual table. Deciding to skip breakfast, he headed for the communications center to pick up any newly arrived messages. He pushed the door to the communications center open, expecting to see his friend, Alexander Yakolev, already at work. Surprised, he saw a man he did not recognize standing behind the counter. Identifying the man by the insignia and name plate on his uniform jacket, Viktor said, "Sergeant Dubkov, I expected to see Junior Sergeant Yakolev. He is assigned to the communications desk during the day watch."

"I am Sergeant Jaroslav Yakovich Dubkov," the man announced. "I was assigned here just an hour ago. May I help you?"

"I am Lieutenant Viktor Zakharov, the senior, cipher analyst. I am here to pickup any new messages. Can you tell me what happened to Junior Sergeant Yakolev?"

"Lieutenant Colonel Meliknikov stormed in here early this morning and ordered Junior Sergeant Yakolev to accompany him to his office," Sergeant Dubkov answered. "I heard others talking. They said Lieutenant Colonel Meliknikov yelled something about a man named Pasha Voronin and then something about him working with a man named Yuri Aleksandrov. You know, the cipher clerk that was murdered."

"Yes, I have heard about Yuri Aleksandrov. I was assigned here to replace him."

"They said Meliknikov was very angry. He grabbed Yakolev and dragged him out the door. The man that overheard the yelling said it was something about finding out who else was involved."

"Did he say anything about what they were involved in?" Viktor asked.

"No. The man said everyone is terrified of Meliknikov. He is even more brutal than Colonel Sokolovsky. The man hid in the other room and did not hear anything else. You should not ask about this matter or you will find yourself in Meliknikov's office."

"Yes, you are correct. Are they any new messages?"

"I will check," Sergeant Dubkov said as he turned and entered the restricted area. "Only these three," he announced a few seconds later as he emerged from the restricted area.

Viktor entered the information in the control log and waited for Sergeant Dubkov to verify the entry.

"Everything is in order, Lieutenant Zakharov," Sergeant Dubkov said, handing Viktor the three new messages.

Viktor left the communication center deeply worried. Too many people were disappearing. If his friend, Alexander, broke during Meliknikov's interrogation, he might only have hours before he was the one being dragged to Meliknikov's office. His emotions screamed at him to flee from the embassy with what he had, go to the authorities, and hope they would believe him. Cautiousness convinced him otherwise. He knew the few messages he had would not be enough to convince anyone of the conspiracy. He must find more evidence.

Viktor became increasingly fearful as batch after batch of old messages had failed to produce one single message that referred to the conspiracy. It was as if the conspiracy had suddenly stopped, but he was certain that was not the case.

Glancing up at the clock, he was shocked to learn it was already mid-afternoon. Time was running out. If he did not find something soon, he would have no choice but to go to the authorities with what he had. When they failed to believe him, he would be turned over to the embassy and then he would face a firing squad for certain. "*What will happen to Anna and little Nikola?*" he asked himself. "I must find something. I must," he muttered under his breath as headed for the secure file room for another batch of messages.

TJ's Market
Pretoria Street
Ottawa, Ontario, Canada

As soon as Nikola had awakened from his afternoon nap, Anna had set out for the market to buy some fresh vegetables. Turning left from Bank Street onto Pretoria Street, she began the final two blocks of the long thirteen block walk to the market. It was a beautiful late summer day. The sun was shining brightly, the sky a brilliant, bright blue without a cloud in sight. Several times during the walk, she had stopped, pretending to fiddle with her shoe or a rusty wheel on Nikola's stroller. So far, she had not seen the car that had been parked on their street every night or the man Viktor had described.

Pushing Nikola's stroller, she crossed O'Connor Street, TJ's Market visible just ahead in the middle of the block. Stopping in front of the market, Anna examined the many crates filled with fresh fruits and vegetables that had been set out on display. She bent over, picked up a luscious looking peach, and held it to her nose. "Delicious," she remarked as she grabbed a paper sack from a basket sitting beside the fruit. She selected four of the best looking peaches and dropped them into the sack. Moving down the line of crates, she stopped and studied several varieties of apples. Squeezing several of each variety, she settled on the Cortland variety, because it was more firm and had a sweet, tangy fragrance.

After grabbing another paper sack, she attempted to drop an apple into the sack, but she missed the sack and the apple tumbled onto the ground. She bent over and retrieved the apple. As she straightened up, she saw a flash of dark gray turn the corner onto Metcalfe Street. "*Could it be the same gray car?*" she wondered. Telling herself there were probably hundreds of gray cars in Ottawa, she added three more apples to the sack and walked into the market to continue her shopping.

Thirty minutes later, her shopping complete, she exited the market. Continuing to follow Viktor's advice, she stopped at the far end of the market, sat on an empty crate, and pretended to tie her shoe. Glancing eastward down Pretoria Street, she saw a dark gray car parked along the street with two men leaning against the fender. One of the two men pointed in her direction. The other man shoved the man that had pointed and they both jumped into the car.

Anna grabbed the handle of Nikola's stroller and rushed across O'Connor Street as fast as the rusted wheels would allow. Part way down the block, she stopped in front of a small bakery, looked in the shop's window, and risked a quick glance back toward the market. There it was again. The dark gray car was driving slowly down the street toward her.

"What am I going to do?" she stammered under her breath.

She lifted Nikola out of the stroller and ducked into the bakery. She waited anxiously while a woman with a flour-covered apron finished with the only other customer in the store. Anna watched as the customer picked up a pink cake box from the counter and hurried out of the store.

"I am sorry to ask of you," Anna panted in broken English. "Afraid. I need from you help."

"Are you Russian, from the embassy?" the woman asked, having heard the Russian accent many times before.

"Me, no. Husband work there. Am afraid."

"Why are you afraid?"

"Two men follow me. From market."

"Why are they following you?"

"They beat husband. He not tell them what they want. They will beat me because they angry. Please help. They come soon."

"Quick. Back here," the woman said, pointing at a doorway behind the counter.

Anna ran around the end of the counter and through the doorway with the woman following close behind. The woman stopped at the bottom of a stairway. "Cecil, get down here, NOW!" she hollered. A short, rail-thin man in a stained tee-shirt and dark trousers, held up by wide black suspenders, came racing down the stairs.

"What is it, Louise?" the man asked. "What's all the hollering about?"

"This poor woman says two men from the embassy are chasing her. Grab your apron and watch the counter. If the two men come in looking for her, tell them she came running into the store and ran out the back door."

The man grabbed a long, white apron from a hook beside the door, threw it over his head, rushed through the doorway, and stood behind the counter.

"Quick, up the stairs and be quiet," the woman ordered.

While Anna ran up the stairs, the woman threw open the door to the alley and then ran up the stairs behind Anna. "Take your little boy into the bedroom and do your best to keep him quiet."

Anna did as instructed. Crouched in the corner beside an old iron bed, she dug through her handbag and located a pencil and a scrap of paper. She handed them to Nikola, hoping they would be enough to keep him entertained. She heard loud voices from downstairs.

"We want woman who ran in here," the taller of the two men barked at Cecil. "She is criminal. Escape from embassy."

"Young woman with a little boy?" Cecil asked with a puzzled look on his face.

"Yes, that is woman," the man answered. "We want arrest her."

"She ran in here and right around the counter," Cecil lied. "Before I could stop her, she ran into the back room and out into the alley. Go look for yourself. The door is still standing open."

"Yes. We go look."

The two men rushed around the counter and into the back room. Seeing the door standing open, they rushed out into the alley and looked both ways.

"She could not run that fast, especially with little boy," the taller man said.

"You are right, Major," the other man agreed. "She could not run that fast. The man in the bakery is lying."

"Let's go find out."

The two men walked back into the bakery. Cecil poked his head into the back room as the men returned from the alley. Somewhat frightened by the angry look of their faces, he backed up and retreated to his position behind the counter.

"Why you lie? Woman not in alley."

"I'm telling you, she ran through here and into the alley. You must have missed her."

"She not run that fast. You lie. We make you tell us where she is."

Louise came down the stairs and entered the bakery, hearing the threat the taller man made.

"Why are you threatening my husband?" Louise blurted out. "You are foreigners here. You have no authority here. I will call the police and have you arrested."

The taller man slipped his hand under his jacket, but the other man grabbed his arm and stopped him.

"Woman is right. You must not cause trouble. We must go."

The taller man removed his hand from under his jacket and glared at the couple.

"I will be talking ambassador," the taller man threatened. "If woman is found here, it is you police will be arresting."

Louise and Cecil breathed a sigh of relief as the two men turned and left the bakery. Cecil sat down on a stool, mopped the sweat from his forehead, and asked, "Who is that woman and why did she run into our bakery?"

"She is frightened to death. She said someone at the embassy beat her husband. When he did not tell them what they wanted to hear, they would beat her to learn what they wanted to know. They were going to kidnap her."

"But who is she?" Cecil asked again.

"I don't know. There was not time to ask her. I have heard stories about how the Russian officers treat their people. She seems like a nice woman and she has a sweet little boy. I will go find out who she is and see how we can help her."

"Okay, Louise. I will mind the store while you do that."

Louise left Cecil standing at the counter, tramped up the stairs and into the bedroom, and said, "The men are gone. You need not be frightened."

"They know where we live," Anna whimpered, holding Nikola tight. "Gray car they drive parked outside our apartment every night. They watch us."

"You said they beat your husband. Do you know why?"

"I not know," Anna answered, unwilling to tell a total stranger why they had beaten Viktor. "They not need reason. Officers beat men under them for smallest of things."

"Well, you're safe here. The Russians have no authority outside the embassy. What is your name?"

"My name is Annusuka Goranovna Zakharov, but everyone calls me Anna. Is much easier. Husband's name Viktor."

"And who is this young man?" Louise asked, holding her hand out.

"Name is Nikola. He is one and one-half years. He is good boy."

Anna put Nikola down on the floor. The little boy looked at Louise and back at Anna. She gave the little boy a slight push and said, "это нормально". He tottered over to Louise and let her pick him up. Louise gently set Nikola on her knee and played the "This little pig went to market" game on his bare toes. Nikola giggled hysterically when she tugged on his little toe and said, "Wee wee all the way home."

"Снова. Снова," he giggled.

Louise looked at Anna with a quizzical look on her face.

"He say, 'again, again',." Anna translated.

After ten more times of playing the silly game, Nikola was still giggling. Louise put Nikola on the floor and pointed him toward his mother.

"If those men know where you live, where will you go?"

"I not know," Anna whimpered. "We only know man and woman across hall. Names are Martin and Sylvie. Last name is Clavet, I think. We know no one else. I have nowhere to go."

"You can stay here," Louise said. "We have that extra bedroom. I'm certain Cecil will love playing with Nikola."

"But Viktor come home and not find me. He be much frightened."

"Where do you live?" Louise asked.

"We live apartment on Somerset Street across from park," Anna answered.

"I know where that is," Louise commented. "It's not far from here. I have an idea. I will tell Cecil to deliver some do-nuts to Mister Clavet and then Cecil can tell him what happened and where you are. Mister Clavet can tell your husband when he comes home."

"You would do for me?" Anna choked, a look of surprise on her face.

"Of course," Louise asserted. "I have waited on several Russian officers here in the bakery. They are always rude and insulting. I do not like them."

"I have only little money. I not able pay much."

"There is no need for money. Cecil and I often help people and I'm a sucker for handsome little boys. You no longer
need to be frightened. Come, let's get you settled."

Louise led Anna and Nikola to the extra bedroom and
then showed Anna where the bathroom was. Louise asked if
Nikola would like something to eat. Anna said something in
Russian and then told Louise that Nikola had said he was hungry.

Louise grabbed a pink box off the kitchen counter and set
it on the dining table. Inside the box was an assortment of
cookies and donuts. She flipped open the lid and said, "Own-
ing a bakery, we always have an ample supply of sweet treats
left over. Help yourself to as much as you want. I'll grab some
milk from the fridge."

Louise set a bottle of milk and two glasses on the table
then went downstairs to instruct Cecil to pack a box of donuts
and deliver them to Mr. Clavet on Summerset Street. She told
him to tell Mr. Clavet what had happened and to tell Mr.
Clavet to relay the information to Anna's husband when he
returned home.

Chapter Eighteen

Russian Embassy
Secure File Room
Ottawa, Ontario, Canada

Viktor rushed toward the secure file room to grab as many messages as he could while he still had time. Slowing down as he approached the security guard sitting in the entry room, he walked up to the desk and said, "Good afternoon, Sergeant. I am here to gather one more batch of messages before I finish for the day."

The security guard opened the entry log, positioned it in front of Viktor, and pointed at the bottom of the open page. Viktor entered the time and signed the log. "I will be leaving as soon as I decipher the messages. I will secure the cipher bag in the cipher room and will not be returning. I will lock the file room door and complete the entry log as I leave. So, you may leave if you wish."

"Is that allowed?" the security guard asked.

"The storage unit in the cipher room will be locked," Viktor lied. "I will also lock the cipher room door as I leave and I will be back early in the morning. If anyone questions you, I will advise them I gave you my permission. It will be fine. You may leave."

"Very well," the security guard replied. "If you say it is allowed."

The guard quickly gathered his belongings and hurried out of the room. Viktor rushed into the secure file room and unlocked the safe. Only five new messages remained to be deciphered. He stuffed those into the cipher bag and snatched a group of thirty old messages. After locking the safe, he pulled the secure file room door shut, checking the door to be certain it was not locked. He signed the entry log and rushed back to the cipher room.

He quickly deciphered the new messages and then sorted the old, already-deciphered messages into sequence number groups as he had before. Working furiously, he deciphered the thirty old messages. Unable to believe his eyes, there was not one single message of interest. None of the messages referred to anything remotely related to the conspiracy.

"What am I going to do now?" he gasped.

Perhaps there simply was no more evidence. Had he invented something in his mind simply because he wanted it to be true? NO! There had to be evidence somewhere, but where? The list of traitors and their cover names was not a figment of his imagination.

Frantic and with fading hope of finding the evidence he desperately needed, he rushed back to the secure file room, stopping by the incinerator to destroy the thirty newly deciphered copies. After putting the old messages back in the safe, he locked the secure file room door, pulled it shut, and rattled the door to be certain it was secure. Left with no choice but to go to the authorities with what he had, he trudged down the hallway and started down the stairs. He put his hand on the railing and stopped.

A thought flashed into his mind. *"Either Colonel Sokolovsky had destroyed the old messages or he had hidden them somewhere else."* His last hope was to search Sokolovsky's office and find the evidence he needed. There was a spare key for Sokolovsky's office to be used in case of an emergency. Excited, he turned and started back toward the secure file room, but Viktor's excitement was short-lived. The security department controlled access and had the only spare key to Sokolovsky's office. There would be no way to lie his way into Sokolovsky's office.

About to give into panic, he frantically searched through his mind for another way to gain access to Colonel Sokolovsky's office. He remembered the door to Sokolovsky's office was an original door dating back to the construction of the building. The door's lock was a simple plunger mechanism, which should make it easy to pick, or so he hoped. He reversed direction and rushed back to the cipher room. Digging through the tools he used to setup the cipher machine, he selected a long, thin screwdriver and an alignment tool. He slid the tools into his trouser pocket and flew out the door. Ignoring the pain in his sore leg, a quick sprint down the second floor hallway, up the stairs three at a time, and another sprint down the third floor hallway and he was standing in front of Colonel Sokolovsky's office door.

"What if I get caught breaking into Colonel Sokolovsky's office?" he thought as he lifted the screwdriver out of his pocket. He hesitated for only a second because it really did not matter. There were no other options. The evidence he had was not nearly enough. When Sokolovsky returned and learned he had been ordered back to Moscow, he would be on his way back to Russia within a day. He would never see his beautiful Anna and little Nikola again.

Glancing down the hallway to be certain he was alone, he slid the screwdriver between the door and the jam. The screwdriver's blade stopped short of the plunger, too thick to pass through the narrow gap. Trading the screwdriver for the alignment tool, he eased the tool into the gap and tried to force the plunger back. The point of the tool scraped along the surface of the plunger, but it refused to budge, the narrow gap between the door and the jam restricting movement of the tool. He jammed the screwdriver into the gap and pried against the door, being careful not to mar the surface of the door jam. The gap opened enough that the point of the tool pushed the plunger back out of the way and the door popped open.

He yanked the door open, stepped inside, and eased the door shut as quietly as he could. His heart pounding inside his chest from the fear of getting caught. He stood still listening for sounds of movement. Being late in the afternoon, the light had begun to fade, but he dared not turn on the light. He would have to search quickly in the semi-darkness before the light faded completely.

Tiptoeing around the room he searched through piles of papers on Colonel Sokolovsky's desk, desk drawers, and file cabinet drawers. His search turned up nothing. No messages of any kind. Slowly turning in a circle, he looked for anywhere else he might search. Viktor's shoulders drooped. He had searched everywhere. There was nowhere else to look. Terror began to swell within him as his last hope of finding more messages had failed.

Startled by a shadow passing in front of the frosted glass of the office door, Viktor held his breath and crouched down beside the desk. The shadow stopped directly in front of the door. The door knob rattled as the person shook the door. If the person opened the door, there would be nowhere to hide.

The shadow moved away and Viktor heard footsteps growing fainter. Being past six o'clock, the security guard had started making his rounds. "*What if the guard had come while I was breaking into the office? How could I have been so careless?*" Viktor chided himself. Viktor slowly let his breath out, slid down to the floor, and leaned against the desk, his heart beating wildly in his chest. He sat motionless for several minutes, breathing deeply. Knowing he needed to leave the office quickly, he pushed himself up from the floor and crept over to the door.

Viktor twisted the lock slowly to avoid making any noise. He grabbed the doorknob and turned his head, pressing his ear against the glass to listen for movement, causing him to stare directly at Sokolovsky's closet. Easing his hand off the doorknob, he tiptoed over and pulled the closet door open. An extra uniform and an umbrella hung on the closet rod. Two hats sat on the top shelf. There on the floor against the wall sat Sokolovsky's leather dispatch case. Viktor could not believe it. Sokolovsky never went anywhere without his leather dispatch case. He must have been in a hurry and forgot it when he and Karpanov went out of town.

With renewed hope, Viktor unfastened the leather straps and flipped the top of the case open. The case was crammed with papers. He pulled out several sheets, but was unable to read them in the darkness. Moving over beside the door, he held one of the sheets up in the dim light filtering through the frosted glass.

"Yes," he whispered. "This is what I have been searching for."

Viktor went back to the closet, picked up the leather case, and moved back to the door. Message after message referred in some manner to the conspiracy Viktor had uncovered. He checked several more messages, trying to decide which ones he would take. The sixth message made him stop and draw in his breath. Angling the message for better light, he quickly read the message a second time. He stood there shaking his head, unable to believe what he had just read.

> *To Grant:*
> *There is one great enemy we must yet defeat, and that is capitalism. Everything in the Soviet Union, at least what the regime is doing now, is designed for that single purpose. The Central Committee is secretly preparing for the third world war. To meet this war, we must continue to build in democratic countries, including Canada and the United States, a fifth column, a network of espionage agents and party agitators.*
> *It is critical that you take measures to arrange for acquisition of documentary materials on the atomic bomb! You must obtain technical process, drawings, and calculations. Obtain from Alek information as to the location of the United States Atomic Bomb Plant.*
> *Anyone who violates strict secrecy turn over to Neighbor and see they are never found.*
> *Director*

"How can the leaders of our country do this?" he stammered. "This is not the country I have served."

Rather than take the time to read through all the messages and select individual ones, he decided to take the entire stack. He laid the stack of papers on Sokolovsky's desk, grabbed a handful of random papers, stuffed them into the leather dispatch case, and set the leather case in the closet exactly as he had found it. Standing in front of Sokolovsky's desk, he picked up the stack of messages, estimating there had to be at least one hundred documents in total. He stared at the papers in his hands, and asked himself if he was doing the right thing. Even though he had been planning to smuggle out additional messages for several days, he battled with uncertainty.

Viktor faced the ultimate moral quandary: doing what is right when everything seemed wrong in his mind. Everyone in the embassy and those back in Russia would call him a traitor. He feared his friends would also consider him a traitor. Viktor stood frozen, knowing he and Anna would never again be able to return to their beloved homeland. He vacillated back and forth between his love for his homeland and his duty to the enslaved and exploited citizens in Russia, the millions who had no voice. He felt he had no choice. He had to speak out against the treachery he had uncovered. If he did not take the evidence in his hand to the authorities and the world descended into another world war, millions more would die and he would be responsible for their deaths.

Once he took the documents and left the embassy, Canada would become his home. At the very least, he hoped he would be able to bargain for a better life for himself and his family. One more glance around the office and his decision became final. He shoved the large stack of documents into his pants, tucked his shirt over the stack of documents, and buttoned his uniform jacket. Once he exited the office and pulled the locked door shut, there would be no turning back.

Viktor twisted the doorknob and pulled the door open a tiny crack, listening intently. The hallway was quiet, the only light coming from one lone light fixture hanging from the ceiling near the stairway. Slipping into the hallway, he eased the door closed. The lock clicked into place. There was now no turning back. Hurrying down the hallway, he stopped at the stairway and froze when he heard someone call out his name.

"Lieutenant Zakharov, what are you doing on the third floor?" the duty security guard called out, walking toward him from the other end of the hallway. "You are assigned to the cipher room on the second floor. You have no reason to be here."

"Sergeant Barkov, it is you," Viktor said as the man stopped in front of him. "I assumed you would be able to quit for the day when I released you from the secure file room."

"Captain Bagoran said it was much too early," Sergeant Barkov answered. "He assigned me to the first watch. I will ask you again, Lieutenant. What are you doing on the third floor?"

Viktor fought to control his breathing, leaning forward slightly to prevent the stack of documents hidden under his uniform jacket from showing.

"One of the messages in the last batch I completed was addressed to Colonel Sokolovsky," Viktor lied. "It is marked important. I thought perhaps Colonel Sokolovsky might have returned by now. I came up to check his office."

"Lieutenant, I am certain you are aware no one is allowed on the third floor after hours without approval and then you must be accompanied by a security escort," Sergeant Barkov said with a stern look on his face. "Security protocol says I must report you."

"Yes, I am aware, but I only walked down the hall and right back after I learned he was not here."

"The security protocol is clear," Sergeant Barkov declared, raising his weapon slightly.

"It will not happen again," Viktor promised, hoping it would change the sergeant's mind. "I was only here for a few seconds."

"Because you are a good officer, I will not report you, but just this once."

"Thank you, Mikhail," Viktor responded, using the man's first name. "I will hurry back to the second floor so you do not get in trouble."

Before Sergeant Barkov could say anything, Viktor turned and rushed down the stairs as fast as he could without dislodging the papers stuffed in his pants. Upon reaching the second floor, he slowed his pace and hurried down the stairs to the first floor. He walked up to the embassy's main desk and stopped.

"You are very late, Lieutenant Zakharov," Captain Grigorri Bagoran, the embassy duty officer, observed.

"That is true," Viktor answered. "But this should be the last time. I stayed later than usual and was able to decipher all the waiting messages. Colonel Sokolovsky will be very pleased the backlog has been eliminated."

"You are flushed Lieutenant Zakharov," Captain Bagoran observed. "Are you not feeling well?"

"It must be because I have rushed to complete the last batch of messages. I am in a hurry to get home. My Anna is preparing a special dinner for tonight."

"I am glad for you, Lieutenant. Sign the control log and hurry home to your family."

Viktor scribbled in the time, signed the entry log, bid the captain good evening, and headed for the main entrance. Knowing he would soon become a hunted man, he pushed open the heavy door and crossed the street in the middle of the block. After crossing Heney Street, Viktor half walked, half ran through the park. Stopping at the edge of the park in the cover of the darkness, he looked in both directions to see if he could spot the dark gray car that had been parked near his apartment every night for several days. Not seeing the gray car, he stepped out of the darkness and started down the street.

Out of the darkness, Martin Clavet's blackout Buick turned left from Charlotte Street onto Tormey Street. As the Buick passed Viktor, Mr. Clavet hollered through the open passenger window, "Go to Chapel Street and Rideau Street. I'll wait." The Buick sped by, turned left at the corner, and disappeared.

Viktor continued walking south on Charlotte Street, constantly glancing left and right looking for the dark gray car. At the next intersection, rather than continuing to Laurier Avenue East, his normal route, he turned right onto Rideau Street and increased his pace. As he approached the intersection with Chapel Street he saw Martin Clavet's Buick approaching the intersection from the south. The Buick stopped even with the sidewalk, Viktor scrambled inside, and the Buick sped off, heading north.

During the drive to Louise and Cecil Emerson's Bakery on Pretoria Street, Martin explained to Viktor the reason for the unannounced pickup near the embassy. Martin told Viktor about the two men from the gray car that had attempted to kidnap Anna and Nikola and then how the Emersons had hidden Anna and the little boy when the two men entered the bakery and demanded they tell them where they were. Martin also told Viktor the two men had threatened the Emersons if they learned they were harboring a criminal that had escaped from the embassy.

"Are Anna and Nikola okay?" Viktor asked, fear tingeing his voice.

"Mister Emerson, told me they were fine," Martin answered. "I will take you to them and you will see from yourself."

Chapter Nineteen

Emerson's Bakery
Pretoria Street
Ottawa, Ontario, Canada

Martin Clavet slowed his blackout Buick as he turned left from O'Connor Street onto Pretoria Street. He drove slowly past Emerson's bakery while Viktor watched for the dark gray car. At the next intersection Martin turned right onto Bank Street and drove around the block. In the middle of the block, he turned off Isabella Street and into the alley.

"When I stop behind the bakery, jump out," Martin advised. "Mister Emerson will be waiting for you. If you need anything, he will deliver some bakery goods to me with instructions inside. Good luck, Viktor." Martin stopped the car behind the bakery and shook Viktor's hand.

"I not able to say how much Anna and I owe you," Viktor said as he climbed out of the car and dashed inside the open door leading into the bakery's back room.

"I'm Cecil Emerson," the man said, holding out his meaty hand. "I'm sorry we have to meet this way."

"I am Viktor Zakharov," Viktor answered as he took Mr. Emerson's hand and shook it heartily. "I am most grateful you and your wife have protected my Anna and little boy."

"We are glad to do it. Frequently, we have embassy officers here in the bakery as customers. They are always rude and arrogant."

"Sadly, that is true," Viktor agreed, nodding his head up and down. "May I see my family?"

"Of course. They are in our spare bedroom upstairs. Let me lock up first. Stay here. I'll be right back."

Viktor waited at the foot of the stairway while Mr. Emerson locked up the bakery and turned the lights off. When Mr. Emerson returned, Viktor followed him up the stairs and into the spare bedroom. Little Nikola came running when he saw his daddy walk into the room. Viktor scooped the little boy up into his arms and squeezed him tightly.

Anna rushed over to Viktor and said, "We were so worried. It is very late. I thought you might have been caught looking at Sokolovsky's private messages."

"I'll leave you folks alone," Mr. Emerson said as he backed out of the room. "If you need anything, Louise and I will be in the kitchen."

"Thank you for your kindness," Viktor responded. Viktor watched as Mr. Emerson pulled the bedroom door shut. He turned toward Anna and said, "No, I did not get caught. I went through all the messages in the safe and found nothing. Sokolovsky and Karpanov have not yet returned to the embassy, so I decided to look in Sokolovsky's office to see if I could find the evidence I need."

"Viktor, you should not take such a risk," Anna protested. "If you were to be caught, they would have you executed."

"It was after hours and it is forbidden for anyone to be on the third floor. I knew it would be deserted and I would not be seen. Sokolovsky's office door is old and I was able to quickly defeat the old lock."

Anna shuddered, thinking about what would have happened to Viktor if he had been caught. She watched as Viktor unbuttoned his uniform jacket and pulled the large stack of documents out from his pants. She asked, "Did you find *all those* in Sokolovsky's office?"

"Yes. I was about to give up and leave his office when I noticed a closet door. When I looked inside, I found Sokolovsky's personal, leather dispatch case sitting against the wall. I have never seen him leave it unattended. He must have forgotten it when he left the embassy. The case was crammed full with these messages."

"Did you find the evidence you need to convince the authorities there is a conspiracy?"

"That and much more," Viktor exclaimed. "I stood there in Sokolovsky's office with these papers in my hand uncertain I could continue. As I stood there, I felt as if I would be a traitor to our beloved homeland. I even thought about putting them back in the dispatch case."

"What changed your mind?"

"Partly the lies and treachery I have discovered that is occurring here, but mostly what is in this one message," Viktor answered as he handed Anna the top sheet from the stack of papers.

Anna quickly read the short message and looked up at Viktor, her reaction changing from shocked horror to bewilderment to anger. She shook her head and asked, "Who is the *Director*?"

"From what I have been able to learn, that is the Military Intelligence Headquarters in Moscow. They answer directly to the Central Committee."

"How can they believe this?" Anna quavered, the paper shaking in her hand. "How can the leaders of our country believe another world war would be good? Have they gone mad?"

"I asked myself those same questions," Viktor sighed. "I have no answers. To deliberately start another world war would be utter madness. I believe our leaders have become blinded by their own ambitions and desire to rule the world."

"Why would they want another world war?" Anna asked.

"I have heard devoted members of the Party say they really wish for it. They say they believe it to be a necessary part of a process that would create a general upheaval throughout the world which would allow them to then establish Communism everywhere."

"Viktor, they must be stopped before they can do this terrible thing," Anna exclaimed, handing the paper back to Viktor.

"I agree. I will go to one of the local newspapers with some of the documents. I will expose what is going on."

"The newspapers?" Anna said, a bewildered look on her face. "Why would you not go to the police?"

"The police are not to be trusted," Viktor asserted. "It is almost certain that the N.K.V.D would have infiltrated the police. If that were the case and I went to them, they would immediately turn me over to the embassy. I cannot risk that. In order to try to improve my understanding of English, I have read articles in the *Ottawa Journal*. I was surprised by how they openly criticized the government. The writers say that they search for the truth. I believe they will be eager to see what I have discovered."

"But, Viktor, these papers are in Russian. They will not be able to understand and they will not believe you."

"I will point out words and tell them what they mean. I will make them understand."

"When will you do this?"

"I believe I should go yet tonight while it is dark and before Colonel Sokolovsky discovers the papers are missing."

"How will you do that? Do you know where the newspaper is located?"

"I do not know. Perhaps Mister Emerson would know where the newspaper is located and then he could take me there."

"But, Viktor, they have done so much for us already. Is it right to ask them to take such a risk?"

"There is no other choice. Maybe Martin Clavet could help, but it would not be safe to walk there. The men that tried to kidnap you will be watching the bakery. I would probably not make it more than a few blocks before they grabbed me. I will go talk with Mister Emerson."

With a resigned look on her face, Anna nodded her head and went back to playing with Nikola. Viktor left the bedroom and walked into the Emerson's kitchen. Louise saw Viktor walking into the kitchen and punched her husband on the arm.

Mr. Emerson turned toward Viktor, pulled out an empty chair, and motioned for Viktor to sit down.

"What can I do for you, Viktor?"

Viktor hesitated, not knowing how much he should reveal to Mr. Emerson. The Emersons had already taken a huge risk when they hid Anna and Nikola. He had told Anna he had no other choice, but he battled internally, wondering if it was proper to involve them even more?

"I can see that something is troubling you," Mr. Emerson observed. "You can tell me. Louise and I have talked and we agree we are *not* going to turn you over to those men no matter what."

"I am most grateful for your help," Viktor said. "What I have to tell you is most serious. If I tell you, it will put you in great danger."

Seeing the look of deep concern on Viktor's face, Mr. Emerson faced Viktor directly and said, "Out with it. We cannot help you if we do not know what the problem is."

"I have uncovered a conspiracy between high-ranking officers at the embassy and important people in Canada. They provide secret military information to Russian agents."

"Do tell, and how do you know this?"

"I am embassy cipher analyst. I decipher all inbound message traffic and sometimes outbound messages also. I have seen many documents proving much spying. Just tonight, I leave embassy with big stack documents stuffed under shirt. I also have document that lists secret cover names Russians use and real person's name each one refers to."

"Where do you have these documents?"

"They in bedroom with Anna. Mister Clavet pick me up near embassy. I come straight here."

"Is that why those two men were so anxious to grab your wife and child?"

"No, that not reason. My superior officer, Colonel Sokolovsky, is away from embassy. Nobody will yet know documents are missing."

"What do you intend to do with the papers?"

"I go to newspaper. They will listen and then they will expose them."

"You should go to the police," Mr. Emerson suggested. "If what you say is true, they can at least arrest the Canadians. The embassy personnel have diplomatic immunity. I do not believe the police can arrest them."

"No, No police," Viktor protested. "Russia has secret police, called N.K.V.D. They work here in secret. Is common for to infiltrate local police. I not trust police. They would turn me over to embassy. I would be executed."

"Okay, no police," Mr. Emerson responded. "Which newspaper are you going to?"

"I think *Ottawa Journal*. I try read some. Try improve English. They criticize the government. They will be eager to learn what I know."

"How are you going to get there?" Mr. Emerson asked. "The *Journal* is on Baxter Road. It must be at least six or seven kilometers from here."

"I know is big favor," Viktor answered sheepishly. "I hope you would take me."

"I don't know," Mr. Emerson wavered, a strained look on his face. "Louise and I are willing to protect you here in our home, but to do what you ask has a great risk."

"I know is great risk," Viktor agreed. "I know no one else. I have no other choice. When Colonel Sokolovsky returns to embassy, he will discover missing documents. They will come here looking for me. They will not care you protest. I must do tonight."

"I will call the police. I will have…."

"You not understand," Viktor interrupted. "These men are expert assassins. Are unfeeling and vicious. They come in the night. If you not give what they want, they kill you and family."

"I don't know," Mr. Emerson wavered, unconvinced he should risk getting caught with a Russian defector carrying stolen documents.

"I not want show you this. This bigger than spying. Russian officers want more war."

Viktor slipped the document he had shown Anna from under his shirt, unfolded it, and handed it to Mr. Emerson. He watched as Mr. Emerson looked at the short message, waiting for his reaction.

Mr. Emerson looked up at Viktor with disbelief clouding his face and said, "I can't read this. You say Russia wants more war? Surely that can't be true. I can't believe they would actually do this."

"Yes, is very true," Viktor countered. "I hear many officers at embassy say they hope for this. Back in Russia many thousands of people tortured and murdered for slightest offense. Communist party knows *only* desire for world domination. Two of men on list of secret names are atomic scientists. They are providing information on how to make bomb. You must believe me before is too late."

Mr. Emerson sat there silently, looking into Viktor's face. The idea of another world war seemed unthinkable. He could not believe the Russians would really push for another war. Viktor waited. When Mr. Emerson did not respond, Viktor shared the hideous events he had witnessed in Königsberg, not leaving out a single gruesome detail. Anger flared in Viktor's voice as he told the Emersons how the commanding general had authorized rape and looting as a reward to the Russian soldiers.

"That is sickening. How could soldiers do such things," Mr. Emerson gasped when Viktor finished.

Mrs. Emerson dug a handkerchief from her apron pocket and wiped tears from her face, shaken by the story of horrible brutality Viktor had recounted. She laid her hand on her husband's shoulder and sputtered, "Cecil, I believe what Viktor says. You must help him get this information to the newspaper. This madness must be stopped."

"Yes, I have to agree," Mr. Emerson concluded. "Viktor, are you going to take all the messages?"

"No, just this one and a few others."

"Go grab what you need. Hurry, we must do this quickly while there is still someone on duty at the newspaper."

Viktor scrambled out of his chair and hurried into the bedroom. As he picked through the stack of messages, picking out those he wanted to take, he explained to Anna that Mr. Emerson had agreed to take him to the newspaper.

"Where do we hide the rest of the messages?" Anna asked.

Having been in the Emerson's home for less than two hours, Viktor had no idea where to hide the stack of messages. He rushed back into the kitchen with the stack of messages in his hand and asked Mr. Emerson if he knew of a good place to hide the messages. Before Mr. Emerson could respond, Mrs. Emerson suggested he wrap them in an oil cloth and hide them in the flour bin down in the bakery.

"That's a great idea," Mr. Emerson blurted out as he kissed his wife on the cheek. "Viktor, you go say goodbye to Anna while I go hide the messages. Meet me downstairs in the back room."

Mr. Emerson plucked the stack of messages out of Viktor's hand and headed for the stairs. Viktor turned and hurried back into the bedroom. He hugged Anna and told her how much he loved her. He kissed her, turned, and rushed out of the bedroom, headed for the bakery's back room.

Viktor waited in the back room for several minutes before Mr. Emerson rushed in, brushing flour off his arms. He instructed Viktor to wait while he backed the bakery's panel van, used for deliveries, up to the back door. Mr. Emerson lifted a white apron off a hook beside the door, dropped the neck band over his head, looped the ties around his back, and tied them. He exited the bakery into the alley and climbed into the old panel van. Mr. Emerson stomped on the old van's starter, but the engine refused to start. After several unsuccessful attempts, he switched the ignition off, mashed the accelerator pedal twice, turned on the ignition, and stomped on the starter again. The old engine chugged, blew a cloud of bluish-black smoke out the exhaust pipe, and rumbled to life.

Mr. Emerson revved the engine several times, shoved the transmission into reverse, and backed up till the van's rear doors were even with the door leading into the bakery. After setting the parking brake, he slipped the transmission into neutral, climbed out, and walked around to the back of the van. He opened the rear, double doors, propped them open, and entered the bakery's back room.

One block away in the alley behind a closed business, on the other side of O'Connor Street, a dark gray car sat idling with its headlights off. Having noticed the back door of the bakery swing open and a man walk out, the driver raised a pair of binoculars to his eyes, peering intently in the direction of the bakery.

"Someone got into the van and backed it up to the bakery's door," the man said to a second man sitting in the passenger seat.

"What is he doing?" the other man asked.

"He is parked so close to the building I cannot tell," the driver answered.

In the bakery, Mr. Emerson picked up two large cake boxes and handed them to Viktor.

"Viktor, take these," Mr. Emerson instructed. "We will go out the door sideways. Be sure your feet stay lined up with mine. When we get behind the van, throw the boxes in and climb in. Lay down on the floor. No one will be able to see you. I will come back in and get some more boxes to make it look like I am making deliveries."

Viktor took the boxes and positioned himself even with the door. Together they sidestepped through the door and stopped behind the van. Viktor tossed the boxes inside, climbed in, and laid flat on the floor as he had been instructed. Mr. Emerson, slammed the van's rear doors closed, went back into the bakery, and grabbed two more cake boxes. Holding the cake boxes with one hand, he exited the bakery and pulled the door closed. He walked to the front of the van, placed the cake boxes on the passenger seat, and climbed in.

Mr. Emerson released the parking brake, shifted the van into gear and drove slowly down the alley. At O'Connor Street, he turned right, drove half a block, and turned left onto Strathcona Street, heading toward *The Ottawa Journal*, their destination.

"What are they doing?" the passenger in the dark gray car asked.

"A man put some boxes in the back and also in the passenger seat," the driver answered. "I only see one man. It looks like he is going out to make some deliveries. Do we follow him?"

"Yes, follow him," the passenger replied. "It seems rather late to be making deliveries. I do not trust him. We will see where he is going."

The driver put the car into gear, drove down the alley, turned left onto O'Connor Street, and switched his lights on. After turning onto Strathcona Street, the driver followed the bakery's van. Being careful to stay at least one block behind the van. The traffic on the streets was light, making it easy to keep the van in sight.

As Mr. Emerson turned right from Strathcona Street onto First Avenue and headed east, Viktor cautiously eased his head up and watched behind the van to see if they were being followed. Not long after the van passed the intersection with Lyon Street, Viktor saw a pair of headlights turn onto First Avenue. He continued watching as the car passed through the light from a streetlamp. The car was dark gray. Just like the car Anna had described. Viktor knew that could not just be a coincidence.

"I think men from embassy following us," Viktor hollered. "Dark gray car turned onto street behind us. Turn right next intersection. Find place to hide."

Mr. Emerson did as instructed. He sped up, turned right onto Percy Street, then left onto Glebe Avenue. In the middle of the block, he spotted a large building on the left. Just past the building, he turned into a parking lot, parked the van beside a large truck, and turned the lights off. Viktor watched the street to see if the car continued to follow them.

A few second later Viktor saw the dark gray car speed by the parking lot. He had been correct. The men from the embassy were following them.

"The dark gray car just drove past," Viktor announced. "They have been following us."

"What should we do?" Mr. Emerson asked. "Would they suspect we are going to the newspaper?"

"No, I do not think so," Viktor replied. "They would have no reason to think that. They will probably go to our apartment and wait there. Do you know a different way to get to the newspaper?"

"Yes. There are many ways to get there. I will drive south for a while and then head toward the newspaper."

Mr. Emerson started the van, pulled out of the parking lot onto Glebe Avenue and continued east. At the intersection, he turned left onto Bronson Avenue, heading south. He drove south for nearly two kilometers. Confident the men were no longer following them, he turned east and headed toward their final destination.

The Ottawa Journal
Baxter Road
Ottawa, Ontario, Canada

After thirty-five minutes of left turns, right turns, narrow streets, driving down alleys, and doubling back to avoid being followed, Mr. Emerson pulled the bakery's van up in front of the *Ottawa Journal*. Viktor opened one of the rear doors and jumped out. He trotted around to the driver's side and tapped on the window.

"I go inside," Viktor said. "Who I speak to?"

"Ask for the night editor."

"Who night editor?"

"He is the one who manages the news department after hours."

"You go now. You have done enough. I will see if one of paper's employees take me back to the bakery."

"Not on your life," Mr. Emerson objected. "What if they don't believe you? They might call the embassy. If that happens, you would need to get out of here in a hurry. I refuse to leave you here alone.

"I not believe you do this for me," Viktor exclaimed, grasping Mr. Emerson's hand tightly. "You good friend, Mister Emerson."

"Go quickly before the men from the embassy show up. I will find a place to park the van. I will drive up here to the front of the building when I see you coming out of the door."

Viktor ran around the front of the van. Not dressed for the late summer chill in the air, Viktor shivered as he hurried up the steps and yanked open the front door to the newspaper. Once inside the building, Viktor looked left and right trying to locate the night editor. The signs on the various doors were meaningless to Viktor. Viktor could speak some English, but still had much difficulty reading English.

He saw a young man carrying a stack of papers in his hand emerge from one of the doors and hurry down the hallway toward him.

"Where night editor?" Viktor asked as the man passed him.

"Go up the stairs at the end of the hallway, then turn right. It's the first door on your right," the young man called out as he continued down the hallway, disappearing through a large swinging door. Viktor sniffed the air that escaped from the room the young man had disappeared into, trying to identify the strange mixture of smells. Of the combination of newsprint, ink, solvents, and machine oil, the aroma of machine oil was the only one familiar to him.

Viktor walked down the hallway, located the stairway, and scurried up the steps two at a time. He turned right and stopped in front of the first door. Staring at the word *Bullpen* painted on the frosted glass panel, he mistakenly assumed it said 'Night Editor'. He knocked lightly and waited. Receiving no response, he knocked again, more forcefully than the first time.

"Come in," a male voice yelled from the other side of the door.

Viktor twisted the doorknob and walked into the room. Startled, he found himself standing in a large room filled with desks pushed together front to back, less than half of which were occupied due to the late hour. Several of the men closest to the door looked up as Viktor entered the room and quickly went back to work. Viktor stood frozen, not knowing what to do. After several minutes, one of the older men punched a young freckle-faced young man on the arm and said, "Andrew, go find out what the gentleman wants."

The young man, who could not be a day over seventeen, rolled his chair back, stood up, and walked over to where Viktor was standing.

"May I help you, sir?"

"Are you night editor?" Viktor asked.

"No. I'm Andrew Welch, the night office boy," the young man replied. "I write up the obits that come in during the day."

"Obits?" Viktor repeated, a puzzled look on his face. "Not know word *obits*".

"Do you speak English?"

"Yes, only little."

"Okay. Obits is short for o-bit-u-ar-ies," the young man pronounced the word slowly. "They come in from funeral homes when someone dies. They describe how the person lived their life and who their relatives are."

"Oh, death notices. I know that. We have back in Russia. I need speak night editor."

"The night editor is down in the lunchroom, but he won't talk to you unless you have an appointment. Tell me what you need and maybe I can direct you to someone that can help you."

"I have paper," Viktor sputtered, his English becoming more broken due to his nervousness. "Much spying. Russia want war."

"Russia doesn't want war," the young man laughed. "The war is over. Why would they want war?"

"Is true," Viktor insisted. "I have paper."

"Show me the paper."

"No. Only night editor," Viktor demanded, becoming agitated. "Must be private. Russia have spies everywhere."

"I assure you there are no spies here, Mister…. What is your name?"

"Not tell you name. Spies everywhere. Men follow me. Must speak night editor, now."

Mark Hall, the night city editor, annoyed by the increasing volume of the discussion between Viktor and Mr. Welch, looked up from his typewriter. He stared at the two men, wondering what all the commotion was about. Pushing himself back from his desk, he rose and started toward the two men.

"Hang on Mister," the young man said. "The night city editor is headed this way. Maybe he can help you."

Mr. Hall walked up and looked Viktor over. Viktor presented a less than inspiring appearance. Standing there in borrowed clothes from Mr. Emerson that were old, worn, and two sizes too small for him, Viktor looked like one of the crackpots that showed up at the paper on a regular basis with some cockamamie story that almost always turned out to be false.

"What's going on Andrew?" Mr. Hall asked.

"This gentleman's English is very poor. He is saying something about spying and that Russia wants war."

"The war is over," Mr. Hall scoffed. "Russia doesn't want war. What does he know about spying?"

"He claims he has a paper, but he won't show me. Says he must speak to the night editor."

"Can you show me the paper you're talking about?" Mr. Hall asked Viktor.

"You night editor?" Viktor asked.

"No. I'm the city editor," Mr. Hall answered. "The night editor is away from his desk. Most of the news stories go through me, so I should be able to help you."

"No," Viktor protested. "I speak night editor and must be private."

"Andrew, where is Morrison?" Mr. Hall asked the young man.

"He went down to the lunch room about twenty minutes ago."

"Go down to the lunchroom and tell him someone in the bullpen is demanding to speak with him."

Viktor listened intently to the exchange between the two men, trying to determine what they were saying. He watched as the young man exited the bullpen headed for the stairway.

"Wait right here," Mr. Hall instructed. "Andrew is going down to get the night editor."

"Yes. I speak night editor."

Mr. Hall returned to his desk and resumed his typing while Viktor stood waiting for Andrew to return with the night editor. Several minutes passed. Viktor turned and faced the door when he heard it open. Andrew held the door open for Mr. Roger Morrison, the night editor. Mr. Morrison glanced at Viktor and had the same reaction as Mr. Hall had.

"I'm the night editor," Mr. Morrison announced. "What's this about spying and Russia wanting war?"

"I have paper," Viktor asserted for the third time. "It show much spying."

"May I see this paper?" Mr. Morrison asked.

"Not here. Need private. Russia have many spies."

"I don't know," Mr. Morrison said. "I'm very busy. I thought I could handle this quickly."

"You must read," Viktor pleaded. "Is much important."

"Okay, I'll give you five minutes. Follow me."

Mr. Morrison turned to his right and crossed to the far side of the bullpen, stopping in front of a door labeled *Morgue*. He held the door open and motioned for Viktor to enter. He followed Viktor into the room and pulled the door shut.

"Sit," Mr. Morrison said pointing at an empty chair on the opposite side of a long conference table. Mr. Morrison shoved a stack of old issues of the *Journal* aside, sat down across from Viktor., and said, "Now, what is it you want to tell me?"

"I have paper," Viktor repeated. "Much spying. Russia want war."

"The war is over. We are not at war with Russia and we do not expect a war with Russia. In fact, Canada's relationship with Russia is quite normal. You must be mistaken."

"No, you not understand," Viktor insisted. "I have paper. You must see."

"Show me," Mr. Morrison said, holding his hand out.

Viktor fished out two messages from under his shirt, un-folded them, and handed them over. Mr. Morrison quickly read the first message then slid it behind the other sheet of paper and read the second message. He looked up at Viktor and shook his head.

"These are in Russian. I can't read them," he said as he handed the messages back to Viktor. "Where did you get these and what makes you think they indicate spying?"

"I decipher," Viktor replied, pointing at the papers and holding them out toward Mr. Morrison. "I am cipher person at embassy. Names on paper not real. Is…. Is…. You call *cover*."

"Do you mean cover names?"

"Yes, Viktor agreed, nodding his head. "Is cover names."

"How do you know that?"

"I discover list. Is English Shows real names."

"Do you have the list?" Mr. Morrison asked.

"No. Not have list. Is hidden."

"I told you I can't read these. How would I know they show spying?" Mr. Morrison said as he pushed the papers back toward Viktor.

"You must read," Viktor begged, handing him the mes-sage that talked about Russian wanting war.

Mr. Morrison looked at the message and laid it on the ta-ble. He shook his head and said, "I can't do anything with these. There is no reason Russia would want another war. I really can't help you."

Viktor started to protest, but Mr. Morrison held up his hand to stop Viktor. "I'm sorry, but even if I believed what you have is what you say it is, you don't need a newspaper. This would be a matter for the police."

"No," Viktor barked. "Russia secret N.K.V.D. everywhere. No go police. Not trust police. If arrest me, I go back Russia. Face firing squad."

"If you won't go to the police, the only other thing I can suggest is to go to the Crown Attorney's office," Mr. Morrison responded. "Maybe they have someone who can read Russian. If you want it so the Russians can't pick you up, you need to get naturalized."

"What mean naturalized?"

"Naturalized means you become a Canadian citizen. At the Crown Attorney's office you fill out a form requesting Canadian citizenship, but it's after hours and the office will be closed for the day. You could go to the Department of Justice and describe your problem. They are not far from here. I suggest you take your papers and go talk to them. I will have Andrew escort you out. He can give you directions on how to get to the Department of Justice."

Mr. Morrison got up from his chair and held the door open for Viktor. Viktor was dumbfounded, having been certain the newspaper would believe him and be eager to print his story. What would he do now? He could not go to the police. They would turn him over to the embassy. Viktor rose from the chair and just stood there, paralyzed by fear.

"You must believe," Viktor begged. "All I say is true."

"Sir, you need to come with me. I'm sorry but I can't help you."

Viktor's face filled with dread as he shuffled toward the door.

"Sir, your papers," Mr. Morrison said, pointing at the messages laying on the table.

Viktor walked over to the table, picked up the papers, folded them, and stuffed them under his shirt. Crestfallen, he trudged along behind Mr. Morrison to the other side of the bullpen and waited while Mr. Morrison talked with Andrew Welch. Andrew grabbed Viktor's arm and ushered him out of the bullpen and into the hallway.

"Hey Mark, what was that all about?" one of the night copy writers asked, "Was he another one of those drunks from the Bell Claire Hotel with some crazy story?"

"He certainly had a crazy story," Mr. Morrison replied. "But he's not a drunk. I had trouble understanding him. Russian, I think. Claims he has uncovered spying and that Russia wants to start another war."

"We certainly get some crazy people coming in here," the copy writer laughed, returning his attention to the half-completed article on his typewriter.

Andrew Welch walked down the stairs with Viktor and directed him to the main door. Andrew poked his head out the door and described the way to get to the Department of Justice. Viktor heard the words but he really did not listen. He plodded down the steps to the sidewalk.

Mr. Emerson had parked a block away, waiting for Viktor to emerge from the newspaper building. When he saw Viktor exit the building, he started the van, shoved the transmission into gear, and pulled up to the front of the building.

"Get in," he shouted at Viktor.

Gripped by images of being dragged in front of a firing squad swirling in his mind, Viktor stood frozen on the sidewalk, having not heard Mr. Emerson holler at him again. Mr. Emerson leaned over and shoved the door open. The door banged Viktor in the leg, breaking his trancelike state. He climbed into the van and pulled the door shut.

"Well, how did it go?" Mr. Emerson asked.

"They not believe me," Viktor stammered. "Say he not believe documents."

"They didn't believe you? What are you going to do now?"

Viktor, staring straight ahead, said, "Man I talk to say go to crown office or something of justice. He say not far."

"Did he say the Crown Attorney's office or the Department of Justice?" Mr. Emerson asked.

"Man say both."

"Why did he mention the Crown Attorney's office?"

"He say if I ask Canadian citizenship, Russians not be able pick me up."

"I don't know if that is true, but it doesn't matter. The Crown Attorney's office will be closed, but somebody should be at the Department of Justice. They are both in the same building. It's only a few kilometers from here. I'll take you there."

"Is no matter," Viktor groaned. "They also not believe me. Soon, I go back Russia. Is firing squad for me."

"Viktor, you can't just give up," Mr. Emerson urged. "If they do not believe you, we will try someone else."

Viktor did not respond. He sat emotionless, staring out the windshield with a defeated look on his face.

Chapter Twenty

Department of Justice
Wellington Street
Ottawa, Ontario, Canada

Following the same procedure as he had during his drive to the *Ottawa Journal*, Mr. Emerson had followed a random route as he drove to the Justice Building on Wellington Street, arriving twenty minutes after leaving the newspaper. Mr. Emerson let Viktor out of the van and told him he would find a place to park and wait for him.

Viktor looked up at the gray, stone, nine-story building, the top floors disappearing into the darkness. With no real hope in his heart, he lumbered slowly up to the door and pulled on the handle, but the door would not open. It was locked. Cupping his hands against the glass, he peered inside. All he could see was a deserted hallway bathed in dim light. About to give up and go look for his friend, he noticed a button to the left of the door. He looked at the printing above the button, but had no idea what it said. With nothing to lose, he reached out his hand and pressed the button. Impatient, he pressed the button again.

A shaft of bright light spilled out into the dim hallway and a man appeared. The man turned and headed for the door where Viktor stood waiting. Dressed in a dark blue uniform, the man pulled a large ring of keys from a clip on his belt, unlocked the door, and pushed it open a crack.

"It's late. What do you want?" the man asked, obviously annoyed by the interruption.

"I have paper," Viktor announced. "Is much spying. I must speak someone important."

"Spying. What are you talking about?"

"Papers I have say Russia want war."

"Russia is not at war with Canada," the man scoffed. "The war has ended. You need to be on your way."

"You not understand," Viktor exclaimed. "Canadians are spying. Give Russia agents much…. much…. uhh…. details."

"You're not making any sense," the man protested. "You need to leave. Come back tomorrow."

Viktor shoved his hand under his shirt and withdrew the documents, holding them out toward the man. Becoming insistent, Viktor pleaded, "Must listen. Officers at embassy lie. I cipher person. Message on paper say Russia want war. Have proof."

"I said you need to come back tomorrow."

"пять минут!" Viktor blurted out in frustration, slipping into Russian.

"Huh, I don't understand what you are saying."

Realizing he had spoken in Russian, Viktor held up five fingers and pointed at the clock hanging on the wall behind the man.

The man glanced at the clock on the wall and said, "Five minutes? You want five minutes. Is that what you said?"

Viktor frantically nodded his head up and down.

"Follow me to the security office. The assistant deputy minister notified me he would be in the building working late. I will check and see if he is still here."

The man pulled the door open and waited for Viktor to enter. After locking the door, he tapped Viktor on the shoulder and said, "This way."

The man walked to the open door where the light spilled out into the hallway and waited for Viktor to enter the security office. He directed Viktor to a chair and told him to wait. Seated behind a wooden desk, the man lifted the earpiece off a black, candlestick phone, pressed it to his ear, clicked the hook switch several times, and waited.

"Justice Department. Number please," the night phone operator answered.

"Jenny, this is Albert in Security," the man announced into the phone. "Ring up the assistant deputy minister and see if he is still in the building. Call me back in the security office and let me know."

Albert Green, the on-duty security guard, dropped the earpiece back onto the hook switch and turned toward Viktor. "Coffee?" he asked, pointing at the coffee urn sitting on a table against the wall. Viktor shook his head, clutching the papers tightly in his hand. Mr. Green grabbed a coffee cup from a shelf above the coffee urn and filled it half full. He sat down behind the desk and blew across the hot liquid. Several minutes passed. Viktor jumped when the phone on the desk rang.

Mr. Green snatched the earpiece and said, "Albert Green, Security," He listened for a few seconds, then answered, "That's great. Connect me please."

"Assistant Deputy Minister Turner," A voice in the earpiece answered. "Who is this?"

"Sorry to bother you sir. This is Albert Green, the security guard. I have a gentleman in my office that rang the night bell. I really think you should talk to him."

"I don't have time. I was just on my way out when the phone rang."

"But this may be important. He has some papers he says are important."

"I don't care. It is late and I am ready to leave for the day. He will have to wait until tomorrow."

"I really think you should talk to him. He says he has papers that prove Canadians are spying for the Russians."

"What? Say that again."

"He says Canadians are giving information to Russian agents."

"Who is he?"

"Claims he's a cipher person at the embassy."

"Have you seen these papers?"

"I have seen them, but I have not read them. He is holding them in his hands. He seems very agitated and frightened."

"Okay. Bring him up, but it better be quick."

Mr. Green placed the earpiece back on the hook switch and waved his arm at Viktor. "Come on. Let's go. The assistant deputy minister said he would see you."

Heartened by the news that someone would see him, Viktor jumped up from the chair and followed Mr. Green out into the hallway.

"The stairs are this way," Mr. Green said, motioning for Viktor to follow.

Viktor followed Mr. Green to the end of the hallway and hurried up the stairs behind him. The two men arrived on the third floor, panting from the quick dash up the stairs. Halfway down another dimly lit hallway, Mr. Green stopped in front of a door labeled Assistant Deputy Minister of Justice and knocked on the glass.

"Enter," a raspy voice called out from the other side of the door.

Mr. Green pulled the door open, guided Viktor inside, and announced, "Sir, this is the man I told you about."

Seated behind a gleaming mahogany desk, Mr. Ian Turner, the Assistant Deputy Minister of Justice, looked up, surprised by the sloppily dressed man standing in front of his desk. Infuriated that the security guard would bother him with such a lout, he glared at Mr. Green and said, "Mister Green, why did you bother me with this man? You know better than to let any old bum off the street in the building after hours."

"But sir, he claims to have papers from the embassy that prove Canadians are spying for the Russians."

"Look at him," Mr. Turner snapped. "Get him out of here."

Viktor, concerned by the man's outburst, looked at Mr. Green and asked, "What wrong?"

"Mister Turner does not like the way you are dressed," Mr. Green answered, tugging at Viktor's shirt sleeve. "He thinks you are a bum."

"No, not bum. Not mine," Viktor wailed. "I borrow from man at bakery. He hide wife and child. Officers at embassy try kidnap them. I not go out in uniform. I borrow from Mister Emerson."

"Why would Russian officers want to kidnap your family," Mr. Turner asked Viktor.

"For punish me," Viktor responded. "I not tell them what they ask. They beat me." Viktor unbuttoned the cuff of his left shirt sleeve and pushed it up beyond his elbow then unbuttoned the top four buttons of his shirt and held it open. "See. Russian officers trained good at beating so not show."

Mr. Turner stood, leaned forward over his desk, and stared at the ugly bruises covering Viktor's flesh.

"Sir, I think you should listen to what he has to say," Mr. Green said.

"Okay, I'll listen, but I only have a few minutes. Mister Green, will you wait outside please." Mr. Turner sat down in his leather office chair. Pointing toward a leather side chair sitting in front of his desk, he asked Viktor to sit. "What is your name and where do you live?"

"Name is Viktor Zakharov. Me, wife Anna, and little boy, Nikola, live in apartment. Somerset Street."

"Exactly what do you do at the embassy?"

"I cipher person. Decipher messages from Moscow. Sometime also messages go to Moscow."

"Mister Green said you had papers that show spying."

"Yes, have these," Viktor said as he handed two sheets of paper across the desk. "Have many more. Mister Emerson hide in safe place."

Mr. Turner looked at the two messages and laid them on the desk. He looked at Viktor and said, "How do I know these prove someone is spying. I can't read these papers. They're written in Russian. Do you have anything else?"

"Have this," Viktor answered, handing the message that talked about Russia wanting another world war across the desk. "Communist Party want this." Viktor asserted. Mr. Turner shook his head and laid the message on top of the others. The expression on his face did not change, adding to Viktor's fear that the justice department would also not believe him.

"I see you not believe papers," Viktor said.

"Well, it is a rather hard story to believe. I'm not convinced Russia would want another war. The papers you have would need to be translated. You can't prove it is the Canadians that are giving information to the Russians?"

"Russians use cover names. Have big list. Is English. Many names. Shows who each name is. Have also other papers."

"Do you have any of the other papers with you or, perhaps, the list you mentioned? I need to see something I can read before I could believe what you are telling me."

"Not have now. Is hidden."

"You said you have other papers. How many do you have?"

Viktor thought for a moment, trying to remember the English words for numbers. Unable to pull the words from his mind, he pointed at a pencil cup sitting on the corner of Mr. Turner's desk. Mr. Turner nodded his head. Viktor grabbed a pencil from the cup, turned over one of the sheets of paper, and wrote the characters: 1-0-0.

"You say you have that many papers hidden."

"Yes, Mister Emerson hide."

"Who is this Mister Emerson?"

"He bakery man. Bring me here."

Mr. Turner sat back in his chair and stared at Viktor, unable to believe the wild tale he had just told him. He pushed the papers toward Viktor and shook his head. He could not sound an alarm with no evidence.

"Well, I'm sorry," Mr. Turner told Viktor. "I really can't do anything based on papers I can't read. It's well after business hours and everyone else is gone for the day. I believe this is a matter for the Department of External Affairs. I'm afraid you will have to come back tomorrow when the Under-Secretary is in. If you bring the list and the other papers with you, maybe he will be able to help you."

Resigned to his fate, Viktor rose slowly and turned toward the door. Halfway to the door, he stopped and looked back at

Mr. Turner. "Tomorrow may be dead. If not, I come back. Bring more papers." With sagging shoulders, Viktor left Mr. Turner's office and pulled the door shut.

"Well?" Mr. Green asked as Viktor exited the assistant deputy minister's office. "Was Mister Turner able to help you?"

"He say not help. Not read Russian. He not believe me. Say come back tomorrow."

"I'm sorry, Mister Zakharov," Mr. Green said. "I'll escort you out of the building."

Viktor shuffled along behind Mr. Green, fearing what would happen to him and his family when Colonel Sokolovsky discovered the documents were missing. He had no reason to think anyone would believe him even if he did come back tomorrow with additional papers. "**Бюрократы делают только то, что хорошо для бюрократов**," Viktor muttered in Russian as he followed Mr. Green down the hallway.

"Did you say something?" Mr. Green asked.

"Not important," Viktor responded.

Mr. Turner sat motionless behind his desk, disturbed by the bruises Viktor had shown him. He had heard stories about the brutality of the Russian officers at the embassy, but he had always thought they were just that — stories. "*Well, even if it's true, there isn't anything I can do about it,*" he told himself.

He lifted his jacket off the coat rack in the corner of his office, slipped it on, picked up his briefcase, and headed for the door. He put his hand on the doorknob and stopped. Unable to convince himself he should just do nothing, he turned around and walked back to his desk. He picked up the earpiece from the phone, tapped the hook switch twice, and waited for the night operator to answer.

Emerson's Bakery
Pretoria Street
Ottawa, Ontario, Canada

After climbing into the Emerson Bakery's van, Viktor had described his fruitless meeting with the assistant deputy minister. During the rest of the trip back to the bakery, Viktor had not uttered a word. Sitting unmoving, Viktor had simply stared expressionless out the windshield.

Nearing the bakery, Mr. Emerson drove slowly around several blocks adjacent to the bakery looking for the dark gray car. Seeing nothing suspicious, he parked the van in the alley behind the bakery and Viktor and Mr. Emerson entered the bakery through the back door. At the top of the stairs, Anna had been pacing back and forth, worried about her husband and how long he had been gone.

"Viktor," Anna exclaimed as he reached the top of the stairs and stepped into the Emerson's kitchen. "You have been gone so long. I was afraid you had been caught."

"The man at the paper did not believe me, so we went to the Justice Department," Viktor moaned. "But the justice minister did not believe me either. Anna, what do we do now?"

"How could they not believe you? You have the papers that prove there is spying."

"They could not read the papers because they are in Russian. My word is not enough proof of spying. The justice minister say I should come back tomorrow."

"Why did he say come back tomorrow? What would be different?"

"The justice minister told me to bring other papers and the list."

"The list? You mean the list with all the names on it? The one we hid in Nikola's stuffed bear?"

"Yes, that is the list. It is written in English. He want to see the names."

"Let's go get the list right now."

"No. It is not safe. The men from the embassy, the ones that tried to kidnap you, may follow us."

"They followed you?" Anna sputtered, a look of shock on her face. "What happened?"

"Mister Emerson pulled into a parking lot before they did could see us. Then he made many turns and took different streets. We did not see them again. I think they went to our apartment and watched for us there. We will have to wait. We will go to the apartment during daylight."

Viktor noticed the Emersons looking at each other with puzzled looks on their faces. "Sorry," Viktor said. "I speak Russian to Anna. Is hard to tell in English. I tell her about car following us and man at paper and minister at justice not believe me."

"What are you going to do?" Mr. Emerson asked.

"I take papers. Go apartment during light. Get list man want. Then ask neighbor take me to justice building."

"I'm really sorry they did not believe you. When was the last time you had something to eat?"

"Busy. No eat since morning."

"Louise," Mr. Emerson shouted at his wife sitting in the living room. "This poor man has not eaten since this morning. Can you throw something together quickly?"

"I'd be glad to," Mrs. Emerson answered as she rose from the couch and headed for the kitchen.

Mrs. Emerson dug around in their refrigerator and pulled out what leftovers she could find. After heating the leftovers up, she added a thick slice of fresh bread and placed them on the table in front of Viktor.

"I'm sorry," she said, with a tinge of embarrassment in her voice. "That's all the leftovers we have."

"Not be sorry," Viktor remarked, "Is much food. Would be feast back in Russia."

Had it not been for the generosity of the Emersons, Viktor would likely not have eaten, nagged by the fear that the justice minister would not believe him even after he saw the other papers and the list of cover names. Deeply worried by the growing danger threatening to overtake him and his family, he picked at the food and did his best to make it appear he enjoyed what had been placed before him.

Noticing Viktor's nervousness, Mr. Emerson bent over and whispered in his wife's ear. During the rest of the meal, the Emersons alternated asking about Viktor's life and family back in Russia. Viktor began to relax as he recounted his days as a little boy on the small family farm. He described how their life had been hard but satisfying until the October Revolution occurred. The resulting Bolshevik Land Decree, written by Vladimir Lenin, ordered the confiscation of all land without compensation of any kind. The Zakharov family farm ceased to exist, becoming the property of the state. With sadness and more than a little anger, Viktor told how they were *allowed* to remain on the farm, but everything produced on the farm was taken by the state. In return for their hard labor, they were doled out meager rations barley enough to feed one person let alone a hungry family.

Viktor's countenance brightened as he told how his papa adamantly demanded Viktor attend school so he could get a good education and escape the back-breaking life of a Russian peasant. Viktor continued his narrative up to the point a high-ranking official noticed his potential and had him sent to a special school. Viktor yawned as he finished his story.

"I can see you are tired," Mr. Emerson observed. "I would like to hear more, but you need to get some sleep. Tomorrow will likely be another tiring day."

"Yes, am quite tired," Viktor agreed. "Thank you Misses Emerson for kindness and great food."

"We are glad we can help," Mrs. Emerson bubbled. "We have already fallen in love with little Nikola. I have taught him to say a few English words." She took Viktor's hand in hers, patted it, and said, "You are like the family we never had. We will not give you up to those Russian bullies."

Mr. Emerson nodded his head in agreement and patted Viktor on the shoulder. "Now go get some sleep."

Viktor smiled and turned away before the Emersons could see the tears welling up in his eyes.

As Viktor walked into the bedroom, Anna noticed a tear running down Viktor's cheek. "Viktor, what is the matter?" she asked.

"The Emersons say we are like family," Viktor choked. "I cannot believe how total strangers take us in and treat us so well. If only I can get an official to believe me about the spying."

"Come to bed, Viktor. You look like you are exhausted."

Viktor slipped out of his borrowed clothes, letting them drop on the floor right where he stood. He climbed under the covers, kissed his beautiful Anna, and laid his head on the pillow. Despite the heart-wrenching disappointment of the day and the fear building in his heart, in a few short minutes, Viktor drifted off to sleep.

Crown Attorney's Office
Wellington Street
Ottawa, Ontario, Canada

After a hearty breakfast and too many day-old donuts, left over from the bakery, Viktor and Mr. Emerson had set out for the Crown Attorney's office. Mr. Emerson, having already been at work for several hours preparing fresh baked confections for the Bakery's early morning customers, kissed his wife and told her where he and Viktor were going. While bouncing little Nikola on her hip, she had watched as the two men disappeared down the stairs.

During the drive to the justice building, Viktor had seen no sign of the dark gray car that had attempted to follow them the previous evening. Mr. Emerson pulled up to the justice building's main entrance and pulled a small notepad from his shirt pocket. He wrote the name of the office in block letters on a blank page, tore off the page, and handed it to Viktor.

"There will be a big board on the wall just inside the main entrance," Mr. Emerson advised. "Locate the office I wrote on that piece of paper. The board will tell you the floor and office number where the office is located. I will park somewhere and wait for you."

"Thank you. I hurry," Viktor said as he climbed out of the van and headed for the main entrance.

Inside the building, Viktor looked left and right trying to locate the board Mr. Emerson had mentioned. A security guard noticed the bewildered look on Viktor's face and walked up to Viktor.

"You look lost," the guard said. "Can I help you find something."

"Need go here," Viktor answered, handing the man the piece of paper.

"The Crown Attorney's office is on the fourth floor, office number four-one-two. Follow me. I'll escort you to the elevator."

Viktor followed the security guard down the hallway. The two men stopped in front of an emerald green door with shiny brass, vertical accents. The guard punched a button beside the door and waited. Several seconds later the outer door slid open.

"Henry, take this gentleman to the fourth floor and point him toward office four-one-two."

"Step inside, sir," the elevator operator said.

Viktor took a tentative step inside and stood against the back wall of the elevator car. Having never been in an elevator before, he felt as if he had walked into a closet. He watched as the operator slid the outer door closed and then slid the accordion, safety door closed. The operator grabbed the handle of the control rheostat and rotated it to the right. Viktor staggered and pressed his hands against the wall, surprised by the heavy feeling as the elevator began to rise. There was a jerk when the operator moved the rheostat control back to the neutral position.

The operator slid the accordion, safety door open then the outer door. "Watch your step," he advised as Viktor stepped out of the elevator. "Go down the hallway to the left.

It's the third door on the right. Once you're inside, ask for Mary Coulson. She's the Crown Attorney's secretary."

The elevator operator waited as Viktor walked down the hallway and stopped in front of the third door on the right. When he saw Viktor reach out for the doorknob, he closed the doors and answered the latest call for his services.

Viktor entered the office, walked up to an elbow-high counter, and waited. Seated on the other side of the counter, an impressively-dressed woman with the whitest hair Viktor had ever seen sat with a telephone receiver cradled between her shoulder and her left ear. Busy writing on a pad of paper, she did not notice Viktor standing at the counter. Several minutes passed as she continued to write. She flipped the page over and continued writing. After nearly filling another page, she said goodbye and placed the receiver back on the phone.

Out of the corner of her eye she noticed someone standing at the counter. She rose from her chair, crossed the short distance to where Viktor stood, and said, "I'm sorry sir. I was busy on the telephone and didn't see you standing there. Is there something I can help you with?"

"Yes, need see Crown Attorney," Viktor replied. "Want apply Canada citizenship."

"Mister Emory, the Crown Attorney, is not here," she advised. "He just left. He is due in court to present indictments to the grand jury. I'm afraid he will be tied up all day, but that really doesn't matter. You must fill out an application before you can apply for Canadian citizenship."

"Not know application. How I get?"

Realizing the man standing in front of her would not be able to fill out the application without help, Mrs. Coulson waved at a woman working at an adjacent desk. "Jean, can you watch the counter and the phone while I help this gentleman." She pulled a form from a shelf below the counter and said, "Follow me."

Mrs. Coulson directed Viktor to an unoccupied office, instructed him to sit at a small table, and closed the door. She sat in a chair on the opposite side of the table from Viktor.

"What is your name?"

"Name is Viktor Sergeyevich Zakharov."

"Do you live in Ottawa?" she asked, as she wrote Viktor's name on the form.

"Yes. Live apartment on Somerset Street."

"First, I need to determine whether we can accept your application. Do you have your landed-immigrant card?"

"Not understand."

"To be a landed-immigrant, you have to come from outside Canada and have legally entered Canada, or 'landed', at one of Canada's designated ports of entry."

"Yes, I land at Canada. Arrive on large ship then take train to work at embassy."

"You say you work at an embassy?" Mrs. Coulson asked, looking up at Viktor.

"Yes. I cipher person at Russian embassy."

"That's not the same as a landed-immigrant," she explained. "You have to apply and be approved for entry into Canada. Have you done that?"

"No," Viktor answered. "Sent here by Russia to work at embassy."

"We won't be able to accept your application for citizenship."

"What?" Viktor groaned.

"Even if you had applied to be a landed-immigrant, you have to have been a landed-immigrant for one year before you can file a declaration of intent to become a Canadian. Then you have to wait an additional four years before you can apply for citizenship."

"Take five years," Viktor gasped. "But I live apartment here. I live Canada."

"By the law's definition, you really don't live in Canada. The Russian embassy provides your apartment, so, according to the law, you are actually considered to be living on Russian soil."

"No, no more. I leave last night. I not go back. Have many papers prove spying. I want defect. Have wife and small child. I need protection."

"What do you mean you left last night?" Mrs. Coulson asked.

In broken English, repeating the same story he had explained to the *Ottawa Journal* and the assistant deputy minister at the Justice Department, Viktor explained that as a cipher analyst he had learned that many Canadians were spying and giving information to Russian agents and that he desperately needed protection.

Mrs. Coulson shook her head and said, "I'm sorry. I can't accept your application for citizenship. If you need protection, you would need to go to the police."

"Nobody listen," Viktor moaned, putting his face in his hands. "Russia spying but nobody believe. "

"What do you mean?" Mrs. Coulson questioned. "Please explain."

"Have papers under shirt," Viktor offered, pulling the papers out from under his shirt and holding them out toward her. "I decipher myself. Prove much spying. Russian officers want more war. Please look."

Mrs. Coulson took the papers and scanned them. She looked up at Viktor with a confused look on her face and said, "These are in Russian. How do you know they want war?"

"Hear officers talk at embassy. Many say want world war."

"Russians wanting another war is hard to believe," she said. "That would be insane." She looked at the first two sheets of papers again and added, "How do you know any of these people are Canadians? All the names here are only first names."

"Are cover names. Have paper with list. Shows real names. Many important Canada people."

"May I see it?"

"Not have here. Is hidden."

"There's just not enough here to disturb the Crown Attorney. You should take this to the police. If you…."

"Not explain more," Viktor blurted out. You not believe. Nobody believe. I leave."

"Maybe you could come back tomorrow and bring more papers."

"Not come back. Men look for me. They will kill me."

With a look of defeat on his face, Viktor stood up, pushed his chair back, and left the small office without another word. He rushed down the hall toward the elevator and stopped in front of the door. He saw the word *Stairs* at the end of the hall. Knowing what the word meant, he decided to not wait for the elevator. He pushed the stairway door open and rushed down the steps. At the first floor, he exited the stairway into the main hallway. Slowing his pace to avoid arousing attention, he walked briskly to the main entrance and exited the building.

Standing on the sidewalk, he spotted Mr. Emerson in the van and waved anxiously at him. Mr. Emerson started the van, pulled up to the spot where Viktor stood, and waited for him to climb into the van.

"Well?" Mr. Emerson asked, looking over at Viktor.

"Take five years become Canada citizen. They not believe about spying. Nobody believe. Go back bakery."

"I'm really sorry," Mr. Emerson said as he put the van in gear and steered the van into traffic.

Neither man said another word as they drove back to the bakery. Mr. Emerson let Viktor out by the bakery's back door and then parked the van. When Mr. Emerson entered the bakery and climbed the stairs into their living area, he learned from his wife that Viktor had gone directly into the bedroom and had closed the door.

Viktor described the five year requirement to apply for Canadian citizenship to Anna. As he recounted his third failed attempt to get someone to believe him, he became more agitated with each sentence. Anna hugged her husband, knowing there were no words to relieve his worry. She, too, was deeply worried, especially for their little Nikola.

What Anna and Viktor did not know was that after Viktor had stormed out of the justice building, Mrs. Coulson had stayed seated at the table in the small office for a long time thinking about her encounter with Mr. Zakharov. She had not said anything to Viktor, but she was deeply troubled by his statement about Canadians spying for the Russians. She also had seen great fear in Viktor's eyes when he said he needed protection. Viktor's last words, *"They will kill me."* had repeated over and over in her mind. Something inside her would not let her just ignore the poor, frightened man. She had told herself she had to do something.

"Papers," she had exclaimed. "He said he had many papers."

Mrs. Coulson had scrambled out of the chair and rushed back to her office. After lifting the phone receiver up and placing it against her ear, she tapped the hook switch twice and waited for the operator to come on the line.

Chapter Twenty-One

Russian Embassy
Colonel Sokolovsky's Office
Ottawa, Ontario, Canada

Late in the afternoon Major Karpanov and Colonel Sokolovsky walked into the colonel's office, having returned from their trip out of town.

"Have a seat, Major," Colonel Sokolovsky said, pointing at a chair sitting in front of his desk.

Colonel Sokolovsky opened the closet, grabbed a coat hanger, and hung up his uniform jacket. He picked up his leather dispatch case, walked over to his desk, and laid the dispatch case on the desk.

"We need to discuss some of the latest telegrams I have received from Moscow," Colonel Sokolovsky said as he unbuckled the straps on the dispatch case. "What is this?" he bellowed as he pulled out the stack of miscellaneous papers Viktor had stuffed into the case.

"What is wrong, Colonel?" Major Karpanov asked.

"These are not messages," Colonel Sokolovsky yelled. "They are just routine papers. Someone has stolen my private messages. Major, go down to security and get the guard up here. NOW!"

Major Karpanov leaped out of his chair and ran out the door. Colonel Sokolovsky slammed his fist on the desk, snatched the papers, and hurled them into the air. The papers swirled and floated in the air, scattering in disarray across the floor. By the time Major Karpanov returned with the security guard in tow, the colonel was seething. Major Karpanov shoved the guard in front of the desk and backed away. Sergeant Mikhail Barkov came to attention and stood waiting for an expected tongue lashing. Sergeant Barkov grew more fearful as Colonel Sokolovsky rounded the desk, grabbed his arm, and turned him to face the colonel.

Colonel Sokolovsky grabbed Sergeant Barkov's tie and pulled him to within a few inches of his face and screamed, "Sergeant Barkov, my private messages have been stolen. Who has been in my office?"

"Sir, no one has been in your office," Barkov stammered, swallowing hard. "The master key is kept in the security office. No one could have entered."

"Well, do those look like messages?" Colonel Sokolovsky raged, yanking the sergeant forward until he fell forward, landing on his knees on top of the scattered papers.

"Colonel, I swear I allowed no one into your office."

"Well, someone has to have been in my office, or, perhaps, it was you that stole the messages."

"I did not. No one…. Wait….,"

"Out with it, Sergeant," Colonel Sokolovsky demanded, raising the riding crop he always carried.

"I remember one evening after hours I found Lieutenant Zakharov in the third floor hallway."

"That is not allowed. Why didn't you arrest him?"

"But sir, he is a lieutenant and he said he had an important message for you and he had only checked to see if you might be in your office. I had no reason to not believe him."

"You imbecile," Colonel Sokolovsky roared as he swung the riding crop and slammed it across Barkov's face.

Sergeant Barkov wailed and grabbed his face. Colonel Sokolovsky kicked Barkov in the ribs. Barkov cried out in pain and fell over onto the floor.

"Major, get this miserable dog out of my office. Take him to the security office and place him in chains. Inform Captain Bagoran this imbecile is to be demoted to private. He is to be sent back to Russia and is to be assigned to the lowest form of duty available. Then, go to the cipher room and bring Zakharov to my office."

"Yes, sir Colonel," Major Karpanov acknowledged as he grabbed the moaning Barkov and dragged him out of the office. "I will return quickly and then we will discuss what we shall do to Zakharov."

After Karpanov left the office, Sokolovsky, shaking with anger, gathered up the scattered papers and placed them on his desk. As he waited for the major to return, he paced angrily back and forth in front of the window, deciding what punishment Zakharov should receive.

Colonel Sokolovsky heard the door to this office open. He turned around, saw that Major Karpanov was alone, and asked, "Major, where is Zakharov?"

"There was no one in the cipher room. I checked with the main desk and was told Zakharov has not signed in today. I also checked the dining hall and the communications center. No one has seen him."

"Well Major, it seems there is little doubt Zakharov is the one who stole my private messages. Take two men you trust and go to his apartment. Find him and do whatever it takes to make him tell you where the messages are."

"Yes, Colonel. I will take two of my best men."

As Major Karpanov twisted the doorknob, about to exit the office, Colonel Sokolovsky stopped him, leaned close to him, and spoke quietly. "Once you retrieve the messages, kill him and then kill his family. Make sure they are never found."

Office of the Prime Minister
Langevin Block Building
Ottawa, Ontario, Canada

In a lavishly decorated third-floor office of the Langevin Block Building, a telephone rang. The building's richly detailed exterior, had been constructed in the Second Empire style, with distinct traces of Romanesque influence. Situated opposite Parliament Hill, the Langevin Block Building served as the home of the Privy Council Office and the Office of the Prime Minister. The three-and-a-half story building's, limestone pavilion, designed for its visual impact, consisted of rows of round arched windows and a copper, four-sided gambrel-style roof. The building's impressive architectural and ornate design testified of the importance of what occurred within its walls.

Sam Billingsley, the Prime Minister's private secretary, rushed out of the inner office and picked up the ringing telephone.

"Prime Minister's office. May I help you?"

"Mister Billingsley, this is Mary Coulson of the Crown Attorney's office. I know you are close friends with Mister Emory. I have a distressing issue I thought you might be able to help me with."

"I am very busy," Mr. Billingsley advised. "You will have to be brief."

"A gentleman, a Russian from the embassy, walked into our office a few minutes ago," Mrs. Coulson began. "It was obvious he was quite frightened. He told me he is a cipher person. He showed me papers he claimed proved there are Canadians spying for the Russians. He claimed one of the papers said the Russians want another world war. I think someone should talk to him."

"Another world war," Mr. Billingsley scoffed. "You can't be serious."

"I saw the documents," Mrs. Coulson insisted. "He said he deciphered them himself. Even though I couldn't read them, they certainly looked real."

"How many documents did he show you?"

"He showed me three documents."

"Three documents," Mr. Billingsley mocked. "That's all he had?"

"Yes, he only had three with him, but he said he had more."

"And who did those three documents supposedly come from?"

"The documents I saw indicated they came from someone called Director. The documents used cover names. He said he has a list that shows who the cover names really are and there are many important Canadians on it."

"Did he show you this list?"

"No. He said he has it hidden."

"I don't have time for this. Three documents does not make a conspiracy. The Russians are...."

"But Mister Zakharov said he had many more papers," Mrs. Coulson interrupted.

"Did this Mister Zakharov say he was going to bring the other papers to show you?"

"No. He was quite agitated and frightened when he left," Mrs. Coulson confided. "At the time I wasn't sure I believed him. The last thing he said as he was leaving was that men from the embassy were looking for him and they would kill him. I can't get the terrified look on his face out of my mind." She waited for a response. After a long pause, she said, "Mister Billingsley, did you hear me?"

"Yes, I heard you," Mister Billingsley answered. "Misses Coulson, as I was about to say before you interrupted me earlier, the Russians are our allies. I would not consider insulting them by accusing them with so little evidence. I'm certain the Prime Minister would agree."

"But Mister Billingsley, the poor man said they were going to kill him."

"Misses Coulson, do you want to listen to some good advice?"

"What good advice would that be?" Mrs. Coulson grumbled.

"Have nothing more to say or do with this man. If he comes back, send him away. I hate to be short with you, but I have more important business to attend to." Mr. Billingsley hung up without saying another word.

Mrs. Coulson pulled the receiver away from her ear and stared at it, annoyed that Mr. Billingsley had hung up so abruptly. She depressed and released the hook switch then quickly tapped it twice. Placing the receiver back to her ear, she waited for the operator to come on the line.

"Number please," the switchboard operator drawled.

"Betty, this is Mary Coulson in the Crown Attorney's office. Get me the city editor at the *Le Droit Journal* please."

"One moment please."

Mrs. Coulson listened to the faint hum and clicking sounds as the telephone system completed the necessary connections. The city editor answered and listened politely as Mrs. Coulson repeated the story she had told Mr. Billingsley, the Prime Minister's personal secretary. The city editor said that while it was a disturbing story, they could not possibly touch a story with such flimsy evidence. He thanked her for thinking of him and quickly hung up before she could protest.

"That poor man may not be alive tomorrow," she moaned out loud. She sat replaying her encounter with Mr. Zakharov in her mind, remembering the defeated look on the poor man's face as he had rushed out of the room. There was not any reason for him to lie. "*What could he expect to gain*," she asked herself. If there was even a shred of truth to what he said, she had to get someone to listen.

Startled from her musings, she reached out to pick up the ringing phone. Before she could answer, she heard the irate voice of the Mr. Billingsley, the Prime Minister's secretary.

"Misses Coulson, listen very carefully to what I am about to say," Mr. Billingsley warned. "Your earlier phone call about the man from the embassy; forget it. And the meeting with him as well."

"But Mister Billingsley…."

"If you want to remain employed, forget it ever happened," he threatened. "It *did not* happen. None of it. Do I make myself clear?"

"Yes, sir," she answered as the line went dead. She pulled the receiver away from her ear, placed it back on the phone, and sat staring at the phone.

"I most certainly will *not* forget!" she sputtered. "He can threaten all he wants."

Her frustration had quickly changed to anger. "*I have to do something*," she told herself. Refusing to be deterred, she reached out, picked up the receiver, and jabbed at the hook switch. As soon as the operator came on the line, she nearly shouted, "Betty, get me Inspector Haines." Furiously drumming her fingers on the desk, she waited, upset that she could get no one to believe her.

Zakharov Apartment
Somerset Street
Ottawa, Ontario, Canada

After spending several hours playing with Nikola, Anna and Viktor talked about what they should do. Anna finally convinced Viktor that he had nothing to lose by going to the police. Viktor decided to set out for his and Anna's apartment to retrieve the hidden list of cover names, hoping the true identity of the Canadians that were spying would persuade the authorities to believe him. Intending to walk the thirteen blocks to the apartment, he kissed Anna goodbye and started for the stairs. As Viktor stepped out of the bedroom, he met Mr. Emerson coming up the stairs.

"And where are you going?" Mr. Emerson asked, blocking Viktor's path.

Viktor argued and tried his best to dissuade Mr. Emerson from putting himself further at risk by driving him to the apartment. Ultimately, Viktor conceded to Mr. Emerson's refusal to take no for an answer. He followed Mr. Emerson downstairs and out the back door to the bakery's van.

While Mr. Emerson drove, Viktor stared out the back windows of the van, looking for any sign of the dark gray car.

Two blocks from Viktor's apartment, Mr. Emerson slowed down and asked, "Any sign of them?"

"No sign. Not see gray car anywhere."

Mr. Emerson turned left off Kent Street onto Somerset Street and drove the last two blocks to the apartment building. As he drove up to the building's back door, he said, "I have several deliveries to make. I'll be back in a few minutes. I'll meet you across the street in the park when I return."

"I wait by swing," Viktor said as he climbed out of the van and ran for the back door.

As Viktor disappeared into the apartment building, a black car turned off Bay Street and drove slowly into Dundonald Park. The man in the passenger seat looked at the driver and said, "The van from the bakery just stopped behind Zakharov's apartment building. I saw somebody jump out and run into the building. What should we do?"

"Zakharov is alone," the driver answered. "His family must still be at the bakery. He must have come here to get something. Perhaps he has hidden the missing documents somewhere in his apartment. We will go to the apartment and make him tell us where the papers are. Once we have the papers, we will go to the bakery and arrest his family. If necessary, we will kill the bakery owner and his stupid wife."

Viktor crept up the stairs slowly, listening for any sounds. He reached the second floor landing and hurried down the hallway to the door of their apartment as quietly as he could, the key already in his hand. He unlocked the door, stepped inside, and eased the door closed.

Breathing heavily from the fear of getting caught, he stopped, waiting for his eyes to adjust to the dim light in the apartment. Deciding not to turn on a light and possibly signal his presence, he stumbled through the apartment in the semi-darkness. He tripped over one of Nikola's toys that had been left lying on the floor, banging his head against the table beside the couch as he went down. Groaning and rubbing the throbbing knot growing on his forehead, he pushed himself up from the floor and continued into the bedroom. Throwing toys aside, he dug through Nikola's toy box until he came to the stuffed bear.

Laying the stuffed bear aside, he gathered the scattered toys and threw them back into the toy box. With the stuffed bear cradled under his arm, he made his way back to the front door. He eased the door open a tiny crack, held his ear to the crack, and listened. All was silent. He stepped out into the hall and pulled the door closed. As he reached the stairs, he heard a muted squeak from the floor below. The third step from the bottom of the stairs had loose nails and always caused an annoying squeak when stepped on. All the apartment residents had become familiar with the loose step and always skipped over it when using the stairs. Assuming it must be strangers, Viktor drew back from the stairs, leaned against the wall, and turned his ear toward the stairway. Muffled voices filtered up the stairwell. Concentrating on the voices, Viktor was able to make out a couple of words. Terror gripped Viktor's heart. Russian. Whoever was climbing up the stairs, was speaking Russian.

"The men from the embassy must have been waiting. What do I do now?" Viktor's flight response screamed. The stairs provided the only access to the first floor. He could not go back to the apartment, knowing that was the first place they would look, but he was trapped with nowhere else to go. He rushed back toward the apartment. About to slide the key in the door's lock, Viktor heard Mr. Clavet's excited voice behind him.

"Viktor, quick. In here."

Clutching the little stuffed bear, Viktor pivoted on his foot, rushed across the hall, and slipped inside the Clavet apartment. The three men reached the top of the stairs just as Mr. Clavet pushed his apartment door closed and twisted the lock. Panting from running and fear, Viktor leaned against the inside of the door, hoping the men would just knock and then leave. He sucked in his breath and stood still, listening. He and Mr. Clavet heard footsteps come down the hall and stop across the hall.

One of the men banged on the door with his fist and called out, "Zakharov, open up. We know you are in there." After waiting a few seconds, he banged harder on the door again and yelled, "Open up. If you do not, it will go badly for you." The man turned and looked at their leader.

Edwin Manning, a corporal in the Royal Canadian Air Force, who lived adjacent to the Clavets opened his apartment door and poked his head out, concerned about the ruckus going on across the hall. "What's going on over there?" Mr. Manning shouted.

"Is not your business," The leader barked. "Go back in apartment."

"It is my business," Mr. Manning responded, stepping partway into the hall. "We have a sick baby and all that pounding is going to wake her up."

"Shut up. Not care about baby. Go back in."

"I will not….," Mr. Manning started, interrupted when his wife Nadia tugged at his arm.

"Come inside, Edwin," she cautioned, "I know who these men are. Do not argue with them."

"What are you talking about," Edwin asked as Nadia forcefully dragged him back inside their apartment.

"I said I know who these men are," she warned. "One day I was shopping with friends and Tatyana, whose sister works at the Russian embassy, recognized them and pointed them out. The tall one's name is Karpanov. Everyone says he is an extremely violent and cruel man. You must not anger him."

"You speak Russian," Edwin said. "Listen and see if you can make out what they are saying."

Nadia pulled the door partway closed, leaving it open a tiny crack, and listened.

"Kick it in," the leader ordered, seeing the Manning's apartment door close. "We must find the missing papers quickly. We will grab Zakharov. His wife and son must be at the bakery. If we have to, we will kill the owners and grab Zakharov's family. Once we have the papers, we will kill them all."

One of the men kicked the door just below the doorknob, applying all his one-hundred and five kilos. The door jamb split, sending wood splinters flying across the floor.

"Inside quick," the leader barked. "Grab Zakharov, then search the apartment."

"I heard Karpanov say something about missing papers," Nadia told Edwin. "He told the other men they would grab Zakharov and his family. He told the other two men when they had some papers, they would kill them all."

"What?" Edwin exclaimed. "The Zakharov's are such nice people. Why would they kill them Nadia, we can't let them do that!"

Edwin rushed over to a small table in the corner of the room and reached for the phone.

"Stop," Nadia hollered. "Do not use the phone. There are several Russians that work at the embassy living here in the building. They might be listening to the phones."

"I have to do something. I can't just let this happen." Edwin paced back and forth across the living room a couple of times then stopped. "I know," he exclaimed.

Edwin eased the door open and stuck his head out. Seeing the hallway empty, he ran quickly to the stairs, raced down to the first floor, and flew out the back door. He leaped on his bicycle and took off as fast as he could pedal.

Inside the Zakharov apartment, one of the men had kicked the splintered door closed. As he entered the apartment, the leader had pulled a Browning Hi-Power, Pistole 640(b) out from under his jacket and waited for the other two men to search the apartment. The two men searched the bedrooms and rushed back into the living room. One of the men shouted, "He's not here."

"How can that be?" the leader exploded. "We saw him run into the building. Tear this place apart. Find those papers."

One of the men scurried into the bedroom while the other pulled a knife out of his pocket, flicked it open, and began slicing open the furniture. The man in the bedroom yanked drawers out of an old dresser and dumped them onto the floor, spreading the contents across the floor with his foot. Turning his attention to the toy box, he kicked it over and pawed through the various toys.

He flipped the ratty mattress over, carefully inspecting the seams for evidence they had been opened. Angry at not finding anything, he flipped the bed frame over on top of the mattress. "There is nothing in the bedroom," he announced as he ran back into the living room.

"I will go check the apartment across the hall. Perhaps they have seen Zakharov," the leader said. "One of you search the other bedroom and the other search the kitchen. Wait here till I return."

The leader pulled the broken door open, crossed the hall, and stopped in front of the Clavet's apartment door. Seeing movement in the light streaming in under the door, Mr. Clavet held his fingers to his lips, pushed Viktor toward the bedroom, and whispered, "Under the bed. Don't make a sound."

Viktor tiptoed past a large china cabinet on his way out of the living room and into the bedroom. Clutching the stuffed bear tightly under his arm, he scrambled under the bed.

Hearing a loud knock on the door, Mr. Clavet steadied himself and pulled the door open. "May I help you," he asked, looking up at the pinched, animal-like features of the tall man's face. Mr. Clavet took a step backward as his gaze settled downward and he noticed the menacing weapon in the man's hand. "You can't bring guns into this building," Mr. Clavet gulped, uncertain it was wise to challenge the man.

"I from Russia embassy," the man thundered. "Need weapon. Look for criminal who steal papers. Name is Zakharov. He live in apartment other side hall. We see him run in building. You see him?"

"No, I have not seen the Zakharovs for several days," Mr. Clavet replied. Trembling, he called out to the kitchen, "Sylvie, have you seen the Zakharovs?"

"Not since yesterday," Sylvie answered from the kitchen. "Misses Zakharov went to the market, but I have not seen either of them since."

"I not believe you," the man snarled, raising the weapon toward Mr. Clavet. "He run in building. He here somewhere."

"What is this?" Mrs. Clavet shrieked when she walked out of the kitchen into the living room and saw a man standing in the doorway holding a gun. "You can't come into our home waving a gun around and threaten us."

"Sylvie, please," Mr. Clavet warned. "Go back in the kitchen. I'll handle this." Mr. Clavet looked up at the man and repeated, "We said we have not seen the Zakharovs. You must leave."

"I do what I want," the man bristled, talking a step into the doorway.

Chapter Twenty-Two

Dundonald Park
Somerset & Bay Street
Ottawa, Ontario, Canada

Staff Sergeant Otis Davenport, in charge of Division A of the RCMP (Royal Canadian Mounted Police), drove south on Bay Street. After crossing Somerset Street, he turned left into Dundonald Park, located a parking area, and pulled into an empty space. Dressed in civilian clothes rather than his normal bright red jacket, black trousers with yellow stripe, and high-top leather boots, he climbed out of his car and strolled down the line of parked cars. Stopping partway down the row of cars, he noticed a black car with a diplomatic license plate. Thinking it rather odd for the car to be sitting there empty in the park in the middle of the day, he retrieved a small notepad from his shirt pocket and scribbled the plate's numbers on a blank page.

He tucked the notepad back into his pocket, walked over to a park bench facing Somerset Street, and sat down. During a call he had received from headquarters, he had been ordered to take up surveillance on a Russian male described as having thin, light brown hair, distinctive, pale blue eyes, and was last seen wearing tattered clothing.

According to the RCMP's Chief Superintendant, someone at the Crown Attorney's office was very interested in this man's movements. Expecting to be seated on the bench for some time, Staff Sergeant Davenport was surprised when a man riding a bicycle raced into the apartment building's parking lot, dropped his bicycle, and ran into the building. He became more suspicious when an Ottawa City Police car roared into the parking lot and screeched to a stop. The police car's driver scrambled out of the car and also ran into the building. Deciding the suspicious activity warranted investigation, he jumped up from the bench, ran across the street, and disappeared into the building.

Hearing a commotion coming from the upper floor, he ran up the stairs. Upon reaching the second floor, he followed the sound of loud voices, his hand tightly gripping his personal weapon hidden under his jacket. He saw the man that had arrived on the bicycle standing against the opposite side of the hall watching the commotion in apartment number four.

Staff Sergeant Davenport ran down the hall and slid to a stop facing the open door of apartment number four. Inside the apartment, the Ottawa Police officer had his weapon drawn and pointed at three men.

"Royal Canadian Mounted Police behind you sir," Staff Sergeant Davenport called out. "Can I offer assistance?"

"Yes, you may," Constable First Class Richard Maples responded. "Guard these men while I find out who they are and what they are doing here."

Staff Sergeant Davenport pulled his service weapon from under his jacket, stepped into the room, and pointed it at the tallest of the three men. Keeping a wary eye on the men, Staff Sergeant Davenport surveyed the shambles inside the apartment: drawers pulled out, cabinets doors standing open, contents dumped on the floor, furniture overturned, and cushions and pillows sliced open with stuffing strewn everywhere.

Constable Maples holstered his weapon, walked up to the three men, and asked, "Who are you?"

"I am Major Karpanov. Military attaché at Russia embassy. They with me," the man growled, pointing at the two men standing beside him.

"What are you doing in this apartment?"

"No, police person. I ask you what you do here?" Major Karpanov roared. "Apartment rented by embassy. Is Russia property. You must get out."

"This building is owned by a Canadian," Constable Maples asserted. "You cannot come in here and tear the place apart."

"Man live here steal important papers," Karpanov yelled, advancing a step toward the constable. "Papers belong Russia. Must get back. You have no authority. You must leave."

"This is not Russia," Constable Maples asserted. "I tell you again, you must...."

"Constable, the major is correct," Staff Sergeant Davenport corrected. "If the apartment is rented by the Russian embassy, according to the law, it is considered to be Russian property. As the major said, you have no authority inside this apartment. We must leave."

"You listen RCMP," Major Karpanov sneered. "Not answer questions. Leave apartment now!"

Staff Sergeant Davenport slid his service weapon back under his jacket, tapped the constable on the shoulder, and said, "Come on. Let's back out into the hall."

The two men backed out into the hallway as the three Russians glared menacingly at them. As soon as they were completely out of the apartment and in the hallway, Major Karpanov slammed the apartment door closed with such force, the door split down the middle.

"Is there nothing we can do?" Constable Maples asked, turning around to face Staff Sergeant Davenport.

"I'm afraid not, constable. Actually, the major could have you arrested for violating their sovereign soil. By the way, I'm Staff Sergeant Otis Davenport of the Royal Canadian Mounted Police."

Constable Maples extended his hand and said, "Glad to meet you, staff sergeant. I'm Constable Richard Maples of the Ottawa City Police Department."

"Let's go talk to the gentleman standing over there against the wall," Staff Sergeant Davenport suggested.

The two men walked across the hallway and questioned Mr. Edwin Manning about what he had seen and heard. Mr. Manning recounted how his wife spoke Russian and she had heard the Russian leader tell his men after they found some kind of papers, they would grab the Zakharov family and then they would kill them. Mr. Manning told them that is when they heard the Russians kick the apartment door in.

"We hear this all the time," Constable Maples said, shaking his head. "There really isn't anything we can do about these complaints. We know the officers at the embassy are despicable bullies, but, as you said, they are Russian citizens and they have diplomatic immunity. So, if I can't arrest them, I'm going back to the station."

"But, Constable, I think I we should investigate this matter further," Staff Sergeant Davenport protested.

"Good luck, Staff Sergeant Davenport," Constable Maples smirked. "You can waste your time if you want. I have other duties to attend to."

Constable Maples strode down the hallway and disappeared down the stairs. Staff Sergeant Davenport decided to question the neighbor that lived directly across the hall from the Russian apartment.

Listening at the door of his apartment, Mr. Clavet had heard the sound of the apartment door being kicked in and then the loud voices when the police and the RCMP entered the Zakharov apartment. After the commotion settled down, Mr. Clavet had gone into the bedroom to try to convince Viktor into coming out.

"Viktor, the police are out in the hallway," he said, leaning down and looking under the bed. "Come out and talk to them. They can give you protection."

"No. No police," Viktor insisted, sliding further under the bed.

"You can't keep running. Sooner or later those men in your apartment are going to catch you. You must talk to the police."

"No. Not trust police. Russia secret police everywhere. They give me to embassy."

"Okay, Viktor. We'll wait till they leave. Then we'll decide what to do."

Mr. Clavet returned to the living room to find Sylvie, his wife, standing in the middle of the room wringing her hands, frightened by all the noise and yelling. As he tried to calm his wife's fears, there was a knock at the door. He opened the door and waited for the man standing there to speak.

"I'm Staff Sergeant Davenport of the RCMP. Did you witness any of the commotion across the hall?"

"No," Mr. Clavet lied.

"Are you certain, sir? Surely you must have at least heard something."

"Well, I did hear loud voices, but I know a Russian family lives there and I keep my nose out of their business," Mr. Clavet lied again.

"May I come in?" Staff Sergeant Davenport asked, sensing something was off in the man's answer.

Mr. Clavet pulled the door completely open and stepped aside to allow the RCMP sergeant to enter.

"I just have a few questions," Staff Sergeant Davenport advised, pulling a leather-covered notebook from his back pocket. "Names please."

"I'm Martin Clavet. This is my wife, Sylvie."

In the bedroom under the bed, fear paralyzed Viktor as he listened to the man questioning the Clavets. Nearing a state of panic, every fiber of his being wanted to jump up and run for his life, but he was trapped. Images of the N.K.V.D dragging him off to some wretched gulag to be beaten or worse danced before his eyes. Sweat broke out on his forehead, his heart hammering in his chest so violently he was certain the man in the other room would hear it. Still clutching the stuffed bear tightly against his body, an uncontrollable shudder shook Viktor's body as he curled up in a fetal position, waiting for a hand to grab him.

"You say you didn't see anything," Staff Sergeant Davenport questioned, looking directly at Mr. Clavet.

"I already told you we didn't see anything."

Staff Sergeant Davenport scribbled something on the notebook he was holding and continued, "Do you know the family that lives in apartment number four across the hall?"

"We know their name is Zakharov. We see them occasionally as we pass in the hall, but that's all."

As a skilled interrogator, Staff Sergeant Davenport noticed Mr. Clavet fidgeting and picking at the leg of his trousers. He turned toward Mrs. Clavet and asked, "Ma'am, do you know the Zakharovs?"

"Not really. We pass them sometimes in the hall."

Staff Sergeant Davenport, slipped his pen into the notebook, shoved it in his back pocket, and turned back toward Mr. Clavet. He stared at Mr. Clavet for a few moments, then said, "Mr. Clavet your mannerisms and your face tell me you are lying." He held up his hand to stop Mr. Clavet's blustering. Mr. Clavet fell silent, allowing Staff Sergeant Davenport to continue, "I am going to ask you one more time if you know anything about what happened in apartment number four, but be warned before you answer. If you lie to me again, I will turn this apartment upside down and then I will take you both to headquarters for a more thorough questioning."

Staff Sergeant Davenport had observed Mrs. Clavet's eyes darting toward the bedroom several times. Staff Sergeant Davenport suppressed the urge to laugh. People under pressure always look at the thing they do not want you to see. It was an involuntary reflex beyond their control.

"I believe I'll have a look around," Staff Sergeant Davenport announced as he stood and started toward the bedroom. "After you," he said, waiting for Mr. Clavet to enter first.

Dundonald Park
Somerset & Bay Street
Ottawa, Ontario, Canada

After securing the Zakharov's apartment door as best they could, the three Russians had exited the apartment building and had crossed the street. The three men disappeared into the park and hurried to the parking area.

Seated in the back seat of the black car, one of the men spoke up, "We did not find Zakharov or the papers. What do we do now?"

Major Karpanov did not answer. He sat staring out the windshield, angrily tapping his fingers on the steering wheel. Seeing the angry scowl on the major's face, the other two man remained silent.

Major Karpanov started the engine, backed out of the parking space, and drove out of the park, heading east on Somerset Street.

Several blocks down the street, Major Karpanov said, "We will go to the bakery. We know Zakharov's wife and child are hiding there. Lieutenant Zakharov may be there as well. We will watch the bakery. If we do not see any activity, we will go in and take them by force, if necessary."

"But Major, we do not have authority outside the embassy," the man seated in the passenger seat spoke up. "If they call the police, we could be arrested."

"Well, Junior Lieutenant Alekseev, perhaps you wish to tell Colonel Sokolovsky we cannot find his papers or the man who stole them," Major Karpanov asked, glancing over at the lieutenant. "What do you expect would happen when Second Secretary, General Pavlovski, finds out we have failed in our duties?"

"We would be reprimanded," Junior Lieutenant Alekseev replied quickly.

"You are very wrong, my uninformed friend," Major Karpanov mocked. "You obviously have no idea how important those papers are. If we do not find them and return them to the embassy, we would be stripped of rank and sent back to Russia. And then what do you suppose would happen?"

Junior Lieutenant Alekseev shook his head, preferring not to answer and be wrong again.

"We would stand before a firing squad. Do you understand how important it is that we find Zakharov *and* the papers?"

"Yes, sir, I understand," Junior Lieutenant Alekseev gulped.

"I am glad, Junior Lieutenant. Now, we go to find that traitor, Zakharov. When we arrest him, and I assure you we will, if he does not tell us where the papers are, we will make him watch as his wife and child die for his treachery."

Ten blocks later Major Karpanov turned the black car into the alley behind a business across the street from the Emerson's bakery, parked beside a delivery truck, and shut the engine off. He pulled his weapon out from under his jacket, eased the slide back to verify a round was in the chamber, and shoved it back in his shoulder holster.

"Captain Kozlov, you stay here. Junior Lieutenant Alekseev, you come with me."

The two men, dressed in civilian clothes to hide their identity, climbed out of the car and crossed O'Connor Street in the middle of the block, headed for the rear entrance of the bakery. Upon reaching the rear door of the bakery, Major Karpanov noticed the bakery's van was not parked it its usual spot.

"Junior Lieutenant, the delivery van is not here. You stay here in case the owner comes back."

Major Karpanov grabbed the doorknob and twisted it slowly. The catch released with a soft click. He pulled the door open a tiny crack and listened, hearing voices coming from the front of the bakery. Assuming the owner's wife was waiting on a customer, he slipped inside, eased the door closed, and moved silently over beside the doorway leading to the front of the bakery. He waited for the lone customer to leave the store. After closing the cash register, Mrs. Emerson moved over to the middle of the display case, slid the door open, and began rearranging a display of pastries.

Major Karpanov stepped up behind Mrs. Emerson and pressed the muzzle of the sound suppressor behind her right ear and snarled, "Not make sound or cry out or I kill you here. Understand?"

Terrified and shaking, Mrs. Emerson nodded her head ever so slightly.

"Move to door. Put closed sign in window. Then turn lights off. Quickly." Mrs. Emerson complied. "Now, back up slowly."

When they reached the back room, Major Karpanov shoved the muzzle harder against her head and asked, "Are Zakharovs upstairs? Remember, you not do as I say, I *will* kill you."

"Yes they are there," she whimpered. "But only his wife and child. Do not hurt them, please."

"Not give me orders old woman," he hissed, pushing her roughly toward the stairway. "We go up stairs. We reach top, you stop."

With her left arm twisted up behind her back, Major Karpanov forced her up the stairs. When they reached the top of the stairs, he leaned to Mrs. Emerson's right and peered around her. Finding the kitchen empty, he pushed her into the kitchen and over to the table.

"Answer quietly. Where are they?"

"Bedroom by the stairs," Mrs. Emerson replied, trembling like a leaf.

"Sit. Do only as I say." he ordered.

Mrs. Emerson opened her mouth as if to say something, but before she could speak, Major Karpanov slammed his weapon against the side of her head. As she began to fall over, he reached out with his free hand, letting her slump quietly onto the floor. He snatched the dish towel hanging on the stove, stuffed it in her mouth, and tied it behind her head. Afraid he would alarm the Zakharovs, he decided he would finish the old woman later.

He moved silently over to the bedroom door, readied himself, and tapped lightly on the door.

"Who is it?" a voiced called out from the other side. Major Karpanov did not answer. Again the voice called out, "Who is it? Misses Emerson is that you?"

Major Karpanov watched as the doorknob began to turn. When he heard the latch release, he kicked the door in, sending Anna Zakharov skittering backward. She lost her balance and landed on the floor with her back against the bed.

"Do not cry out, Misses Zakharov," Major Karpanov snarled, pointing the menacing weapon at her.

"Who are you?" Anna whimpered.

"I am Major Alexei Karpanov. I am here to recover the papers your husband stole from the embassy."

"Papers? What papers? My husband does not have any papers." Anna lied.

"Do you think I am stupid?" Major Karpanov raged. "We know your husband took papers from Colonel Sokolovsky's office. I demand you tell me where they are."

"Viktor does not have your papers," Anna lied again, knowing Karpanov would not believe her. She could not escape and she was not strong enough to fight off Karpanov. She would sacrifice herself and hope Viktor could find someone that would believe him.

Enraged, Major Karpanov rushed over to where Anna sat, leaning against the bed. He grabbed her arm, jerked her upright, and backhanded her, sending her flying across the bed. Jerking her head up by the hair, he screamed in her face, "Where is the child?"

Terror filled her eyes. "No! You must not hurt Nikola," she shrieked. "He is innocent. He has done nothing."

"Where is the child?" Major Karpanov yelled. "If you do not tell me where the papers are, I will kill him while you watch."

"No, please no!" Anna wailed.

Major Karpanov yanked Anna upright and slapped her again. She tumbled off the opposite side of the bed, landing roughly on the floor. Her foot struck the pile of blankets Nikola was sleeping on, startling him awake. He cried out, reaching for his mother. Anna grabbed Nikola and held him close to her chest.

Hearing the infant cry out, Major Karpanov rushed around the bed.

"Get up," Major Karpanov roared.

Anna scrambled to her feet and attempted to rush past Karpanov. "Please, do not hurt my child," she begged, attempting to flee through the door. "He has done nothing to you."

Major Karpanov beat her to the doorway, blocking her escape. He raised the weapon and pointed it directly at Nikola, his finger tightening against the trigger. Releasing the pressure on the trigger, Major Karpanov turned his head, surprised by a squeak coming from the doorway.

Mr. Emerson reached the top of the stairs and looked into the bedroom.

Chapter Twenty-Three

Clavet Apartment
Somerset Street
Ottawa, Ontario, Canada

Fear raged through Viktor's body like a wild fire when he heard footsteps enter the bedroom. It exploded in his mind with a blinding whiteness. He cringed and hugged his knees. His mouth went dry as panic gripped his throat. Viktor lay frozen, a cold, numbing dread enveloping him, unable to move, barely able to breathe.

"What do you have hidden in here, Mister Clavet?" Staff Sergeant Davenport questioned. "Your wife kept glancing at the bedroom door. That tells me there is something in here you do not want me to see."

"As you can see, Sergeant, there is nothing unusual in here," Mr. Clavet answered. "It is just a bedroom."

"You are lying," Staff Sergeant Davenport shouted. "What are you hiding? Open the closet."

Mr. Clavet walked over to the closet and pulled the door open. Staff Sergeant Davenport leaned into the small closet. Satisfied there was nothing hidden inside the closet, he returned his attention to Mr. Clavet. The bead of sweat running down the side of Mr. Clavet's face did not go unnoticed.

"I can see you are quite nervous, Mister Clavet," Staff Sergeant Davenport said. "I have noticed that since we entered the bedroom, you have deliberately avoided looking at the bed."

Staff Sergeant Davenport bent over, looked under the bed, and exclaimed, "Well, who is this?" He kicked the bed frame and shouted, "Come out from under there."

Prodded from his paralyzing fear, Viktor struggled out from under the bed and lunged toward the door. "No. No. No," Viktor howled, racing toward the door.

Staff Sergeant Davenport dove toward Viktor, catching him by his ankle. Viktor fell face first onto the floor. The stuffed bear went flying. Like a crazed animal, Viktor scrambled across the floor, arms flailing, desperately reaching for the stuffed bear. With the bear safely in his arms again, he pushed himself up against the wall.

"I am not going to hurt you," Staff Sergeant Davenport asserted, trying to calm the wild-eyed man staring up at him. He took a step toward Viktor, causing Viktor to become even more agitated. Viktor backed further away, sliding against the wall until he was trapped in the corner of the bedroom. "Mister Clavet, come over here and help me calm this man down. Why is he so frightened?"

"This is Viktor Zakharov," Mr. Clavet responded. "He lives with his family in the apartment across the hall. The Russian officers have been trying to kidnap him and his family. The Zakharovs fear for their lives. If they are caught, they will be sent back to Russia and then they will be killed."

Mister Clavet kneeled down beside Viktor, put his hand on his shoulder, and looked directly in his eyes. "Viktor, you must calm down. This man is from the Royal Canadian Mounted Police. He will...."

"No. Said no police. Not trust police," Viktor howled. "Russia corrupt all police. Give me to embassy."

"Mister Zakharov, are you the man that went to see the Crown Attorney?" Staff Sergeant Davenport asked.

Hearing the words 'Crown Attorney', Viktor's breathing slowed somewhat and he looked up at Staff Sergeant Davenport. "Yes, talk to woman," Viktor stammered, struggling to get the words out. "She not believe me. Nobody believe."

"She must have believed something you said because she called Inspector Haines. The Inspector then assigned me to watch you."

"Watch me?" Viktor mumbled, a look of astonishment on his face. "She not believe. Send me away."

"The Inspector told me someone is very concerned and wants to see the other papers you said you have."

"Yes, have many papers," Viktor agreed, nodding his head.

"Do you have those papers here?"

"No. Not have here. Papers hidden."

"Mister Clavet, help Mister Zakharov up please."

Mr. Clavet stretched out his arm, grasped Viktor's hand, and helped him to his feet. As Viktor straightened up, the stuffed bear slipped from his grasp, setting off another spell of panic. Viktor grabbed for the bear. He snatched it from the floor, clutched it tightly, and sat on the edge of the bed.

"Why is that bear so important?" Staff Sergeant Davenport asked, looking at Mr. Clavet.

"I don't know. He had it when the Russians were coming up the stairs and I motioned for him to come in here to hide."

"Mister Zakharov, why is that bear so important to you?"

"Hide list inside. It proof Canada people spy for Russia."

"Can you show me?"

Viktor held out the stuffed bear toward Mr. Clavet and said, "Hands shake. Open seam. Here," Viktor said pointing at the seam where Anna had opened the bear. "Anna put list inside. Sew closed."

"Sylvie, get your scissors," Mr. Clavet yelled at his wife.

Mrs. Clavet rushed into their bedroom, tore through her sewing basket, and located a pair of scissors. Not bothering to gather the scattered sewing items, she rushed back into the bedroom, and handed the scissors to her husband. He carefully snipped the stitches, dug inside the opening, and pulled out two folded sheets of paper. Viktor snatched the sheets, unfolded them, and handed them to Staff Sergeant Davenport.

Staff Sergeant Davenport quickly scanned the first page, set it aside, and scanned the second page. He looked up at Viktor and asked, "What exactly is this list?"

"This column code name," Viktor explained, pointing at the left side of the paper. "On other side is name real person."

"You say these people are spying for the Russians. How do you know that?"

"Have many papers," Viktor exclaimed. "I cipher person at embassy. See code names many messages. Messages go Colonel Sokolovsky to Russia and Russia to Colonel. Say Russia want war."

"I can't believe this," Staff Sergeant Davenport groaned. "I know some of these people. This just can't be."

"Is all true," Viktor asserted. "Swear on mama's grave."

"I need to see those papers."

"Not have. They hidden."

"Where?" Staff Sergeant Davenport asked. Viktor did not answer, still uncertain if he could trust Staff Sergeant Davenport. Without the papers he had stolen from Colonel Sokolovsky, he would have no hope of convincing anyone he was telling the truth. Losing them would seal his fate.

"Listen to me, Mister Zakharov. If what you say is true, we must get those papers to a safe place. I need to know where they are."

Viktor remained unconvinced. He shook his head and said, "No lose. Risked life to get. Is all proof I have."

"I assure you the Royal Canadian Mounted Police has not been infiltrated by the Russians. I want to help you. I will protect you, but you have to trust me."

"Viktor, you must trust this man," Mr. Clavet begged. "I believe him. We must hurry. Do you want the Russians to find the papers? If they do, what would happen to you and your family?"

"No. Must not find. My Anna and little Nikola…." Viktor exploded, tears filling his eyes. "Sokolovsky and Karpanov not good Russians. Are vile pigs. Must pay." Viktor looked at Staff Sergeant Davenport. "I tell you. Mister Emerson hide in bakery. I not know where."

"Bakery. Where?" Staff Sergeant Davenport asked.

"I know where that is," Mr. Clavet blurted out. "There is an Emerson's Bakery not far from here. It's on Pretoria Street."

"Let's go," Staff Sergeant Davenport barked. "My car is just across the street in the park. We must get to the bakery quickly"

A white panel van with J & R Mechanical, Ltd. painted on the side in large black letters pulled into an empty parking space in the parking lot adjacent to the apartment building on Somerset Street. Two men dressed in dirty gray coveralls climbed out of the van and walked around to the rear of the van. The shorter of the two men opened the rear door and retrieved a red tool box. He slammed the door and the two men entered the building.

"We must hurry, Jimmy," the shorter man advised the other man. "The boss said the man we are looking for lives upstairs in apartment number four."

Together the two men climbed up the stairs. At the top of the stairs, the shorter man set the toolbox down, retrieved two .45 caliber pistols fitted with Maxim sound suppressors from underneath the top tray. He handed one to the taller man and together then started down the hallway.

The two men were startled when the door to the apartment across from apartment four opened suddenly and three men stepped out into the hallway.

"Get Viktor inside, quick!" Staff Sergeant Davenport yelled, spotting the weapons the men were holding down beside their legs. He ripped his service weapon from under his jacket and fired at the closest man, striking him just below the company patch over his left pocket. Mr. Clavet grabbed Viktor's arm, shoved him inside the apartment, and dove in after him.

The second man fired his weapon. The bullet hit the door jamb beside Staff Sergeant Davenport's right ear. Staff Sergeant Davenport flinched as flying shards of wood stung the side of his face. The man at the stairs fired again. Staff Sergeant Davenport fell forward, firing as he hit the floor. An eerie quiet settled on the hallway as swirling smoke and the acrid, stinging odor of cordite filled the air.

Emerson's Bakery
Pretoria Street
Ottawa, Ontario, Canada

Major Karpanov turned toward the doorway, swinging his weapon toward Mr. Emerson. Having already overpowered the now unconscious and bound Junior Lieutenant Alekseev, Mr. Emerson had crept up the stairs prepared, having grabbed a large metal paddle as he passed through the bakery's kitchen. Gripping the handle with both hands, he swung the heavy paddle as hard as he could. The paddle connected against the side of Major Karpanov's face with a sickening crunch.

Major Karpanov's eyes went slack as he tumbled over sideways. The weapon slipped from his hand, landing on the floor at the same time his head impacted the floor. Three gold-capped teeth lay scattered in front of Karpanov's open mouth. The teeth in his lower jam no longer lined up, the ferocious blow having split his jaw in half.

"Here, bind his arms with this," Mr. Emerson yelled, unbuckling his belt and pulling it through the loops of his trousers. "I'll smash his head in if he so much as twitches."

Anna sat Nikola on the bed, snatched the belt out of Mr. Emerson's hands, and knelt down beside the unconscious Karpanov. "Vile, disgusting pig," she hissed as she spit on his discolored face. She shoved Karpanov's arms behind his back, wrapped the belt around his wrists, and cinched it as tight as she could. "What about his feet?" she asked.

"Grab an electrical cord from the kitchen," Mr. Emerson advised, the paddle raised in a striking position. "There's one by the dining table."

Anna ran into the kitchen and shoved the dining table aside, revealing Mr. Emerson's wife, Louise, lying unconscious on the floor. Anna reached out and touched her. She was still breathing. Anna nudged her. She moaned and began to stir. Anna ripped the extension cord from the wall outlet. The end of the cord bounced along behind her as she raced back into the bedroom.

"Louise lying on floor," Anna panted, breathing hard from her dash to the kitchen and back. "She still breathing. Is moving"

"What?" Mr. Emerson bellowed as he turned and raced into the kitchen.

Anna laid one of Karpanov's legs on top of the other, looped the cord around his legs, pulled it tight, then tied the free end around the bed frame. She lifted Nikola from the bed and ran into the kitchen.

Winded and shaken by the ordeal, Anna uprighted one of the overturned chairs and sat down. "Where Viktor?" she wheezed as she watched Mr. Emerson help his wife to a sitting position. Mr. Emerson removed the gag from Louise's mouth and handed it to Anna.

"Soak this in cold water," Mr. Emerson said, handing the dish towel to Anna.

Anna stood up, stepped over to the sink, and soaked the kitchen towel. She handed the dripping towel back Mr. Emerson and sobbed, "Viktor leave with you. Why he not with you now?"

"He was supposed to meet me in the park across from the apartment building," Mr. Emerson answered, pressing the cold towel on the large knot above Louise's temple. "My deliveries took longer than expected. I waited for him, but he never came. I thought maybe he did not want to wait and came back here."

"Where Viktor?" Anna shrieked again.

"He must still be at the apartment."

"We go now! We find him."

"We will go to the apartment, but first I have to make sure Louise is okay."

"I'm okay," Louise moaned, taking the cold rag away from her husband. "I have a headache, but I'll be fine. Help me over to the couch and then you go find Viktor. We promised Anna we wouldn't let those Russian bullies hurt Viktor."

With Anna on one side and Mr. Emerson on the other, they helped Louise stagger over to the couch. Mr. Emerson moved over in front of her and kneeled down.

"Are you sure you're okay?"

"Yes, as long as I sit here, I'll be just fine. I could use a glass of water."

Without being asked, Anna went to the kitchen and returned with a glass of water. She set it on the table beside the couch. "I so sorry," Anna sighed. "We not mean cause you much trouble."

"It's not your fault, sweetie," Louise replied as she gently repositioned the cold rag. "You and Cecil go find Viktor."

"What we do Russian pig?" Anna asked, pointing toward the bedroom.

"I'll go check and make sure he is still tied securely." Mr. Emerson hurried into the bedroom, knelt down beside Major Karpanov's still body, and pressed two fingers against his neck. He repositioned his fingers and felt again. Returning to the living room shaking his head, he said. "The Major is not going anywhere. He's dead."

"I not sorry he dead," Anna snapped. "He would kill my Viktor. Not blink eye."

Mr. Emerson pulled the bedroom door shut and looked at Anna. "We can't leave Nikola here. Louise is certainly not able to look after him. He will have to come with us. Come on let's go. Viktor may need our help."

Anna followed Mr. Emerson down the stairs. She stopped at the bottom of the stairs, a look of shock on her face, and asked, "Who is that?"

"I have no idea who he is. He was waiting out in the alley. The dim-witted idiot was so busy watching where I usually park the van, he didn't hear me slip up behind him. Broke the handle of my shovel clean off when I smacked him. Guess I should check and see if he's dead too."

He leaned over and put two fingers against the man's neck. The man twitched and his eyes sprang wide open. "Well, he's not dead," Mr. Emerson observed, watching the man struggle violently. The man stopped and lay still, realizing he was bound securely and struggling was pointless.

"We'll see you later, my stupid friend," Mr. Emerson snickered, patting the man's face. "Your boss is dead and you are going to spend a very long time in prison." Realizing the man did not understand, he drew his fingers across his throat and jeered, "Karpanov dead."

Mr. Emerson grabbed the man by the shoulders and dragged him over beside a pallet stacked high with one hundred pound bags of flour. When he let go, the man's head banged sharply against the jagged edge of the pallet.

"Oops," Mr. Emerson snickered. He piled three hundred-pound bags of flour on the man's legs to keep him from getting away.

"Come Anna. The van is parked around the corner."

"Papers!" Anna shrieked. "Must have papers."

"They're right here in the flour bin," Mr. Emerson indicated, pointing toward a wooden bin in the corner of the room. He rushed over to the bin, threw off the lid, and plunged both arms into the flour. Rooting around in the flour, he located a hard object and pulled it out. Clouds of flour dust rose into the air as he shook and pounded the object. He unwrapped the folds of oilcloth, revealing a large stack of papers. Anna snatched the papers and stuffed them into her hand bag.

Carrying Nikola on her hip and the hand bag stuffed with the papers Viktor had taken from Colonel Sokolovsky's office slung over her arm, Anna followed Mr. Emerson as he hurried out the door and ran around the corner. Mr. Emerson started the van's engine, shoved it into gear, and screeched away from the curb, headed toward the Zakharov's apartment.

Chapter Twenty-Four

Clavet Apartment
Somerset Street
Ottawa, Ontario, Canada

Martin Clavet leaned over and pressed his ear against the door. Listening intently, he heard no sound coming from the hallway. He eased the door open and peered into the hallway. All he could see was Staff Sergeant Davenport's motionless form lying in front of the door. Deciding he could not let the man that had saved his life just lie there, he slid out of the way and pulled the door completely open.

Seeing no activity in the hallway, Mr. Clavet stood up and yelled at Viktor, "Come help me. I think Sergeant Davenport has been hit."

Viktor scrambled up off the floor and followed Mr. Clavet into the hallway. Together they rolled Staff Sergeant Davenport over onto his back. Mr. Clavet laid his hand on the man's chest to check for a heartbeat, expecting he would feel nothing. Staff Sergeant Davenport's lifeless eyes stared blankly up at the ceiling.

"He's dead, Viktor," Mr. Clavet sighed, sadness clouding his face.

"No," Viktor wailed. "He only one believe me. Now what I do?"

"Wait! There were two men," Mr. Clavet shouted, reaching for the Walther PPK (Polizei Pistole Kurz) in Staff Sergeant Davenport's lifeless hand. "Where is he? Where's the other man?"

Mr. Clavet looked up and turned toward the stairs just as Jimmy Ellingsworth, the second man, raised his head above the last step. Mr. Clavet yanked the weapon free from the lifeless hand, raised it, and pointed it toward the stairs, but he was one second too late. The man at the top of the stairs fired. The bullet struck Mr. Clavet one inch below his right eye. Martin Clavet dropped the weapon and lurched over backward, already dead before he hit the floor. Reacting by instinct and his military training, Viktor snatched the weapon from the floor and fired repeatedly in the direction of the man that had just killed his friend.

Bang…Bang…Bang…Click…Click…Click. Viktor kept pulling the trigger, spent cartridges spinning across the floor. Despite Viktor's shaking hand, two of the hurriedly fired shots had struck the man at the stairs. The man tumbled backwards down the stairs, breaking his neck as he landed at the bottom.

Viktor jumped up and glanced at Mr. Clavet. Knowing his friend was dead, he dropped the weapon, snatched the papers Staff Sergeant Davenport had been holding, and rushed into the apartment. Looking frantically around the apartment, he located the stuffed bear on the floor beside the couch. He rushed over, grabbed the bear, and shoved the papers inside.

"Sorry, friend Martin dead," Viktor sobbed, stopping beside Mrs. Clavet huddled in the corner of the room. "Must run."

Viktor sprinted out the apartment door and down the stairs. He leapt over the dead body and disappeared out the building's back door. Hearing the wail of sirens in the distance, he panicked and ran down the street in the direction of the bakery, hoping to find Anna and Nikola. He had no idea where they would go, if he found them.

Sprinting down Maclaren Street, Viktor heard one police car scream down the next street over. As he approached the intersection at Kent Street, he saw another police car approaching two blocks away. He crossed the intersection and turned left on Kent Street. Slowing his pace, he turned into the alley, desperate for a place to hide. Other than a large green, smelly dumpster, the alley was vacant. Fortunately, the dumpster was nearly empty. Viktor lifted the lid and jumped inside.

Pulling his jacket over his nose to block out the stench, he closed his eyes and listened.

The wail of the siren grew louder then fainter, finally fading away completely. Viktor pushed the lid of the dumpster up and scanned the alley. Seeing no one, he scrambled out of the dumpster and continued his escape, hoping to reach the bakery with no further incidents.

He backtracked to Maclaren Street and resumed running. Having run only one block, he could not believe his eyes. He saw the Emerson Bakery van headed toward him with Mr. Emerson driving and Anna seated in the passenger seat. He stepped one foot into the street and waved frantically, trying to get their attention. In the van, Anna punched Mr. Emerson on the arm, pointing excitedly toward Viktor.

Mr. Emerson stomped on the brake. The van screeched to a stop, sliding five feet past where Viktor stood. Anna threw the door open, jumped out, and hugged Viktor.

"No time," he panted. "Men kill RCMP police and Mr. Clavet. Other police there now. Must escape and hide."

"Mr. Clavet is dead?" Anna cried.

"No time," Viktor repeated, grabbing Anna's arm and pushing her toward the van's open door. "Talk later."

Viktor pushed Anna into the van, slammed the door, ran around to the rear, and climbed in. "Mr. Emerson, go now," Viktor shouted. "Police must not find us."

Mr. Emerson shoved the shift lever into low gear, mashed his foot against the accelerator pedal, and slipped his foot off the clutch pedal. The old, mostly smooth tires on the old van lost traction, spinning wildly, sending up a cloud of blue gray smoke. The van slid sideways, the worn tires unable to grip the pavement. Mr. Emerson eased up on the accelerator, gaining control of the skid. He mashed the accelerator back down and the van roared down the street.

Slowing slightly to turn at the next intersection, the van's escape was cut off by another car turning in front of it. Mr. Emerson stomped on the brake. The van slid into the other car, breaking one of the van's headlights and creating a large dent in the passenger door of the other car. Mr. Emerson mashed his foot on the starter, but before he could get the van started, two men jumped out of the other car.

"Get out and run," Mr. Emerson yelled. "They have guns."

The van's engine roared to life. Mr. Emerson, turned the steering wheel, mashed the accelerator, and dumped the clutch. The van's front end glanced off the other car, nearly striking one of the men as he leapt out of the way. He threw the van in reverse, backed up, and rammed the car again.

Mr. Emerson's actions created enough of a distraction to allow Anna and Viktor to leap out of the van and disappear around the corner of a building. As the men advanced toward the van, a police car lurched around the corner and slid to a stop in the middle of the street. Constable Maples, having been informed about the gun battle that had occurred at the apartment on Somerset Street, had become concerned. Thinking the Russian he had talked to earlier may not have been lying, he alerted his training cadet and together they had jumped into his assigned police car and had headed for the apartment.

Speeding down Maclaren Street, Constable Maples had arrived on the scene just as Mr. Emerson ploughed the van into the car a second time. He saw the two men advancing toward the van with their weapons pointed toward the van's driver. After the police car squealed to a stop, Constable Maples jumped out, and bellowed, "Ottawa Police. Drop your weapons. Get on the ground."

Neither man complied. They turned and began firing at the newly arrived police officers. "Dixon, take cover!" Constable Maples yelled as he dropped to the ground and rolled over, taking cover behind the open door of his police car. Both police officers quickly emptied their service revolvers as a horrific gun battle erupted. Each man flipped the cylinder of his revolver out, dumped the expended cartridges, and shoved in fresh rounds. Training cadet Ronald Dixon stuck his head up, aiming his revolver through the now missing glass of the passenger window. In his first gun battle with criminals and lacking field experience, Office Dixon took a few seconds too long acquiring his target.

The man on the sidewalk side of the car fired, striking Office Dixon just to the left of the badge on his cap. Office Dixon fell backward, landing flat on his back on the sidewalk. His cap flew off, bounced on the sidewalk, and landed against a building.

Constable Maples, a police force veteran of twenty-four years, had been in several gun battles with desperate men. In their desperation, criminals always made mistakes. Biding his time and conserving ammo, he waited for the opportunity he knew would come, if he was patient. Thinking they had killed both police officers, the two men rose cautiously from behind their car and waited. No gunfire. They started toward the police car. Constable Maples waited, listening to the scraping of their steps on the pavement. He counted their steps: one…two…three. Springing out suddenly from behind the car door, he fired two quick shots.

Both criminals went down. Constable Maples ran over, not stopping to examine the first man who was obviously dead. Rushing to the other side of their car, he found the other man groaning and crawling toward the weapon that had fallen from his hand. Constable Maples kicked the weapon out of reach, grabbed the man's arm, and flipped him over onto his face. After quickly securing handcuffs around the man's wrists, he rushed back to the police car to check on his training cadet.

"Dixon," he groaned. The young man of only twenty-three had been on the force for less than a month and now he lay dead. He eyes were open but unseeing, blood seeping from the hole in his forehead, creating an expanding puddle on the sidewalk. Constable Maples retrieved the rookie's cap and laid it over his face then went to check on the occupant of the van.

The van's occupant had taken a bullet below his right collarbone, but he was still alive. He raced back to the police car, grabbed the radio microphone, and keyed the transmit button. Nothing. The radio was dead. A thin curl of smoke rose from the middle of the dash. Constable Maples ran back onto the sidewalk, jerked open the door of a hardware store, and poked his head inside. "Is anybody in here?" he hollered. "It's safe. The criminals are down. Somebody call the police station and then call an ambulance." The clerk rose up behind the counter, waved at Constable Maples, and reached for the phone. Constable Maples ran back outside and back to the van to tend to the injured man until the help arrived.

Eight minutes passed before the first police car arrived. The ambulance arrived ten minutes after that. The melee had started so suddenly, Constable Maples had no idea there had been more than one person in the van. Ten blocks away, Viktor and Anna walked hurriedly away from the scene on Maclaren Street.

"Viktor, I am tired," Anna panted, struggling with Nikola under one arm and the bag stuffed with papers hanging on the other. "I need to stop and rest."

"I am sorry, but we must not stop," Viktor answered, taking Nikola from her. "We cannot go back to the bakery. We must find somewhere else to hide."

"But where?" Anna questioned. "We have never been this way. Where will we go?"

"I do not know, but we must keep walking. We must not be caught near where the car stopped us. Did you not hear the gun shots and then the sirens?"

"Yes, I heard. We should go back and help Mister Emerson."

"No, Anna. There is nothing we can do. We have no weapons. We must keep going until we find a place to hide."

Block after block Viktor and Anna trudged southward away from the melee. Several kilometers further south, nearing the Rideau Canal, they crossed Woodlawn Avenue and entered a residential neighborhood. It looked like a nice place to live. A frail woman with thin white hair eased her cart off the curb and crossed the street. She smiled at Viktor and Anna as she passed them. They smiled back. A large woman with a purse the size of a suitcase stood waiting at a bus stop, squinting into the late-afternoon sun. A flock of Common Goldeneyes flew overhead, headed for their nesting grounds along the canal.

As Viktor and Anna neared the middle of the next block, Viktor noticed a property that did not fit in with the rest of the neighborhood. The house was an old, two-story, weather-beaten shambles, its clapboard siding weathered and cracked, many shingles missing from its roof. A large outbuilding of some sort stood between the house and a dilapidated wooden fence that bordered the property. The entire property appeared to be abandoned. A dingy mailbox, almost entirely hidden by tall weeds, leaned precariously sideways, next to a rutted drive-way. Overgrown bushes partially blocked the outbuilding's door and obscured its windows. The walls, not stained with grime, were covered with long-ignored, creeping vines, the main stem as thick as a man's wrist.

Thinking the outbuilding would be a perfect hiding place, Viktor handed Nikola to Anna and pushed aside two rotten boards in the dilapidated fence. He wedged himself through the opening and reached back for Nikola. Anna followed him through the hole in the fence and pushed the boards back in place. With his foot, Viktor shoved the building's door open far enough to allow them to slip inside.

Once inside, Viktor pushed the creaky door closed as far as it would go. Dim shafts of light filtered through the decaying roof. Together, they crept over to the far corner of the shed. Viktor located several old wooden crates and stacked them together. They sat down trembling and exhausted from the long walk and fear of being captured.

"Viktor, many people around us have died this day," Anna whispered. "You said Mister Clavet is dead and we do not know if Mr. Emerson is dead."

"At the Clavet's apartment, a man from the Royal Canadian Mounted Police found me hiding under the bed. I thought he would arrest me and turn me over to the embassy. Anna, I think he believed me when I showed him the list of names."

"Viktor, that is wonderful."

"Two other men showed up. They killed Mr. Clavet and they also killed the RCMP policeman. He was the only one that has believed me."

"Oh, Viktor, what are we going to do?"

"For now, we will rest," Viktor answered. "That will give me time to think."

Viktor shivered. The air inside the old building was cold and damp. Even though the building had long ago been abandoned, the smell of manure still filled the air. A dusty horse blanket lay draped over the rails of a stall on the far side of the building. Viktor handed Nikola off to Anna and walked over to where the blanket hung. He dragged it off the rail and shook it gently. Years of accumulated dust fell to the ground. Clouds of dust particles rose into the air, dancing and swirling in the shafts of light. A second blanket lay exposed on the stall's top rail. Viktor grabbed it and dragged both blankets over to where Anna and Nikola sat.

He pushed the crates up against the piles of debris in the corner and spread the first blanket over the crates. Viktor sat down, held the second blanket up, and motioned Anna over. Anna handed Nikola back to Viktor and together they huddled under the old horse blanket.

Viktor held his little boy tightly, rocking back and forth, the old crates creaking under his weight. "*What will tomorrow bring?*" Viktor wondered as the little boy drifted off to sleep.

Abandoned Building
Wilton Lane
Ottawa, Ontario, Canada

Viktor and Anna had slept fitfully in the smelly, damp air of the old building. Viktor awakened as the sun rose and the early morning light began to filter in through the grimy, dirt-streaked windows. He slipped out from under the musty horse blanket and stretched, trying to relieve his aching muscles. Rather than wake Anna and Nikola, he wandered around the building, looking at the various items that had been discarded long ago.

Viktor counted six stalls as he meandered along the west wall of the building. Two of the stalls still had halters and other items of tack hanging on pegs beside the gates. He tried to picture what it must have been like when beautiful horses had loafed in the stalls and stable boys had led them out to be exercised. At the far end of the building, on a narrow shelf beside a large sliding door sat several brushes, likely having been used by a groomsman after a horse returned from the exercise paddock.

Viktor turned and stared at the empty interior of the rotting building. "*How sad*," he thought. What had certainly been a lively, bustling place was now empty, lifeless, and decaying. He shuddered, more from a feeling of sadness, than the damp cold. He sighed and headed back toward the place where Anna and Nikola slept. As he reached the blanket-covered crates, Nikola stirred. The little boy sat up and held his arms out.

Viktor reached down and lifted the little boy up. He tried to sit carefully, but one of the old crates shifted and slipped off the stack.

"What time is it?" Anna yawned, awakened by the jostling of the crates.

"I do not know exactly," Viktor answered. "The sun has not been up long. So, I would say somewhere around seven o'clock."

"How are we going to feed Nikola?" Anna questioned as she stood and stretched.

"I do not know that either," Viktor shrugged. "We have no money to buy anything."

"But Viktor, he needs to eat," Anna fretted.

"I know that," Viktor snapped. He started to walk away, taking two steps before he turned around. "I'm sorry," he apologized. "I don't know what to do. There is no one left to help us. Mister Clavet is dead and we do not know what has happened to Mister Emerson. The only person with the police that believed me is also dead. I just don't know what to do." Viktor threw his hands up in frustration and walked away.

Anna started to say something, but stopped. She could not remember ever seeing such a look of defeat on her husband's face. She wanted to run to him and hug him and tell him everything would be okay, but she knew Viktor was a very proud man. She watched as he tramped across the dust-covered floor. She would wait and see what he decided.

Viktor wracked his brain in a vain effort trying to decide what to do next. His mind was blank. They had no money. There was no one to call. There was nowhere left to run. "What? What? What?" he ranted.

Anna watched as Viktor paced back and forth across the entire length of the old building, swirls of dust rising with each step. He stopped midway through the fourth circuit and returned to where Anna sat watching.

"I could not think of anything," Viktor blurted out. "There is nothing left to do but to call the police and show them the papers again."

"But Viktor," Anna exclaimed. "They did not believe you before. Why would they believe you now?"

"We have no other choice," Viktor insisted. "We have many papers now. They must believe us."

"Okay, Viktor, but how will you call them? There is no telephone here."

"I will check the houses next to this property. If one of them has a phone, maybe they would allow me to call the police."

"Please be careful," Anna cautioned, as Viktor started toward the door. "Viktor, if you take Nikola, someone may be more likely to let you use a phone."

"You are quite correct, my beautiful wife," Viktor smiled.

He bent over, kissed Anna, and lifted Nikola off the crate. They exited the building and slipped through the opening in the fence. Each person that answered the door at the first two houses said they could not help as they had no phone. Viktor and Nikola turned left onto Oakland Avenue and walked up onto the porch of the first house. No one answered.

The next house, a single-story bungalow, painted a pleasant shade of light green, sat far back from the street, beneath three towering pine trees. Viktor followed a curving sidewalk up to the front door, knocked on the door, and waited. He heard footsteps approaching the door. A middle-aged woman with wire-rimmed glasses, wearing a bright print apron over her dress opened the door.

"May I help you?" the woman asked through the screen door.

"Need phone," Viktor announced, excitedly. "Want call police."

"What did you say." the woman questioned, unable to understand Viktor's nervous jabbering.

"Phone," Viktor repeated, making the motions of putting a phone receiver to his hear.

"A phone? You need a phone?"

Becoming frustrated, Viktor slipped into Russian for a few words. "У кого-то должен быть телефон."

"Ruskie?" the woman asked. "Are you Ruskie?"

"Da, I Ruskie," Viktor beamed. "I am Viktor Sergeyevich Zakharov."

"Wait here. I'll get my husband. He's Russian."

The woman returned with a thin-framed man with an oval face. The man's pallid skin sagged around his face and neck as if the body underneath had shrunk. With great effort and talking slowly, he greeted Viktor, explaining, in Russian, that he had emigrated from Russia to Canada five years earlier. Hoping to blend into his new country, the man had changed his name from Bogdan Listunov to Benjamin Linsky.

"Bad men chase me, wife, and little boy," Viktor babbled impatiently. "Hide in empty barn. All night."

"Slow down, Mister Zakharov. Start at the beginning and tell me what happened."

Spellbound, Mr. Linsky listened intently as Viktor described the events of the past few days. When Mr. Linsky heard about the Zakharovs spending the night in the decaying horse barn on the old Zimmerman place, he insisted Viktor go get his wife and bring her back. At the front door, Viktor tried to leave Nikola with the Linskys, but the little boy refused, clinging tightly to Viktor's side. Viktor told Mr. Linsky he would run back to the old barn and bring Anna back as fast as he could.

A few minutes later Viktor and Anna arrived panting and out of breath. Mrs. Linsky, waiting at the door, ushered them inside and directed them into the kitchen, insisting they eat something before they called the police An assortment of breakfast items awaited them on the dining table. Anna slid a delicious looking pastry onto a small plate for Nikola. While the little boy hungrily wolfed down the pastry, Anna poured a glass of milk and set it beside the plate.

Viktor reached out, picked up a Piroshki, a Russian hand pie, and bit off a large chunk. "Delicious," Viktor mumbled, his mouth full of flaky pastry. "Is like my Mama used to make."

Between bites of pastry, Viktor elaborated on how no one had believed him or the documents he had shown them. Mr. Linsky nodded his head in agreement as Viktor described the sadistic behavior of Colonel Sokolovsky and the other Russian officers at the embassy.

"I understand exactly what you are saying," Mr. Linsky interjected as Viktor stuffed another bite of Piroshki into his mouth. "I, too, have suffered under the hand of a sadistic officer. I still carry the scars on my back."

Viktor stabbed another pastry with his fork and dumped it on his plate. He devoured the pastry in silence, then drained the glass of milk Mrs. Linsky had set by his plate. Satisfied that his guests had been fed, Mr. Linsky led Viktor into a small den-like room and closed the door. "Let me call the police," Mr. Linsky said. "I will explain to them exactly what you just told me."

Mr. Linsky sat down behind a small oak desk, lifted the telephone receiver, placed it against his ear, poked the tip of his finger in the zero, and spun the dial all the way around. When the operator came on the line, he asked to be connected to the local police. Viktor listened as Mr. Linsky spoke, understanding only a few words of the conversation.

"Mister Zakharov, the desk sergeant said they have been looking for you and they would send someone right away," Mr. Linsky advised as he placed the receiver back on the telephone.

"Thank you, Mister Linsky," Viktor responded. "We are most grateful. Please, you call me Viktor."

"Very well, Viktor," Mr. Linsky replied. "Then you must call me Ben."

"Please, can you translate these?" Viktor begged as he handed Mr. Linsky several of the documents. "Nobody believes me because they cannot read these documents."

Mr. Linsky grabbed a pencil and began translating the documents. When he finished, he handed the documents back to Viktor and the two men returned to the kitchen to rejoin Mrs. Linsky, Anna, and little Nikola, still working on his second pastry. Viktor and Anna joined the Linskys in light conversation about life in Russia while they waited for the police to arrive. Ten minutes later, hearing the sound of screeching tires, Mr. Linsky rose from the table and pushed the kitchen window curtain aside.

"They're here," he announced.

Mr. Linsky opened the front door and watched a uniformed man climb out of a police car and make his way up the sidewalk. Mr. Linsky pushed the door open as the man reached the house's narrow porch.

"Come in," Mr. Linsky said, holding the door open.

"I'm Sergeant Charles Seward of the Ottawa City Police Department," the man announced.

"Sergeant Seward, follow me," Mr. Linsky said. "The man I mentioned on the phone is in the kitchen."

Mr. Linsky turned and led Sergeant Seward into the kitchen. After introducing his wife, Betty, and the Zakharovs, Mr. Linsky explained that the Zakharovs spoke very little English and he would serve as interpreter. After giving a brief repeat of the events Viktor had described to him earlier, Mr. Linsky informed the police officer that individuals from the Russian embassy had tried to kidnap the Zakharovs and that they should be taken into protective custody immediately.

"Before I take them into custody, I have a couple of questions," Sergeant Seward insisted. The sergeant pulled out a chair, sat down, and laid a notepad on the table. "Why would someone from the Russian embassy want to kidnap these people?"

"As Mister Zakharov explained to me, he has uncovered evidence of a conspiracy between high-ranking Canadians and senior officials at the embassy," Mr. Linsky answered. "That league of traitors does not want this information to become public. Mister Zakharov believes if he is caught, the Russians will kill him and his family."

"How does Mister Zakharov know this?"

"Mister Zakharov is a cipher analyst at the embassy and he has copies of coded messages between Communist Party officials in Russia and certain individuals here at the embassy."

"Does he have these copies now?"

"Yes, he told me has many such copies."

"My last question, Mister Linsky," Sergeant Seward said. "How is it these people come to be in your house?"

"They hid all night in an abandoned building not far from here. Mister Zakharov knocked on the door and asked to use a telephone. I offered to help him because I speak Russian."

"That is quite a tale," Sergeant Seward remarked as he closed the notepad and slipped it into his hip pocket. "These people will need to be questioned more thoroughly down at headquarters."

Sergeant Seward stood up, pushed the chair back, and reached for Viktor's arm.

"No," Viktor shouted. "Not arrest."

"Calm down, Mister Zakharov," Sergeant Seward ordered. "You are not under arrest. There will be no handcuffs." Sergeant Seward looked directly at Viktor and said, "You and your family need to come with me down to headquarters. Before we can put you in protective custody, we will need to go over your story in detail."

"Mister Linsky come too," Viktor stammered.

"Mister Linsky cannot come," Sergeant Seward answered. "At the station we will arrange for our own interpreter. Come on let's go."

Sergeant Seward took Viktor's arm and directed him toward the front door. Sergeant Seward moved over beside Anna and Nikola and spread his arms as if he were corralling farm animals. He nodded his head toward the front door, directing them to follow Viktor.

"Thank you and your wife for all your kindness," Viktor spoke in Russian to Mr. Linsky as he was pushed out the door.

Once outside the house, Viktor and his family were herded down the sidewalk toward the police car sitting on the street. As they approached the police car, the front passenger door opened and a man climbed out. The color drained from Viktor's face and his jaw went slack.

"Lieutenant Zakharov, my friend, it is good to see you again," Colonel Sokolovsky taunted, a menacing grin on his face. "You and I shall have a long talk."

Colonel Sokolovsky yanked the rear door open, grabbed Anna's arm and shoved her into the car. He looked at Viktor and snarled, "Get in the car or your child dies here!"

Defeated and left with no hope of escape, Viktor complied. Colonel Sokolovsky slammed the door and climbed into the passenger seat. Sergeant Seward started the engine, shifted the car into gear, and sped off.

Viktor's face had gone pale, his eyes glassy with fear. His arms trembled. His hands clasped tightly between his knees. "*What have I done?*" his mind screamed as he glanced over at his precious Anna. He desperately wanted to tell Anna he was sorry, but the words would not come. His mouth was frozen. He turned back toward the front, his gaze fixed on the floor. Tears of anguish filled his eyes and ran down his cheeks, "*If only I had just been quiet,*" repeating over and over in his mind.

Chapter Twenty-Five

Constable First Class Richard Maples sat behind an old, scarred, metal desk in his office going over the incident report from the previous day's shootout on Maclaren Street. The report was still incomplete, lacking sufficient details describing the events leading up to the shootout. The lone survivor driving the Emerson Bakery delivery van had been rushed to the hospital in critical condition. He survived a ten-hour surgery and was recovering, but he was still unable to talk. Reliable eye witnesses were few, their statements so varied they were mostly unusable. Two of the bystanders interviewed had said they *thought* there might have been additional people in the bakery van. However, neither one of them could give a usable description or say in what direction they had disappeared. He flipped the folder closed and leaned back in his chair.

Deciding he would go to the hospital to see if the lone survivor of the shootout had improved enough to answer some questions, he slipped the folder into the top drawer of the desk. About to push back from the desk, he looked up when Constable Third Class Oscar Jenkins stopped and leaned against the door to his office.

"Constable Maples, I overheard the desk sergeant talking with Sergeant Seward," Constable Jenkins announced, surprised to see Constable Maples sitting behind the desk. "I think it may have something to do with the case you're working on."

"What did you hear?" Constable Maples asked.

"As I walked by the booking desk, I heard the desk sergeant tell Sergeant Seward he received a call from a man by the name of Linsky, lives over on Oakland Avenue not far from the river. Mister Linsky said a man and a little boy showed up at his door asking to use a telephone. Said the man was Russian and something about people from the embassy were trying to kill him and his family."

"What?" Constable Maples shouted. "When? How long ago?"

"Maybe fifteen or twenty minutes ago," Constable Jenkins replied. "Sergeant Seward ran out of the station like the Devil himself was chasing him."

"Where on Oakland Avenue?" Constable Maples barked as he jumped up out of his chair and snatched his service weapon from the bottom drawer of the desk.

"Huh?"

"The Linskys, dummy. Where on Oakland do the Linskys live?"

"All I heard was second house," Constable Jenkins shrugged.

"Why didn't you come and tell me about this sooner?" Constable Maples exploded as he rushed through the door.

"It's your day off. I didn't think…," Constable Jenkins' voice trailed off as he watched Constable Maples's disappearing back, already half-way across the police station's lobby.

Constable Maples flew out the police station's front door and raced around the corner of the building, nearly falling as he sprinted toward the parking lot. He yanked the door to his assigned squad car open, scrambled into the seat, and mashed his foot on the starter. Slowly the engine turned over, chugging slowly, pumping clouds of black smoke out of the exhaust pipe. Constable Maples pumped the accelerator pedal several times to get the engine running up to speed. With the engine running smoothly, he stomped on the accelerator pedal and slipped his foot off the clutch pedal.

The squad car's tires squealed loudly, leaving two black streaks as it roared through the parking lot. As the squad car approached the sidewalk, a pedestrian dove sideways to avoid being rundown. The squad car bounced over the curb, lurched into the street, and sped off down Catherine Street. An on-coming car swerved up onto the sidewalk to avoid a collision and crashed into a telephone pole. The driver of a car coming from the other direction stomped on his brakes, slide sideways and glanced off a parked car. Pieces of headlight glass and clods of dirt littered the street. A wayward hubcap rolled across the street and landed in the gutter. Constable Maples looked in the rear view mirror and saw two angry drivers shaking their fists at him.

Returning his attention to the street in front of him, he reached for the radio microphone hanging on a clip on the dashboard. He put the microphone to his mouth, took a breath, and stopped. Knowing Sergeant Seward could possibly be listening, he tossed the microphone aside, not wanting to forewarn him.

Three blocks later, siren blaring and red light flashing, Constable Maples, slowed slightly and jerked the steering wheel hard to the left. The squad car slid through the intersection sideways, lifting precariously off the passenger-side wheels. Constable Maples eased off the accelerator and the car settled back onto the pavement with a loud whump. Jamming the accelerator back to the floor, the squad car flew down Bank Street toward the river.

Two kilometers later as he approached Holmwood Avenue, Constable Maples turned off the siren and red light and slowed to a normal speed, not wanting to signal his approach. He continued for four blocks then turned right onto Wilton Crescent. Following the gentle curve to the right along Brown's Inlet Park, he turned right onto Wilton Lane and drove slowly down the street.

"I've missed them," constable Maples exclaimed, seeing no cars parked along the street. A sudden flash of red at the intersection one block ahead caught his attention. He down-shifted and rolled slowly up to the intersection. Two blocks ahead a black and white car passed through the intersection.

"It has to be him," Constable Maples muttered.

After turning onto Monk Street, Constable Maples matched the speed of the black and white car, maintaining enough distance to not be noticed. He followed the car as it turned onto Holmwood Avenue then quickly onto Bank Street. Constable Maples became puzzled when the black and white car passed through the intersection with Catherine Street and did not turn toward the police station. He continued following and watched as the black and white car turned right on Somerset Street.

"Where on Earth is he headed?" Constable Maples muttered out loud.

Six blocks later the black and white car turned left onto Queen Elizabeth Drive.

"He's headed for the embassy," Constable Maples shouted.

Determined to not let that happen, he turned left onto Metcalf Street, reached over and flipped on the siren and red light, and mashed the accelerator to the floor. Six blocks later he slowed slightly, turned right on Laurier Avenue West, and jammed the accelerator back to the floor. Flying past Marion Dewar Plaza, he reached the intersection with Queen Elizabeth Drive one-half block before the black and white car. Steering his car sideways across the street, Constable Maples blocked the black and white car's path.

Sergeant Seward jammed on his brakes and skidded to a stop mere inches from Constable Maples's squad car. Wild-eyed and in a rage, Sergeant Seward scrambled out of the car and raced to where Constable Maples stood.

"What is the matter with you?" Sergeant Maples screamed, the veins on his neck distended.

"I want to know where you are taking those people," Constable Maples challenged. "They may be part of my investigation. I need to speak with them."

"I outrank you," Sergeant Seward bellowed. "They are my prisoners."

"Prisoners? What have they done? What crime are they accused of?"

"That's none of your business, Constable."

"They are part of...," Constable Maples stopped, seeing Sergeant Seward reaching for the revolver hanging at his hip.

Constable Maples kicked Sergeant Seward's hand and planted his beefy fist square on the man's jaw with a crushing, round-house right. Sergeant Seward's limp body slammed against his patrol car and slid to the ground. Constable Maples grabbed the revolver that had fallen out of the sergeant's hand and stuffed it in his belt.

A man dressed in civilian clothes jumped out of the passenger seat and raced around the rear of the car.

"What meaning of this?" Colonel Sokolovsky yelled. "These are criminals. Steal papers from embassy. I take them embassy, NOW!"

"No, you will not take them anywhere," Constable Maples warned.

When Colonel Sokolovsky took a step toward him, Constable Maples drew his weapon and pointed it directly at the colonel's face.

"Sit down and shut up!" Constable Maples roared. "I said you are not going to take these people anywhere. Grab the sergeant's hand."

Looking at the business end of Constable Maples's weapon, Colonel Sokolovsky complied. He grabbed the sergeant's limp hand and held it up. Constable Maples pulled out a pair of handcuffs, handed them to the colonel, and ordered, "Put one on the sergeant's wrist and one on yours. Make sure they are tight."

Satisfied the two men were no longer a threat, he opened the back door of the black and white car. The Zakharovs sat huddled against the far side of the car, wild-eyed with fear.

"Come out quickly," Constable Maples ordered, beckoning with his hand.

Viktor shook his head. "No. I not know you. Why I come out?"

"I'm trying to save your life," Constable Maples answered. "Something is fishy about this mess. I've got to get you out of here. Come quickly. Get in my car. I'll take you back to the station. I need to find out if you know anything about the incident on Maclaren Street yesterday."

Viktor said something to Anna in Russian. She nodded her head in agreement and shoved Viktor toward the open door. They climbed out of the car and ran over to Constable Maples's car. He opened the back door and waited for them to climb in. Anna, holding a frightened and crying Nikola, climbed into the back seat. Viktor jerked the front door open and hopped in. After slamming the front door, Constable Maples raced around the car, jumped into the driver's seat, and shifted the car into reverse. He backed up a few feet, changed gears and sped away from the scene.

As the squad car roared down the street, Constable Maples's mind raced trying to decide what exactly he was going to tell the inspector. He had just assaulted a superior officer. His career as a police officer would likely be over.

Driving much too fast to make the turn onto Elgin Street, he continued down Laurier Avenue West. At the end of the block, he eased off the accelerator, downshifted, and turned left onto Metcalf Street. Three blocks later, driving at a normal speed, he heard the radio crackle to life.

"Attention, all officers, Division T. This is Sergeant Seward. Constable Richard Maples has assaulted a superior officer and threatened a high-ranking Russian official with his firearm. He abducted two Russian criminals by force. He must be stopped. Consider him armed and dangerous. Shoot on sight if necessary, by my authority."

"Great! Just great!" Constable Maples exclaimed, knowing the police station was now the last place he could go.

He jerked the steering to the right, turning onto Cooper Street. He reached over, flipped on the siren and flashing red light, and stomped on the accelerator.

"Somewhere to hide. I need somewhere to hide," Constable Maples muttered under his breath. Knowing he had to get out of the city, he made a sharp right onto Bay Street, turned off the red light and siren, and slowed to a normal speed.

"Police person sir, light down street!" Viktor Zakharov yelled from the passenger seat, pointing straight ahead.

Constable Maples saw the flash of red five blocks ahead turning off Albert Street onto Bay Street and headed toward them. A small park just past the next intersection afforded the only possible hiding place. He squealed around the intersection and roared into the first parking area at the edge of the park.

"Get down," he yelled.

Viktor reached over the seat, grabbed Anna's arm, and pushed her down. Little Nikola fell down onto the floor. He sat there smiling thinking this was just a game. Constable Maples leaned over on top of Viktor. Breathing hard, they listened to the sound of the siren growing louder until the siren's wail sounded as if it was right outside their vehicle. As quickly as it came, the siren's wail grew quieter and faded out completely.

"Wait until I check to see if it's safe," Constable Maples whispered as he straightened up and peeked out the window. "They're gone," he panted, pushing himself up straight.

He backed the squad car out of the parking space, edged up to the intersection, and looked both ways. No sign of police cars in either direction. He turned right onto Bay Street and drove eight blocks to the western edge of downtown Ottawa. After turning left onto Wellington Street they crossed the Portage Bridge over the Ottawa River into the province of Quebec. Less than one kilometer later, they connected with Boul de la Carriere and then to Highway One-Zero-Five. Constable Maples increased his speed as he passed through the northern outskirts of the city of Gatineau. The houses and business thinned out and finally gave way to the forested hills that lay along the Gatineau River.

Constable Maples drove north for ten kilometers and began to look for a place to get off the major highway and hide. He needed a place where he could talk to his passengers and find out why they were so important and whether throwing his career away had been worth it.

He turned off the highway onto a narrow gravel road named Pine Loop Trail. Traveling slowly along the rutted gravel road, they crossed a narrow bridge over a small babbling creek. Five hundred meters further along the road, Constable Maples turned off the road and drove down a tree-shrouded lane that led to a small cabin. No light glowed from any of the windows of the cabin and there were no cars parked in sight. He pulled his car behind the cabin to be out of sight from the road and turned off the engine.

"We should be safe here," Constable Maples said as he turned, looked at Victor, and offered his hand. "My name is Richard Maples. I am a constable with the Ottawa Police Department."

"My name Viktor Sergeyevich Zakharov," Viktor responded, shaking Constable Maples's hand. "In back seat is wife, Anna, and son, Nikola."

"Who was the Russian gentleman back there with Sergeant Seward?"

"His name Colonel Vasily Yevgenovich Sokolovsky," Viktor sneered, a look of disgust on his face. "He Military Attaché Officer at Russia Embassy."

"Why did he want you so badly?"

"Have many papers. Show much spying by Canada people. He want back. Not want people see."

"So, you did steal papers from the embassy. That would make you the criminal he said you are."

"No!" Viktor wailed, thinking yet another person did not believe him. "He is criminal! He with other men kill friend Martin Clavet and RCMP man."

"I read the report about that. I was there at the apartment earlier. The man there called himself Karpanov."

"Karpanov is pig. He take orders from Sokolovsky. Together they get important Canada people to give big secrets to Russia agents."

"Can you prove any of that?"

Viktor looked over the seat and had a short conversation with Anna in Russian. Fortunately, Anna had been able to snag the handbag crammed full of papers before she climbed out of Sergeant Seward's car. She reached into the bag, grabbed the messages Viktor had shown to the people at the Crown Attorney's office, and held them out toward Viktor. He snatched them out of her hand and handed then to Constable Maples.

"I can't read these," Constable Maples remarked. "They're written in Russian."

"Turn over," Viktor said. "Mr. Linsky translate on back."

Constable Maples turned the paper over, quickly scanned the messages, looked up at Viktor, and said, "While this *might* indicate spying, there is no way to know who the names on these papers are."

"Дай мне список кодовых имен," Viktor shouted.

Anna dug furiously through the papers in the bag, not finding what she looked for. Terrified, she began rifling through the papers a second time. Breathing a sigh of relief, she pulled out the list she was looking for and handed it over the seat to Viktor. Viktor handed the two-page list to Constable Maples and said, "This paper English. On side paper, look for names: Grant, Frank, Gray, and Foster. Look across. See real names."

Constable Maples took the list and ran his finger down the column of code names on the left side of the pages. He located each of the names Viktor had mentioned, a queasy feeling growing in the pit of his stomach. Staring at the top of the first page he scanned down through the real names, stopping on the last entry on the first page. He couldn't believe his eyes. There, next to the code name 'Chester' was the name Charles Seward, Sergeant, Ottawa Police Department.

Shaking his head, he asked, "May I see more of those?"

Viktor spoke in Russian. Anna handed Viktor the bag stuffed with papers. Viktor set the bag on the seat.

"I cipher person at embassy. I decipher messages. Are all true. I hear officers talk. Many want more war."

Constable Maples pulled out random pages, read them, and laid them aside. After reading a dozen of the messages, he had had enough. He felt physically sick. If he had not read the messages with his own eyes, he would have refused to believe it. High-ranking officials in the government *and* in the military were selling out the country he loved.

"Viktor, We have to get you to the Justice Department."

"Have talked people at justice. Nobody believe."

Chapter Twenty-Six

Colonel Sokolovsky sat behind his desk fuming, his hands balled into tight fists. He lifted up his hands and slammed his fists on the desk. "Only a few blocks and that criminal Zakharov would have been inside the embassy walls," he raged. Seward had let that other police officer overpower him and escape with the Zakharovs, a mistake for which he would pay with his life. But even worse, the incriminating papers had been lost, but only temporarily if he had anything to do with it.

About to place the telephone receiver to his ear, he was interrupted by a knock at the door to his office.

"Enter," he called out as he dropped the receiver back on the cradle.

A frightened and trembling Captain First Rank Bagoran, not wanting to deliver the news he had just been given, opened the door and stepped into the office. He swallowed hard and just stood there.

"Well," Colonel Sokolovsky growled, waiting for the man to speak.

"Sir, I... Ahh... I...,"

"Out with it or get out of my office," Colonel Sokolovsky yelled.

"I am afraid I have bad news, Colonel" Captain First Rank Bagoran stammered. "I have just been told Major Karpanov has been found dead."

"What?" Colonel Sokolovsky bellowed as he stood up and leaned forward, a look on his face that would melt carbon-hardened steel. "Where?"

"They say he was found in the second floor of a bakery shop on Pretoria Avenue. The side of his head was bashed in."

"Who is responsible?"

"I was not told," Captain First Rank Bagoran gulped, visibly shaking.

"Go find out who is responsible!" Colonel Sokolovsky screamed. "NOW! Or you will join him."

Captain First Rank Bagoran turned and sprinted through the doorway, down the hallway, and down the stairs three at a time. Most might consider Colonel Sokolovsky's outburst an empty threat given in anger, but Captain First Rank Bagoran knew better. Colonel Sokolovsky *never* made threats he did not intend to carry out.

Colonel Sokolovsky slumped down in his chair and slammed his fists on the desk again. "**боже мой**", he swore. "This must be stopped!"

He ripped the phone receiver from its cradle, dragging the phone halfway across the desk. He stabbed at the hook switch three times and waited. "I need Lamont, NOW," he shouted into the phone, not waiting for the operator to answer. Viciously banging his riding crop on the desktop, he waited for his adjutant to answer.

"This is Lamont. What is it, Colonel?" Lamont questioned.

"Karpanov has been murdered."

"Colonel, that is awful. Who is…,"

"There is a far more urgent matter," Colonel Sokolovsky interrupted. "Another police officer assaulted Seward and has taken the Zakharovs. Worst of all, they have the papers. We *must* find them."

"What should I do, Colonel?"

"Contact all our agents. Describe the Zakharovs and tell them to scour the city. They must be found."

"Should I contact locals, Beck, Leader, or others?"

"No, I will contact the undersecretary directly," Colonel Sokolovsky answered, not using the proper code name and completely violating his own required security protocol. "We need someone much higher for when they are found."

"We shall find them, Colonel," Lieutenant Colonel Radomir Ivanovich Meliknikov answered.

Colonel Sokolovsky stabbed the hook switch repeatedly again then waited for the operator.

"Yes, Colonel," the embassy operator answered.

"Get me the undersecretary, quickly."

Two minutes later, a male voice answered "Hello, who is this?"

"Grant," Colonel Sokolovsky answered.

"Huh... Ahh... Wait."

Colonel Sokolovsky heard a clunk through the receiver then silence. After a long silence, the male voice returned.

"You are never to call me here. I had people in my office for a very important meeting."

"More important than stupid meeting," Colonel Sokolovsky snapped. "Seward let other officer take Zakharovs *and* take private papers. They escape. Not know where they go. Big trouble if papers get found."

"When did this happen?"

"One hour now."

"What are you doing to find them?"

"I alerting all agents. You inform resources or what you call them. Zakharovs must be found quickly."

"I will make the necessary calls. You are never to call me here again."

Colonel Sokolovsky wanted to reply but the line had already gone dead. He slammed the receiver back into its cradle at the same time Captain First Rank Bagoran stopped in front of the open doorway. Colonel Sokolovsky motioned the captain into the office and waited.

"I have learned the police suspect the owner of the bakery, a Mister Emerson, is the one who murdered Major Karpanov," Captain First Rank Bagoran said with all the courage he could muster.

"Send someone to kill him," Colonel Sokolovsky snarled.

"That is not possible."

"And why not, Captain?"

"Emerson was trying to escape in the bakery's van. There was a shootout. Kozlov and Alekseev are dead. Emerson survived, but he is in the hospital and is not expected to live."

Colonel Sokolovsky's shoulders sagged. "*What else could possibly go wrong?*" he wondered. "Shut the door," he groaned, ordering the captain out of his office with a dismissive wave of his hand. Swiveling in his chair, he stared out the window. Despite his belligerent mannerism, deep inside he was very worried. What would happen if he did not regain possession of his private papers?

Ottawa Police Station T
Elgin Street
Ottawa, Ontario, Canada

Enraged and desperately wanting revenge, Sergeant Seward leaned back in his office chair with an ice pack pressed gently against the side of his face, an ugly, reddish-purple hue spreading up toward his ear. "*When I get my hands on Maples, I'm going to beat him to a bloody pulp,*" he promised himself. With a handkerchief in his other hand, he dabbed at the corner of his bleeding mouth.

Sergeant Seward sat forward when he noticed someone enter his office.

"Wha is ehh?" he whimpered through his cracked and swollen lips, wincing from the pain coming from the deep split at the corner of his mouth.

"There's a call for you at the booking desk from a Mister Grant," the young man announced. "He said it was urgent."

"Haa em puu hea," he said, wincing again as he pointed at the phone, shifting the bloody handkerchief around in his hand, trying to find a clean spot.

The young man turned quickly to prevent the sergeant from seeing the smile growing on his face. Nearly everybody in the station detested Sergeant Seward because of his snarky attitude. As far as he was concerned, the sergeant got exactly what he deserved. He hurried over to the booking desk and relayed the sergeant's request.

Sergeant Seward cringed when the phone on his desk rang. He dropped the handkerchief on the desk, grabbed the receiver, and held it to the uninjured side of his face.

"Hea-oo," he answered, squeezing his eyes closed as a tear formed and ran down his face.

"Who is this?"

"Is Sew-aaa," Sergeant Seward answered, struggling to get the words out.

"You not make sense. Tell me who is or I hang up."

"Seward." The sergeant squealed as he reached for the handkerchief, having reopened open the cut.

"This is Grant. Whatever takes. You must find Zakharov and papers. Your fault. Not listen excuse. Have one day or you pay. Big price."

Before Sergeant Seward could attempt to answer, the line went dead. He threw the receiver in the direction of the phone, missing completely. Not bothering to pick it up, he grabbed the ice pack and placed it against his throbbing face.

"*What am I supposed to do?*" he whined in his mind. "*I have no idea where Constable Maples or the Zakharovs are and I can't talk.*"

Pulling the center drawer of his desk open, he rooted around until he located a pad of paper. He laid the pad on his desk and pushed the drawer shut. Laying the ice pack aside, he wrote out instructions he would give to the desk sergeant on his way out of the building. He tore the top sheet off the pad and stood up. He opened the bottom draw, retrieved his back-up weapon, and headed for the booking desk.

The desk sergeant looked up when Sergeant Seward rapped on the side of the booking desk. He leaned over and took the slip of paper Sergeant Seward was holding out. After quickly reading the short note, he looked at Sergeant Seward and said, "Will do, Sergeant. I will notify all stations in the city and have them put all units on high alert. Is there anything else?"

Sergeant Seward shook his head, turned, and started for the front door. Unable to resist, the desk sergeant snickered. Sergeant Seward whipped around and glared at the desk sergeant.

"Ah gea yuu," Sergeant Seward mumbled.

Walking toward the main exit, Sergeant Seward heard the snickers and saw several people turning away, trying to hide the smiles on their faces. He kicked the swinging door open and stepped into the vestibule. Leaning against the wall, he pulled a fresh handkerchief from his pocket and dabbed his still bleeding mouth. He muttered something unintelligible then pushed the front door open and headed for his car parked at the far end of the parking lot.

Deserted Cabin
Pine Loop Trail
9 Km Southeast of Wakefield
Quebec, Canada

In the dark shadows behind the forest cabin, Constable First Class Maples stared out the windshield deep in thought, contemplating his next move.

"What we do, Richard?" Viktor asked.

"I don't know, Viktor," Constable Maples answered. "Given the level of people on that list, I'm trying to decide if there's anybody inside the Justice Department I can trust. If I don't call anyone there, who else can I call?" Banging his hand against the steering wheel, he asked himself over and over, "Who? Who? Who?"

After several minutes of scanning through images in his mind of people from his past, he shouted, "That's it! I'll call Owen Sammons."

Digging way back in his past, when he had served in the Royal Canadian Navy, he remembered that his division head,

Command Chief Petty Officer Owen Sammons, had mustered out and had joined the RCMP. If he remembered correctly, Owen had recently been promoted to the rank of CSM (Corps Sergeant Major). His immediate objective changed to finding a telephone.

"I'm going to see if there is a telephone in that cabin," Constable Maples announced as he pushed the car door open. "Stay here. I'll be back."

He pushed the door closed and walked partway down the lane toward the main road looking for evidence of overhead wires. He stepped off the left side of the lane into the trees. Pungently scented spruce branches slapped against his face and snagged his jacket. Pushing a large branch out of the way, he stepped deeper into the trees. The branch slipped out of his hand and snapped back, hitting several other branches. He shrieked and drew up his shoulders as cold water from the dew soaked branches dripped down his collar. "Nothing," he complained as he turned and headed back to the lane.

Being more careful, he ducked under the branches on the right side of the lane and entered the trees. Dodging under tree limbs, five meters in from the lane he saw what he was looking for. Three meters up in a large spruce tree, he saw a single black wire attached to a porcelain standoff. Following the wire through the trees, he arrived at the northeast corner of the cabin. The wire attached to a point under the eve and ran down to a rectangular box at the base of the cabin.

Constable Maples walked over to the car, tapped on the window, and waited for Viktor to roll the window down. "There's definitely a phone in the cabin. I'm going to go see if I can get in."

Constable Maples tramped along the narrow moss-carpeted strip between the trees and the cabin. From under a layer of leaves, came the rustling sounds of small animals scurrying away. Thick ferns lined the edge of a small clearing on the other side of the cabin. Narrow beams of sunlight streamed through a few widely-scattered openings in the dense canopy of trees, creating polka-dots of light on the ground. Rotting tree trunks lay crisscrossed deeper in the trees. Shelf fungus sprouted from the decaying logs, growing as large as dinner plates.

He was surprised to see that a brand new door with a six pane window had been installed. As he placed his hand on the doorknob, a black-capped chickadee skittered out of the trees, landed on the edge of the roof, and peered down at him. He looked up, whistled, and watched as the bird flitted away into the trees. Planted just off the corner of the cabin, stood a Common Winterberry shrub, covered with clusters of vibrant, red berry-like fruits. A black-masked Cedar Waxwing sailed out of the trees, landed in the shrub, snatched a berry in its beak, and darted back into the trees. In the distance Constable Maples heard the harsh 'jeee-ahh, jeee-ahh' of a blue jay.

He twisted the doorknob. As he had expected, the door was locked. Walking completely around the cabin, he found no other doors. Left with no other choice, he would have to gain entry the hard way. He turned away from the window and jabbed the pane of glass closest to the doorknob with his elbow. The glass did not break. He jabbed the glass harder. Shards of glass tinkled on the tile entryway's floor. Reaching in through the missing pane, he twisted the lock button. He withdrew his arm and twisted the knob and pushed the door open.

A quick scan of the cabin's three-room interior revealed furnishings far newer and nicer than existed in his own home. Beautiful paintings on the walls and color-coordinated accessories, confirmed this was more than just a weekend cabin. "*There must be a telephone somewhere*," he told himself. A quick scan revealed a phone sitting on a small table in the corner of what appeared to be the living room. Constable Maples picked up the phone, delighted to hear dial tone in his ear. He tapped the hook switch three times and waited.

"Operator, may I help you?"

"Yes, operator, this is Constable Maples, Ottawa Police badge number three-seven-four. This is an emergency," he exclaimed, hoping word of the assault had not yet reached the phone company. "Connect me to the RCMP Division O, CSM Owen Sammons. Please hurry."

"Right away, Constable," the operator answered.

Constable Maples coiled and uncoiled the phone wire around his finger as he waited for his old shipmate to answer.

"CSM Sammons. The operator said this was an emergency. Who is this?"

"This is Richard Maples. We served together in the Royal Canadian Navy. I worked under you when you were the division command chief. Do you remember me?"

"Yes, vaguely. What is this about an emergency?"

"I am now a Constable First Class for the Ottawa Police Department. Earlier today, I prevented a Russian cipher clerk and his family from being kidnapped. From the papers he has with him, I have learned of an unbelievable conspiracy. I am in trouble and I desperately need your help."

"We received a province wide alert. The alert said a family of Russians had been kidnapped and an Ottawa Police officer had assaulted a superior officer. Was that you?"

"Yes, but they're lying. It was not an assault. The police sergeant was taking these Russians straight to the embassy without notifying anyone. There was a Russian colonel with him. When I confronted them, the Sergeant Seward started to pull his weapon. I had no choice. Please believe me. I desperately need your help."

"Okay, Richard, I'm listening," CSM Sammons said.

"CSM, you better sit down. You are not going to believe what I am about to tell you."

For the most part, CSM Sammons listened patiently to Constable Maples's recounting of what Viktor Zakharov had told him and the documents he had personally read. He also told CSM Sammons about the shootout that had occurred the day before, leaving two men, carrying no ID but assumed to be Russians, dead and another man severely wounded and fighting for his life. CSM Sammons interrupted several times for clarification of whom a message had been sent by or who received it.

Constable Maples finished revealing what he knew of the conspiracy and waited for his old shipmate to say something.

"Richard, that's a pretty wild tale," CSM Sammons asserted. "I can certainly understand why nobody wanted to believe Mister Zakharov."

"That's all I know at this point, Sergeant Major. I believe him. He has more messages he says also reveal the conspiracy. A whole bag full. There has to be a hundred or more."

"What exactly is it you want from me?" CSM Sammons asked.

"Considering the list of code names I told you about, I'm afraid to call anyone at the Ottawa Police Department or the Justice Department. The Zakharovs and I need protection. Once we're safe, we can decide who to call."

"You realize you are asking me to jeopardize my career and, very possibly, a lengthy prison sentence."

"Yes, I know that and I'm sorry. If I had any other options, I would not have called you."

"Okay, let's say I believe you, for now," CSM Sammons replied. "Where exactly are you?"

"We are about halfway between Gastineau and Wakefield. Off highway one-zero-five on a gravel road named Pine Loop Trail. A cabin on the south side of the road a quarter mile before Vallée-Meech Parc. You can't see the cabin from the road."

"I know where that is," CSM Sammons acknowledged. "Sit tight. I'll be there as soon as I can."

"Thank you, Owen. I really appreciate this," Constable Maples responded as he laid the receiver back on the phone.

Constable Maples dug around in the drawers of various cabinets until he found a pad of paper and a pencil. He wrote a note, giving his name and the reason for his forced entry. Apologizing profusely for any damages, he promised to pay for any damages he had caused. He tore off the top page and laid it in the middle of the kitchen counter. After sweeping up the shards of broken glass and dumping them into a trash can, he stepped outside, locked the door, and pulled it shut.

Constable Maples returned to the car and explained to the Zakharovs that someone he knew in the RCMP was on his way to take them into protective custody. Relieved that someone might have finally believed them, the Zakharovs relaxed for the first time in days and began to chatter back and forth about the freedom they hoped to find in Canada.

Anna's first thoughts were about the abundance of food and how easily it was obtained. Viktor's thoughts were more personal, relieved that he would no longer have to constantly look over his shoulder.

For nearly an hour Constable Maples answered the Zakharovs questions about different aspects of what life would be like in Canada. Often, Viktor would have a puzzled look on his face, unable to fully comprehend being able to move around so freely *and* with no papers. Expecting CSM Sammons to have already arrived, Constable Maples became concerned. He climbed out of the car and walked back to the road to see if anyone was coming. Standing in the middle of the road, he watched for ten minutes. Seeing nothing, he turned and headed back toward the car. Halfway back to the car he heard the distant sounds of an approaching car.

He walked up to the car, leaned against it, and waited. Completely unprepared, he watched as two cars turned off the road and parked side by side, completely blocking the driveway. CSM Sammons and another man jumped out from the car on the left and one man jumped out from the other car. All three men drew their weapons and surrounded Constable Maples and the Zakharovs.

"Sorry, Constable Maples," CSM Sammons announced. "Hand over your weapon and be *very* careful. Remember, you are considered a dangerous fugitive. Based on the Ottawa Police alert, we would be fully justified to shoot you right where you stand. Corporal Woodham get the constable's weapon."

Constable Maples knew he was severely outnumbered and outgunned. He carefully withdrew his weapon, holding it with two fingers, and handed it to the corporal. The corporal stepped backward and handed the weapon to CSM Sammons.

CSM Sammons stuffed the weapon behind his waistband and said, "Corporal Woodham , take Corporal Keen and go get the Russians out of the car."

Corporal Woodham and Corporal Keen ran around to the other side of the car and ordered the Zakharovs to get out. With a look of abject defeat on his face Viktor opened the passenger-side door and crawled out. He held the rear door open while Anna crawled out with Nikola clinging tightly to her.

"Please do not hurt little boy," Viktor begged.

"Shut up Ruskie," Corporal Woodham shouted. "Make any trouble and I'll shoot him first."

"Please, no," Anna shrieked, turning her back toward the man to shield Nikola.

Corporal Woodham poked Viktor in the back with his weapon and ordered him around to the other side of the car. Corporal Keen forcibly shoved Anna causing her to stumble and fall against the car. Enraged, Viktor took a step toward the man. Corporal Woodham smacked Viktor on the side of the head with the barrel of his weapon and yelled, "One more step and you die right here, Ruskie!"

Viktor stopped and rubbed his bleeding ear. Holding his temper in check, Viktor helped Anna up. Together they walked around the car as ordered. Constable Maples made eye contact with Viktor and mouthed the word, "Sorry."

"Owen, why are you doing this?" Constable Maples asked.

"Because you assaulted a superior officer," CSM Sammons answered.

"But I explained that. I told you I had no choice. The sergeant was reaching for his weapon."

"I don't believe you, Richard. Corporal Woodham personally talked to Sergeant Seward and got the true story. The sergeant said he was not going to the Russian Embassy and that you attacked him for no reason. The sergeant said it is you that is collaborating with the Russians."

"If that's true, why would I call you and ask for help? I would have gone straight to the embassy."

"I don't know. Maybe to throw the police off the trail while you got away with the Zakharovs."

"That wouldn't make any sense. If I had the Zakharovs, why wouldn't I just go to the embassy?"

"It doesn't matter. I'm taking you in. Corporal Woodham will take the Zakharovs back to the embassy."

"You must not do that. They will be killed."

"Why would the Russians kill their own people?"

"Do you know what Viktor Zakharov does at the embassy?" Constable Maples questioned.

"No, but why would that matter?"

"He's the cipher analyst. He deciphers coded messages that come and go from the embassy. Like I told you on the phone, he has discovered messages that reveal a high-level conspiracy. He found a list of cover names that fell out of the embassy's military attaché's private diary. The list shows who the cover names really are and also the positions they hold. And, guess what? Sergeant Seward's name is on that list. Owen, Sergeant Seward lied to the corporal."

"Do you have that list?" CSM Sammons asked.

"Yes, plus over a hundred messages that confirm what I have told you," Constable Maples answered.

"Corporal Woodham, you and Corporal Keen go put the Zakharovs in your car. Richard, I want to see these papers."

Corporal Woodham pushed Viktor toward the car sitting on the west side of the lane. Corporal Keen followed with Anna and Nikola. Upon reaching the car, Corporal Woodham opened the rear driver-side door and motioned toward the rear seat with his weapon. Viktor climbed in slid across the seat to the far side. Corporal Keen shoved Anna inside the car and slammed the door. Before Corporal Keen could turn around, Corporal Woodham jammed his weapon against the back of Corporal Keen's head and fired. Corporal Woodham raced back to where CSM Sammons stood, pointing his weapon at CSM Sammons's face.

"Both of you stand still. Do not move."

"Woodham what is….,"

"Shut up and hand over your weapons," Corporal Woodham bellowed. "I'm tired of taking your orders. I can't let you see those papers."

"You'll never get away with this," CSM Sammons challenged.

"Oh yes I will," Corporal Woodham smirked. "I will kill you with the constable's weapon and then the constable with your weapon. I'll take the Zakharovs to the embassy and then I'll tell headquarters you and the constable had a shootout and I barely escaped with my life."

Back in Corporal Woodham's car, Anna watched in horror as the ambush played out before her eyes. A combination of terror, panic, and anger churned inside her. Once again she saw the freedom she so desperately wanted for her husband and little boy slipping away. "*No! No! Not again!*" a voice screamed in her mind.

Chapter Twenty-Seven

Crown Attorney's Office
Wellington Street
Ottawa, Ontario, Canada

Mrs. Mary Coulson, secretary to the Crown Attorney, slammed the door to her office and hurled her purse at the chair sitting in the corner. Smoldering with frustration and irritation that Inspector Hines had not yet returned her call to him the previous afternoon, she sat down heavily in her chair and angrily shoved a stack of papers out of the way. She had made it perfectly clear that the matter she wished to discuss was urgent. "Why hasn't he called back?" she groused.

Before leaving her house and while finishing her morning coffee, she had happened across an article in the morning newspaper describing the shootout that had occurred on Pretoria Street. According to the article, two unidentified men were dead and a man named Emerson was in the hospital in critical condition. About to set the newspaper aside, the last paragraph had caught her attention. One witness had said he thought he saw two people get out of one of the cars and disappear. The article ended with a quote from the only other witness, "One of them, a man I think, was wearing baggy, tattered clothes. I can't be sure, but I think one of them was a woman. It looked like she was carrying a small child. People were shooting. I only got a glance before I ducked for cover."

Mrs. Coulson remembered that Mr. Zakharov had been wearing clothes that looked like they were two sizes too small for him and they were definitely old and tattered. What if the people seen running away were the Zakharovs? If so, it would confirm what Mr. Zakharov had told her. Someone *was* trying to kill him and his family. Determined to get someone to listen, she decided she would not wait for Inspector Hines to call her back. She would call someone else and she knew exactly who to call; her husband's brother, the Deputy Commissioner of the RCMP.

She snatched up the phone receiver and jammed it to her ear, poked the hook switch several times, and waited for the operator to come on the line.

"Number please," the switchboard operator drawled.

"Betty, this is Mary Coulson in the Crown Attorney's office. Get me Arlo Murray, the Deputy Commissioner, RCMP Headquarters, Division C. Tell him to call me right back. It's important."

"Right away, Misses Coulson," the operator answered.

Less than two minutes later, the telephone on Mrs. Coulson's desk rang. She picked up the receiver and said, "Hello."

"Hey, Mary," Deputy Commissioner Murray chimed. "I was surprised when the operator said you needed to talk to me and that it was important. What can I help you with?"

"Thanks for calling back so quickly, Arlo," Mrs. Coulson said. "Did you hear about the horrible shooting that happened in Ottawa yesterday?"

"Yes, I saw that on the morning's action report. Why do you ask?"

"I believe I know the two people that were seen disappearing from the scene. I called Inspector Hines yesterday, but he still has not called me back."

"How would you know those people?"

"A man named Zakharov came to my office two days ago claiming he had uncovered a conspiracy between high-ranking Canadians and Russian Agents. Even more concerning, he said the Russians want another world war. He had several papers that supported his story. He said he went to the Ottawa Journal and the deputy minister at the Justice Department, but nobody believed him. He came here asking to apply for citizenship. I tried to help him, but I couldn't because he works at the embassy and he is not a landed immigrant."

"What does he do at the embassy?"

"He said he is the cipher analyst. I suggested that he come back the next day and bring more papers. I can still see the look of terror on his face. As he was leaving, he said someone from the embassy would kill him."

"I'm sorry, but I…."

"Oh, but there's more. After he left, I just couldn't forget the look on his face, so I called Mr. Billingsley, the Prime Minister's private secretary. I explained Mister Zakharov's story to him. He scoffed and said he didn't believe it. Well, he called back a few minutes later quite upset and told me to forget it ever happened."

"That seems odd," the deputy commissioner observed.

"Then he threatened me," Mrs. Coulson exploded. "He said if I wanted to stay employed, I would forget it."

"He threatened you. Are you sure?"

"Yes, Arlo, I'm sure," Mrs. Coulson snapped.

"Mary, I'm sorry," the deputy commissioner apologized. "I didn't mean to accuse you of lying, but you must admit that story is a lot to take in."

"I know, but I swear every word of it is true and I believe Mister Zakharov. Arlo, you have to do something to help those poor people."

"Okay, Mary, I will do some checking and see what I can find out. First, I am going to call Inspector Hines and find out why he did not return your call."

"Thanks, Arlo. Let me know what you find out." Mrs. Coulson replaced the receiver and turned toward the pile of work on her desk.

Deserted Cabin
Pine Loop Trail, 9 Km Southeast of Wakefield
Quebec, Canada

Intense anger continued to churn inside Anna as she watched Corporal Woodham pointing his weapon at the only man that had said he would help them. Not just anger, rage boiled up inside her like molten lava threatening to explode from a volcano.

"Viktor," she screamed. "Do you see what is happening?"

"But we are unarmed," Viktor cried. "There is nothing we can do and what about Nikola?"

As the raging vortex of anger swirled inside her, she made a choice. The freedom she craved was worth fighting for. Ignoring the risk, there was no doubt in her mind that she would rather die than go back to Russia.

Anna handed Nikola to Viktor and grabbed the door handle.

"Anna, what are you doing?" Viktor wailed. "You must not…."

"Viktor, be quiet," Anna cautioned. "If we do nothing, we shall all go back to Russia and die and we will never know freedom."

Anna slipped out the door as quietly as she could and gently let it close. She crouched down and crept to the front of the other car. Corporal Woodham's attention fixed on CSM Sammons, he stood with his back toward Anna. Measuring the distance in her mind, she convinced herself she could cover the distance quickly enough. She took two deep breaths, sprang out from behind the car, and lunged toward the corporal, pumping her legs as hard as she could.

Anna hit Corporal Woodham square in the back. The weapon fired as it flew out of his hand. Corporal Woodham landed face first on the gravel lane with Anna on top of him. Anna rolled off and sprang to her feet. Corporal Woodham rose to his knees, his chest heaving, desperately trying to refill his lungs with air. CSM Sammons lashed out with his foot, landing it against the corporal's chin. Corporal Woodham lurched backward and landed flat on his back, unconscious.

"Constable, handcuffs quick," CSM Sammons hollered. "Then go check on Corporal Keen."

Constable Maples grabbed a pair of handcuffs from a pouch on his belt, tossed them to CSM Sammons, and ran to the car where Corporal Keen lay motionless on the ground. He looked down at the corporal and shook his head, knowing instantly there was nothing he could do for the man. He returned to where CSM Sammons stood.

"Sorry, the corporal's dead," Constable Maples said. "Now, maybe you'll believe me."

CSM Sammons waved Viktor to join them. When Viktor arrived, he handed Nikola to Anna and took the weapon CSM Sammons held out toward him.

"Here, take this weapon and guard this criminal," CSM Sammons ordered. "And thank you…. Ah…."

"My name Anna."

"Thank you, Anna, for saving my life," CSM Sammons exclaimed, turning toward Constable Maples. "Now, let's go have a look at those papers."

"Follow me," Constable Maples responded.

Constable Maples walked over to his car, opened the door, and retrieved the bag of papers. He dug through the cache of papers, looking for the one with the list of code names. After locating the list, he ran his finger down the column of actual names.

"Ahh, here it is," he exclaimed. "Just as I thought. Next to the code name 'Martin' is the real name 'Maxwell Woodham'. Seems our fellow officer over there is part of the conspiracy. Sergeant Seward's name is on here also next to the code name 'Chester'."

"Let me see that," CSM Sammons barked.

He grabbed the list, examined both pages thoroughly, and said, "I don't believe it. I'm looking right at it and I don't believe it. The names on here are shocking."

"Is all true," Viktor asserted. "I see code names on many messages. Many in bag you hold."

"We don't have time to look at all those messages," CSM Sammons remarked. "If this is all true, and it certainly appears it is, there are many people that would kill to keep this from getting out. We are going to need help finding a place to hide, and quickly. Is there a phone in that cabin?"

"Yes, there is," Constable Maples replied.

"Come on, let's go," CSM Sammons barked. "Viktor, you and Anna stay here. Richard, let's drag that mutt over to his car. We'll dump him in the front seat and handcuff him to the steering wheel. Then we'll go make a phone call."

After securing the unconscious Corporal Woodham, they rejoined the Zakharovs and headed for the cabin. For the second time, Constable Maples stuck his arm through the missing window pane and unlocked the door.

"Phone's over there," Constable Maples advised as they walked into the cabin's living room.

CSM Sammons walked over and put his hand on the phone. He turned, looked at Viktor, and said, "Mister Zakharov, the constable here mentioned earlier that you had already talked to several people about the papers you have. Can you tell me who you talked to?"

"I talk man name Morrison at *Ottawa Journal*. He not believe. Then I go Justice place. Talk man name Turner. Not help. Say come back next day. I go back. Talk woman name Coulson. Ask to be citizen. She say take five years. I go back bakery. Man name Emerson take me apartment to get more papers. Karpanov show up. RCMP man name Davenport also come. Find me in neighbor apartment. He believe me. Other men show up kill RCMP man and neighbor. I run. Emerson see me on street. Men with guns shoot Emerson. Anna and me run. Hide in old barn. Knock on houses. Find Russian man, name Linsky. He call police, but Sokolovsky come. Taking us embassy. Maples save us. We come here cabin. Sorry, I no English speak good."

"You say a man by the name of Davenport talked to you?"

"Yes. I hide across hall in Martin Clavet apartment. RCMP man knock on door. Find me hide under bed. Say he believe me."

"I heard about an RCMP staff sergeant being killed in a shootout, but the Ottawa Police report said it was a robbery."

"Two men, shoot him and neighbor. Police lie. Not robbery."

"That is quite a story, Mister Zakharov," CSM Sammons said. "I had considered calling someone in the Department of Justice, but after hearing your story, I don't think that would be a good idea."

CSM Sammons stood silently going over in his mind who he should call. He, Constable Maples, and the Zakharovs needed help and they needed it quickly. Unable to think of anyone else, he decided he would call his superior. He lifted the receiver, punched the hook switch three times, and waited.

"Operator, how may I help you?" a shrill, female voice asked.

"This is Command Sergeant Major Sammons. Get me the RCMP detachment at Ottawa. Hurry this is an emergency."

"Royal Canadian Mounted Police, Ottawa Detachment," a female voice answered. "This is Lenora. How may I direct your call?"

"Lenora, this is Command Sergeant Major Sammons. I have an emergency. Connect me to Inspector Hines."

"Right away, sir."

"I hope I can get the inspector to believe me," CSM Sammons shrugged as he waited.

"Sergeant Major, Lenora tells me you have an emergency," Inspector Hines announced. "I was notified you and two corporals left the station in hurry. Something about escaped Russians. Is that your emergency?"

"Yes, that's it exactly, Inspector," CSM Sammons replied.

"I heard about an Ottawa Police Constable assaulting a superior officer and then abducting a pair of Russians. Are you involved in that?"

"Yes, Inspector, but that is only part of it," CSM Sammons continued. "The constable and the Russians are here with me. Corporal Woodham threatened to kill me. He's handcuffed to his steering wheel. Corporal Keen is dead. The Russians have...."

"Hold on," Inspector Hines interrupted. "You're not making sense. Slow down and tell me exactly what happened."

CSM Sammons took a deep breath and, as briefly as he could, recounted the events of the past thirty minutes, including the conspiracy Viktor Zakharov had uncovered and the papers he had smuggled out of the embassy.

"Sergeant Major are you crazy?" Inspector Hines roared into the phone. "That is the wildest story I have ever heard. If you tell that story to anyone else, your career will be over and they'll lock you up in the Looney Bin. Do you *really* expect anyone to believe that?"

"Yes, Inspector, I do expect you to believe that because it is true. Mister Zakharov is the cipher analyst at the embassy. He deciphers the embassy's message traffic and he has a stack of messages that prove what he is saying."

"I don't care if he's the….," Inspector Hines stopped talking abruptly when he noticed his administrative assistant waving wildly in the doorway to his office. "Hang on Sergeant Major. My assistant says she has something urgent." The inspector placed his hand over the mouthpiece, preventing CSM Sammons from hearing what had caused the interruption.

CSM Sammons turned toward Constable Maples, shrugged, and said, "The inspector just stopped talking. Something urgent, but I don't know what."

"Sergeant Major stay on the line. Do not hang up. The deputy commissioner says he must talk to me immediately."

CSM Sammons heard a clunk in his ear as the inspector laid the receiver on the desk. He could hear muffled voices, but could not make out what they were saying. "He's talking to the deputy commissioner," CSM Sammons informed the constable. CSM Sammons fidgeted as he waited for the inspector to return. "I don't know how long it will be before he comes back on the line. You all just as well sit down."

Constable Maples sat down on a straight-back wooden chair beside an enormous natural stone fireplace. He shivered in the damp air, thinking how nice it would be if there was a roaring fire in the fireplace. The Zakharovs took a seat on a dark green, tufted sofa on the other side of the room. Anna set Nikola on the floor, took a small toy out of her jacket pocket, and handed it to the little boy. The cabin was quiet except for the sound of Nikola pounding the toy on the floor. They all looked up when they heard CSM Sammons say, "Yes, I'm still here."

"I wouldn't have believed it, Owen," Inspector Hines stammered, breaking protocol and reverting to the sergeant major's first name. "I just got dressed down by the deputy commissioner. Seems somebody in the Crown Attorney's Office had talked with a Mister Zakharov. That someone believes there is ample evidence to believe his story. The deputy commissioner instructed me in no uncertain terms that I am to put the Zakharovs in protective custody. The order came from the Prime Minister himself. The deputy commissioner's last order was that I am to make certain those papers are seized and protected. He warned me that if I fail, I will be demoted to corporal and sent to the Northern Territory. I hope you understand how important this is."

"I understand, sir," CSM Sammons replied. "I am sorry this has caused you such trouble."

"Let's just ignore that and make certain the Zakharovs are protected. Stay put. It will be dark in a little over an hour. The Prime Minister is scrambling a special ops team to come and escort you, the constable, the Zakharovs, and the papers to a secure location. The team will also tidy up the area. Protect the Zakharovs and those papers. Whatever the cost, Owen."

"Yes, sir. I will," CSM Sammons answered. He hung up the phone, walked over to the fireplace, and sat down on the hearth.

All eyes had followed the sergeant major as he walked slowly across the room and sat down. The Zakharov's expression quickly turned to disappointment and fear as the sergeant major sat there staring at the floor. After a long pause, he looked up at the Zakharovs and said, "Somebody at the Crown Attorney's Office has believed you. Deputy Commissioner Murray told me the Prime Minister himself is sending a special ops team to take you and your papers into protective custody. Constable, you and I are to accompany them."

Viktor and Anna leaped up off the couch and hugged each other, hardly able to grasp that someone had finally believed them and that their ordeal was nearly over. Smiling from ear to ear, they rushed over to CSM Sammons and grabbed his hand, pumping it wildly and thanking him profusely. Only by their expressions could he tell they were elated, because they were jabbering in Russian. They rushed over to where Constable Maples sat and thanked him also.

"Constable, the special ops team won't arrive here for a little over an hour. They want to wait until after dark to move us," CSM Sammons advised. "Will you stand watch while I see if I can find something to eat for our Russian friends. The deputy commissioner said we are to make certain they reach a secure location. No matter what the cost!"

"I'll be glad to," Constable Maples responded. He lifted his weapon out of its holster, pulled the slide back to make certain a round was in the chamber, and headed for the door.

"Hey, Richard," CSM Sammons called out. "the deputy commissioner said someone would signal you with a red light. Two flashes."

"Got it," Constable Maples acknowledged as he slipped out the door, weapon in hand.

Chapter Twenty-Eight

Camp X
Deep in the North Woods
Undisclosed Location

Late in the evening of Friday, August 14th, 1945, a heavily armed contingent of Canadian Special Forces, driving all black vehicles delivered the Zakharovs, CSM Sammons, Constable Maples, and a bag stuffed full of papers to the commanding officer of Camp X. Located deep in the woods, far from any population centers, and heavily fortified, Camp X served as a top-secret wartime school to train Canadian and Allied soldiers in sabotage and counterintelligence techniques. The camp also often served as a secret location for the interrogation of military and civilian defectors.

CSM Sammons and Constable Maples were interrogated for several hours and then loaded into one of the black vehicles and transported to an undisclosed location. They would be hidden away until all potential threats related to the revealed conspiracy had been neutralized. At that time, they would be returned to their units for duty.

Temporarily, the Zakharovs were settled into a somewhat ramshackle three-bedroom farmhouse used to house various military assets or other persons of special interest. An intelligence officer and a stenographer, both fluent in Russian, were assigned fulltime to the Zakharovs to be present anytime they were questioned or interrogated. An enlisted staff member was assigned to deliver fresh clothes, toiletries, food, or other personal items they might need.

The Zakharovs marvelled that they were allowed to take baths and use as much hot water as they wanted. A special surprise for Anna was the brand new bar of perfumed soap perched on the edge of the tub. She was especially thrilled as it was so much better than the harsh Russian soap that dried her skin out. Dressed in brand new clothes, Viktor munched on fresh fruit and made a sandwich with the most delicious sliced meat he had ever tasted. Anna watched as little Nikola happily splashed in the tub. Tears formed in her eyes and rolled down her cheeks, knowing her little boy would grow up knowing true freedom, a dream that she had thought was unattainable. After thirty minutes, she lifted Nikola out of the water kicking and screaming and wrapped him in the softest towel she had ever felt.

Viktor and Anna jabbered back and forth in Russian in between bites as Anna and Nikola gobbled down the sandwiches Viktor had prepared. After getting Nikola settled down and asleep, they undressed and climbed under deliciously fresh smelling sheets. Asleep in mere minutes, they had the best night's sleep either of them could remember.

The next day proved to be arduous for the Zakharovs as they were scheduled to be interrogated by multiple teams from Canada's RCMP, the United States FBI, and England's MI5 and MI6. The questioning was slow going as everything had to pass through the assigned interpreter. Often, questions and answered had to be repeated several times to be certain accuracy was maintained.

At the end of day one, everyone on the first two teams, the RCMP and the FBI, were completely stunned by the number of individuals involved and the level the conspiracy rose to. The assigned leader from each of the two teams met separately to discuss the first day's findings and develop a plan for the days to come. Horrified by the level to which the conspiracy rose, they ordered an immediate lock down on all information pertaining to the interrogation. All transcripts, documents, photos, and conversations were to be considered ultra-secret and Eyes-Only to a very small and select group of individuals.

Inspector Boris Bartos, the RCMP interrogator, and Greg Miles, the FBI interrogator, concluded it was imperative that a sampling of the massive amount of evidence be delivered to

Brice Winthrop, Canada's Prime Minister ASAP. They photographed the two-page list of code names and nine other documents that had been translated. The film was rushed to the camp's photography lab for immediate processing. Less than an hour later, a phone call was made to the Prime Minister's residence. A courier with the photos locked inside a leather case handcuffed to his wrist and an armed escort sped out of the gate of Camp X.

Office of the Prime Minister
Wellington Street
Ottawa, Ontario, Canada

The following day, Leonid Grigoryovich Volkov's personal limo screeched to a stop in front of the executive office building of the Canadian government. The limo driver climbed out, hustled to the passenger side of the car, and held the door open for the Russian ambassador. A security guard stood waiting at the building's front entrance, ready to escort the ambassador directly to the Prime Minister's office.

Swearing under his breath, the ambassador was not happy about being summoned like a school boy to the principal's office. He had absolutely no idea why he had been ordered to the hastily called meeting. Vowing the Prime Minister would get an earful, he stomped up the steps, stopping abruptly when the security guard stepped in front of him.

"Get out of my way," Ambassador Volkov bellowed.

The security guard placed his hand on his weapon and warned, "I would lower your voice if I were you, Mister Ambassador. I am to escort you straight to the Prime Minister's office. You only are allowed to enter. Your escort is to stay here."

"My escort goes where I go," the ambassador snarled.

"No sir," the guard answered. "You are to be escorted in alone. If you resist, I have the authority to arrest you. Is that what you wish?"

"Your superiors will hear about this," the ambassador growled.

He turned and spoke in Russian to the uniformed man standing beside him. The man did an about-face and returned to the limo. The security guard pulled the door open and waited for the ambassador to enter. Inside the building's entrance, two more security guards stood at attention with weapons at the ready. The ambassador did not speak another word as he was escorted up three flights of stairs. The security guard opened the door to the Prime Minister's office.

"Ambassador Volkov, come and sit down," Prime Minister Brice Winthrop ordered, pointing to a chair positioned in front of his desk.

"I want to know the meaning of this."

"I suggest you be quiet and listen, Mister Ambassador," the Prime Minister snapped.

"You cannot speak to me like that."

"You sir, are a guest in my country. I will speak to you however I choose." The Prime Minister held up his hand to silence the ambassador and continued, "We have uncovered a disturbing conspiracy being perpetrated by officers from your embassy."

"That is a lie," Ambassador Volkov roared. "We have done no such thing."

"Oh, really," the Prime Minister shouted as he slammed the photos from Camp X down on the desk. "And just what do you suppose those are?"

The ambassador leaned forward and studied the photos one by one. Once the ambassador had finished with the photos on the desk, the Prime Minister handed him two more.

"What are these photos?" Ambassador Volkov challenged.

"They are photos taken of a two-page list of individuals involved in a conspiracy to steal military secrets," Prime Minister Winthrop answered.

"That proves nothing," Ambassador Volkov scoffed.

"Oh, really. Where do you suppose that list came from, Mister Ambassador?" The ambassador glared at the Prime Minister, but did not answer. "That list fell out of Colonel Sokolovsky's private diary."

A look of shock spread across the ambassador's face then disappeared before he answered, "I don't believe you."

"We have the individual that discovered the list. In addition, we also have over one hundred documents that were in Colonel Sokolovsky's possession. As we speak, those documents are being photographed and translated. I have been told there are some very disturbing things on those documents. Once we arrest all the Canadians on that list, I am certain they will have much to tell us. Would you care to comment, Mister Ambassador?"

The color drained from the ambassador's face as he settled back in his chair. His shoulders sagged and he shook his head, the bluster and arrogance gone.

"I can see you now understand why I called you here?"

Hands trembling in his lap, he looked up at the Prime Minister and said, "But Prime Minister, I swear I knew nothing of this conspiracy. Had I known, I would have stopped it."

"For your sake, I hope that is true. Otherwise, you are going to spend a very, very long time in prison."

"But we have diplomatic immunity."

"Not for war crimes. I am certain the Crown Attorney's office and the courts will consider the stealing of military secrets to be war crimes. You will likely die in prison."

"Please believe me, Prime Minister. I know nothing of this. I would never allow such a thing to happen. We are here to be Canada's ally."

"For now, let's say I believe you," the Prime Minister said, glancing up at the clock on the wall. "As of five minutes ago, all telephone and telegraph lines in and out of the embassy have been temporarily disconnected. A brigade of Canadian Army soldiers have surrounded the embassy. Any Russian personnel currently outside the embassy will be allowed to reenter. Once they are inside, no one, and I mean no one, will be allowed to leave. If anyone sets foot outside the embassy, they will be shot. Is that understood, Mister Ambassador?"

"Yes, Mister Prime Minister," Ambassador Volkov answered, knowing that only inside the embassy walls did he have any authority.

"One other thing, Ambassador Volkov," Prime Minister Winthrop added as he handed him a piece of paper. "You are to have every officer in the embassy write this sentence on a piece of paper. I will send somebody by the embassy tomorrow morning at eight am sharp to collect the papers. If it is not ready, the repercussions will be severe. Do you understand?"

"Yes, Mister Prime Minister."

"Very well. Now, get out of my office," Prime Minister Winthrop barked. "A military escort is waiting to accompany you to the embassy to make certain you contact no one. Once our investigation has concluded, you will be notified of any charges that will be filed. Sergeant get him out of here."

Ambassador Volkov seethed inside as he stomped down the stairs and out of the building with the security guard one step behind him. He climbed into his limo without a word. During the entire trip back to the embassy, he planned what he was going to do to Colonel Sokolovsky for the embarrassment he had just endured.

Camp X
Deep in the North Woods
Undisclosed Location

The interrogation of the Zakharovs lasted two more days because of the required repeating of questions and answers and the tedious translation of the one hundred eight documents Viktor had escaped with. A number of the documents had been handwritten by someone with incredibly poor penmanship, slowing down the translation process even further. The handwriting samples Prime Minister Winthrop had demanded would be used to identify the authors of the handwritten documents to further corroborate Viktor's testimony.

At the end of the third and final day, Inspector Boris Bartos, the RCMP intelligence officer, sat down with Viktor to answer some follow up questions generated by a review of the transcripts of the first two days of interrogation. The session lasted a little over two hours. Satisfied with Viktor's answers, Inspector Bartos had one final task. He spoke slowly and directly to Viktor in English, "You and Anna are to be given new identities. Do you understand?"

"Yes," Viktor replied. "Get new names."

"That is correct," Inspector Bartos said, sliding a piece of paper across the table. "Your new names are Stanley and Evelyn Krysac. You are of Czech descent. In a few days you will receive new citizenship papers. They will indicate that you and your wife emigrated to Canada four years ago. A new birth certificate will indicate that your son, Nicolas, was born here."

"Canada citizens?" Viktor remarked, a puzzled look on his face. "Woman at Crown place say take five years. How can this be?"

"In this special situation, our government will make an exception. From this day forward, you will be the Canadian citizens written on that paper. Do you understand?"

"Yes, exception," Viktor acknowledged, pointing at the names. "We now these people."

"Good. Practice saying and writing those names so they become automatic."

"Yes, I Stan-ley Kry-sac," Viktor beamed. "Viktor and Anna Zakharov gone. No more."

"Okay, I believe we are done with the questions at least for now. Someone will meet with you tomorrow to begin English lessons." Inspector Bartos stood, held out his hand, and said, "I admire you for your courage. Mister Stanley Krysac, may I be the first to welcome Canada's newest citizen."

Stanley jumped up from his chair, grasped the inspector's hand, and said, "Am happy to make acquaintance, Inspector Bartos. We glad be Canada Citizens."

Inspector Bartos and the other individuals in the room watched as Stanley was escorted out of the room. Soon Stanley and Evelyn Krysac would learn that their last name, Krysac, means rat, or mole, in the Czech language. The idea for their name probably came from Inspector Bartos as he was Czech-born, emigrating to Canada with his parents many years earlier.

"I dare say this information is going to cause some raised eyebrows when it gets out," Inspector Bartos remarked.

"That may be the understatement of the century," Greg Miles, the FBI interrogator, joked.

Prime Minister's Office
Wellington Street
Ottawa, Ontario, Canada

Prime Minister Brice Winthrop grabbed the large official-looking envelope that had just been laid on his desk. He opened the middle drawer of his desk, picked up a letter open-er, and sliced through the seal on the envelope. Scanning quickly through the flowery greeting, he came to the purpose of the letter. He read the sender's demand and nearly fell out of his chair he was laughing so hard.

"Ken, come in here," the Prime Minister chuckled. "You aren't going to believe this."

Ken Caldwell, the Prime Minister's new private secretary, pushed back from his desk, stuck his head through the door-way to the Prime Minister's office door, and asked, "What is it, sir?"

"Come over here. You have got to read this."

The Prime Minister handed the letter to his secretary and watched his eyes flit back and forth as he read.

"You have got to be kidding," he sputtered. "Is this for real?"

"Yes, it's for real," the Prime Minister answered. "The Russians are nothing if not predictable. They seem to think if they bluster loud enough and long enough, we will give in to their demands."

The Prime Minister plucked a red pencil from a cup sitting on his desk and underlined the portion of the letter that had made him and his secretary laugh:

> *I, Leonid Grigoryovich Volkov, Ambassador for the Embassy of the U.S.S.R. demand that the Department of External Affairs take immediate and urgent measures to locate and arrest V. Zakharov and to hand him over for deportation as a capital criminal, who has stolen money belonging to the Russian Embassy.*

The Prime Minister grabbed a sheet of paper and wrote a short note to be sent to Ambassador Volkov.

> *Canadian authorities have no knowledge of where Mister Zakharov is or might be. An RCMP All Points Bulletin will be issued to all RCMP offices across the country to be on the lookout for a Mister V. Zakharov.*

"Here, type this up and then I will sign it," Prime Minister Winthrop snickered as he handed the paper to his secretary.

Epilogue

Three days later, for their protection, Stanley, Evelyn, and Nicolas Krysac were moved from Camp X to an undisclosed location with their new government-provided identities. Having been moved under the cover of darkness, the Krysac's had no idea what to expect when they awakened the next morning. Stanley had trouble pronouncing the name Evelyn, so they agreed to shorten it to Evy.

"Evy, come quick," Stanley bubbled. "You must see this."

Evy scooped up little Nicolas and hurried over to the window. She looked through the window as Stanley held the curtain out of the way.

"Oh, my," she exclaimed. "That is beautiful. Let's go outside and get a better look."

Stanley pulled their bedroom door open and they rushed across the living room toward the front door, surprising the duty watch seated on the couch.

"Whoa folks. Where are you going?" the uniformed man asked.

"We go out look at the lake," Stanley answered.

"See that you go no farther," the man instructed, following them out the door. The man stopped and sat in a chair at the edge of the porch where he could observe the Krysacs.

The three Krysacs strolled down to the water's edge.

"Vik… I mean Stanley, water is so clear can see clear down to bottom."

Stanley reach down and stuck his hand in the crystal clear water. "Hey, that's really cold," he exclaimed in Russian, pulling his hand back and wiping it on his trousers.

"Stanley, you must remember speak only in English," Evy admonished.

"I know, but is hard find words," Stanley complained.

"Yes, but will get easier with practice," Evy said as she took hold of his hand.

They wandered along the shore of the lake until the man on the porch yelled at them to go no farther. They reversed direction and returned to where they had started. Stanley spied a fallen log not far away and pushed Evy in that direction. They spent nearly an hour sitting on the log watching the glistening water and listening to the birds calling to each other in the trees.

"Come, Evy, we must go before guard comes after us."

Stanley stood and offered his hand to help Evy up. As they began to walk away, Stanley turned back toward the lake and said slowly in English, "I believe we like it here very much."

Eight days later, special squads of RCMP officers and Justice Department agents spread out across several provinces. At precisely five o'clock in the morning, in a finely orchestrated operation, those squads arrested fourteen individuals identified as key perpetrators in the Soviet spy ring. The suspects were seized and hauled away as quickly as possible and with no explanation to minimize the possibility others involved in the spy ring would find out and disappear.

In theory, Canadian civil rights were still suspended under the War Measures Act, which had not been revoked as the war had only recently ended. Using the War Measures Act as legal justification, the suspects were taken to multiple locations, held incommunicado, and interrogated.

All but two of the fourteen suspects quickly broke down under interrogation after being shown incriminating copies of the documents Viktor Zakharov had turned over to the Canadian government. Threats of death by firing squad also convinced a number of the suspects that their continued silence carried far too high a price. The two holdouts ultimately relented when confronted with the sworn and notarized statements of the other twelve. Their statements filled in several gaps in the spy organization.

Two weeks later, twenty-six other Canadians were arrested for spying. A complete list of the names and the positions of those involved in the Soviet spy ring was compiled and delivered to Prime Minister Brice Winthrop. After reviewing the list of names and the sworn statements, the Prime Minister called an emergency meeting of the Privy Council.

Armed with multiple copies of the RCMP interrogation findings, one for each of the Privy Council members, Prime Minister Winthrop walked into the conference room and called the emergency meeting to order. He handed the copies to the gentleman seated on the left side of the long mahogany table and told him to pass them around. After tapping the glass of water in front of him with a pen and getting the attention of the council members, he advised them to review the last two pages of the findings report.

The fourteen individuals that had already been arrested were listed first, followed by the twenty-six additional individuals that had been identified during the interrogation of those already in custody. Audible gasps and outbursts of angry shouts filled the room. The Prime Minister let the outbursts continue for several minutes before quieting the room.

As expected, the Prime Minister's request to issue arrest warrants for each of the twenty-six individuals and to invoke a Royal Commission of Inquiry to investigate the espionage were approved unanimously and immediately by all members. Every council member shook their head in disbelief as they discovered how high the spy ring went. A partial list included: a clerk at the Canadian Foreign Ministry, a captain in the Canadian Army, a squadron leader in the Royal Canadian Air Force, a radar engineer working at the National Research Council, a manager at the Department of Munitions, an explosives expert from McGill University, and even a sitting member of the Parliament. However, the most shocking of all was the Secretary of the War Production Board.

"Gentlemen, what we have here is a despicable League of Traitors the likes of which has never been seen before," the Prime Minister thundered.

In near unison, the council member's voices rang out, "They should all hang for this treachery and treason!"

Once order was restored, the Prime Minister cautioned the council members to leave the copies of the findings on the table and to not speak a word of what had just transpired. The Prime Minister dismissed the council members and hurried back to his office to begin selecting individuals to serve on the Royal Commission of Inquiry which was to be called to order in just three days.

When word ultimately leaked out to the media that the Soviets had been successfully operating a large spy network inside Canada for months, if not years, in which Canadian citizens passed classified information to agents of the Soviet government, the outcry was enormous and it was loud.

The Royal Commission of Inquiry learned that some of the information passed to the Soviets was of public knowledge. The Canadian government was less concerned with that information. However, because Canada played a large role in the research and development of nuclear bomb technology, officials were deeply concerned that vital secrets might have slipped into the hands of their enemies.

Viktor Zakharov's defection and the evidence he turned over to the RCMP ushered in the modern era of the Cold War. The final report of the Royal Commission of Inquiry alerted other countries around the world, such as the United States and Great Britain, that Soviet agents almost certainly had infiltrated their nations as well. For many long months, government officials around the world slept fitfully, wondering just how much atomic bomb information made its way to Russia.

Carefully selected parts of the Royal Commission of Inquiry's final report was shared with Leonid Volkov, the Russian Ambassador. Ambassador Volkov was informed that Prime Minister Winthrop, with full agreement of the House of Commons, was seriously considering expelling the entire Russian embassy and taking back the land and building.

After testimony confirmed that Ambassador Volkov knew nothing of the conspiracy and after several pointed conversations between him and Prime Minister Winthrop, they worked out a truce of sorts. All of the Soviet personnel involved in the conspiracy, from Second Secretary Pavlovski down would immediately be returned to Russia for appropriate punishment. Ambassador Volkov immediately agreed and signed an official agreement stating the Prime Minister's terms.

Over the course of two days all except two officers and eight enlisted men were packed and loaded onto two trucks for the long trek to Trois-Rivières, Quebec, to meet a passenger steamship bound for Königsberg.

When the expelled Russians finally arrived in Moscow, they were off loaded from the trucks and ordered to stand at attention in a steady, pouring rain. Two hours later, a red-faced, senior member of the Central Committee stomped back and forth and screamed at the terrified men for an hour. They would be severely punished, not for the crime of spying, but for the unpardonable crime of getting caught. They were all, except for one, to be stripped of rank and sent to various gulags where they would spend the rest of their lives performing menial tasks.

One man, a disconsolate, former, Colonel Sokolovsky was singled out and ordered to stand still while the other men were loaded into trucks for the last journey of their lives. The heavy-set general walked up to Sokolovsky and stared at him for several minutes. Shaking his head, the general informed Sokolovsky that he had selected a very special punishment for him. One that would fit his failure. Sokolovsky's heart sank in horror as he watched Dmitri Maksimov, restored to the rank of major, walk out and stand beside the general, glaring at him. Sokolovsky learned that he was to be Maksimov's personal steward and he was to do anything the major demanded. Maksimov turned, snapped his fingers, and walked toward his waiting car. Junior Lieutenant Sokolovsky shuffled along, head down, wishing the general would have just shot him.

Two months later, Stanley and Evy Krysac were progressing well with their lessons in English. Little Nicolas was growing like a weed. He loved the walks with his father into the woods that bordered the rear of the two-acre tract of land their three-bedroom house sat on.

One sunny day around mid-morning an official looking car drove down the lane and stopped in front of the porch. Stanley rose from the rocking chair in which he was sitting and stepped off the porch. He walked to the car and waited for the man inside to climb out. The man handed Stanley a small yellow envelope. Without a word, the man climbed back into the car and sped off down the lane.

Stanley slid his finger under the seal, ran it along the length of the envelope, and pulled out a folded sheet of paper. He unfolded the paper and read the short message. He dropped the envelope, crumpled the paper in his hand, and walked toward the lake.

Evy had heard the car drive up and stop. She had watched the man hand Stanley the envelope. She became concerned when she saw his reaction after reading what had been in the envelope. Something was terribly wrong. She could tell by the way her husband walked. Hurrying out the door, she stepped off the porch and ran after Stanley. When she reached the lake, he was just standing there looking out across the water.

"What is the matter?" Evy asked.

No answer. He just stood there, the breeze ruffling his hair. She saw a lone tear roll down his cheek. Stepping in front of him, she asked again, "Stanley, what is wrong?"

He handed her the crumpled paper, but did not say a word. She quickly read the message on the paper. "Oh, Stanley, I am so sorry," she sobbed as she dropped the crumpled paper. Stanley reached out and pulled Evy close to him and began to weep. Together they stood there weeping as the crumpled pa-

per, carried by the breeze, skipped across the ground and landed in the water.

The telegram notified him that the Soviet Supreme Court
had sentenced the defector, Viktor Zakharov, in absentia, to
death. That first line did not cause the grief he was experienc-
ing because the death sentence had been expected. However,
when he read the last paragraph, he felt as if a dagger had
struck him deep in his heart.

The telegram informed him the Soviets had swiftly retali-
ated against his family in Russia. Anyone related to him or Evy
had been rounded up. One by one they were executed for the
treasonous acts of one Viktor Zakharov. The public executions
were carried out as a warning to anyone who might consider
defecting in the future.

Viktor Zakharov's defection was an event that led to a
major change in the collective political thinking of the entire
Western World. That single event turned out to be a major
wake-up call for the West.

What would have happened if Viktor Zakharov had not
had the courage to walk out of the Russian embassy with over
one hundred documents stuffed in his pants? The world will
never know. It can only speculate and that speculation is
frightening, indeed. Had the Soviets not been caught and had
they achieved a deliverable atomic weapon sooner, perhaps,
even years sooner, they very well might have achieved the
world domination they desperately yearned for. Or worse, the
world could have been destroyed by a worldwide nuclear holo-
caust.

In hiding, with his new identity, Viktor Zakharov (Stanley
Krysac) could never receive the recognition he deserved for his
harrowing sacrifice or even a thank you from a grateful nation.

Instead, Stanley and Evy Krysac stood alone, consoling
each other over the deep and horrendously painful loss they
could only share with each other.

THE END

Appendix I

The facsimile images of Russian messages and notes that follow are examples of the documents that were smuggled out of the Russian embassy in Ottawa, Canada.

ТО: Коминтерн - После прочтения, сжечь

~~Edmonds~~ Benson согласился с моими первоначальными просьбами и представил материалы для прилагаемого доклада. Он предлагает заполнить любые недостающие детали повторно: военные движения. ~~Edmonds~~ Benson и ~~Holland~~ Gray чувствует необходимость поддержания очень высокой степени безопасности и принятия повышенных мер предосторожности в их необходимы обычные встречи. Поскольку в настоящее время они не помечены какой-либо политической принадлежностью, они обеспокоены ге: введение новых членов в группу, и чувствовать, что это может поставить под угрозу их собственную тайну. Пожалуйста, проверьте ~~Wagoner~~ walter, ~~Sargent~~ Leader и ~~Selasst~~ Foster через Коминтерна и ответить.

Facsimile of Message, page 91

Если же о прибыли ссссуд...
Беле сошлются на свою хранящуюся принадлежность и на указания следователя свое обеспечения о деньгах свяжутся с каналией коммунистической партией, и пусть назовет фамилии той чиновника, которой дал ему эти указания. Никаких манускрипта от Беле не берите и никого интереса не проявляйте к каким либо информации.

Facsimile of Handwritten Note, page 102

---

1. Фамилия, имя, отчество _____ SAM CARR.

---

2. Псевдоним _____ " FRANK ".

3. С какого времени в сети _____

4. Адрес:
   а) Служебный _____
   б) Домашний 14 Moutrose,TORONTO.Tel.Ll-7847(brook).

5. Место работы и должность "РАБОЧЕ-ПРОГР. ПАРТИЯ"-полит.деятель.

6. Материальные условия Материально обеспечен,но деньги берет.
Необходимо иногда помогать.

Биографические данные:

    Подробный материал по биографии имеется в ЦЕНТРЕ в КОМИНТЕРНЕ.
Прекрасно знает РУССКИЙ язык,окончил ЛЕНИНСКУЮ школу в МОСКВЕ.

Facsimile of Registration Card, page 140

"ФРАНК" идентифицирован как лицо, желая предоставить секретную информацию. Имеет веру в коммунистическую идеологию или симпатию к ней. Завербован, потому что он является национальным организатором "Труд-Прогрессивный"Коммунистическая партия Канады. Показал большую изобретательность в получении потенциальных агентов в "NET".

Установил отношения с людьми, которые могут быть используется в качестве контактов, которые имеют присущие слабости, которые могут быть использованы Методы подхода будут варьироваться в зависимости от человека и от занимаемой должности.

Продемонстрировал сверхъестественный успех в наборе высокообразованных лица, желающие предать свою страну и предоставить совершенно секретную информацию, к которой они имеют доступ в ход их работы советским агентам, несмотря на их клятвы верности и секретности, которые они приняли.

Facsimile of Message, page 136,37

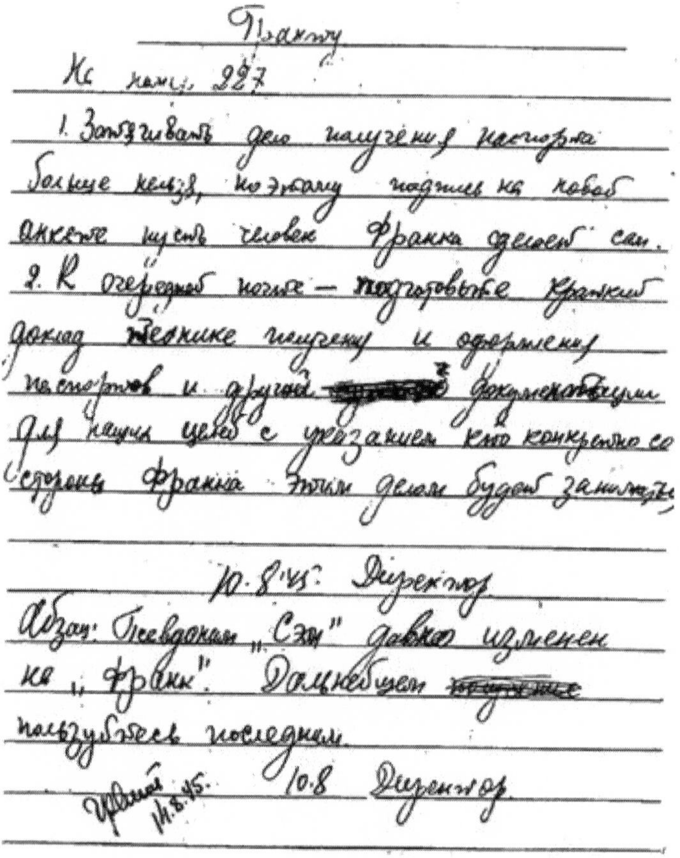

Пахну

Кс нам. 227

1. Затягивать дело получения паспорта больше нельзя, поэтому подшей на новой анкете пусть человек Франка делает сам.

2. К очередной почте — подготовьте краткий доклад технике получения и оформления паспортов и других [illegible] документации для наших целей с указанием кто конкретно со стороны Франка этим делом будет заниматься.

10.8.45. Директор

Абзац: Псевдоним „Сэм" давно изменен на „Франк". Дальнейшем [illegible] пользуйтесь последним.

10.8 Директор

Прочитал 11.8.45.

Facsimile of Handwritten Note, page 168

Если же в пределах месяца
Бенеш сошлется на свою кар-
ранную принадлежность и на
указания ~~[illegible]~~ своих [illegible]-
[illegible] о [illegible] связаться с ка-
надской контрразведкой, и пусть
назовёт фамилию того человека,
который дал ему эти указания.
Никаких материалов от Бенеша
не берите и никакого интереса
не проявляйте к каким либо
информации.

Сообщите как обстоит дело
с выполнением ранее поставлен-
ных задач для лейтенанта
Skидах.

Facsimile of Handwritten Note, page 216

Bibliography

What follows is a sampling of the books and articles I found most useful in researching this novel. I found the lengthy, detailed report published by Canada's Royal Commission to be particularly revealing and fascinating.

I am presenting these references to assist any reader who would like to delve into the unbelievable, yet absolutely true story that forms the basis for this novel.

Bonikowsky, Laura Neilson, Igor Gouzenko Defects to Canada, https://www.thecanadianencyclopedia.ca/en/article/igors-choice-feature, March 4, 2015 (Accessed 12/09/2020).

Budenz, Louis F. *The Techniques of Communism: Invading Education*, http://www.biblebelievers.org.au/ (Accessed 08/29/2020).

Editor. Lone Sentry, The Red Army Infantryman, http://www.lonesentry.com/articles/redarmyinf/ 07/24/2020).

Editor, WW2Today, *The rape and loot of Konigsberg*, http://ww2today.com, http://ww2today.com/11-april-1945-the-rape-and-loot-of-konigsberg-capital-of-prussia (Accessed 07/12/2020).

Encyclopedia.com. *Comintern - Communist International*, https://www.encyclopedia.com/history/modern-europe/russian-soviet-and-cis-history/communist-international (Accessed 08/07/2020).

Knight, Amy. *How The Cold War Began - The Gouzenko Affair and the Hunt for Soviet Spies*, New York, New York, Carroll & Graf Publishers: 2006.

Lenin, Vladimir. Lenin on the Komsomol, http://soviethistory.msu.edu/1924-2/young-communists/young-communists-texts/lenin-on-the-komsomol/ (Accessed 06/19/2020).

Reuvers, Paul & Simons, Mark. *The Fialka M-125 Reference Manual*, https://cryptomuseum.com/crypto/Fialka/m125/index.htm (Accessed 09/09/2020).

Royal Canadian Mounted Police. *Ranks of the Force*, https://www.rcmp-grc.gc.ca/depot/orientation/prep-preparer/things-to-know-choses-a-savoir/ranks-grades-eng.htm (Accessed 12/04/2020).

Sawatsky, John. *Gouzenko: The Untold Story*, Toronto, Canada, Macmillan of Canada: 1984.

Sly, Gordon. The Gouzenko Affair - A wake-up call for the West, The Kingston Whig-Standard, June 7, 2004, https://www.nemacolin.net/igor/#wake-up (Accessed 07/06/2020).

Taschereau, Honorable Robert, Kellock, Honorable R. L., et.al., *The Report of the Royal Commission* Appointed Under in Council P.C. 411, (Ottawa: Edmond Cloutier), June 27, 1946.

About the Author

Keith Hoar writes fiction that transports you beyond the mundane into worlds of intrigue and suspense, mystery and terror.

Writing that plunges you into the story, makes you hold your breath, and interrupts your sleep.

Keith Hoar is a writer and former IBM Certified Business Intelligence Expert who consulted for numerous Fortune 100 companies. He designed executive suite business intelligence dashboards and real-time reporting systems. Keith also owned his own consulting company that designed custom software systems and sophisticated data-driven reporting systems.

Keith proudly served his country in the United States Navy for ten years. At Naval Submarine School, New London, Connecticut he assisted in training crews from both Fast Attack and Ballistic Missile submarines that patrolled the world's oceans in defense of freedom.

Keith is a PADI certified SCUBA diver with 100+ dives all over the Caribbean. Keith has published three previous novels, *Edge of Madness, RAGE*, and *DEADLY SECRETS*, edge-of-your-seat, hold-your-breath thrillers. He has also published a nonfiction book, *DECEIVED: The Assault of Revisionist History*.

Thank you for taking the time to read about the author. Keith is most grateful for fans of his books, and would love to correspond with readers like you. For more information, visit https://keithhoarbooks.wixsite.com/home or you may reach him at his author email - kahoarauthor@email.com

Made in the USA
Columbia, SC
15 February 2021

32992436R00221